Praise for The Helg

'Standout
Weekend Sport

'A dark mystery in a dark age brought vividly to life.
For lovers of the *Vikings* TV series and Lindsey Davies
alike. I look forward to more of Helga Finnsdottir'
Robert Fabbri, author of the bestselling Vespasian series

'Kristjansson has an evocative style that
is easy to get caught up in'
The Eloquent Page

'An exciting new voice. With his Viking mystery, Snorri has
created a new and interesting sub-genre of Icelandic noir'
Ragnar Jonasson

'For Vikings done right, come to Snorri Kristjansson'
Mark Lawrence, bestselling author of *Grey Sister*

'Praise Odin, it's a terrific mystery! With Viking family
values and a sharp-witted heroine, Snorri Kristjansson
delivers a first-rate chronicle of intrigue and murder'
Stephen Gallagher, bestselling author of *Red, Red Robin*

'*Council*'s depiction of Viking life, practices and Norse
mythology is its strength . . . [it] brings something to the
table which will appeal to readers of different genres'
Crime Fiction Lover

Also by Snorri Kristjansson

THE VALHALLA SAGA

Swords of Good Men
Blood Will Follow
Path of Gods

HELGA FINNSDOTTIR

Kin

SNORRI KRISTJANSSON

COUNCIL

Jo Fletcher
BOOKS

First published in Great Britain in 2019
This edition published in 2020 by

Jo Fletcher Books
an imprint of Quercus Editions Ltd
Carmelite House
50 Victoria Embankment
London EC4Y 0DZ

An Hachette UK company

A CIP catalogue record for this book is available
from the British Library

PB ISBN 978 1 78429 811 1
EB ISBN 978 1 78429 812 8

This book is a work of fiction. Names, characters,
businesses, organizations, places and events are
either the product of the author's imagination
or used fictitiously. Any resemblance to
actual persons, living or dead, events or
locales is entirely coincidental.

10 9 8 7 6 5 4 3 2 1

Typeset by CC Book Production
Printed and bound in Great Britain by Clays Ltd, Elcograf S.p.A.

MIX
Paper from
responsible sources
FSC® C104740

Papers used by Quercus are from well-managed forests and other responsible sources.

For Morag.

Contents

Chapter 1

BOY

The girl, seven winters of age, pressed her slight frame up against the wooden fence and peered past it in horrified fascination, caught between curiosity and fear.

'What is she *doing*?'

The boy next to her rolled his eyes and made a face. 'My father says something's wrong in her head. She thinks she's an animal.' Everyone knew Mad Ida was just that: mad. Gone. Away with the trolls and the fairies.

The girl didn't even spare him a glance. 'It looks pretty uncomfortable.'

The clucking grew louder.

'Probably is. Beaks are much better for pecking with. Won't last long, though.'

'Why not?'

His voice had the hard-earned wisdom of all of his nine winters. 'She's scaring the hens and Auntie won't have it.'

The girl opened her mouth to speak, but a woman's loud voice drowned whatever she'd started to say.

'Shoo! Shoo! Get out!' The formidable woman who came striding from behind a nearby shack barrelled past the children and stormed into the chicken pen. She stopped and stood in front of the scrawny figure, not much bigger than a child, who was flapping her arms within oversized, scrappy clothing and squawking back at her. 'Ida, get *out*!'

The woman called Ida squawked angrily at the intruder and squeezed all her features into the middle of her face, as if she could form a beak through willpower alone. She pecked once in Auntie's direction, then flapped away, scattering chickens as she went.

The big woman groaned with frustration. 'Get OUT, Ida! You're scaring my animals!' Happily ignoring her, Ida just kept flapping around the yard, jerking her head this way and that in her poor imitation of the chickens' walk. But the chickens clearly weren't impressed; every time she tried to get close, they moved off in a flurry of feathers to another corner.

Snorting like an angry bull, Auntie stormed off, slamming the gate shut after her.

'Where is she going?' the girl whispered, shrinking back.

'She's probably gone to fetch—' He stopped as voices drifted towards them from the direction in which Auntie had disappeared.

One was loud and rapid, the other slow and rumbling. The first voice spoke a lot more than the second.

Auntie rounded the corner again, this time with a big, broad man in tow.

'Is that your uncle?'

'Absolutely,' the boy said with no small satisfaction. 'He sailed with Greybeard, you know.'

2

'Wow,' the girl said. 'Who's that?'

The boy caught his breath. 'You don't even know who Grey-beard is?'

'Is he the man who came two days ago to ask about the council?'

The boy was indignant. 'No! That was just some dumb traveller. And he wasn't even *old*. Greybeard is the scariest raider there ever was! He sailed to the Southern lands where they have people with ash-black skin and he took all their gold – *everyone* knows he was the biggest, meanest—' He stopped. His audience of one had lost interest, because Auntie and Uncle were now in the pen with Ida.

'You go right and I'll try to shoo her to you,' Auntie said, and this time she stepped gently towards Ida and almost cooing, said, 'Ida, we're going to go into the house and have some stew. Would you like some stew?'

'SQUAWK!'

'I don't think she wants stew,' the girl whispered.

Inside the chicken pen, the chase was on: Auntie dashed, Uncle shuffled – and Ida darted with surprising speed between the two, squawking madly as she went. Twenty chickens getting underfoot did not help the pursuers' cause.

After a couple of rounds Uncle roared in frustration, 'Enough of this!' The big man spread his arms and approached Ida, slowly but deliberately. 'Out!' he ordered firmly.

Ida stopped, looked at him and blinked. 'Squawk,' she said, reproachfully as the farmer caught and embraced her, none too kindly. The girl on the fence shifted out of the way as the big man lumbered out, carrying the old woman, and made for the longhouse.

3

'Nils!' Auntie shouted after him, hurrying to keep up, '*don't*—!'

'If she wants to be a chicken—' the farmer shouted over his shoulder.

'What's he going to do?' the girl whispered, shaking.

'NO!' Auntie was running now.

The boy and the girl watched them disappear into the barn but they could still hear the shouted argument, interspersed with increasingly frightened squawking.

The girl's brow furrowed and she pursed her lips. 'They're *really* angry.'

'Look,' the boy hissed suddenly, staring over her shoulder and pointing at the path leading down to the farm. 'In the woods—'

'What is it?' The girl turned.

'A rider!'

Sure enough, where the trees thinned out they could see a figure on a horse making its way towards them at a leisurely pace.

Nils scowled. 'I will have no more of this.'

'You can't just snap her neck!' Hertha was standing in front of the rust-stained block, broad forearms crossed, scowling back at her husband. Ida was squirming in his arms, her head twisting backwards and forwards, but with less and less fervour; she'd noticed the well-worn axe resting by his feet.

'She'll be the end of us—'

'No, she won't – look at her . . . what could she do to us?'

'She'll open the gates and let out the cows,' Nils snapped. 'Or she'll decide she's a fox and eat the chickens. Or she'll vanish off into the woods with the children and drive you crazy trying

4

to find her. The gods don't like her, Hertha.' He inched closer to the block.

Hertha's scowl turned to a sneer. '"The gods don't like her" – listen to yourself! Just because my mother's sister is a little strange, you want to end her life? What's next, Nils? Do I have to send the girl home to her own farm just because she might say something wrong?' The big woman mimed a troll snapping a neck. 'And don't you dare think about picking up that axe.'

'You're twisting my words,' Nils snarled. 'And anyway, you know I'm right. She can't stay here.'

'Anyone home?'

The voice from the other side of the barn door was followed by a very polite knock on the wall. Hertha's eyes widened and Nils strengthened his grip on Ida's neck.

'Is that—?'

'Yes, it's me.'

Hertha smiled suddenly. 'Oh, but you can pick a moment, girl.'

A young woman stepped around the corner and smiled at the assembled group, then swiftly slapped her cheek and looked at the flattened sting-fly in her palm. A satisfied grin lit her face. 'Got him! This bastard's been buzzing around my head ever since I passed the pond.' She wiped the corpse off on the leather pouch tied to her belt next to bags of various sizes. 'Hello, Nils!' Smiling at the big Viking, she reached back to re-tie the rider's knot in her black hair.

'Well met, Helga,' Nils muttered, looking at his fidgeting captive with a hint of embarrassment.

5

'And hello to you, Ida.' The old woman muttered something, shaking her head this way and that.

Helga looked at Nils, smiled and raised her eyebrows a fraction. 'Can I—?'

As if he'd suddenly realised he was holding a burning log, Nils let go of Ida and almost pushed her towards the tall young woman. 'Of course,' he stammered. 'I was never – I – anything you could—'

'You've done the right thing.' Helga held Nils' eye and after a few moments his heart stopped pounding and his shoulders lowered.

'She will be fine.' Helga's voice was calm as she reached out slowly to the old woman. Ida's frantic head movements slowed as Helga talked to her in a low, rhythmic voice, the words only half-heard by the interested onlookers. She clasped the old woman's bony shoulders before stroking her arms, the movements deliberate, firm, moving her hands down to the wrists, then holding the fingers. She let go and rested the back of her hand on Ida's forehead, swept her fingers down the cheek to the chin, then repeated the action on her other cheek. Finally, tipping Ida's head upwards, she looked into the old woman's eyes. 'Hertha?' she said softly without taking her attention off Ida.

'Yes?' The big farmwife snapped to attention. Behind her, her husband watched intently but silently.

'Do you have any daisies nearby?

Glancing at Nils and smiling nervously, Hertha said, 'Yes indeed. Whole field of 'em, out by the treeline.'

'Very good,' Helga muttered, almost as if she was talking to herself, stroking Ida's arm again, not losing contact with her for a moment. 'Very good indeed. Perhaps we should have some tea?'

The sun had not moved far at all when the children came sprinting back, each with their small bag full of daisies. 'Thank you.' Helga beamed at them. 'You are fantastic workers.'

'Thank you,' the girl said solemnly, proffering the bag.

The boy muttered something and looked at his feet.

'And fantastic workers get paid for their efforts,' Helga said, mirroring the girl's serious voice. Reaching into one of the small pouches by her hip, she pulled out two amber-coloured pebbles. 'I think you might like this. And I have a very special request, which I could only ask of someone really trustworthy, like you two are: would you take care of Grundle for me?'

Their eyes widened and the boy put his hand forward, eager and nervous. The girl, after a quick glance at him, followed his lead. As Helga handed over the payment, she murmured, 'I am sure you have many things you need to do.' The children didn't need to be told twice; she'd barely finished speaking before they were bolting off to see to her horse.

Helga turned to Hertha and Nils. 'Honey sweets with a little bit of dried ground beet. Good for busy bees. Now for Ida. You know how daisy tea calms the mind?'

Hertha crossed her arms. 'We've tried that.'

'I would expect nothing less of you and Nils,' Helga said. 'For most, that would have been perfectly effective.'

'What do you mean, "most"?' There was hesitation in Nils'

7

voice; he still wasn't sure he wanted to be involved in this discussion, but the young woman wasn't giving him much choice.

She looked at them briefly before turning her attention back to Ida, who was almost drowsing in her arms. 'You are very lucky: Ida has been touched by the gods. She will bring great fortune to your farm if you show them the respect they are owed.'

'How?' Hertha's arms remained crossed and at her belligerent tone, Ida's mutterings grew ever so slightly louder. Behind them, Nils tensed up again.

Helga's smile was not remotely shaken. She pulled out a small but sharp-looking blade, a carving knife with a wicked point, and produced a tile from another of her bags. 'The gods . . . well, sometimes they're a little hard of hearing,' she said conspiratorially. 'And sometimes we need to shout in different ways. Pour the tea.' The command in the young woman's voice had Hertha moving before she'd quite decided whether she was going to.

It wasn't long before she was back, clutching a rough-hewn tree-bowl filled with steaming tea.

The knife made a scritching sound as it lanced into the thumb-sized tile in Helga's hand, quick, deft movements sending blink-thin slivers of wood drifting to the ground until a rune appeared. Gently, she reached out and took the bowl from Hertha, passing her the tile in return.

'Is that – *magic*?'

Hertha shushed her husband, none too gently. 'What do we do with it?' she said, respect in her voice.

'You keep it on you,' Helga said, 'and touch it when you are making the tea.'

'I don't know this one,' Hertha said, turning it around in her fingers and studying the mark.

'I would be surprised if you did. I learned it some years ago from my m— It came from a family I stayed with when I was younger.'

'And this works?' Nils said hopefully.

Helga looked him straight in the eye. 'Yes,' she said. 'And if the gods change their minds and it stops working, you come and find me immediately. There are other things that we can do as well.' She turned back to Hertha. 'Meanwhile, set Ida to simple tasks, preferably with counting – things she can actually do – and make sure she eats her food. Four flowers to each bowl, like I did; when you're down to one flower in a footprint you need to move on and find a new patch. If you run out, come and see me – I always have some dried at home.'

'I usually put two in the bowl when she's bad . . .'

Helga smiled. 'I think she's worth four, don't you?' She reached into her bag and produced a handful of the honey sweets. 'I'll leave these here to bribe your workforce.' She winked at Hertha.

Ida shook her head forcefully, her breathing quickening. 'Nnnaah!' she muttered more loudly.

'Now,' Helga said, her voice still level but the words coming out more quickly, 'you have the rune, and the gods are watching. What do you need to do?'

Hertha stiffened. 'I, uh—'

A large, callused hand appeared and plucked the bowl out of Helga's hands.

Nils kneeled down in front of the woman and spoke softly. 'You are going to have some tea, Ida,' he intoned, with the calm voice of someone who had dealt with skittish horses all his life. Ida's eyes darted from him to Hertha, then back to the farmer. 'There's a good girl,' he murmured softly, raising the bowl to Ida's lips.

'*Nnnh!*' Ida shook her head.

'No,' the Viking said, unmoving, 'drink.' He tilted the bowl slightly, Ida's head stayed still, then she tasted the tea with her tongue. Nils tilted the bowl again and this time the old woman's lips started moving. Before long the bowl was drained.

'Now what?' Hertha asked.

'Just wait.' Helga smiled and reached for Ida's hands, feeling with her thumbs past the old woman's gnarled knuckles to the sinewy wrists. Her eyes closed slowly.

'. . . hungry,' Ida whispered.

'No wonder,' Helga said, opening her eyes.

Hertha stared at them both for a moment, then she disappeared through the door.

'How are you feeling?' Helga scanned the frail old woman as she talked. 'Headache? How is your stomach?'

'I just said I was hungry, stripling,' came the tart reply.

'Oho! She's better,' Nils said, a smile breaking out on his bearded face, as Hertha emerged from the longhouse with two fist-sized rolls of bread, a dollop of butter and some quartered plums on a plank.

'Here,' she all but barked, handing it over to Ida, 'eat.'

Helga glanced over at Nils, who was looking at the two women with affection. 'The shrews of Rowan Glade,' he said. 'Never a kind word to each other, no one more true.'

He smiled as Hertha fussed over her old aunt. 'This is good,' he told Helga, and grabbing a hand-axe, left the women to it.

The farmwife turned from her aunt and looked Helga up and down, almost as if sizing her up. 'You know, for a Norsewoman you're not bad.'

Helga grinned. 'Thank you,' she said, looking down. 'I should be going. Just remember, send for me if you need anything, or if Ida gets bad again.'

'I will.'

Overhead, swallows swooped and dived on the summer wind.

The horse moved slowly, gently picking its way down the shadow-striped path from Rowan Glade. The sun sent cascades of green light shafting through the leaves to the forest floor, which was still moist and fresh from the night's rainfall. She drew in a deep breath, feeling like she was sensing nature with every fibre of her body.

Beneath her, the horse snorted.

'I agree,' Helga said. 'It's beautiful here.'

Content with the response, the horse tossed her mane and continued walking. The rocking motion and the warmth of the big body set Helga to thinking, and she felt a familiar, pleasant tingle rise in her cheeks. 'Only one day now,' she said softly to the horse, then hummed, '*Tomorrow, tomorrow, tomorrow*.' There was an ache running throughout her body, which was almost unbearable. *Almost.* In a sense, the wait was sometimes nearly as delicious; it reminded her of the joy and relief of quenching a hard thirst with cool spring water.

'Right, girl,' she said, 'enough of this dallying. So where do we find our bounty?'

The horse tilted her head and looked sideways at her.

'Oh, forgive me, your Highness. Of course I should not bother you with such mundane questions.'

Grundle pulled on the reins and Helga stroked her neck. 'All right, then – if that's what you want, we'll go down that way.' The horse stepped away from the broad path; the thick underbrush meant the going was harder, but the beast was right. Her prey was more likely to be found away from the beaten track.

She peered through the trees until she spotted a sun-dappled glade, the perfect spot. The henbell's distinctive long stalks, drooping cross-hatched flowers and spiky leaves were nestling in the grass away from the pine trees. She dismounted, but she didn't need to tell the mare to stay clear; Grundle was already moving a little way back as Helga picked her way towards the flowers with her knife in hand, breathing shallowly as she muttered the old rhyme,

Touch of death and odours fell
When you pick the dreaded Bell.

She tried to ignore the bitter taste to the air around the plants as she knelt down and wrapped a long rag around each hand before going further. Only then did she slice the first stalk in half, taking care not to get any of the sticky juice on her flesh. That was bagged, then a little digging yielded the root too. She quickly dealt with another two plants, then retreated thankfully, already starting to feel giddy and slow. If she'd stayed much longer she might have had to deal with hallucinations, even nausea too. But once dried and used carefully – a tiny portion of the leaves to calm and soothe; a shaving of the roots to help with sleep – henbell was invaluable for any healer.

'If I'd fallen asleep, you'd have had to come and get me,' Helga said to Grundle. She got a snort in reply as they ambled back into the forest.

When they came across a field of motherwort beside a stream, the stern voice of the woman she'd thought of as her mother for most of her life came back to her: *Stop fussing and drink the tea, girl.* The cramps had been so bad she'd been doubled over, clenching her teeth so hard she thought they would break, but instead of sympathy – not that Hildigunnur had ever been big on sympathy – she had been brusquely assured that she wasn't dying, offered a clean rag and then the tea. The smell had been bitter and the first sip unpleasant on the tongue, but then Hildigunnur had made great show of stirring a generous dollop of honey into the bowl, a high treat.

The jagged spikes of pain had dulled immediately and while the soreness and the squeezing feeling had remained, it had been nowhere near as unbearable. Thinking back on it, she wondered if that had been the moment – that actual tangible result – which had made her love the idea of being a healer. A day later, the cramps and tearing pains had all but vanished; there was still the blood, but nothing that couldn't be managed.

She smiled at the memory as she sliced off the first of a dozen plants and bundled it into an empty bag.

Riverside had been kind to her, and so had the woman who had adopted her; she could admit that now.

Grundle turned a corner and Helga drew her breath in at the sight of the sun hitting a clump of tall, bright pink spikes. She dismounted and stroked the rough leaves beneath the speckled bell-shaped flowers hanging in ordered rows around a firm stalk; it looked like someone had taken great pains to arrange them in a regular pattern. 'So who do you think named them foxgloves?' she asked the horse, who sensibly ignored her.

Out came her knife and she cut a handful of the rough, thick leaves just at the base of the plant. A little could make a racing heart beat a little slower, but you couldn't use more than two leaves at a time. 'Quick and slow and big and small is far more good than none at all,' she muttered to herself, smiling wryly at the memory of being forced to repeat the words over and over and over until she was sick of them.

Memories of Riverside had softened now. The first year away from the place she'd always thought of as home, at least until her siblings had come back for a family reunion, had been difficult. First she'd stayed with Thyri, Bjorn's widow, and their idiot son Volund, a nice boy even if he'd long lost the wits the gods gave him. He was going to be a huge bear of a man like his father and as long as instructions were clear and simple and repeated enough times, he'd be able to help Thyri on the farm. However, when winter broke and spring started carving paths through the snow, Helga had felt the need to move on. She had fonder memories of the next year; Groa, the Eastmen's cranky old healer had pretended not to like her for the longest time, but Hildigunnur had taught her to read people and she could see clear as day that the old woman had enjoyed the company. When Helga had found out that gossip was the old woman's favourite thing, all manner of life wisdom had been grudgingly dispensed in return for rumours and stories, thinly disguised as chiding.

Decide at night, do in the morning.

If you find good water, drink it.

Leave the boys alone.

Well – two out of three wasn't bad. She blushed at the sudden images in her head, although funnily enough, it was her skin that remembered most of it: strong bodies under fur, the feel of hot flesh on flesh, the pull of taut muscles, the heat, the musk ... There had been a little blood at first, but Hildigunnur had warned her about that too, and ensured she'd never forget the recipe for particularly strong juniper tea that was 'good for decision-making'. No young woman who came to Riverside left without the makings and instructions on what kind of night to use it after. It was months after she'd joined the Eastmen that she suddenly recalled how often she'd seen her mother brewing juniper tea for herself; what she'd learned by then made her smirk at the memory – and then she'd wondered, in a way that made her feel sad and happy at the same time, whether she looked anything like Hildigunnur when she did.

But the woman she'd come to know as her mother had lied to her and deceived her and there could be no returning. With all mothers and daughters there had to be some evasion of truth, she knew that much – but there was a limit.

Too much foxglove stops the heart.

Grundle walked up to her and nudged her shoulder.

'Yes, yes,' she said, 'I know. I'm getting moody in my old age.' She looked into the horse's long-lashed eyes. 'So you want to get going, girl, do you? You want to go home.' She rose stiffly and remembered, too late, as always, that too much time foraging always turned her knees to wood. 'Well, so do I.'

She hauled herself a little gracelessly onto Grundle's patient back and moments later they were heading home at a nicely paced walk.

The forest gave her all it could: rich scents, riotous bird song, surprise patches of blooming flowers. She smiled and allowed Grundle's rhythmic motion to lull her half asleep, her thoughts idling like fish lazily circling in a pond. On occasion the sun would pierce the leaf cover, bathing her in bright light and a gentle warmth.

Life is good, she thought, feeling the herb bags bouncing gently against her hips, stuffed with the day's bounty, and that in turn made her think again of what was to come when she got home and somewhere just under her navel there was a tingling and a tightening of muscles.

Life is good indeed.

The gaps between the tall trees gradually widened, letting in more sunlight, and what had been a beaten path more used by beasts than men was unmistakeably now a road. Helga could see familiar shapes in the woods now – a crooked branch, signs of a stag sharpening his horns – which she greeted like old friends.

I'm home. Even though three years was no time at all in the kingdom of King Eirik, as she was so often reminded, and even though the older ones still weren't quite sure about her, on account of her coming from the west – most of them still called her 'that Norsewoman' or, she strongly suspected, 'that Norse witch' when she was far enough away – she still felt at home here.

And there it was: the first flash of bright light shining through the trees. She still wasn't used to how the chains sparkled and twisted in the wind like living things, but she recalled how frightened she'd felt when she'd first seen the enormous hall. Back then Uppsala had felt so terrifyingly big and crowded, with people shoving and swearing at her at every turn. She'd managed to keep a brave face, that first day, until she knew she had to get away; she'd told her travelling companions she was going to tend to the horses and ran off to the stable, where she'd indulged herself in a short but heavy bout of tears, then worked on fighting back the rising fear and the throbbing headache. Her overwhelmed senses had been so crowded with sights and smells and the sheer weight of noise, all intermingling and overlapping.

It had taken a horse, nudging her from behind, gently reminding her that she was within reach of feed, to help her overcome that cold fright.

She reached down and patted Grundle's flank. 'That's where we met, wasn't it? You were my first friend.' The horse snorted. 'And even though I really wanted to, I didn't run away.' She could see more blue sky now, and ahead, fields of green and gold. 'I didn't,' she repeated, more forcibly.

She relaxed in the saddle and allowed the horse to lead,

thinking happily, *I could fall asleep right now and wake up at home.* Everything was alive around her. She drew a deep breath and closed her eyes, taking in her surroundings: the air was fresh, with a hint of sun-warmth and the smell of pine resin. Helga put out her tongue as if to taste it, then wet her lips. *To anyone watching I'd look like an animal,* she thought, which made her giggle, picturing herself on the horse, eyes closed, tongue darting in and out like an adder. 'It's a good thing there's no one around,' she said to Grundle, who was studiously ignoring her. 'Come on, then, girl. Take us home.'

The mare needed no encouragement, first settling into a gentle trot, then picking up speed, pushing into a canter, while around them the sunlight flooded through the increasing gaps between the trees, bringing with it a delicious smell of heat on leaves mixing with the soil being kicked up under thudding hooves. Even the air tasted different at this speed, almost like honey. *Do I have any at home?* Helga wondered, and another thought followed immediately which made her scalp tingle.

She leaned over the horse's muscular neck, feeling the solid warmth radiating, and urged her on as the forest disappeared behind them and the plain opened up before her. The sight thrilled her now: Uppsala, the Halls of the King, sat proud on the hill overlooking the farms far in the distance. The light flashed on the temple chains, drawing the attention of the gods to the bustling life below, the longhouses linked by walking boards, the fence-lines demarcating territory. There was always something happening there.

At last she could just make out her own little house, nestled away near the northern treeline. Grundle did too, for she picked up the speed and the two of them thundered on towards home.

'It's good to run sometimes,' Helga told Grundle. The smooth, even strokes of the brush were sending both of them into a trance of sorts. *This is all that matters,* she thought. *Home and horse and life.* There was something so powerfully good in coming home, in knowing every angle, curve and line of your environment, feeling like your small but sturdy house and one-horse barn were a part of you. *This feeds me*, she thought. Grundle's hide was feeling smooth and kempt now, and judging by the soft snorting, the mare was happy. She gave her work a critical once-over and thought about Einar; he and his father Jaki had taught her how to treat a horse right. *He'd have approved.* Her feelings were still mixed when she found her mind drifting back to her life at Riverside. The first year she'd moved to Uppsala, she'd asked every traveller from the west for news of the valleys, but there had been precious little to hear: small kings and minor skirmishes, that was about it. Unnthor was the big man, and not just in his valley, and he and Hildigunnur kept a firm lid on trouble for miles around, so of course there'd be precious little news coming to the town.

The moment she opened the gate, Grundle flicked an ear in farewell and walked in, immediately dropping her head to graze. With the herb bags bouncing satisfactorily against her hip, Helga visualised the interior of her storeroom, the small shed next to her house. She'd built the whole thing herself, even though there'd been no shortage of men – of all ages! – offering to help her with pretty much whatever she needed when she'd first arrived. But Hildigunnur had always been a great believer in self-sufficiency, and *not being beholden* – especially to men – so with her mother's tart voice echoing in her ear, she had turned them all down. Her time with the Eastmen had taught her that a firm but friendly denial served best.

Time to sort the harvest. The contents of her storeroom could be the difference between life or a slow, agonising death, so she always memorised exactly what she had and, just as importantly, what she needed.

Patting the bags, she murmured,

> *Henbell, hyssop, meadow-rue;*
> *Lungwort, foxglove, good and true.*

Almost as if she'd invoked them, the scents started tickling her nose.

The shed had a normal front door, but she'd turned the whole back wall into a big set of swinging doors that opened onto the herb garden, her pride and joy. Rows of verdant green and dusky silver stretched away, the beds arranged neatly by type. Groa had taught her a lot about planting, but she in turn had surprised her crotchety instructor with her vast knowledge of forest herbs and an unerring nose for finding them, thanks, of course, to her mother's lessons. *Old witches,* Helga thought, grabbing a handful of thyme, *have taught me all I know of life.*

She knelt by the rosemary, inhaling its sweetly bitter scent as she twisted off some stems, then moved on to the juniper at the end of the plot. A good handful of berries and she was done.

Back in her shed, she dealt with the forest's bounty first, then tied up the freshly picked garden herbs and hung them off a nail in the top corner.

Last week's picks were nicely dried out; a flash of her blade and rosemary, juniper and thyme were chopped up and tied neatly into in a small muslin bag. 'One stew mix, ready to go,' she said to no one in particular, repeating the actions until she had two dozen piled beside her. She did good trade, selling the ready-mixed herbs to travelling merchants; the bright ones knew guards worked better on tasty food and the investment was small. She'd even started getting return customers: one Dane who made the trek up just after winter to trade honey for pelts had come to her for the third year in a row. He'd even offered to marry her, but when she'd pointed out he wanted to marry her herbs he'd had to agree.

'They're all fools,' she said, not unkindly, but they were fun; life would certainly be duller without them. If less loud. She looked around at her shelves, not so much counting as confirming that she'd not run out of anything. It made her happy to see everything just so.

Her hand went to the runestones around her neck. *She did teach me a lot.* Closing her eyes, she muttered the combinations. Nauth, need, and Gebo, giving, Sovilo, the sun, and energy, life, and Jera for patience. She stroked Ehwas and Mannas, the last two, smiling: horse and man, all a girl needed. When she'd first noticed the runes in Groa's hut she'd been surprised – she always kept her own hidden – and she was wary about turning the conversation to the magic of the inscriptions, but when at last she summoned up the courage, quite expecting to be thrown out or ignored, the old woman had been more than happy to talk. She'd been waiting for a promised apprentice, although she never told Helga who had made her that promise.

That had been a fascinating night, the first of many. They'd started with single runes before moving on to the really interesting part: the ways in which they could be combined, opening up all manner of possibilities, like a flower garden blossoming in spring. Nothing had been quite the same for Helga after that. Some of them had stuck with her – mostly the things to do with growing and healing – but she couldn't quite lose the feeling that she'd forgotten some important things as well. 'They'll come to you when you need them,' Groa had wheezed. She'd been a patient teacher – most of the time. Out of habit, Helga felt her side, that one particular area the old witch had delighted in pinching, even though it didn't hurt any more.

I still have so much to learn. But the old woman had told her it was time to make her own way in life, and Groa was never one to brook no for an answer, so here she was in Uppsala, making her own way . . .

Lost in thought, she collected a pile of seedpods and returned to the herb beds. Kneeling on the ground, she rubbed the damp earth between her fingers, enjoying the feel of it, before scattering the seeds and covering them gently with a fine tilth of soil.

She felt the rider long before she could see him.

Sometimes she imagined that she could tell his hoofbeats from those of any other horse, which made her remember watching Hildigunnur console lovelorn young women whose men had gone a-Viking. How stupid they had looked to her younger self. *You'll never catch me crying over boys*, she'd sworn, and she winced a little at the memory as she kept her eye trained on the rider, waiting for him to come close enough to admire.

No one sat a horse like he did.

There was a wiry strength to him that always made her heart beat a little faster, a grace in how he didn't fight the movement but rolled with it naturally. When she'd first seen him she'd felt like her heart had gone quiet. It was something in the way he'd dismounted, strong, but light on his feet. She'd hung back, that first time, unable to tear her eyes off him.

And now he was coming to her, grinning broadly and waving at her as he urged his horse faster. She waved back, a little annoyed to find she was blushing, but unable to hide her own smile of welcome. He pulled up a dozen steps away and was airborne before the big animal had fully stopped; five long strides brought him to her. She had only a moment to drink in his features – the long blond hair, the close-cropped beard and the twinkle in his eye – before she was enveloped in his strong arms and then their lips were touching. The scent of him filled her nostrils and she forgot everything else. Grabbing him around the back of his neck, she pulled him even closer, soaking him up as they staggered in a drunken dance towards the house. He stuck out one hand and shoved the door open and then they were falling to the floor, her legs wrapping around him, hips thrusting with pure want. She could feel the pulse between her legs, an almost unbearable urge.

He broke the kiss. 'Missed me?'

'Shut up,' she said, yanking at the rope holding up his trousers, grunting in frustration when it failed to come unknotted quickly enough. He moved with her, wriggling to free himself while staying as close to her as possible. After some quick fumbling, her skirts were up above her waist. She felt the air on the soft skin of her hips, and with it the goosebumps rising on her forearms, and then he found the heat and the wetness and slid in. A warmth flowed through her with his first thrust.

They gazed into each other's eyes in the half-light. She breathed him in again, that delicious man-smell of him mixed with sweat and horse and sun. He was hers and she was his. As the waves within picked up speed, the world outside their connection seemed to slow down. She turned her head and gazed at his arm, a solid pillar supporting his weight on her, and she reached out, pushed aside the thin layer of rough-spun cloth to rest her hand on warm skin and hard muscle beneath. She trailed her fingers up his arm, always conscious of that delicious tightening inside, and stroked his shoulder, his broad back, thrilling to her lover swelling up inside her until, *there*, *there!* – and she felt herself tense almost to the point where she couldn't bear it another instant . . . and suddenly sweet release swept through every pore of her body. She could see eyebrows over half-closed eyes rise, then he shuddered and groaned and sighed and lowered himself carefully down into an embrace and feeling the weight and admiring the size and power of him, she felt herself lazily drift off, as contented as a cat basking in the sun.

'So how was it?'

'Hm?' He was searching for a boot that had gone missing in their haste.

'The trip. I didn't expect you until tomorrow.'

'Oh,' he said, waving a hand, 'that. It was reasonable, I guess. Met some people, but few of them were talking.'

'Will Alfgeir not be disappointed?' She stirred the pot, wrinkling her nose at the pungency of the bitter leaves, but needs must. Her body felt all soft and relaxed and she revelled in it. *As long as you don't forget to drink the bloody tea*, a sharp voice reminded her.

'I said few, not none.'

Somewhere in the back of her head there was a tingle. She glanced over to see him looking at her, half-dressed, relaxed and smiling impishly. A ray of light caught his blue eyes. *You are too beautiful, you bastard.* She beamed at him. 'I am sure my mother warned me about silver-tongued charmers like you.'

'Well, my mother didn't warn me at all about Norse witches who get you drunk, make you twist your ankle and then offer some *very* unconventional healing methods!' It was his turn to grin.

You won't forget me in a hurry. The thought was there, shocking and thrilling in its confidence. She put on her best innocent face and was rewarded with an adoring look.

He came over and put his arm around her waist. 'I missed you,' he said, voice soft.

'Shouldn't have gone away then,' she said.

'I had to.'

'I know.' On occasion the king's right-hand man would send for Freysteinn to go riding; he'd call in on farmers and seek out news. He rarely told her much about what he'd learned. She kissed him

25

on the cheek, just above his beard line, then leaned over and filled her bowl. As she rubbed against his crotch, his hand quested up towards her breasts.

'Save some for later, horse boy,' she purred, but he just grinned at her and left his hand where it was – then there was a sudden shift in him and his voice was gentle again when he asked, 'How has the sleep been in the last week?' He pulled her to him and hugged her.

The tea was scalding hot on her lips, and so bitter, but she forced it down, really wishing she couldn't hear Hildigunnur saying, *The hotter the better – and get it done with quickly. Unlike the fucking.* Her mother's joy in giving advice had usually been linked to Helga's mortified expression.

'It's not been bad,' she said.

He reached up and stroked her hair. 'If you have more of those dreams, I'm sure people would like to know.'

Even though everything he did to her put her body at ease, she felt the words like a fishbone in the throat. 'I'm not a fortune-teller,' she said. 'I don't know what any of it means. It's just dreams.'

'Of course, of course.' His voice was soothing. 'Have your little patients behaved while I was away?'

'They are people,' she said, more sharply than she'd intended. 'Although of course they have their problems. Old Ida thinks she is a chicken now.'

Freysteinn chuckled. 'The Rowan Glade lot have always been' – he caught her glance and amended his statement – '*unusual*, I'm told.' He clucked sternly to emphasise his point, which made her laugh. He let her go, leaned back and gazed at her. 'You love them, don't you?'

She felt the tingling in her scalp again and wasn't quite sure what it was. 'I do, yes – they may be annoying, but we're all neighbours, after all, and we have to help each other.'

'You do what has to be done,' he said softly. 'There should be more people like you, Helga. It would make everything . . .' He trailed off, frowning.

'What?'

'Someone's coming—'

And now she could hear it too: the very faint, rhythmic thud of hooves on the ground, growing closer.

The dot on the green plains was trailed by a cloud of kicked-up earth. Her easy mood faded quickly. Whoever it was, they were riding hard – and that usually meant one thing only. 'I have to go,' she said.

'I'll come with you.'

'Really?'

He smiled. 'I keep hearing – *everywhere* – what a great healer you are. I might as well come and see it for myself. Also . . .' He leaned in and whispered, 'I love watching you.'

By the time Olver's son Hugin had arrived, sweaty and exhilarated, they were ready to go. He turned his mount around with not much of a word and led the way back across the plains, south, then eastwards, not quite straight to the coast but in that direction. Giving the horses their head, they'd crested a hill at a speed that made Helga's stomach churn with excitement, but it wasn't until they'd crossed a sizeable stream that the boy slowed his horse some.

'We found him in the copse,' he said finally, gesturing to a stand of trees around a bend in the river. 'He's in a bad way and Pop said not to move him.'

'What's wrong with him?'

'He's lost a lot of blood – and he's been in the river.'

Her heart sank. There were times when she could do things and there were times when there was absolutely nothing to be done. They all dismounted and she tied Grundle up next to old Olver's horse, who was standing stolidly staring into space.

'We're over here,' came a shout and there was movement in the bushes.

'I got her, Father!' the boy shouted back, but Helga was already rushing to where the old farmer crouched.

''e's all but gone,' he said, almost apologetically. 'I sent the boy for you the moment we found 'im.

At his feet was a young man, shivering and pale. She couldn't immediately put a name to his face. 'Who is he?'

'Never seen 'im before,' Olver said. 'Not from round 'ere.'

The young man – not much more than a beardless boy, really – was short and pudgy, and what had probably already been a fair-skinned complexion before he fell in the river was now the colour of dead flesh, contrasting with a big birthmark standing out on his cheek. His thin reddish hair was plastered to his skull. The only thing alive about him was his eyes, which darted between Helga and Olver – then suddenly rolled up into his head as he started to shake violently.

Helga rushed over and grabbed his arms. 'Pin him down,' she ordered, and father and son did so without question. 'Now, get on top of him.'

'Wha—?' Hugin started, but his father was quick to understand.

'Warm 'im up,' he snapped. 'Get to it, boy. 'e's fading.'

Looking deeply uncomfortable, Hugin shifted until he was lying on top of the stranger. At Helga's direction, he hugged the youth close, until at last he stopped shaking, but it didn't appear to be making much difference. Whatever life there'd been left in him seemed to have leaked out.

She could feel Freysteinn approaching behind her, cautiously. 'Is he . . . er . . . gone?'

Before she could answer, the boy's eyes opened lazily, like someone drifting out of sleep, alighted on Freysteinn's form towering over them and widened. The boy's mouth moved, but he was too weak to breathe now and no air passed his lips.

'Looks like 'e's tryin' to tell you summin',' the farm boy said.

'Me?' Freysteinn sounded surprised, but then he too dropped to his knees and leaned in close. He put his face next to the stranger's mouth, but nothing happened. 'What is it?' he asked the youth. 'I can't hear – can you speak up?'

There was no sound. Freysteinn stood up and all four of them looked at the prone youth, watching the life fading out of the body in their midst until his eyes rolled up into his head and stayed there.

Olver's stubby fingers reached for the boy's eyelids and closed them, surprisingly gently. 'Shame,' he said. ''e was young.'

'Who was he?' Freysteinn asked. 'He doesn't look familiar.'

'Never seen 'im,' Olver said again, but now he sounded almost dismissive. The body between them had changed so quickly from a man who might be saved to a dead thing just . . . lying there.

'Hm,' Freysteinn said, looking around the clearing. 'There have been no stories of travellers recently, apart from—'

'That's not yet,' Olver said with authority, 'and besides, 'e's far away from the main paths. Regardless of who 'e might've been representin', 'e would've been quite lost.'

'Mm. Helga . . . ? What are you doing?'

She heard Freysteinn's voice, but it was almost a background sound. Something about the youth was . . . wrong. After a moment, she realised that Freysteinn was asking her why she was still kneeling over the body. 'Just looking,' she said, absentmindedly. *Tell me your secrets*, she commanded the boy-shaped mound before her.

But there were none, or at least, none she could find. No necklace. No jewellery of any sort. No pouch, no knife, no markings of any kind. He'd clearly never been in battle – his thin lips looked like they would have bent naturally into a nervous grimace.

And no wound.

Had he just fallen in the river? So why then did he get so cold so quickly?

Her fingers, questing up from the shoulder to the neck, finally found what she was looking for.

'Someone has . . .' She felt around the back of his head. 'Someone's bashed his head in.' Another moment's pause. 'With a rock.'

'What makes you say that?' Olver said.

'There's a circle where the rock hit.'

'Why not a tree branch?' Freysteinn said. 'He could have been, uh, climbing? Maybe fallen down and hit—?'

No. I love you and you're beautiful, but this is what I do. 'No splinters. Even a treated club will leave something in the wound.'

'Sword?' Hugin suggested nervously.

'No, it wasn't any edge that did this, nor hammer, nor mace: they leave the same kind of mark – and this is not it. It has to have been a rock.'

'So he must have fallen . . .'

She could practically hear Freysteinn thinking, and thinking fast, which made her smile. *Do not underestimate me, horse boy. I am easily your equal.*

'. . . off a horse – somewhere else? So he hit his head, fell in the river and managed to crawl up onto the riverbank. So it was an accident.'

She glanced at him. He was looking very happy with his answer.

'Come,' she said softly, and when he knelt down by her, she took his hand and guided it to the spot where the skull had been hit. 'Feel.' She watched his face.

'What is it you want me to feel? His head is pretty bashed.'

Disappointment blossomed in her. *We share many things, but an interest in wounds is clearly not one of them. Ah well. Perhaps I shouldn't be surprised.* 'I guess,' she said, feeling strangely subdued.

'We'll take 'im and send 'im off,' Olver said. 'Our god-house is close.'

'Thank you,' Helga said, gratefully; he hadn't needed to make that offer. The boy had no connection to them, so they'd have

31

been well within their rights to leave the corpse where it was, let it feed the forest. But she couldn't help but notice that the victim was of an age with Olver's own son. Sometimes fathers couldn't choose their feelings.

After they'd said their goodbyes, they left the horses to find their way home, needing little prompting. She held on to Freysteinn for as long as she could, talking of this ailment and that cure, stroking his hair and cheek and chest, trying to keep at bay the image of the pale youth in the copse. She only allowed him to leave when he'd promised he'd be back by sundown and even so, her body was aching with loneliness as she watched him ride away.

Convincing herself that it was a good kind of hurt, she went back to her storeroom, mentally tallying her herbs and running through recipes, but thoughts kept intruding: *Who was the boy? If it was an accident – why did he have nothing on him?* Almost unbidden, her hand found its way to the back of her head.

Her voice sounded muted in the shed. 'Unless he fell off the horse, cracked open his skull, mounted the horse and fell off again, there's no way he could have sustained injuries here' – she pushed her finger to the first indentation, then three fingers across to the other side of the head – 'or here . . . not at the same time.'

Before he died, he had looked like he'd wanted to say something to them. She badly wanted to know what his last words would have been – his name, maybe? The place where he'd been murdered, where they could find a horse and saddlebag and a pool of blood on rocky ground?

She could imagine Hildigunnur sneering contemptuously, *Accident, my arse.*

That boy had very deliberately been hit from behind, with a stone.

Twice.

Chapter 2

GUESTS

Twenty miles north of Uppsala, a line of horses trudged on with slow, regular steps. Ingileif had made them follow the river since dawn, but when it turned to the west they'd entered the long shadows of the pine forest.

Breki was bored out of his mind.

He looked at the backs of his fellow travellers. Wrapped in travel cloaks of some indeterminate colour between green and brown, Ingileif's retinue looked less like fearsome warriors of the North and more like rug piles on horseback. The woman they called the North Wind rode up front, as befitted a jarl, stubbornly clad in the white fur of the northern bear despite the summer heat. Legend had it she'd taken it from the King of Bears himself; before they'd left for Uppsala Breki's father had whispered that he'd seen the merchant who'd sold it to her, but no man with any sense would argue the point. He'd told Breki that in the big world, nothing was as it seemed.

So far, the old man had been right. As usual.

When the king's messenger had arrived at Ingileif's longhouse with the summons, Breki had been hardly able to contain himself, but oddly, none of the adults had shared his excitement. On his first trip away from home, Breki was expecting adventures, skirmishes with bandits and encounters with mythical monsters roaming the countryside. Maybe even the chance for a rescue of some high-born maid or discovery of some long-hidden treasure. So far he'd seen nothing but fur-clad backs and felt nothing but his own arse, which was by turn hot, cold and sore. Now he understood the grim, exasperated faces he'd seen in the North Wind's longhouse when they'd been summoned. Turned out, travelling was waking, sleeping, cooking, eating, sitting, shitting – and boring. And added to that, there was one traveller, smaller, more hunched over, who moved a lot less than the others. She generally remained hidden in her covered cart, but once he'd glanced towards it – entirely by accident – and caught sight of two eyes peering out from somewhere deep in the folds, sparkling like a hunting beast spotting prey in a cave-mouth. He'd made sure he did no more accidental glancing in that direction.

'Uppsala.'

He wasn't sure which of the cloth piles had grunted, but as they came out of the forest, there it was nonetheless: lazy smoke trails from far too many cook-fires to count snaking their way skywards from so many longhouses and huts all scattered higgledy-piggledy, as if someone had thrown them from the hill.

Breki's eyes widened.

On the summit of the hill was the biggest building he'd ever seen. He'd heard stories of the temple at Uppsala, of course – who hadn't? – but none that did it justice. The midday sun broke out from the clouds and suddenly silent lightning erupted from the big tower in its centre and went flashing across the wooden structure, shooting towards the far corners of the great building.

Big Rolf leaned over to him and said, 'You might want to consider closing your mouth some time soon before a bird decides to nest in it.'

Breki shook his head and shrugged. 'I . . . wasn't . . . I mean . . .'

'Yes, you were,' Big Rolf chuckled. 'Gawking like you'd seen the eight-legged horse hisself. And that won't do for a Northern lord in Ingileif's retinue, and even less for a squirt like you.'

'But . . . but . . . the lightning . . .'

'Yes. It's an awesome sight, for sure, knocks anyone sideways the first time. Do you know why?' When Breki shook his head, Big Rolf laughed and told him, 'There are golden chains strung from the top of the tower to the corners to catch the light and make it look like the gods are touching us. Looks incredible, in truth, but really, it was just some poor sod up a ladder with a hammer and nails.'

Breki looked back at the temple and snorted. 'Nothing is as it seems, is it?'

'Exactly.' Big Rolf looked him up and down, as if the old man had just remembered who he was. 'Maybe there's hope for you yet, little Breki.'

Breki couldn't help but smile. Even two summers ago the man they called Big Rolf had barely reached his shoulders, and by now Breki was nobody's idea of little. He'd been awkward for his age, a gangly tree of a boy, until his eleventh summer, when he'd suddenly gone through a great spurt which included more than his share of muscle. Wrestling had been so much more fun after that. Now, even though he was a good head taller than most of the grown men, Big Rolf still called him little Breki, and while he always took care to pretend to be offended, he didn't stray too far from the old man. When he was a little boy he'd told his father that Big Rolf had the grey hairs of a coward. His father had cuffed him soundly, then explained that two kinds of men got grey hairs: cowards, and wise men. He'd asked whether Breki wanted to call Big Rolf a coward to his face and of course Breki hadn't, and that was that.

Big Rolf broke into his memories. 'Let's go through it again.'

Breki rolled his eyes. 'Why?'

'Because the building material that was spent on you all went to the shoulders and arms and I'm not sure what's inside your massive head. *What are you supposed to do?*'

'Stay quiet and look dumb.'

'Excellent. You're doing well at that already. Lots of practise, huh? And what else?'

'Remember everything.'

'That's right.' The old man leaned back in the saddle, apparently satisfied. No one had bothered to explain to Breki exactly why this was so important, but judging by the number of times Rolf had broken up the journey just to drill it into him – stay quiet, look dumb, remember everything – it was apparently crucial to the success of the mission. That was a better conclusion than the other possibility: that the old man was just as bored as he was.

As Ingileif's party made its way slowly across the fields, more of Uppsala came into view. The temple dwarfed its surroundings, but Breki could not help but be impressed by the sheer number of houses. There were more of them on the hill and dotted around than he'd ever even imagined, let alone seen.

'How many people live here?' he asked Big Rolf.

'It depends on the season. Now? I reckon King Eirik's court counts about sixty followers in summer: some lords, some younger sons from strong families, mercenaries, of course, and fortune-hunters. They have servants, karls and retinues, say about seven to a man, give or take. That's already around four hundred—'

'Four hundred and twenty, twenty-one if you count the king,' Breki replied without thinking.

Big Rolf pretended not to hear him. 'Around four hundred. He'll have blacksmiths, tanners, farmers, merchants and thralls for that lot – about a hundred more. Give or take. Then you have the wives, children and useless, lumbering boy-oafs. And soon, we'll add to that tally.'

Breki whistled. 'That's a lot of people in one place.'

'It is,' said Rolf, eyes twinkling. 'Any number of vagabonds and young glory-seekers just like you, all hoping to pick up crumbs from the king's table.'

'But why are we here now, if it's so busy?' asked Breki.

'Because the king sent for us, that's why.'

'I know that. I saw the messenger just as much as you did. But *why* did he summon Ingileif?'

'He can call on his council whenever his spotty Majesty pleases – he did, so we're here. Councils are important: we go, we trade, we hear news and we argue a lot before we agree on anything. King Eirik may be young, but he is no fool. He knows that the North goes as she goes.' Big Rolf nodded up towards the figure in the front. Ingileif, called the North Wind, was a square shape of a woman, a little older than Breki's parents. He couldn't remember ever seeing her do anything out of the ordinary, but she'd been the chieftain of his valley and the surrounding area for as long as he could remember and no one had ever challenged her or spoken against her. A year ago, when he'd said as much to Big Rolf, the old man had told him to glance, when he could, at Ingileif's knuckles. A little later Breki had had the chance. He'd not had to ask for more explanation since.

A child came out of a hut, saw them and immediately sprinted away, but none of the riders up front so much as raised a finger; they just sat there, letting the horses set the pace. It looked like the North Wind didn't much care to make a lord's entrance, Breki thought.

As they drew closer, the arrangement of houses started to look less haphazard. A road snaking around the hill rose towards the entrance to the temple on the far side. The houses that had looked to be scattered around just anyhow were in fact all connected to this road by steps and walkways and smaller paths. The whole place reminded him a little of a tree – he almost expected to see a squirrel scampering up and down.

A small group of men had appeared on the road and were walking towards them.

'That'll be the welcome, then,' Big Rolf mumbled. 'Let's see what they think of us.'

Breki thought the North Wind must have seen them, but Ingileif made no move to hurry. Nor did she dismount or in any way recognise the fact that she was riding into the king's home town. 'Why isn't she doing something?' he whispered to Big Rolf.

The old man smiled. 'It's much better to do less and have them wondering what we are about. Makes it more likely that they'll make mistakes. In negotiations it never hurts to let your opponent make the first move.'

'Opponent? But we're all from the land of the Svear, aren't we?' Breki whispered back. 'And the Svear stay together. Don't we?'

Big Rolf just pointed towards the Uppsala group, who had stopped a little way away. The locals were facing them, waiting for the visitors to approach. 'Watch and learn, little Breki.'

The one at the front was one of the biggest men Breki had ever seen. He was more than a head taller than the men at his side, with a chest to match. He looked less like a human and more like a bear to Breki's eyes.

'Who's that?' he muttered, trying to keep his voice as quiet as possible so the man-mountain wouldn't notice him. Behind the big man was a group of four strong young men who all looked like pups in comparison.

Big Rolf frowned. 'That's Alfgeir Bjorne, the king's right hand. This is interesting.'

'Why?' asked Breki.

'Quiet. I'll tell you later.'

'Well met, North Wind!' the big man boomed.

'Well met, Alfgeir Bjorne,' Ingileif replied. She was looking more like a grizzled old troll herself, something that had just walked out of the forest, than a woman.

After a short silence the Uppsala man spoke. 'I trust you've had a good journey?'

Breki noticed that two of the men behind Alfgeir were exchanging quick glances. A third wore just a hint of an ironic smile.

'Good enough,' the chieftain replied after a pause of her own. 'Always an honour to come at the king's request,' she added. 'Always an honour.'

'Yes,' Alfgeir replied, 'and the king is very pleased to see you. The others are on their way. There will be a feast for your men. Follow me! We'll see that your horses are seen to before you're fed. The northern stables should do,' he added over his shoulder to the young man who had appeared at his elbow.

Without another word, the welcome delegation from Uppsala turned and started walking up towards the top of the hill.

Big Rolf poked Breki's shoulder. 'You're the youngest, so you get the horses. We'll go and make sure the maidens are all locked up for when you return.'

Breki grinned. 'If the stories are true they'll be all in the same room and you in the middle, hiding from shadows and Norsemen.'

'You'll need a bigger mouth than that to fit my—'

'Enough,' said Ingileif, who'd somehow circled round unseen. 'Shut up, Rolf. You talk too much; always have. You're with me. Eldar' – she turned to a tawny-bearded, broad-faced man – 'take the cart. Stake out a camp, then return to the longhouse. You know what to do.' This was followed by a significant glance at the cart up front, which somehow managed to look threatening even though it was not moving at all. 'Boy—' Breki didn't know if the chieftain had trouble remembering his name, or if she simply didn't care. Best not think too much on that. 'Boy, we'll walk from here. You'll see to the horses – Alfgeir's man will show you the way.' With a grace that belied her years and stature, Ingileif dismounted.

Following her lead, three of her men followed suit. Rolf reached up and clapped Breki on the shoulder. 'You heard her, so do as you're told.' Eldar was already heading away with the cart and the remaining men.

Within moments, Breki was left with six horses and one thoroughly unimpressed local boy who looked bored of waiting and uninterested in helping. Grabbing three reins in each hand, he asked, 'Where's the barn, then?'

Without replying, his guide walked off.

'What's wrong?'

Helga's chest tightened. Just his voice was enough to create a reaction and now he was standing by his shovel, leaning on it and looking at her as well. The way his hips and his shoulders lined up like that, the slight bulge of muscle in the arm he was flexing, was making it a little difficult for her to get any words out.

'What do you mean?' she managed after a moment, although of course she knew full well what he meant. She'd been out of sorts all morning, closed off in her own head. He'd offered to help her dig out a new bed, but for all they'd been working side by side since daybreak, she'd not laughed at any of his jokes or risen to any of his more ribald suggestions, or even engaged in any sort of meaningful conversation.

'You're still thinking about it, aren't you?'

So he did know. 'Yes,' she said quietly, wondering why this death had affected her more than the others she'd seen. *They were old men, old women and drunks – oh, and two fighting men, murdered by their own kin . . . but this one? He was just a boy. A soft, harmless boy.*

'There's something *wrong* about it,' she admitted at last. *Maybe it will help to talk it through.* The soft soil felt alive in her hands and she could feel the pressure as she drove the seeds into the ground, perhaps a little harder than was strictly necessary. 'I think he was attacked without reason and killed without any honour.'

She glanced up at Freysteinn, but he didn't move. *Come over here, you bastard. Come over here and touch me and tell me I'm wrong and make me believe it.* But if he could hear her thoughts, he didn't obey but just stood there, looking concerned. *For me, or the dead boy?* she wondered.

'Are you sure?'

'Of course I'm sure,' she snapped. 'I wouldn't say it if I wasn't. He was hit twice from behind, with a rock, stripped of his possessions and thrown in the river.' She looked at him, eyes flashing – and something in her sank. *I've stung him.* Freysteinn was looking shocked at her sharpness and somewhere she felt a flash of fear. *He'll leave.* The thought was gone as soon as it was born, but the bitter taste of it remained. She wished fervently that she could

43

take it back, or maybe just say it more gently. *Would Mother have apologised to a man?* The thought slipped in like a scent on the wind, followed by another: *She'd never have put herself in a position to need to.*

Freysteinn gave her an appraising eye. 'Maybe I could tell Alfgeir the next time I see him, if you want,' he said finally. 'And he could tell the king.'

But you don't believe me. She took a breath and forced the tension out of her voice. 'I want to tell King Eirik as soon as possible, and I want to do it myself – but I'd be very happy to have you by my side as I do so.'

He smiled. 'Of course, my love.'

She could feel herself blush, and for some reason that made her furious. The feeling was warm and tickly and tight, but somehow she didn't feel like it was hers. She scanned his face for smugness, a knowledge of what he was doing to her – but there was none. Just that beautiful, beautiful mouth . . . In her mind she made a note to use all the tricks she could think of to reduce him to a quivering wreck at the earliest opportunity. 'What do you say we finish this and then ride into town?'

His eyes sparkled, but he checked himself. 'Yes,' he said after he had pushed whatever he wanted to say first to the side. 'We'll ride in. By then maybe the Northmen will have arrived.'

The bloody Northmen! She bit down hard. Since the council had been announced she'd been preparing herb bags, tinctures and mixtures and various other handy things to trade, but the boy in the forest had completely knocked them all out of her head. Feeling a sudden burst of energy, she grinned up at Freysteinn and this time set to planting with a will. There were trades to be made, and a conversation to be had with the king.

The northern stables were bigger than any longhouse Breki had seen, but the familiar sharp smell of horse dung reminded him of home.

'You can bed them down here,' the boy said, friendlier now his task was done. He took one set of reins from Breki and tying them loosely to a post just inside the door, pointed down the length of the barn. 'The guest stalls are up there, at the far end. Take any of the empty ones; they can have one each, there's plenty of room. You'll find buckets, combs and brushes, picks and the like all over there.' He pointed vaguely at some rough-hewn shelves barely visible in the dusky gloom. 'Come to the King's Hall when you're done. It's the big one – you can't miss it. There'll be food.'

'Thank you,' Breki said, but his host was already walking silently away. He sighed and walked over to the shelves. His back and legs were aching, but the animals needed seeing to. He grabbed a couple of the brushes, a bone pick and some rags before untying Ingileif's mount and leading it to the far end of the building. Sure enough, there were plenty of empty stalls; it looked like almost half the stable building was empty. He started brushing the horse clean, just like he'd done every day since he'd been big enough to reach over the back. *How many horses would four hundred people need?* he wondered idly. They'd brought four packhorses themselves, even though that had left only a handful at home.

Ingileif's horse whinnied softly, interrupting his thoughts, enjoying the firm brush strokes. When he'd finished grooming, Breki checked the hooves. They were fine, as he'd expected, for they'd been travelling on soft grass the whole way. He loaded the trough with hay and made sure the animal was contented before fetching the next one.

They were all standing patiently at the pole he'd tied them to. 'You're not really that concerned, are you?' Breki said to them, and when one of the mares snorted in reply, 'All right, all right. It's your turn next.'

He worked in silence, remembering spring days at the farm, finding the mindless, repetitive task oddly soothing. It felt good to be doing something useful after the interminable days of slow, boring riding.

As he led the last animal in, an odd scuffing sound and a deep snort told him he was no longer alone in the barn. He looked around, confused, and called, 'Hello? Is someone there?' No one replied, but the feeling of unease didn't leave him. It suddenly occurred to him that he was to all intents and purposes a stranger in someone else's stable and he might quite easily be killed for a horse-thief.

He wasn't able to shake the feeling that something was out of place . . . *There*. He was positive he'd glimpsed a shadow in one of the stalls. He sidled across and looked in – and immediately took two steps back. The animal within was massive, easily four times the size of a regular horse, the colour of a stormy night in winter. And there was something wrong with its legs. There were far too many of them.

He blinked and the image was gone.

The stall was still occupied, sure enough, but this horse was a regular one, with the normal four legs, and none too spectacular at that. A wiry old man with thin, wispy hair and a white beard was humming tunelessly to himself as he brushed it down. He wore layers upon layers of tattered grey travelling clothes. A wrist-thick quarterstaff with a slightly pointed end was propped up in the corner.

How did I miss him? Breki shook his head to clear it and was about to move along when the old man noticed him.

'Well met, stranger,' he said.

'Well . . . met,' said Breki, wondering when the old man had come in. 'The name is Breki, and I am—'

'—one of Ingileif's men, aren't you?' the old man replied.

Breki found himself blushing. 'I – I suppose I am.'

'Suppose?' the old man said, smiling. 'That's not what heroes do, is it? They rarely *suppose*. A proper young hero *knows*. So . . . ?'

'I am a Karl of the North Wind's court, come here to stand by her at the King's Council.' The words were out before he could stop them, leaving Breki mortified. He didn't have any sort of right to call himself a karl. He was just the oldest of Berg's sons; he had been allowed to sit in the longhouse twice because he was good at wrestling. If Big Rolf had been there he'd have cuffed him round the head, and he'd been right to. If his father had been well enough to travel and heard him say that . . .

He winced.

But the old man was nodding to himself. 'Go then, Breki

Bergsson, Karl of the North Wind. Do your work and go and stand by that fine figure of a woman. I have no doubt she'll need your strength and wisdom.'

Breki walked off in a daze, leading the mare. His mind didn't focus for a long time, but luckily his hands knew what to do and so he unharnessed the beast and stacked the tack in the corner, rubbed her down and moved onto the brushes. *Karl of the North Wind.* Why had he said that out loud? He had no hoard. He had no name. He was just a stupid boy, no more than thirteen summers of age, with a big mouth that was going to land him in trouble. The horse whinnied, protesting at the unaccustomed roughness, and Breki, coming to himself, mumbled an apology, his ears burning. There were names back home for men who took their moods out on animals, none of them pretty.

Pushing all other thoughts aside, he concentrated on the mare, softening the strokes and enjoying the warmth of the hide and the play of muscles under skin as the mare flexed, nudging his arm with her great head, approving the improved treatment. After he finished up he walked the length of the stables, but he was definitely alone. Somewhere at the back of his mind a memory of an old man teased him, but there was no one there. The more he looked, the less he was certain of what he was looking for. Had he imagined something?

In the end he just left, shaking his head.

Uppsala was a strange place and no mistake.

'What do we know?' King Eirik leaned against the back wall of the longhouse and looked to the south, lazily scanning the plains.

'Not much,' Alfgeir Bjorne rumbled. 'Ingileif is here. Her horses are being stabled. Her men are quiet and keep to themselves. An old woman travels with them, in a cart.'

The king smiled. 'I'd expect nothing less of them. If the Northmen have brought a Finn-witch with them, they want us to know they mean business.'

'I don't like it,' the big man said.

'You don't like anything. That's your job.'

'Yes – but I *really* don't like this. There's something in my bones.'

'Old age,' the king said, grinning. 'You never thought you'd get through half of your fights.'

'True enough. But Ingileif is wily: she usually knows what she can get out of a situation before she starts.'

'Always has – but she doesn't burn her crops. We have dealt with her before and we'll deal with her again, if need be.'

'How?'

King Eirik smiled. 'Every chieftain wants one of three things: gold in their hand, grass of their own or glory to their name.'

The big man snorted. 'I hope you're right. Some of them, however, are harder to buy than others.'

'And Ludin of Skane will be here soon enough to prove you right.'

'I'd hoped he'd mellow with age.'

'Not likely,' the king said. 'Last I heard, he was running raids on the Rus just for fun. Apparently he only needs half a boat's worth of blades these days – his reputation sails before him and does the rest. The stories had him burning villages and putting children to the stake.'

'Sounds about right. I'll tell the boys to keep one eye on them and save the other one for the Dalefolk.'

'I'd worry more about Ludin and Ingileif. Grim is coming, isn't he? He's reasonable.'

'He's not.' Alfgeir's voice had a hard note to it. 'I just heard. They've hired a negotiator.'

'Hired a *negotiator*?' King Eirik frowned. 'You mean old Grim of the Dales will no longer hand-shake his own bargains? Must be bad then. Who's coming in his stead?'

'I'll tell you after.' He glanced down towards the foot of the hill. 'Heads up: North Wind's blowing.' Below them was a group of large figures in heavy furs, heading up the winding path towards the temple and the King's Hall.

'We'd best get to our oars, then,' King Eirik said. 'Lead them through the front, will you? I'll be inside.' With that, the king ducked through a small door in the back wall and disappeared from sight.

Alfgeir Bjorne looked down on his town. The sun was shining and one by one, the villagers were drifting towards the gathering square, where the traders had set out their carts. 'I don't like this,' the big man muttered as he moved towards the corner of the longhouse, ready to greet their guests from the North. 'I don't like this at all.'

Helga, seeing the big man come around the corner, called out, 'Alfgeir!'

He stopped like a bear catching a new scent. 'Helga,' he said after a moment, walking towards her.

'I have information for the king.'

He looked down at her and frowned. 'Now is not the time for talk. We have the Northmen coming in.'

'I just need a moment with him.' She saw his eyes glide up her and above her head; he was scouting down the path. 'He needs to hear this. A boy has been slain.'

Ah, that caught your attention, you big oaf.

She felt a small twinge in her stomach when he looked back down at her. Alfgeir might not be quite as big as Unnthor or Bjorn, but there was a strength to him and an economy of movement that always made her a little uneasy. A man his size could crush her if he wanted to – but now he just said, 'Be quick!' and set off towards the front of the hall, moving so quickly that she was hard pressed to keep up with his powerful stride. Within moments he was flinging open the doors of the longhouse. 'He's in his seat.'

The doors slammed behind her and she felt like she'd fallen off a cart. Without blazing fires in the pits and people filling the place, feasting and singing, the longhouse looked like the inside of some great sleeping animal. In the distance, on the other side of the hard-packed floor, King Eirik sat on his dais. The throne was simply made, carved out of one great oak tree and decorated only with the eagle, his chosen animal. The noise of the doors slamming had alerted him, because he was leaning forward and peering at her.

'Who's there?'

'Helga, daughter of Unnthor.'

'Come into the light.' There was a warmth in the king's voice; the longhouse suddenly felt impossibly big around her and mixed

51

with a remembrance of another place far away. *No time for this*, she told herself as echoes of carousing and fighting rang somewhere in the back of her head. Biting down on the memories, she forced the dizziness away and walked with haste to the dais. The king struck a lonely figure on his throne, but he was regarding her with curiosity. 'Well met, Helga.' She bowed her head. 'What do you need?'

What do I need? The question surprised her and she found herself faltering. 'It's not about what I need. A boy has been killed.'

This caught King Eirik's attention. 'Killed? Where?'

'In the forest, near old Olver's farm.'

'. . . hm. That's out east.' He sounded like he was talking to himself. 'Mm.' He frowned, then asked her, 'Who was he?'

'I don't know,' she said.

'And you are sure he was killed?'

'He'd been in the river. He died in Olver's arms.'

And there it was. The twist of the king's mouth, from serious thought to wry smile, gave Helga a sinking feeling. *Stupid woman,* his face said, *fearing the shadows.* 'The Fates will have cut his strings for a reason. If you can't tell me who he was or who attacked him, I am afraid we will have to leave him to them. Now I must ask you to leave me, as I am expecting a delegation of Northmen led by a tough old boot of a woman.' He smiled at her and glanced towards a smaller door on one side.

'Thank you,' Helga muttered, chastened. As she turned her back on the king, the pale, sickly face of the boy came back. She had more than a suspicion that it would stay there until she figured out who killed him.

*

Two days' ride south of Uppsala, a hard-faced man with short hair and a close-cropped grey-white beard looked at the sky, watching the afternoon turn into evening in the west. In the east, darkness had crept up, higher and higher.

'Camp,' he snapped.

Behind him, seven men cut from the same cloth moved as one, dismounting from their horses. Nods and other gestures, with the occasional two-word questions, bounced back and forth. Three men disappeared into the forest. Another two went to the back of their line, grabbed reins and led the heavily laden cart into the centre of the encampment.

'Food,' the greybeard said, and within moments, a large pot had been suspended on trestles over the speedily constructed fire. One of the three men returned bearing a dead hare, legs still twitching, which he skinned, gutted and jointed with confident flicks of his short, sharp blade. The meat was thrown into the pot, snarking and spitting on the hot metal. Water-skins appeared, but a portly man with auburn flecks in his beard who had taken up position by the fire raised a meaty hand and grunted, 'No. Roots first.' Another bag was emptied and the contents chopped. There was more snarking from the pot. The cook leaned over and sniffed deeply, waited for a moment, then, 'Water. One skin.' The water went in, hissing and steaming as it hit the sides. He produced two small leather bags, one of salt, carefully hoarded, the other of dried herbs of some sort, and added a few pinches of each, then pulled out the long wooden spoon tucked into his belt and stirred, intently breathing in the aroma all the while. Some moments later he gestured for another water-skin, stopping the pourer halfway through with a gesture and one word. 'Enough.'

While the cook went back to stirring and sniffing and finally tasting, some of the men brushed down and fed the horses while others erected tents.

With a gesture, another skin of water was added.

Still nobody spoke.

Finally, after a last monumental sniff, the cook glanced at the greybeard. 'It's ready.'

'Any slower and I'd've taken a bite out of you, Alvar,' said a thick-necked man with a broken brawler's nose, moving towards the pot.

No one else had shifted a muscle.

'Oh, come *on*,' he said, looking around. 'Surely we're not waiting for her – she's way up ahead by now. We've not had any food since sun-up, but you're going t—'

The cook cleared his throat, looking pointedly over the brawler's shoulder.

The ninth man, who had not moved from his horse nor taken any part in setting up the camp, dismounted in one fluid motion. His dark green robes, very different from the others' utilitarian travellers' clothes, fluttered about him for a moment before settling. Black eyes sparkled out of dark brown skin above a hooked nose and thin lips, currently pursed in displeasure.

The brawler curled his own lip in disgust and took a step forward. 'Do you know what I think?' he said, conversationally, flexing broad shoulders and cricking his neck. 'I think your horse got spooked. She'll never know. Whatever colour, skulls break just the same.' He took another step towards the man in green, glaring down at his slight frame.

'Lars,' the greybeard snapped, 'stop right now.'

But the man in green raised a hand and glancing at the greybeard, shook his head gently. Then he turned his eyes upon the advancing brawler and smiled.

'What?' Lars growled. 'Fucking *say* something! You ain't said a word since you joined at Hedeby. Do you even understand me, you fucking little shit?'

The dark-skinned man's smile widened.

'I'll wipe that off your shitty f—'

Lars Larkwood had pretty much punched, kicked and bit his way through life to this point and as a result, he had a fighter's quick reflexes.

They were nowhere near quick enough.

Coughing and choking and clawing at his neck, Lars fell to his knees, his face turning purple as he tried desperately to draw a breath.

Opposite him, the dark-skinned man had settled back into his relaxed stance, his right hand drifting softly back down to his side. No one else had moved.

The sound of thundering hooves fell neatly into rhythm with the coughing man and as one, the men straightened up. The cook made sure to rest the long spoon across the pot.

The man in green took two steps backwards and bowed his head.

The horse pulled to a halt, snorting and pawing at the air. The woman astride it asked, 'What happened?'

Greybeard answered, 'Lars stepped out of line.'

She sighed and looked at the man in green. 'Nazreen. Will he live?'

The man in green considered the question. The woman on the horse barked something at him in a harsh, guttural language and this time the man with the odd-sounding name shrugged, then smiled and nodded. He walked back to the shaking, red-faced Lars, kicked him unceremoniously to the ground, grabbed his shoulders as he fell and twisted him down onto his back. Ignoring the flailing arms, Nazreen put a hand on the back of Lars' neck and tilted his head backwards.

The wheeze in his lungs as he dragged in air sounded like winter wind through a holey wall. Lars coughed violently and gulped again, and again. 'You *bastard* . . .' he rasped hoarsely. 'Fucking near killed—'

Then something must have connected in his head, for he tilted his head up and saw the woman on the horse.

'Lars . . . ?' she said sweetly, dismounting. She walked towards him and the bruiser stared at her, his eyes wide open. The woman knelt by his head, speaking calmly. 'If I ever have a reason to so much as glance at you for the rest of this trip, I will open you up myself. Do you understand me?'

He nodded, still gasping.

Moving infinitely slowly, she held the index finger of her right hand up in front of his eyes, then placed it gently on his sternum. 'From here' – she traced a line down his large frame, across a soft belly, down towards the hips, over the damp patch in his trousers until it rested between his balls – 'to here. Do you understand me?'

She pressed down, none too gently, and the bruiser winced and shuddered before nodding for the third time. He blinked furiously, as if to hide incipient tears.

'Good,' she said, smiling and rising. 'It hurts, doesn't it?' When he inclined his head again, she told him, with not a trace of sympathy in her voice, 'So shut up for a while. You're still breathing, which means Nazreen didn't crush your throat. That's because he is a good man.'

The dark-skinned man next to her smiled and bowed his head, black eyes sparkling in the dusk.

Now the woman turned to the man with the grey beard. 'Aegir. Explain.'

'I gave the command,' Aegir said, scratching his chin. 'I would have stepped in and disciplined him, but your man told me not to.'

'He told you?'

'Well, not so much. He . . . well . . . gestured.' Aegir winced.

The woman looked over at Nazreen and barked a question at him. He looked at her and she shook her head. 'Men,' she said. 'Violence is always the solution with you lot.' She examined the assembled faces. 'Could I *please* ask you not to kill each other? At least not until we're back from Uppsala. We have things to do.'

The men watched her impassively.

. 'I'll take that as a promise,' she said. 'Now, hand me a bowl. I'm starving.'

Chapter 3

GATHERING

'That's not good enough.'

King Eirik leaned back and sighed. 'Come now, Ingileif. You cannot ask me for forty men in the harvest season, thirty sacks of feed *and* a new bridge.'

The grizzled chieftain leaned back, mirroring the young man's movements. 'That's odd.' A thoughtful pause. 'Because I am quite sure I just did. And after a visitor has asked, it is polite of the host to answer.'

The king smiled. 'Indeed. And as you know I will, I offer you half of that.'

'And I refuse.'

'But knock off one of this and five of that for your next offer.'

Ingileif smiled. 'Of course.'

Eirik glanced over at Alfgeir, a hulking study in silence. 'And that's only the first verse.'

'What can I say? I like the song.'

Breki craned his neck and tried his very best to follow the finest points of the conversation. He had been told to go stand by the wall – a position befitting his importance, Big Rolf had said as he'd told him yet again to shut up and listen, and yet again tasked him with remembering the exchanges word for word. *Every word,* the little man had said. *Every single bloody word. And* exactly *the word, and don't make anything up. And remember how it was said as well.*

Breki had promised, and had tried to look suitably chastened, even after Rolf had repeated himself for the third time, and then added, *And especially if that bastard Thorgnyr pipes up.* The man in question, Thorgnyr the Lawspeaker, had until now done nothing Breki could see to merit the venom in Big Rolf's voice; he'd just sat there next to Alfgeir Bjorne, looking faintly bored. There was no threat in him, Breki decided. Apparently he'd come from Iceland, which was, at least the way Big Rolf described it, a strange island far to the northwest full of crude men and criminals, but Breki reckoned he must've been kicked out for being a little runt. Next to Alfgeir, the law-man looked like a child who'd been kept indoors for too long: his skin was pallid and his left eye twitched as if it had a mind of its own.

Breki dragged his mind back to the negotiations. Even though he was bored, he had decided he would force himself to watch and listen and remember. After all, Rolf had promised him all manner of punishments if he got so much as a word wrong and Rolf was, generally, a man of his word.

'And the bridge?' the king asked. 'Who'll be providing the materials?'

'You will, of course.'

The king scoffed and went to speak, but a different voice cut across his and he shut up.

'Who benefits most from the bridge?' The Lawspeaker's voice was reedy, but it carried surprisingly well.

Ingileif frowned. 'What do you mean?'

'If the bridge gets built, who profits more?'

'You do,' Big Rolf chimed in for the first time. 'We bring metals from the north—'

'—for which you are handsomely paid,' Thorgnyr interrupted. 'And if the bridge isn't there, how will you get your metals to market?'

'The usual way,' Ingileif said, 'as we do now: we go down the valley and cross at the ford.'

'And who feeds your horses? And who feeds your men?' Thorgnyr was still looking faintly bored, and almost as if he felt sad that no one else had thought to bring this up. 'The bridge would save you two days' travel, would it not? Which is two days' worth of food that would go to your wives and your children. Unless things have changed – which, last I checked, they hadn't – the north doesn't do so well when Freyr doesn't sneeze on your crops.'

'How we do in the north is our business,' Big Rolf snarled.

'And it will continue to be, unless you build a bridge,' Thorgnyr said. 'A bridge that opens up a path straight to us, a bridge which makes it easier for you to get your wares to the biggest market in the land, a bridge which saves you travel – a bridge which makes it much easier for us to send fifteen strong men up your way come harvest-time.'

The silence swirled around Ingileif for a long time. 'Twenty-five.'

For a moment it looked like Thorgnyr had forgotten what they were talking about, but then his face slid back into boredom.

'Twenty sounds about right to me. They'll meet twenty of yours midway and we'll build the bridge together. And we'll leave the feed to be traded as and when. With all the money you'll make off the bridge I'm sure you'll be able to pay us a sensible amount for every bag you need.'

Breki thought Big Rolf's head might explode, so furious was he. 'You want us to— And with no guarantee—'

Ingileif's massive paw rose and he stopped talking.

'This can be done,' she rumbled. Then she eyed the king. 'Eirik's generosity is noted.'

'As is the North Wind's cunning,' Eirik said.

Breki might have caught the briefest flicker of amusement in the corner of the old woman's eye, but it was gone so quickly it would be easy to think he'd imagined it.

'We will talk more about this,' the chieftain rumbled. 'The river has not yet run to sea.'

'No doubt we will,' Eirik agreed.

Breki wondered if he'd missed a joke somewhere, but Ingileif was rising, Big Rolf had followed and within moments the entire Northern delegation was moving towards the door.

No one smiled, no one spoke.

As the door closed behind the Northmen, Alfgeir looked at Eirik. 'Well . . .'

'That went about as expected,' Eirik said, leaning back.

'Hm.' Thorgnyr offered an annoyed half-sneeze.

'Are you not happy?'

'It's boring,' the reedy man said. 'You said as much. We followed

61

the script. She says this, you say that, then I have to step in and slap some sense into her and we both walk away with exactly what we had decided beforehand would be perfectly acceptable.' He peered at the king, then Alfgeir. 'Boring.' After a moment's thought, he added, '. . . your Majesty.'

Alfgeir cleared his throat. 'In that case, you might be pleased – or at least entertained – to hear what's coming.' Thorgnyr's head inclined ever so slightly towards the king's right-hand man. 'Grim of the Dales is ill.'

'Oh yes.' King Eirik looked interested. 'You said they'd hired a negotiator?'

'They've hired Jorunn.'

The longhouse went silent.

King Eirik paused, then, '. . . and when you say "Jorunn", you mean . . .'

'Yes, I do. Jorunn daughter of Unnthor, wife of Sigmar son of Goran, last heard of travelling down by Miklagard. She's back, and if the stories are to be believed, old Grim was only too happy to hand his responsibilities over to her.'

'I must remember, next time I spill blood for the gods,' King Eirik said wearily, 'to ask them what in the nine worlds I have done to anger them so.'

'Never saw a rat-hound go after its prey like she did,' Alfgeir said.

'Remember Olthor?'

Alfgeir's brows knit, then he gave a heavy chuckle. 'The poor boy who was so certain they were about to be married?'

'Until she claimed his land, his farm and his pelts in court. She spoke so well that he ended up thanking her for her generosity in allowing him to keep half a blanket to sleep under.' King Eirik smiled. 'I suspect we'll have to count our words, lest she takes half of those too.'

'And find some new ones,' Alfgeir said. He looked at Thorgnyr. 'Still bored, Lawspeaker?'

Thorgnyr peered thoughtfully up at the rafters. 'No,' he said, after a moment. 'I heard about Olthor's case and how she argued it. I am . . . not bored.'

He turned his head and glared towards the door, utterly missing the look that passed between King Eirik and Alfgeir.

Helga watched from afar as the delegation of Northmen walked down the hill, chatting and laughing. Only one of them looked a little confused: a tall, lumbering boy walking by himself at the back. She thought of Volund and smiled. Some boys were just oxen without a nose-ring, big and meaty and waiting to be led. And others . . . For a moment she imagined she could sense where Freysteinn was, how he moved, how his hard, warm thighs felt under the fabric of his trousers. *I'm sure Hildigunnur would like him.* She thought of her mother again – or rather, the woman she'd known as her mother – and let her mind wander as she made her way down the hill towards the market-field. There was sunlight and she would have it on her skin. There would be trades to be made and she would make them. And then there would be the night . . .

Enjoying the feel of the soft grass even through sturdy leather boots, she let herself drift. Just telling Eirik what was on her mind had lifted a weight off her chest and she felt a lot less responsible for the boy who had died. His face briefly visited her again but she shook his image away and continued resolutely enjoying the day.

It is summer, I am about to make some money and I have tamed an animal of my very own. Smiling, she let her feet guide her to her cart.

It took her a moment to notice the tension. Only when Grundle, standing patiently beside the cart, whinnied and shook her head twice, then stamped her feet, snorting, did she register that a number of her fellow traders were huddling together in small groups, whispering and trying not to look at a handful of people on horseback at the far end. *I thought the Northmen had already tied up their—?*

The memory of a snarling face and a wielded blade hit her like ice in the gut, her knee buckled and her breath caught in her throat. She knew that profile, that wave of the hand, that arch of the back. Stiffening herself, determined not to fall, she edged across until she was leaning casually on her cart, her clenched fingers tucked out of sight.

Remember to breathe. The voice – her own, but calm – came to her. As if a dream, she watched Jorunn dismount, graceful and lithe. *Pay attention*, Helga told herself, although she had no need of such a reminder, not with Jorunn.

The riders were following Jorunn's lead. One was a big bruiser, clearly no stranger to violence. Another, with close-cropped grey hair and beard, looked like he'd seen and survived a lot. In fact, they all looked like hard men. *Hardly your normal trade delegation, this*, she noted. *Well, unless they're planning on trading blows.* The echo of her mother's voice made her heart beat a little slower and brought a half-smile to her face – then the last man joined them. He was small, maybe a head shorter than the grey-hair, but he moved like a cat. *Or a snake*, her internal voice helpfully added. *And the others are having none of him.* Most of them were Svear, or near as, and fighting men the likes of whom she'd seen any number of, although none the likes of her father. But this man, he was different, and not just his skin, which was darker. He was lighter on his feet and graceful, and where the others suggested strength, danger and quick tempers, he radiated calm.

For some reason, that did not put Helga at ease at all.

She busied herself re-organising her already perfectly laid-out wares in the cart so she could keep the newcomers in her field of vision without being seen to be staring. *Where is Freysteinn?* she wondered, suddenly wanting him to be there, wanting someone to whisper with, but she was alone – and Jorunn Unnthorsdottir most certainly wasn't.

She was forced to watch from a distance as bindles and bundles were unloaded at speed, the men all moving in near-silence and marshalled efficiently by the grey-haired one. Jorunn stood watching them, not moving but occasionally snapping a command, with the small, dark-skinned man at her side, relaxed but observant.

Like a well-trained attack dog.

'This is unusual.' Freysteinn sounded casually interested.

Helga had to school herself to not let on how annoyed she was that she hadn't noticed him come up behind her. 'What is?'

'We've got visitors and you're here, rearranging bags of herbs that were perfectly fine when I left, rather than fleecing them for every last bit of metal with your legendary market-wit.'

He had a smirk on him that suddenly annoyed her. *You weren't there*, she thought, and the bitterness of it surprised her. *The leader of 'those visitors' wanted to kill me.* For some reason, though, the words stayed unspoken; the urge to tell him everything about that night, the satisfaction of watching Jorunn walk into her carefully laid trap, immediately followed by the very real fear of death, had somehow vanished.

Instead, she found somewhere within her a controlled smile. 'It is not always wise to rush in,' she said coolly. 'Better to give them some time to sniff around first. If they know what's what, they'll come to me.'

His smirk turned into a smile and she found herself warming to him again. 'What are you grinning at?'

'I know how great you are,' he said, 'and I like it when you know it too.'

She made a face at him and was about to retort when movement caught her eye. *Now there's a thing.* 'Look who else is out and about,' she muttered.

Freysteinn turned, and she wondered fleetingly why the surprise on his face made her happy. 'Indeed,' he murmured. 'Thorgnyr Lawspeaker in the trading field long before any dispute has been called – have you checked for carrion?'

She grinned in response, then turned her attention back to the Lawspeaker. They weren't the only onlookers to have noticed his arrival and she watched the ripples of his presence ruffling moods. Some traders strapped on fake smiles, others, muttering, were crossing their arms and rolling their eyes. She took particular note of a few people sidling towards their wares, especially those who were trying to look innocent while surreptitiously pushing things out of sight. A couple had very convenient side compartments built into their cart, something she hadn't noticed at first, which set her wondering what might need to be hidden from the Lawspeaker's sight . . .

But Thorgnyr ignored them all.

'What's he doing?' Freysteinn muttered.

The tingle hit Helga's spine. 'He's waiting,' she whispered.

And sure enough, just a short time later, the newcomers had finished setting up their stall and Jorunn stepped out in front and started, 'People of Uppsala!' Her voice rang out, clear and strong, with just the right mix of command and invitation. 'Come and see the finest that the Dales have to offer: amber jewels to melt your heart. Mead to warm your soul. We have—'

'No permit.' Thorgnyr's nasal whine grated across the end of her sentence.

Helga's heart stopped for a moment. The interruption was somehow made more insulting by the boredom in the Lawspeaker's voice.

He knows what he's doing, Hildigunnur whispered in her ear. *He intends to rile her up and then outwit her.* Surprisingly, this annoyed Helga. She couldn't help it: for all she hated his opponent, the Lawspeaker, however clever he might be, was an innately unlikeable man.

Like a cat spotting a rival, Jorunn shifted and faced Thorgnyr. 'Permit?' she asked, her voice laced with honey.

Helga could feel the warmth of Freysteinn as he sidled up next to her. She revelled in it.

'You can't trade without a permit,' Thorgnyr said. 'King's rules.'

'King Eirik granted me a permit to trade freely in Uppsala and adjacent lands seven years ago. That would have been . . . before your time.' In her voice was the cold suggestion that her permit was not only more valid than the Lawspeaker, but would also last longer than Thorgnyr. A lot longer.

Freysteinn glanced at Helga. 'Was that a threat?' he whispered.

Yes. 'I don't know,' she whispered back, but no one was paying them any attention; all eyes were on Thorgnyr.

'Not before the time of laws,' he answered, distinctly unimpressed. 'That permit was given to your husband Sigmar and you cannot expect to use it just because you are his wife. The speech of a maiden should no man trust,' he added, turning to the crowd and winking.

Helga looked at Jorunn and her blood ran cold. *Thorgnyr had just quoted the* Hávamál *at her. That . . . was a mistake.*

There was no sign that she had taken the insult to heart. Instead, the blonde woman looked up and to the right, biting her lip just slightly, as if she was trying to remind herself of something. When she spoke again, her voice was clear and calm. 'King Eirik pays you.'

Thorgnyr blinked, almost as if surprised, and looked Jorunn up and down. 'I eat. I drink. I solve disputes and make arrangements.'

'So he pays you for your legal work in food and board.'

The Lawspeaker hesitated. Helga glanced at Freysteinn, who was staring at the two debaters. 'He does not,' Thorgnyr said slowly. 'He follows the rules of the *Book of Wisdom* and offers me guest's rights.'

'A greedy man, if he be not mindful, eats to his own life's hurt,' Jorunn said, smiling.

'That was *definitely* a threat,' Freysteinn explained breathlessly, as if Helga hadn't already worked out the implications herself. 'She's forced him to swear that he isn't getting paid, but that's meant he's had to mention guest's rights.'

I know. 'No better burden than the mother's wit,' Helga muttered. Night after night of repeating long verses full of laws about how to behave, how to treat guests and how to deal with life, came back to her, along with the image of Hildigunnur's stern face staring down at her from a height. 'You never know when it'll come in handy,' her foster-mother had said, forcing her to learn the *Hávamál*, the *Book of Customs*, by rote. *Just like her four children before me.*

'And does it not say in the *Hávamál*,' Jorunn continued, 'of your friend, that you should share thy mind with him, gifts exchange with him, fare to find him oft?' She bowed with a flourish of her cape and suddenly held in her hand a finely carved figurine, two hands tall and glistening black. Like a skald she held it still just long enough for the people close enough to get a good look at it. 'There are things we have to trade that I will swear Uppsala has never seen the like of. If I and my men may speak to the subjects of King Eirik again' – she looked around, nodding at some of the older, more respected traders, some of whom nodded back, curtly – 'I will sell, buy and bring profit and prosperity.'

And then, with a flick, she sent the figurine flying gracefully through the air. Thorgnyr flinched and flailed at it, but it landed two steps in front of him.

A perfect throw. Just close enough to force him to move and nowhere near close enough to catch. A throw designed to make him look weak and feeble.

Jorunn was polite, respectful and, above all else, devastatingly correct. Her face, carefully impassive, very loudly said, *That's my fucking permit right there.*

Then Helga glanced at Thorgnyr's face. The snide, arrogant Lawspeaker looked down on the statue as if it was a pile of rotting dung, but he was trapped in custom. He had been played at his own game and outwitted, forced to take the trinket as a guest's gift. Although quite against her will, at that moment Helga couldn't quite muster the full extent of her fury at Jorunn Unnthorsdottir.

The Lawspeaker bent down awkwardly, picked up the figurine and made a show of being unimpressed with its exquisite features. 'I will present this to King Eirik – as a gift,' he said, turning around.

Jorunn watched him turn, then without missing a beat continued her introduction. 'As we sell more from our cart, who knows what we will uncover? Come on over – and if you remember me from old, there will be a cup of mead on offer. On *that*, you can trust the speech of a maiden.'

Helga had to fight to stop herself smiling. The barb had been pitched perfectly, delivered when Thorgnyr was out of earshot and underplayed with great accuracy. She watched as the town split – not quite down the middle, because for all his faults, Thorgnyr was thought to be wise and mostly fair . . . but still, there were quite enough people in the market-field who had lost out because of his rulings, and of course anyone that close to the king would accumulate enemies. Furthermore, the people of Uppsala might have their own opinions on this, that and the other, but few would turn down free mead.

Freysteinn whistled softly. 'I can't remember seeing Thorgnyr trounced like that since . . .' He fell silent.

'Ever?' Helga said. Despite the rising morning sun, she felt like winter. It wasn't hard to imagine Hildigunnur thirty years ago, straight-backed and unflinching, arguing her way around fat traders and bearded chieftains and besting them all. It was much harder to shake the image of the feral, furious Jorunn, in a hut with her and Einar, brandishing a knife and bragging about having stabbed her brother in the back. But it was even harder to deny a touch of admiration for her foster-sister. Helga had endured Thorgnyr's grating, nasal and supercilious manner on more than one occasion, watched him parading around, safe in the knowledge that he had the king's favour and was unquestionably the wisest legal mind for as far as the eye could see, and she somehow couldn't find it in herself to side with the man who had just now, and in front of an audience to boot, been knocked down a peg or two.

Lost in her thoughts, it took her a while to notice that Freysteinn was no longer by her side. Dimly, she registered a faint warmth from her rune necklace. 'Dagaz and Laguz,' she said softly to herself. 'Hope and mystery.'

Much less calmly than she would have liked, she cast her eye around. When she finally spotted him, walking over to Jorunn's cart, her insides turned over again. By the tying post, Grundle snorted and stamped the ground again.

'I know it's fine,' she said out loud, but her words lacked conviction. Instead, she was silently cursing her location. She'd set up where experience had taught her she would attract the most customers, at the centre of the field, but Jorunn's crew had set up their cart at the edge, which meant it was too far to hear even snatches of conversation. It took some careful, *casual* movement to position herself where she could keep an eye on her wares and the customers . . . and Freysteinn's back.

The moments dragged on, slower than a winter moon – and still he stayed. *He must have seen everything she has to offer, and twice over!* Anger flared within her, but she couldn't say why, exactly.

'He can look at what he likes,' she muttered, rearranging her bags of flavour-enhancing herbs for the fifth time. 'And he can buy a statue from her and shove it up his—'

Grundle whinnied, and Helga caught herself.

'Fine, fine,' she grumbled. 'You're right and I am being stupid.' Rooting around, she found the brush and went over to comb the horse's mane. The animal nudged her gently. 'I have you,' she muttered, 'and you are honest and true.' Feeling the horse's head against her cheek was comforting, as was the blast of hot breath as the mare snorted in pleasure. 'And you have me, and it's us against the world.' Grundle blew out more air in agreement and reached her head down towards the grass, gently head-butting Helga's hip in the process.

Helga glanced over the horse's neck. *He's still there.* Before she could check herself, her feet were moving. *Too late to turn back now.*

She sent the brush sailing through the air to land in the cart. Fear and anger jostled for control within her, until both were lost to a cold, hard emotion she didn't recognise. She was dimly aware that she was walking past people she should greet, but whatever was pulling her towards the visitors' cart was pushing her away from sensible decisions.

And then she was there, looking straight at the side of Jorunn's face.

'Welcome.' The voice was lightly touched with the honey of a well-practised merchant: not too much, not too little. Enough to make you feel special, not enough to suggest she was desperate. And all without so much as a hint of recognition, because Jorunn was not taking her eyes off Freysteinn.

'Welcome to Uppsala,' Helga replied, fighting hard to keep the grimace off her face. Her voice sounded hollow, somehow – like she was outside herself, listening in on the conversation. 'Have you come from afar?' In her mind she saw Hildigunnur, rolling her eyes and throwing her hands up in the air in disgust as she started walking away from a hopelessly dim pupil. *'Come from afar?' Is that the best you've got?*

But this time, the scorn neither worked nor mattered.

'We came from the Dales,' Jorunn replied, turning to face her. 'The ride was uneventful.'

Did she just—? Helga felt her heart lurch. Did she just put a tiny bit too much emphasis on the word 'ride' and make eyes at Freysteinn?

'That's good,' Freysteinn said, sounding oblivious to the under-currents swirling between the two women.

'Oh, I don't know.'

Oh, she definitely did. Helga's blood felt dangerously close to boiling. *She's almost bloody purring.*

'It was boring, if I am to be honest. I don't mind a bit of . . . action.'

Helga felt the swelling in her breast like a breath that she never stopped taking. Within it, her heart was thudding so hard that she was sure it could be heard across the field. It took her the full blink of an eye to remember words again, and another blink to be anywhere close to being able to speak. 'You certainly did well with our Lawspeaker,' she stuttered.

'You usually get one free strike with men like that,' Jorunn replied. 'He'll be ready next time.'

'Does that worry you?' Helga listened to the words coming out of her mouth and hanging in the air between them. She sounded petty and shrill and weak. *Why won't you recognise me? You threatened to kill me, you yammering bitch!*

Jorunn looked at her fully now, and Helga suddenly felt small and powerless and childish. *She can take me and everything I own.* The thought lanced through her, carved through years of confidence and cut her to the core.

'No.' The reply was dismissive and final.

And with that, Helga let go of everything she'd tried to control. Running her hand over a row of belts beautifully coiled around a wooden block she relaxed into the cold current of her fury. 'With pricing like that, you should.'

Jorunn's manner cooled demonstrably. 'How so?'

'You're selling these—'

Jorunn interrupted, '—masterfully crafted belts, from Araby—'

'Not unless Sven from Fjarndal has changed his name to Araby in the last few months. He came through here two years back, and that' – she lifted up one of the belts and pointed to a tiny scratch, almost hidden by the buckle – 'is his rune there.'

Jorunn looked at her like someone who had just discovered a bug in their corn. 'That is kind of you to mention, but I am sure no one would think that that *clearly* exotic rune looks anything like this . . . "Sven" of yours.'

But you'll know, and you'll know that I know. Helga asked, almost as if an afterthought, 'And how much are your healing herbs?'

'We trade them on an exchange basis.'

A warmth inside made her feel like someone who has just set their own house on fire. 'So, what would I need to give you for that bag of herbs?' Jorunn made to speak but Helga held up a hand to stop her and continued, 'I ask only for curiosity, as I trade in herbs myself.'

Jorunn scowled. 'If so, then you should hope your customers will come back to you after they've seen what I have to offer,' she snapped back. Her men had gathered behind her, with the dark-skinned man standing slightly apart, looking decidedly displeased.

But with what? Helga wondered.

'And they won't, because our stuff is better than yours,' the biggest of them, the bruiser, rasped. His beady eyes glared at her from above a nose broken at least three times.

He reacted to her tone of voice like a dog to a whistle. Helga had just about enough time to form the thought when a familiar voice sounded behind her.

'Easy there, big man,' Freysteinn moved up to her side and then stepped in front of her. There was steel in his voice. 'We'll see how we go.'

'I'll see how you go,' the bruiser growled.

The dark-skinned man shifted on his feet, just a slight . . . *readiness* – then stopped. The movement had been tiny, but Helga had caught it: a sudden flick of Jorunn's fingers. A signal. *Don't.*

The big man took a pace forward, then another, more decisive this time, and squared off in front of Freysteinn. 'You jumped-up little shit, coming over here and getting in the way of us being traders, trading – uh, honestly—'

They weren't words so much as noises to start a fight, but it made no sense. *Why wouldn't she command him to stop?* She glanced at the dark-skinned man, but he'd slinked back like a morning shadow and was now standing behind Jorunn, glaring at the back of the big man's head.

She wants this. The realisation spread through Helga's blood like cold water. *The game isn't going her way, so she's changing the rules. But why?*

'Those are big words,' Freysteinn said, calmly, 'and strange ones, for a guest of the king.'

'Well, you're not making us feel very welcome,' the bruiser growled. 'And you need to show some respect.' Two quick steps and a meaty hand was on Freysteinn's chest. 'Step back and let other people through.' He pushed.

Freysteinn slapped his hand away, scowling. 'You give no orders here.'

'Neither do you, squirt,' the big man said.

'Lars . . .' Jorunn's voice was quiet and there was a low note of caution. That was the command to stop – but it was so softly spoken.

Helga wasn't even sure the man had heard her. *She has to know that he's far past listening! He's about to start a fight – what is she playing at?*

'And I will not be spoken to like this by a sapling little shit like you,' Lars growled, winding himself up even further, 'so you need to do right and apologise.' Another step and he was chest to chest with Freysteinn, but the younger man neither budged, nor replied.

'Apologise.' This time the man pushed hard, but still Freysteinn didn't shift.

Helga was desperately trying to work out what she'd missed, because this was about to get nasty if she couldn't stop it.

'Lars.' Jorunn snapped at him this time, but there was no response; she might not have spoken at all for all the attention her man was paying her.

'*Apologise!*'

'Lars – back off!' This time Jorunn did lace her voice with command, but far from obeying, Lars growled and swung at Freysteinn, his big, meaty fist clenched to do real damage.

But Freysteinn effortlessly swung out of the way of the punch – and then Helga felt the heat moments before something – no, some*one* – crashed past her.

There was a muted thud, an eye-blink of silence – and then a collection of noises as Lars hit the ground, hard.

Alfgeir knelt over the fallen man. 'In my town,' the king's right hand growled, '*I* start things, and *I* finish them.'

'Get up and shut up, Lars.' Jorunn's voice was cold.

The dark-skinned man behind her looked impassive. *He's neither flexing nor scowling. He's just . . . ready*, Helga realised. The man's unusual reactions, his *differences*, were unnerving her.

Lars sat up and glared at Jorunn, then Alfgeir. 'He disrespected me – and you! You have no right to—'

The rest of the sentence was cut short as Alfgeir delivered a vicious kick to the man's side, then grabbed him by the neck and pounded him back down. 'Was something I said *unclear* to you?'

This time, Lars didn't move. Neither did anyone else, for that matter. Lying on the ground, the man shook his head slowly.

'Good,' Alfgeir growled. 'Now you will listen to me, and this time you will *hear* me. If you so much as look at anyone funny from now until you leave, your friends may have to search the woods for a while before they find all the parts of your body. What do you say?'

He muttered something into his chest.

'I didn't hear you.'

'I will,' Lars hissed between gritted teeth, 'respect the peace and the king's rule.'

Alfgeir stood up and took a couple of steps back. Only now did he appear to notice Jorunn's delegation and maybe it was Helga's imagination, but his shoulders stiffened somewhat.

But Jorunn didn't see the reaction to her presence, for her

attention was fixed on her man on the ground. 'I thought we'd had a conversation,' she said. Without waiting for his answer, she snapped, 'Stand up.'

Lars did as he was told and Jorunn slapped him across the face.

It took him a moment to realise what had happened. Helga couldn't see his expression, but the sudden set of his shoulders told the tale and stung into shock, he made as if to move towards Jorunn – then he suddenly stopped in his tracks. A slight movement from the dark-skinned man had apparently convinced him that acting on his impulses would be, at this moment at least, a very bad idea.

'You do not disobey my orders. You do not bring the Dales into disrepute. And' – Jorunn's lips were pursed so hard that her mouth looked ready to break – 'you do not step in front of me. Ever.'

For a moment the bruiser looked ready to speak, but he reconsidered and head bowed, stomped back to his place behind the grey-haired commander, who was glaring at him.

Jorunn turned to Alfgeir. 'On behalf of the men of the Dales, I would like to ask that you forgive Lars. He has a hot head and little wit to fill it with.'

Helga watched her, a mixture of emotions swirling through her. The first, and strongest, hurt her the most. *Jorunn is Hildigunnur's. I was never her real daughter.* Jorunn looked regal and commanding. She spoke with absolute certainty and would never back down.

Helga turned to Alfgeir, and her mood improved drastically. *And Alfgeir Bjorne is decidedly unimpressed.*

'Words are cheap, Jorunn Unnthorsdottir, and the gods know

you have enough of them.' Alfgeir did not take so much as a half-step to meet Jorunn's attempt at reconciliation and the grizzled band behind Jorunn, recognising it, bunched together a little tighter. They were trying hard not to betray emotions, but Helga thought she had caught one or two of them flinching. *Do they like her – or just fear her?*

'I had hoped for a better welcome, Alfgeir,' Jorunn said.

'After your husband ran away from a wergild negotiation?'

'It was never proven,' Jorunn snapped. 'It was their word against ours.'

'And yet you did not stay long enough to let the sitting council clear your name.'

'We had business to attend to. I've done nothing wrong.'

'Never said you had.' Alfgeir smiled. 'You can come and go wherever you please, without any worry for your reputation.'

Helga found she was wincing as a shadow of anger flickered across Jorunn's face at the insult, but then the mask of control was back in place.

'But if you do, prepare to see your name in the mud. And if you cannot keep your dog on a leash . . .'

The threat was the worst kind: a *polite* one. Helga watched as glances passed between Jorunn's travelling companions. More than one of them stole a look at the dark-skinned man. *Jorunn's camp might be tense tonight.*

Alfgeir continued, 'King Eirik confirms that you have licence to trade. Do not overstep the bounds of his hospitality, and do not test my patience. There is a lot more of one than the other.' With that the big man nodded, shot Helga a glance that clearly said, *Get away from here if you know what's best for you!* and walked off.

The moment his broad back was turned, everyone around Jorunn's cart did an incredible job of pretending nothing had happened. After a moment's indecision, Helga decided that Alfgeir was correct: it would be the right thing to walk away as well, and without prompting, Freysteinn followed her. Neither of them spoke as they made their way across the field to where Grundle stood, thoughtfully chewing on grass.

Finally, Freysteinn broke the silence. 'I've never seen you go after another trader like that.'

'No.' After a while, 'I don't think I ever have.'

'So why her?'

'Because I know her.' It was out of her mouth without warning. She felt the lump in her throat growing.

'You know her?' Freysteinn sounded almost alarmed. 'How?'

She couldn't name either of the feelings clashing within her, but one won over the other. 'I grew up on a farm in the Norse dales. Jorunn's mother took me in once all her children had left. In my seventeenth summer they all came back for a kin-meet – only none of them wanted to meet the others; they just wanted their father's treasure. After a hard feast the oldest, Karl, was killed in his sleep by his younger brother.'

Freysteinn just stared at her, his mouth hanging open. She waited for a moment, but he didn't ask any questions.

'Unnthor, the man I called "father", threatened to kill anyone who left, so there we were. Jorunn lied, manipulated and eventually stabbed her brother in the back. I found her out and made her confess. She threatened to kill me – she probably would have done, if Unnthor and his men hadn't heard her through the walls. I laid a trap – and she walked straight into it. She is rotten to the core, that one. There is more to the story, of course, but that is the bones of it.'

Helga took a deep breath, like she'd just come up after a long swim underwater, and noticed that Freysteinn seemed to be looking at her . . . differently. *He sees me as an equal.* The thought was thrilling. She was feeling . . . light, almost as if she'd launched herself off a cliff, tumbled head over heels in the air and landed on her feet. The show-down with Jorunn felt like she'd been tested, and had passed.

Around them, the other traders had all packed up and left. Jorunn's people were long gone, as was their cart.

Grundle swished her tail, just to remind Helga of her existence, and Freysteinn touched her arm, gently, as if to reassure her that he too was still there. 'We can discuss that . . . later.' His glance told her where to look. One of the multitude of boys Alfgeir occasionally tipped to run his messages was making his way across the field.

Helga was relieved. Now that Freysteinn knew, the world was level again. He would know to look out for Jorunn and not be taken in by her particular brand of magic. She didn't have to carry it all on her own. And if she didn't have to do that, she could cope with Eirik and Alfgeir. When she thought back on Riverside, she remembered standing between Unnthor, Hildigunnur and their children and feeling quite alone in the world.

She glanced at Freysteinn. *Not alone any more.*

'Alfgeir wants to see you.' Satisfied that they'd heard and understood, the boy turned and ran off without offering any further explanation.

Freysteinn looked mildly amused. 'Maybe he wants us to compose a ballad to honour his slaying of the impudent Dalesman.'

'That's fine,' Helga said. 'I'll sing. You can do the words.'

· 'Because I am a skald by nature?'

'Because you have the voice of a wounded goose.'

'Filthy Norse-witch!' He took two steps towards her and aimed a slap at her backside, which she nimbly dodged. As she went skipping towards the hill, he followed her, calling, 'Wounded goose? I will keep silent from now on.'

'Oh, please don't,' she said. 'A girl needs something to amuse her.'

'I should have gone hunting and found myself a fox for a pet instead. Save myself the grievous wounding.'

This is too easy. 'You'd have to come to me anyway and explain why you needed salve for claw-marks on your thighs.'

'Hey!'

She giggled as he gave chase, resolving not to run too fast.

From his spot on the hill just outside the longhouse, Breki took in the view, watching the sun setting in the distance sending shadowy talons from the eastern tree line raking along the path towards them. He was standing at the back of Ingileif's group, only half-listening to the mutterings of the men. When they'd got back to the camp, Rolf had forced him to relay the entire conversation, word for word, as promised, and while he hadn't been quite impressed enough for Breki's liking, the promised punishments – overly elaborate, to his mind – hadn't materialised, so he'd had to be content with that. Big Rolf had also taken the trouble to explain to him that the negotiations had gone well and that they'd got what they wanted – but he'd asked why the old woman still looked so sour and Big Rolf had said that it also showed that trouble was brewing, because otherwise the king would have driven a much harder bargain. Breki had seen the sense of this.

But the day wasn't done yet. Now they had to go back to eat, drink and make merry with all these people. But he was tired. He'd seen more men in one day than in his whole life and the sheer size of Uppsala was making him feel a little sick. All the mumbled half-sentences, sideways looks and intensely furrowed brows weren't helping.

'You might need to wrestle.' Big Rolf had suddenly appeared at his elbow.

'. . . uh . . . what?' Breki almost had to shake himself out of the enveloping line of darkness creeping towards them.

'Wrestle – you know, grab someone, twist them and throw them to the ground? You've done this before, yes?' The short man slapped him on his muscular forearm, as if to remind him what it was for.

Breki frowned. Thinking back, he remembered his father looking unhappy when Big Rolf had said they 'might need the big lad' but he'd been focused on the adventure and hadn't given it much thought. But on the other hand, unlike trade conversations where every sentence apparently meant something entirely different, wrestling was something he did understand.

'I see. Could've told me earlier.'

'And while you were listening and paying attention, you could also have been a good boy and tried to think for yourself,' Big Rolf replied crisply. 'And to get ahead of the next question desperately trying to crawl out of your thick skull: you have to wrestle because there will be drinking, and there will be folk from other parts who will have their own wrestlers, and we will be putting on a show for the king. During this show, a lot of business is done. Also, screaming and sweating and drinking together makes friends out of enemies. Well, most of the time.'

'Fine.' His shoulders were beginning to tense up, so he flexed them, enjoying the feeling of coiled strength. He stretched his spine and his thigh muscles as well – then without warning, he grabbed Big Rolf by the hips.

'Stop it,' the old man muttered, but Breki just grinned, bunched the material of tunic and trousers in both hands and started to lift.

'Stop it!' The mutter had turned to a hiss as Big Rolf's feet left the ground.

Breki affected surprise, letting go and raising his hands in the air. 'What? You can't just tell me to wrestle and then not expect me to warm up.'

Safely back on the ground, Big Rolf adjusted his trousers in the crotch with a look of disgust. 'I am told by reliable sources that your grandparents lived in a cave in the mountains and filed their teeth.'

'After eating your grandparents for a late morning snack, no doubt,' Breki retorted.

A flicker of a smile, gone in an instant. 'Just . . . watch yourself,' the old man said, before scuttling away to retake his place at Ingileif's side.

Watch yourself. Breki chewed it over. He'd not had a great need to watch himself since he'd reached his full height, which had happened a good three years before his peers. This summer, his thirteenth, he'd been half a head taller and a good two hands wider than the next biggest boy in the village and more than happy to take on all-comers when it came to wrestling. His body was that of a full-grown man, and then some. After easily throwing a huge Finn at Spring Festival, he'd noticed Big Rolf pull his father aside for a quick talk, and not long after that, he'd received the invitation to eat at the North Wind's table. That had been three months ago and now he was here, getting ready to wrestle in King Eirik's own longhouse.

He blinked, realising he'd been so lost in his own thoughts that he hadn't noticed half of his group had already gone inside. He followed them in – and stopped dead, astounded by the change. It looked exactly like he'd always imagined Valhalla to be.

Earlier that day the king's hall had been a big, functional box of a room, all hard benches, cold light and sharp words. Now mounted torches sent golden light flickering off the walls and dancing up to the rafters and the smells of rich broth, cured meat and honey perfumed the air. A soft but persistent hum of voices, all speaking at once, bounced off the walls, that somehow looked more substantial in the living light. The benches now pushed back around the walls were already half-full with the men and women of Uppsala.

At the end of the room sat King Eirik, flanked by the Bear and the bored Lawspeaker. A young man pushed past him, towing a willowy woman, and Breki found his eyes lingering on her supple frame and raven-black hair for a moment, enjoying the way she moved with such lightness and grace – they both did. They were making their way towards a seat very near the king's dais. He would have stopped and stared for longer, but for the fact that his group was taking up position on the far side of the longhouse and Big Rolf was gesturing fiercely at him. Just as he took the seat Big Rolf was pointing at, he heard the door creak open behind them and a wave of silence spread out towards the end of the hall.

'Ludin of Skane greets King Eirik and the people of Uppsala!'

The voice rang out, filling the room, and Breki turned to see, but the king was already rising from his seat and calling, 'Well met, Ludin – come, join us!' He waved the newcomers towards an empty table on the opposite side from where the Northmen had settled.

There were twelve of them, but only a couple stood out: a woman, dressed in blue from head to toe, with a wide belt that looked expensive even from a distance. Her hair was bunched up in a traveller's bun and she moved like a rider. By her side walked a man who looked much more like a king than the king himself. The line of his nose and the trim of his beard spoke of riches, just like his embroidered cloak – but nothing said more than the long-sword resting in a hilt off his left hip. Breki glanced at Big Rolf. *A sword!* He'd never seen one, only heard about them in stories of men who went a-Viking, although few enough of them came back to their villages. There were some tales of swords buried in warrior hoards too, but he'd never seen one of those either.

This is what a king and queen look like, he thought.

Then a third man caught his eye: a gaunt, twitchy fellow who was scanning the room this way and that. He reminded Breki of a frightened but dangerous dog.

Ahead of them walked a servant, or a thrall, maybe, a tired man in middle age, unremarkable in every way, dressed in traveller's garb and half a head shorter than the rest of the group.

'How did you find the ride up here, Ludin?' The king sounded almost deferential.

Breki watched the swordsman intently, but oddly, it was his servant who spoke up.

'Oh, it was fine. We have been up for a while.'

Breki squeezed his eyes shut then opened them quickly, wanting to make sure he'd seen aright, before casting another glance at Big Rolf, who rewarded him with a scowl and a not very subtle reminder to keep watching.

'Oh?' King Eirik sounded surprised by this.

'Yes,' said the servant, who must after all be Ludin of Skane himself, as his group sat down behind him. He searched for the right words, then smiled. His smile was not a pleasant thing.

'I have been enjoying your forests for a little bit of hunting.'

Chapter 4

FEAST

The heat was overpowering, the noise was awful, the conversation mindless, but of all the things that were getting to her, the smell was the worst: a hundred and fifty warriors sitting and sweating together was a special kind of unpleasant. *A herd of cows farting would make this better, not worse.* Freysteinn had long since left her to go and howl at the moon with the other hounds. In a cold way, she was quite enjoying plunging into the depths of her own foul mood.

Ever since Ludin of Skane had entered the longhouse, her mind had been racing. *I have been enjoying your forests for a little bit of hunting.* The pallid face of the boy, the too-cold feel of his skin on her fingertips, wouldn't leave her mind. Had he encountered Ludin and his men? Had he surprised them during . . . *something*? She glanced covertly their way again. They all looked like they could bash someone's brains out with a rock without a second thought. Every last one of them looked battle-hardened, even the woman in blue and the over-decorated tree trunk with the sword. As if her thoughts were drawing him, the tree trunk turned and caught her eye. A slow, hungry smile formed on his lips as she looked away. She thought of what Hildigunnur would have said and blushed bright red. *Subtle as a bull in a knot-hole*, or something equally bawdy, of that she had no doubt.

The faces of the women sitting next to her announced his arrival before he did. He was dressed in rich blue with a dark cape to match, well-worn, but ornately decorated. *That's some riding outfit.* It had clearly been layered with gold with the intent of catching every possible ray of light. 'Gunnar,' he said. He was clearly someone who was thoroughly pleased to wake up as himself every morning. Even the arch of his neck and the way he looked down his nose at her was irritating.

Helga searched herself for any wish to speak to him and found herself coming up empty. She looked up at him, willing him to understand that she wanted him to take a running leap into a nettle field – but he did not.

'Gunnar of Skar,' he repeated, and when that addition didn't change anything, his face clouded over with confusion for a moment – then comprehension appeared to dawn on him. 'You . . . haven't heard of me.'

The temptation to carve him up with words was like a bad itch, but she forced herself to remember what Hildigunnur had taught her: *Don't break branches until you have to make a club.* She was still an outsider in this town and she didn't know the women next to her well enough. Cutting down this trumped-up cock might be satisfying tonight but it might cause her trouble later. She pulled on an apologetic face she found somewhere hidden away and bowed her head a fraction. 'I am afraid not, m'lord. Sometimes important news takes a while to reach us.' *Which is true, and in no way suggests that you are important, but . . .*

'I see,' he said, beaming.

But you clearly think so and that could be . . . useful. She reminded herself to remember the benefits of patience next time without having to have Hildigunnur's voice in her head doing so. Gunnar of Skar sat down uninvited and, looking none-too-subtly at her breasts, started, 'Well, down south they sing of the victories of Ludin, and my part in them.'

I'm sure they do. 'You must give us an example!' She stopped short of touching him – the very notion made her skin crawl – but she sensed from some of the more reticent women around her that she, as apparently unelected spokesperson for the group, had done the right thing. *Men are mostly bears, but women are many animals.* She wondered idly if Hildigunnur's words would ever stop coming back to her. There had been a lot of learning at Riverside, not all of it obvious. *And you weren't the only one to benefit,* she told herself again as a burst of laughter indicated where Jorunn was currently holding her own small but entirely devoted court.

'Oh, well,' said Gunnar. He settled into his much-told story like a greybeard into his pile of mangy furs and Helga braced herself to be patient and let the river flow. She'd learned that a lot of men liked to talk a lot, and when they did, they rarely watched all the words that came out. She made sure she was gazing at him whenever he remembered to look at his audience – which now included three other young women, one of whom Helga sort-of recognised, who had turned around on their bench to join her – and spent the rest of the time scanning the crowd. Jorunn, surrounded by men, was controlling a lively conversation much like a farmer would his dogs. The dark-skinned man was hovering nearby, still and poised in an ocean of increasingly erratic movement.

In front of her, Gunnar was still talking. '. . . and then they came for us, all twelve – actually, no, I misremembered; it was fifteen of them, and—'

Might have started as three. Will probably end as thirty. Truth is rarely present when we write our own stories.

Ludin was now sitting up on the dais, talking with King Eirik and Alfgeir Bjorne, who was leaning in, watching and listening with attention. In an otherwise crowded hall, for some reason few people were coming anywhere near to the unassuming old man. She kept studying the crowd, while Gunnar prattled on, '. . . course, we knew we had to get to the ship, and quick! So I drew steel—'

The Northmen were not quite clumped together, but none of them had strayed more than seven steps from the next one. Dimly, she recognised that something had changed. Sound. Sounds. *Shit. He's stopped talking.*

'That is incredible!' She coated her voice with adoration and gazed at Gunnar.

He beamed. 'Oh, it was only what any man of honour would do. It's nothing like when I—'

'Gunnar. It's almost time.' The hand on his shoulder was slim and pale, but not in any way fragile. Helga glanced up – and up – and up. The blonde woman was almost as tall as Gunnar, and

her eyes were sharper by far than his carved features. She looked
Helga straight in the eyes and smiled. 'I am Drifa Styrsdottir, of
Ludin's party.'

'She packs our lunches and counts our chickens,' Gunnar bur-
bled happily.

She keeps you alive, you idiot.

Helga did not break gaze with the blonde woman. The negotiation was quick, but pleasant. 'I am Helga Unnthorsdottir, healer
of wounds and—'

'—seller of herbs. Your name is known, and I have been
meaning to seek you out. Gunnar, go and see to the men. They
need to be in good voice.'

Like a trained dog, the tall man rose, but he still took the time
to wink at Helga before he turned away and strode across the
floor, swishing his gold-adorned cape.

The moment he'd gone, the other three young women found
reasons to drift away from the bench.

Drifa waited until everyone was gone before asking, 'Did he
tell you about a raid on King Aethelstan?'

Helga made a quick judgment. 'Um . . . probably?'

The tall woman laughed, and they were friends. 'I think he
thought you were giving him the eye.' The face made by this
admission told more than any words and Drifa laughed out loud
again, a bright, pleasant sound. 'To be fair, he sees that everywhere he goes. Your three friends' – Helga grimaced, and Drifa
lifted her eyebrows – 'and a more than reasonable number of
other young women do get blinded by the gold. He's hopelessly
vain, but even though he might preen like a songbird, I will say

there is some truth to some of the stories. That thing dangling by his leg is not just for decoration.'

'Really?'

'There are a fair number of widows and fatherless children because of him.'

For some reason, that gave Helga a little bit of satisfaction. Given all his posturing, she had not immediately had Gunnar of Skar pegged as an effective mass-murderer, but she had suspected that underneath there was an edge to the man. Drifa, on the other hand . . . her edge was somewhere else.

'I am still relatively new in these parts,' Helga said. 'I have spent most of my time here finding out just how much I don't know.'

'Everywhere is like that, I guess. Every place has stories that will kill you if you aren't aware of them.'

'Precisely.' *Was that a threat? Or a warning?* 'That is why meeting people from other places and talking is important.'

Drifa glanced out across the King's Hall, where large, well-feasted, drink-filled men were either bumping into each other, howling out the words to half-remembered songs or laughing raucously. 'Is that your . . . ?'

In the middle of the floor, Freysteinn was leading a complicated combination of dance and song that looked to be two parts mead, one part mortal danger and all parts joy. Helga smiled. 'Yes.'

'Well done. Tamed yourself quite the horse there.'

Yes. Yes indeed. Well done. 'He's the one I want to walk with. He makes me . . .' Her eyes met Drifa's and no other words were necessary.

*

94

Breki looked out at the sea of humans and felt thoroughly sick. Big Rolf had offered him a cup of mead, but he'd only accepted once it was clear that it was heavily watered. Alcohol didn't help with balance, and while he could probably get away with that at home, this felt . . . different.

'Scared?' Big Rolf had silently appeared at his elbow again, but the question had none of the usual gentle mocking attached to it.

'No,' Breki said, on reflex.

'Then you're an idiot,' Big Rolf said affectionately. 'A lumbering baby idiot.'

'Whereas you are only the size of a baby.'

Big Rolf smirked. 'Everywhere but my trousers.'

Breki relaxed, the familiar banter somehow a comfort. 'What can I expect?'

'You're going up against the best wrestlers in the three other corners of the land of the Svear. What do you think you'll get?'

'They'll be strong,' Breki mused.

'And?'

'I don't know. Very strong?'

Big Rolf looked at him. '. . . yes. But you are no weakling yourself.'

Breki thought about how he'd felt his own strength growing, the way he'd started finding things were suddenly easier to lift, and something within him uncoiled a little. 'That is true,' he said.

'And you have speed, and you know where to put your feet,' Big Rolf said, which also made Breki feel better, until he added, 'But one thing you don't have is experience, and that is harder to get.'

'So where do I get experience?'

Big Rolf pointed to the raucous crowd in the middle of the longhouse. 'By taking on the best.'

'Are you Northmen?' The voice belonged to a squat man with a reddish beard.

'Our balls are as frozen as they get,' Big Rolf replied. 'This bear-child is Breki and I am Big Rolf. He keeps saying that I am not his father.'

Some emotion flitted across the man's face, but it was hard to tell what it was. He was slurring his words a little, but there was determination in his voice. 'Have you travelled around south of Uppsala?'

Breki watched as Big Rolf's manner changed. 'We have not,' he said. 'Not recently, at any rate. Why?'

'My name is Alvar Dal and I am looking for my son,' the man said. 'He left our home in the Dales to find his fortune, but he always promised he'd come back. I heard he'd been seen in Hedeby, but then he disappeared without a trace – but I know he is out there somewhere.'

'Tell me more about him.'

Breki almost didn't see it happen, but somehow Big Rolf had quickly moved them so that they were facing away from most of the shouting, almost cocooned in a little pocket of quiet. He'd also somehow conjured a bit of dried meat, which he was offering to the red-bearded stranger.

'He's not a fighter, not as such. Smart boy, though,' the man was saying, and Breki could hear the hope and pride in his voice as he accepted the gift. 'He's got this big birthmark on his left cheek, and red hair like mine. He enjoys his food too, like his

Da.' At this the man patted his significant belly and smiled, but despite that, something in his face struck Breki as sad and broken.

'If I see him, Alvar Dal, I will tell him that he should return home.' Big Rolf's voice was calm, strong and reassuring.

The man clapped him on the shoulder and thanked him before ducking back into the crowd.

'What was that about?'

Big Rolf was thoughtful. 'That was a man searching for something I fear he will not find.'

As the great mass of men swallowed Alvar Dal, Breki wondered yet again at the sheer number of people in the world, until Big Rolf broke into his ruminations.

'Now you need to get your head back to where it needs to be, got it? We are about to begin.'

They must be able to smell the impending violence. Helga watched with interest as a space cleared in front of the dais in the middle of the floor. Nobody was ordering anyone around or giving any commands, but soon enough cups had been refilled and the benches which had been pulled up around the space were crowded with eager men. The hush spreading around the hall was not quite silence, but sounded like a hundred conversations being taken down to just above a whisper. Suddenly the delegations from the west, south and north were clearly visible, each standing slightly apart from the crowd.

Helga smiled wryly to herself as she examined the potential combatants. *They might as well have arranged themselves on a map.* Alfgeir had told her about the wrestling, warning her she should be ready to help if there were any – and he'd chewed on the word – *accidents*.

Of course she'd agreed, completely ignoring the possibility that real harm might be done to someone in the cause of entertainment . . . but now she wasn't so sure. Usually the worst you'd get after a drunken scuffle was a sprain. Weapons were very rarely drawn, and if they were, the situation would change very quickly, but there was usually someone around with clout enough to stop things before anything turned really nasty. There was a definite benefit to making sure that it was in no one's interest to go brandishing weapons about the place.

I really hope that holds here, she thought, not entirely convinced, for there was definitely something in the air and it wasn't good.

'Well met, friends!' King Eirik shouted over the crowd, which was met with a lusty roar. 'We are gathered here to trade, to talk' – he paused for a moment to make sure everyone was hanging on his words – 'and to answer a very important question!'

This time the roar was even louder; they knew what was coming.

'North, west, south – or indeed, east! – who is the best . . . at *wrestling*?'

The noise threatened to shake the King's Hall apart.

They really do like shouting. Helga fought to keep the grimace from her face and her hands from covering her ears.

'And so first up, we go to the Dales! Dalesmen, who is your champion?'

'Lars Larkwood!' Despite the crush, Jorunn had of course found herself a space on one of the benches; now she stood on it, head and shoulders above her men, and shouted, 'A sweet and humble soul from the valleys, Lars is; he has never hurt a fly. We can only hope that he is treated gently!'

The laughter that followed her words was rough, knowing and mean.

Lars stepped forward and pulled off his shirt. As he tied his trousers with the thick cord required for the grapple, he flexed.

Helga frowned. *The man looks like a carthorse.* She thought for a moment about Freysteinn, and how he hadn't budged an inch when faced with the big Dalesman, and a thrill went through her.

'Well met, Lars! Although I am given to understand that you have already met our champion.' King Eirik was calm, almost friendly, and his insult landed softly, but it landed true. Surrounded by smirking faces, Lars stiffened.

When Helga looked at the dais, she saw that Alfgeir's seat was empty.

Moments later, the king's right-hand man stepped into the ring, finishing up the knot on his own wrestler's cord. Without his tunic he really did look like some sort of beast from the old tales: a huge, hairy half-bear with long, powerful arms ending in paws that could probably crush a man's skull.

She could feel the bowstring of anticipation pulling taut in the hall.

In the centre, Lars looked at Alfgeir and scowled.

'Well met, Alfgeir Bjorne!' Jorunn cried, looking over the heads of the enrapt audience towards King Eirik, and she raised her arm.

Up on the dais he did the same.

They shouted as one, both their arms fell – and the noise of the crowd rose to meet them. The two men immediately started circling, their arms wide, meaty hands spread. Helga tried to pick out Freysteinn from the crowd, but it was just a mass of frantic red faces, arms flailing, mouths moving in sounds that were drowned in the general hubbub. Then there came a great roar and when she turned back to the wrestlers, the big man from the Dales was clutching his left upper arm, his face contorted in a grimace. His eyes were trained on Alfgeir, even as his muscles were visibly pulsing with fury.

Lars launched himself again at the king's man, swooping in this time, his hands dropped to Alfgeir's waist – and were stopped in mid-air as Alfgeir's palms met his chest with force. Moments later, Alfgeir's hands were clenching Lars' belt and he was pushing, *pushing*, as Lars flailed for his own purchase on his rival's cord. He battered away at Alfgeir's arms, their legs straining, and for just a moment they were perfectly balanced, the one against the other – until Lars started to move backwards, then his feet left the ground and, slowly at first – slow enough for his brain to catch up with what was happening and for his face to register fury, then horror – then faster, Alfgeir's hip swivelled, his arms heaved, and with a twist, Lars went flying.

The man from the Dales landed with a great crash, to the roar of the home crowd. Helga's eyes went to Jorunn, expecting to see anger, disappointment, disgust – but instead, there was closely guarded triumph. It was so frustrating: there was a game being played, and she didn't know the rules. The calm smugness on the other woman's face did nothing to improve Helga's mood and it took her a moment to realise that she had been distracted, for in that eye-blink, cheers of celebration had turned to roars of outrage. Her eyes were drawn to the ring once more, where Lars was back on his feet, red-faced and coughing. He managed no words, but an accusatory finger was pointed straight at Alfgeir Bjorne. He coughed again, violently, and Helga winced. *That's going to hurt in the morning.*

'You fight without honour!' Lars rasped at last.

Oohs and indrawn breaths swept the room, but Alfgeir looked entirely untouched. 'Please say that again. I couldn't hear you . . . over the noise of me putting you on your back like a fishwife.'

Loud laughter from some of the more sober among the audience amplified the insult. Helga could only see his broad back, but the snigger in his voice carried loudly enough.

Lars didn't take the offered exit route but repeated, 'You have no honour!'

This time the crowd fell silent, and it was not a good silence. It didn't take a Lawspeaker to know that Lars was breaking the rules. They'd fought; he'd lost.

Alfgeir leaned forward. 'What was that last word?'

'Honour!' Lars was all fury now, red-faced, muscles taut – and apparently completely oblivious to the growing outrage and chorus of jeering and booing from the crowd.

'I thought so,' Alfgeir said. 'In *my* county we teach our ill-mannered children not to use words they don't understand.'

The big Dalesman screamed and charged. Helga saw the muscles tense in Alfgeir's broad back and braced herself for a crunching sound, the smell of blood and screams of pain. Despairingly, she thought, *Why do they always have to do this?*

But it was all over in a moment. She heard a big roar from Alfgeir, followed by the thud of someone dropping a carcase from a great height. There was half a heartbeat of silence – and the longhouse filled with a roar even louder than before.

'Helga!' The shout snapped her out of her daze. Freysteinn appeared in her field of vision, gesturing for her to come quickly. She fought her way through the drunken masses to Lars, who was lying flat on his back once again, but this time he was holding his throat, looking anguished. His face was turning from red to purple, but he wasn't shouting at anyone ... in fact, he wasn't making any sort of breathing sounds.

Oh, for fuck's sake.

She stilled the part of her mind that always thought too much, let irritation over the sheer stupidity of men be her flame and acted. The sharp little knife was in her hand in a blink while part of her was noting that the crowd had gone quiet, expectant, almost. Killing a man in the ring would probably do nothing to lessen Alfgeir's fame.

They're waiting for him to die. Well, not on my watch. Sorry to disappoint you.

'Hold him down,' she snapped at Freysteinn, who immediately and silently did as he was told. 'Keep him still.' She placed the knife at Lars' throat.

'Hey—!' someone shouted from the crowd – a warning? But a hard-snapped command from a woman's voice stopped whoever it was in their tracks.

Jorunn? She couldn't think about that, not now. She pushed – *just there, gently ... gently now ...* until a fat drop of blood rose to meet her. She remembered when Groa had shown her how to do this, the bony hand grabbing hers that first time and forcing her to push through when she was being too weak, too tentative. She remembered the thud of her heart in her chest, how she'd screamed out loud that she *couldn't*, that she was *killing her*, and her absolute shocked surprise at the wheezing, bubbling sound of breath the girl on the ground made, followed by the sudden rising of her chest. She let the thoughts drift through her mind as she finished the work, making the incision *just* so, right there between the two nubs on the throat, then easing her little finger in until she found the hollow space.

'Straw,' she snapped at Freysteinn.

'. . . what?'

She looked up to see him standing there, all clueless and worried. 'Get. Me. A. Straw. The roof is covered in it. You'll find some in the corners. Needs to be hollow. And clean! Go – NOW.'

He darted away, slinking through the crowd like a dog after a rat, and returned surprisingly quickly with three long, coarse straws. Helga examined them. *Ah well. If he dies, he dies.* She picked the cleanest one, sliced off an end, blew through it and eased it into the bloodied incision. The big man's chest fell – then it rose again, ever so slowly – and fell. She felt for the end of the tube and placed her finger very carefully over it. The faintest hint of air tickled her finger.

The crowds parted and Jorunn appeared, flanked by four of her men. 'He'll live.' Not a question but rather a statement of fact.

'Yes.' Try as she might, she couldn't suppress her annoyance. *She has stolen control of the situation.*

'Odin will have to do without a great warrior for another night!' The line was delivered perfectly, and got the response she had no doubt calculated. All the crowd's attention was on Jorunn now and no one was sparing Helga even half a glance as Jorunn's men bent down to pick up their injured friend.

'Careful,' Helga snapped at the nearest one, taking back control, at least for a moment. 'You – hold the head. And hold it still. If that straw slips, he's for the dogs tonight.' She looked at the next and barked, 'Stay with him, and watch him carefully.'

Under her critical gaze, Lars was gently lifted and carried carefully out of the ring, two men going ahead to clear a path.

'The brave man of the Dales lives to fight another day – but the east has shown its might!' King Eirik's voice cut through the throng as the ring cleared.

Feeling invisible and suddenly exhausted, Helga got up and moved out of the way. *No one needs me any more, so back in the pen I go.*

A warm hand touched her elbow, her body knowing before she'd registered his presence. 'You saved his life,' Freysteinn said, the sweet smell of mead on his breath, and the tone of his voice told her a hundred other things, and there was hope and joy again.

How can you be such a sun in my day? She felt almost angry at him for being able to take away her darkness. That was a perfectly good black mood he'd ruined.

'Come. Sit with me.' She looked at him and couldn't find words, for he was looking her in the eyes and everything around them had faded and he was stars and heat. 'Because I'm proud of you and want to be seen with you,' he added, and she let herself be led by him to a raised seat near the dais. They settled down just in time to see Gunnar of Skar stand up and step towards the ring.

Breki was watching Big Rolf, who looked like he was trying to see everyone in the hall at the same time.

'Are you ready, boy?' The old man punched him in the arm twice. 'Ready to wrestle?'

'Yes,' he replied, although it was a lie, and they both knew it. Breki had had to work hard to keep looking when the two big men had crashed together, feeling suddenly very much like a pup among wolves. Who was he to think that he could be considered anyone's equal here, in this place of chieftains? He was just a boy, nothing more.

The sting of the slap was sharp, jerking Breki's head to one side. Big Rolf was staring at him now, straight at him and through him, and there was no way he could look away.

'Listen,' he growled, 'I've seen my share and your share and twice anyone else's share of fighting and it is *never* the size of the fighter that wins it. Do what you know how to do and do it with honour, and if anyone gives a frozen yak-shit whether you win or lose, I'll make them eat it. Do you understand me?'

'Yes,' Breki said, and this time Big Rolf didn't slap him.

Instead, the old man smiled. 'Good. Now get up and enjoy yourself.'

Across the hall a tall, blonde woman had risen. 'From the land of Skane, we present one of our finest: a fighter of fame and a favourite of the skalds.' Next to her, the equally tall man who looked like a king was unbuckling his sword.

Big Rolf was looking past the woman. Suddenly all colour drained from his face and he started muttering, 'Shit. No. Shit. No no no no no NO!' He hissed and spat and disappeared.

Breki looked around to see the woman had stopped speaking and was looking down at Ludin, for the jarl himself had stepped up and put his hand gently on the fighter's arm. The taller man almost wilted, shrinking back into his clothes. The woman started to say something, but the chieftain made a motion with his hand and she fell silent, as did most of the rest of the hall. Breki looked around for Big Rolf and eventually spotted him in heated conversation with Ingileif. Big Rolf looked furious, but the North Wind was shaking her head and although she was a bit of a way away, Breki thought she was almost sad.

Were the Southerners withdrawing? The thought took root in Breki's head and blossomed like a flower in spring. He could escape with his honour intact. There would be stories to tell back home and none of them would involve him being thrown around like a rag doll to the North Wind's everlasting shame. Relief flooded his veins—

—until Ludin of Skane himself stepped forward, the wrestling cord already snug around his waist.

There was no announcement this time, no banging on benches or stomping on the ground. Instead, Ludin just walked from his table and into the ring, nodding towards the place where the Northmen were gathered. A lot of very large men shrank back to let him pass untouched. All eyes were fixed on the man in the ring, but he did nothing: no shouting, no flexing, no show; he just quietly removed his shirt.

Big Rolf's voice rang out to meet him. 'And to meet Ludin of Skane we have a boy we found under a pine tree! Raised by bears, we suspect that he is part human – but we rarely step close enough to him to find out. Step aside – for Breki Bjarnason!'

Breki touched his cord, checking it, then looked up.

Like a big beast waking up, the King's Hall greeted him with loud cheers and a path cleared for him towards the open space in the middle of the great room. Breki started moving, but everything was feeling unreal, like a dream. Ludin was a creature from tales, mostly of wars with Rus wildmen. He had been killing people for twice the summers that Breki had even been alive. There were *songs* about him. He couldn't be real, so this couldn't be either.

The noise washed over Breki, buffeting him from side to side, until someone slapped him hard on the back and the sting of it woke up something within him. Big Rolf's words echoed in his head: *Enjoy yourself.*

Breki stepped into the ring and found that up close, he positively towered over the notorious warlord. Furthermore, the little man was *old*: he had to have cleared forty winters, easily. There was grey in his hair and his face was creased. He had little muscle to speak of; his upper body looked like over-boiled chicken meat. Either of the other two men would have snapped him like a twig.

But here he was, standing in front of him in the ring and looking almost . . . bored.

Breki removed his shirt to appreciative hoots from the audience. At least he looked like a wrestler. Behind Ludin, he could see the tall blonde woman had raised her arm. The Hall held its breath – and then the crowd erupted with encouragement as her arm dropped. Without thinking, he dropped into his wrestling stance, weight low, arms out and strong, but not too far apart; keep them close enough for leverage. Learning that lesson had been painful. He had taken three sideways steps when his head caught up with his feet and realised that something was wrong.

Ludin hadn't moved.

There was no stance, no movement, nothing. He was just standing there, still looking bored.

Breki stepped closer and snatched for a handful of belt, but the expected slap did not come; instead, Ludin stepped aside, lazily, and now he was looking up at him, almost as if he'd just noticed his opponent for the first time.

Breki looked into his eyes and suddenly felt a lot colder. There was nothing there.

Just . . . darkness.

Fear turned to fury and Breki lashed out again, properly aiming for the belt this time. How dare the old man mock him like this? He deserved to go down. *End it – end it quickly.* He slapped his hands down quickly on the old man's cord and—

—the slash of pain in his right wrist was a river in winter. Instinctively he hardened his grip, but for some reason his fingers would not obey and he felt the cord slipping from his hand. Cold sweat broke out on his forehead just as Ludin twisted to his other side, grabbed his left hand and forearm – and then something snapped and he lost his grip there too.

The old man looked down as if looking for his belt, then Breki's nose and mouth burst into flaming agony as Ludin's head connected. He reeled backwards, finally realising that the old man's hands were on his belt, then the horizon was falling away and the ceiling stretched up above him. There was a hard thump as he landed.

'Ludin wins!' King Eirik's voice rang out over a confusion of angry sounds.

Feeling his mouth filling with blood, Breki started rolling over to spit it out – and immediately regretted it the moment he put his weight onto his left hand. He spat blood and lay back down, only to see a long figure standing above him, staring blankly down at him – and then moving – moving towards him—

'LUDIN WINS!' The shout rang out again, louder this time, followed by cheers. Breki thought they might have sounded a bit forced, then he thought perhaps he wasn't thinking quite straight, because the face of the man who had hurt him was coming closer still, until it was blocking the wooden beams of the roof from view. Breki wondered about lifting his hands to cover his face, but he found he was frozen by terror and pain. He tasted death on the air as the bare-chested man knelt next to his head.

The warlord's stare was cold and deep. 'Lives . . . lives are hard to live and easy to take,' he said, almost thoughtfully.

Through the haze of pain, Breki wondered idly how many people had been in this position, hurt, defenceless and looking up at Ludin of Skane.

'You won, Ludin. Step away.' The North Wind's growl was unmistakeable – and close. Very close. It was a voice which ended fights.

The warlord rose, looking bored again. As he disappeared from view, the sights and sounds of the Hall rushed back to fill Breki's senses as another wave of pain washed over him. He bit the inside of his cheek hard. It wouldn't do to bring even more shame to the North, to his chieftain, to his family and everyone else. He could feel a lump forming in his throat. Fighting to hold back tears, he let the pain take him. His nose and mouth were throbbing, he could feel his lower lip swelling, but worse by far was the agony in both his wrists, which felt as if the cold fires of Hel were burning within.

Another figure appeared in his field of vision, but this one swiftly knelt down beside him. He tried not to wince as his wrist was grasped in strong but unexpectedly gentle fingers.

'Calm down.' The voice was soothing – a woman's voice. She was young, but she looked stern. A halo of dark hair was tied back from a sharp face. Now he remembered her from earlier – the graceful girl with the lithe, handsome man – but it felt strange to be so close to her.

'Your face is properly bashed, but you'll be fine.'

As she examined him closely, the shame returned. He braced himself for a cutting comment of some sort, but instead, her face softened. Lowering her voice so only he could hear, she said, 'It was an unfair fight and the fact that you are alive speaks to your strength.' She put a slim hand on his bare chest and he suddenly became uncomfortably aware that everyone was watching him. He blinked twice, to show her that he was listening, and she smiled.

From a belt she produced a rolled-up brown cylinder and looked at his chest, then into his eyes. 'I am going to test your wrists. I know you're tough, but you might want to bite down.'

The smell told him what it was before the taste did.

'How bad is this?'

When the agony exploded in his left wrist, he bit down so hard on the leather he almost expected to chew through it. He could feel the cold sweat on his forehead and breathing hard through his nose, had to concentrate to bring his attention back to the girl. He managed to still his racing heart enough to see she was frowning.

'Hm. How about this?' His right hand hurt too and he chomped down on the leather again, but the pain wasn't quite as bad this time. He hoped that was a good sign.

'Mm. Okay.' She looked away from his face and spoke to someone out of sight. 'Lift him up carefully. The right is badly sprained, but the left is broken. He'll need to come and sit with me while I bind him up.'

Strong hands felt for his shoulders and Breki was lifted from the floor. People started clapping, a lot of them, but he wanted to sink into the ground. He'd lost, and ignominiously at that. There was nothing to applaud. Horribly ashamed, he glanced over towards where the North Wind had stood – and found the old woman staring at him, straight in the eye. The weathered face and permanently furrowed brow made her look like an old hill-troll, with piercing blue eyes hewn out of the ice. Ingileif held his gaze for a moment, then nodded, very slowly.

Breki had to clench his jaw not to burst into tears. Everything hurt and he'd lost against an old man, but he wasn't dead and the North Wind wasn't angry and there were just too many people in Uppsala by half.

'Come on,' the dark-haired woman said, like she was leading a skittish horse, and he followed her to a seat near the dais.

A man rose to meet them, concern on his face. 'Is it serious?'

'No,' she said, with a smile in her voice. 'They breed 'em big and strong up north.' The compliment didn't make Breki feel as good as he suspected it was meant to do. He felt stupid and stuck in some kind of nightmare troll house and now that he wasn't fighting he felt stupid without his shirt. A wave of anger came out of nowhere and smashed around inside his head. Why couldn't he have won? Maybe then she wouldn't be treating him like a kid who'd fallen down and hurt himself. He gritted his teeth and forced a grimace that would hopefully be seen as a smile in kind.

The woman sat him down and placed his arms gently in his lap. 'Hold still,' she said. 'I am going to wrap you up to make you heal quicker.'

'Thank you,' he muttered.

She placed the leather roll back in his mouth and busied herself with his left wrist, the most painful one, and although he'd wanted to ignore it, he couldn't stop himself biting down hard again. The pain made him feel like he was sitting too close to a raging fire.

The young man leaned in and through a fog of pain and exhaustion, Breki realised it was the graceful one, the man he'd seen with the healer earlier. He had long blond hair and a kind face, like someone's friendly older cousin.

'One of you won,' said the man, 'but the other has the honour.'

'What do you mean?'

'He didn't want to wrestle. He just wanted to hurt you to prove a point.'

A sudden intense blaze from his left hand broke Breki's concentration, but fighting to stay conscious, he caught a glance and a smile passing between the two of them – then the crowd roared again, distracting him.

'—between the north and the south!' King Eirik finished off. In the centre of the longhouse the ring had formed again, but it was even bigger this time. Alfgeir Bjorne's huge frame swayed as he stretched his arms and rolled his neck from side to side. Across the circle, Ludin was once again standing almost still, but his poise and the set of his shoulders was reminiscent of a cat waiting to pounce.

A heavy feeling settled in Breki's stomach and for a moment he forgot about the jagged throbbing in his left wrist.

Someone was going to die tonight.

Helga felt the muscles in the boy's arms relax for a moment, then he tensed up again. He clenched his teeth on the leather, but he couldn't stop the tears welling in his eyes or the sweat glazing his forehead.

'Relax,' she murmured. 'Keep your hand still and try to ignore the pain. It will go away soon.' Considering how much juniper root she'd shaved into the mixture she'd coated the leather with, it was a miracle that the big ox was still awake at all. *They really do breed 'em big in the north.* She smiled despite herself, until a cacophony of screaming men nearby ruined her brief moment of levity. Clearly Alfgeir and Ludin were squaring off. She turned to speak to Freysteinn, but he too was caught in the moment, staring with rapt attention at the wrestlers.

In the circle, Alfgeir had spread his big arms wide. 'Ludin! It must be unfamiliar for you to fight like this – without your swordsmen and facing your enemy!' It was a calculated insult, just short of being a declaration of war, and it worked like kindling on the flame for the home crowd, who started hollering and stamping their approval as they stared hungrily at Ludin.

But apart from a brief tensing of the lips and a flare of the nostrils, the old warlord was still in control. 'I may lose the occasional fight,' he said in a tone that was honed to carry across battlefields, 'but I'm not weak – and careless enough – to lose both my sons.'

Helga realised that her hand had risen to her mouth as if to hold it shut, and she wasn't alone. There was a moment's utter silence as the people gathered in the King's Hall took in Ludin's statement – and the outrageous accusation – and then she watched as Alfgeir's hairy back flexed, he gave a rising howl and charged his opponent, accompanied by a swelling tide of noise from the audience.

In an instant the whole longhouse was engulfed in a blood-frenzy, with men squaring off against each other, every single one of them determined to pound the other into the ground . . .

It's a herd gone mad—

That was the only thought she had time for, for Freysteinn had swooped in and bending as close to her face as he could, he was bellowing something. It took her a moment to work out that he was saying, 'YOU NEED TO GET OUT – TAKE THE BOY – RUN—!'

But Helga was already moving; almost without thought she'd

got Breki on his feet and with her arm around his thick waist to steady him, she'd started kicking a path to the little door behind the dais, trying to find the spaces between the surging crowd so she could get them to the wall. Men and women alike were pushing and shoving each other out of the way, apparently desperate not to miss out on the action. She could smell the excitement and fear in the air and wasn't surprised to see fighting had already broken out here and there. She twisted Breki to the left just as something rushed past: someone moving at speed towards the fighting, not away, with something glinting in his hand.

King Eirik.

Helga watched the king leaping like a stag, finding footing wherever he could – a bench, a table, the bent-over back of a man stamping on someone's leg, then onto shoulders, even, she'd have sworn, a man's head. He paused nowhere longer than a blink and she was reminded of stories of raiders doing Njordur's Dare, running up and down the length of a ship on upturned oars. And then he was through the throng and standing in the middle of the ring, loudly banging together a shield and a short, stubby axe.

'THE FIGHT IS OVER! THE FIGHT – IS – OVER!'

The astonishing volume of the king's voice and the sharply unpleasant clang of metal on metal served remarkably like cold water on the heated combatants. A lot of them were also wise enough to take into consideration the fact that the king was the only man on the floor holding a weapon and looking angry enough to use it. A line of sight cleared to the centre as embarrassed men shifted from one foot to another.

At last Helga caught sight of Alfgeir. *He's holding himself together, but only just.* She had never before seen the big man positively vibrating with fury like this; she had only known him as the king's calm right-hand man. Watching him now, she had no trouble imagining him going a-Viking, striding ashore, battle-axe in hand, ready to slay.

Ludin of Skane, opposite him, might not look like a giant from the tales, but there was no less murder about him. His arm was moving oddly by his side before falling unnaturally still.

Like someone trying hard not to reach for something.

'A Viking fights with strength,' King Eirik declared, 'and Ludin has showed enough strength to withstand Alfgeir's flyting and drive him mad with fury. In the spirit of friendship,' he added, eyeing them both sternly, 'I will stop the match and declare that the north and the south are evenly matched – in strength and in cunning.'

More than a few disbelieving shouts came from the crowd, but the king hadn't finished. 'And those who have both strength and cunning should work *together*, rather than trying to kill each other.'

'KING EIRIK IS WISE!' one of the Northmen, a short, grey-haired man, shouted loudly.

'All hail the wise king!' the Northern chieftain bellowed out in immediate response.

'All hail the wise king!' Freysteinn shouted just after her, his voice louder still.

The cry picked up pace and volume until the crash of axe-head on shield disrupted it again. This time the crowd fell silent much more quickly.

'And nothing brings friends together quicker,' the king declared, 'than MORE ALE!'

The crowd roared, someone in the direction of the Northmen struck up the song about Sigurd's sister and the goose and the wrestling circle was soon replaced with milling bodies as the men started lumbering back and forth again in what they probably considered to be dancing. The rising smell of ale and mead being dished out and consumed at pace soon joined the reek of sweat, but at least Helga could no longer sense the anger and fear that had permeated the room just a little while ago.

Freysteinn kissed her on the cheek and disappeared in the direction of Alfgeir and King Eirik.

Hm. So maybe our king is not entirely un-wise. Helga settled the drowsy young wrestler down with his back against the wall, noting his drooping eyelids with pride. *You'll sleep well tonight, young cub.* A little blush of fondness stirred, surprising her, then a faint memory of another lost soul in a big frame ghosted away as soon as it had arrived and she wasn't surprised any more. She wasn't in any sort of rush to have children, but she could be a big sister for a while.

Alvar Dal pushed through the crowd, oblivious to the tears welling in his eyes, just impatient to get outside. 'Seen him in Hedeby,' he muttered to himself, 'and knows where he went – at last! I can't believe it . . .' He had finally asked the right question of the right person at the right time and now he was just a few steps away from finding out where his son was.

Whispering a word of thanks to the Fates, he twisted the narrow silver ring on his finger, running his thick finger over the well-worn pattern as if it were a talisman, and stepped out into the cool night air.

Chapter 5

COUNCIL

'Helga!'

Smoke. Grey tendrils curl and swirl around my ankles, creeping up my calves, my thighs, towards my hips.

Pulling me, pushing me around.

There is something behind me, too. It's close – close and dangerous. But it doesn't matter how much I twist and strain, I can't get a good look at it. The grey smoke has risen like mist in the morning. It's making it hard to see anything—

'Helga!'

I can feel leaves crunching under my feet. I can smell the damp soil on the riverbank, rich with leaf mould. When I pinch my fingertips together, they stick with the all-too-familiar sensation of blood—

'Helga, come quickly!'

Everything is all of a sudden tilting sideways and—

—she saw the light slithering in through the skin screens on the wall. Beside her, Freysteinn stirred but didn't move.

'Helga!' Someone rapped on the wall and she blearily realised the calling and knocking had been going on for a while.

'What?' she mumbled, too tired even to scowl as she pushed her way out from under the pile of furs.

'Helga, the king has sent for you!'

Still mostly asleep, she rolled off her bed and dragged on a shift before padding to the door, but when she dragged it open, she was hit square in the face with the full morning sun. She could just make out the silhouette of one of Alfgeir's multitude of messenger boys, sitting astride the big man's horse.

'Why by the flaming arse of Thor would he do that?'

Wait. He's on Alfgeir's own horse. That means . . . What? What does it mean?

The boy looked down at her and almost proudly reported, 'There's been a . . . well, they've found a body. A dead'un.'

The comforting *thud-thud, thud-thud* of Grundle's hooves on the grass helped wake her up, and once her thoughts were behaving themselves again, she tried to summon up a picture in her mind of what she might see. The boy had been vague on the details and while Freysteinn had been keen to accompany her, the colour of his skin and the stink of mead on his breath had convinced her that she'd be better off going alone. Besides, if someone was wounded she'd need to see to them, and most of the time Freysteinn didn't exactly help her concentration.

Her hair whipped behind her as Grundle gladly picked up speed. *I don't often ride as fast as I used to*, she mused, wondering why that was as she looped the reins round the pommel and reached back to tie up her hair in a loose tail. Once secured, she leaned forward again until Grundle's mane was almost tickling her nose, stroking the powerful neck and breathing in the comforting smell of horse.

'Good girl,' she murmured softly. 'It's time to push on now.' She could feel the strength beneath her as the mare lengthened her stride and her hooves started furiously pounding the ground. She looked back as the boy behind her let out a yelp and lurched in the saddle as Alfgeir's mare took off after Grundle, clearly determined not to be left behind.

Helga grinned. *Even though I may have slowed down a bit, you are going to have to ride harder if you want to keep up with me, boy.*

The forest gave way to plains spreading out in front of them. Up ahead rose the hills of Uppsala and at the very top stood the mighty temple. The sun catching on the chains was sending jags of flashing light everywhere, but the sight had long since stopped striking awe into Helga's breast. *Gods can't be called with glittering metal. The temple is beautiful, but it is still just a house.* The thought had a bitter aftertaste. Something shifted inside her head and she could feel a throbbing heat, along with the weight of the fingernail-sized runestones hanging around her neck. There were seven now, and she knew when to use each one: *Thurisaz*, for settling conflicts in the body. *Hagalaz* to build strength. *Nauth* for what you wanted most and *Laguz* to clear the murky water of the future. She was proud of every single one of them.

They were given.

The words were there, spoken just by her ear, clearly audible above the din of the hooves: a man's voice, amber-deep and warm with age.

They are a gift to be used.

It was a familiar voice, but one without a face or a memory attached to it. *No, the gods don't need big houses. They're here – whether we want them or not.* The headache faded and left her space to enjoy the speed. The hill was closer now, but she could see no sign of anything different in the cluster of houses around it, just the normal relaxed purpose in everyone she saw. The day was warming up, so the old people had taken themselves outside to bask like cats in the sun while mending whatever needed mending – cloth, nets, pans . . . In the distance she could see farmers working the fields with the steady rhythm of those who knew that rushing achieved nothing more than tiring a body out. Children – who hadn't yet learned this valuable lesson – were engrossed in games that involved little more than a great deal of running and screaming.

And somewhere in the middle of it all there is a dead body.

Death was just part of life. Everyone knew that. But death had its place: it was meant to wait for illness, war or old age. This was the second time in a short while that death had come unbidden to Uppsala.

Grundle tossed her head and Helga looked over her shoulder. She had to stifle a laugh at the sheer terror on the face of the boy clinging on to Alfgeir's mare for dear life, but she waved back at him and didn't comment when Grundle slowed, just a tiny bit. 'Well done – you've caught me!'

He was too winded to speak, and in any case, the din of their hooves would have swallowed his words, so he just pointed to the left. Helga, gesturing agreement, pulled Grundle up a little to let the boy take the lead. Alfgeir's mare looked happier to be in front, even if he didn't. The boy slowed the mare to a grudging trot and Grundle, less grudging, followed suit, happy to let him lead the way.

Helga frowned as he passed the main path up to King Eirik's hall, wondering where they were going.

The morning sun had disappeared behind the rising ridge and the light was changing, but Alfgeir's big frame was still visible from quite a distance. The mare, spotting her master, quickened her pace, forcing the boy to pull on the reins and shout at her, which changed absolutely nothing, but he did manage to stay on, even when she stopped dead at Alfgeir's feet and nuzzled him as he took hold of her rein and muttered a low greeting.

The boy didn't wait for orders, just jumped off swiftly and gracelessly and walked away without a backwards look. *You'll be feeling that in the morning,* Helga thought without an ounce of sympathy, dismounting smoothly, then turning at once to the king's right-hand man.

Alfgeir dropped his head in wordless greeting and pointed to the foot of the cliff where three of King Eirik's men stood, looking for all the world like they'd just stopped for a chat.

Only none of them are actually talking and all three are on alert. She watched them looking out over each other's shoulders as she followed Alfgeir towards the cliff.

The dead man lay sprawled at the foot of the ridge. *He looks like he's sleeping.* He was older than she'd thought he'd be, for some reason. There was more than a touch of silver in his beard and crinkles around his mouth. When Helga looked up, she could only just see the awning of the longhouse. She glanced over at Alfgeir, who was watching her closely, then turned her attention back to the dead man. *Look at the body. Learn everything you can.*

Uncomfortably aware that everyone was staring at her, not just Alfgeir, she dropped carefully to her knees and bent into the reek of the man. 'He had his fill last night.'

'He did.' Alfgeir's voice was dark.

'Who is he?'

'Name's Alvar Dal. Travels with the Dalefolk.'

His face came to her now: she'd seen him, one of Jorunn's mute henchmen in the market. In death, there was nothing at all threatening about him. Big, scabbed hands with thick and oft-broken fingers suggested that he'd been able to take care of himself in a fistfight, but in death his face held no killings. Compared to the wrestler, the grey-haired captain and the dark-skinned one, he couldn't have been much more than an afterthought.

'He manned the pots,' Alfgeir offered.

'I see.' A pause. 'He looks a little . . . um . . . worn for a . . . um . . .' She paused and twisted her head to peer up at Alfgeir. 'For a trade delegation.'

There was a flash of a cold, steely smirk that disappeared again almost immediately. 'If you were to ask Jorunn, I am sure she would tell you something about invaluable experience.'

'I'm sure she will,' Helga said. Something had passed between them. Alfgeir's stance had changed, ever so subtly. *He . . . doesn't dislike me.* Helga felt an odd flush of pride, then tried to push it away; this was not the time.

'I saw him last night,' Alfgeir continued. 'He was all over the hall, talking to everyone he could find. He was drinking hard too, even more than most.'

'What was he talking about?'

'He was wanting to find his lost son.'

The bottom felt like it had dropped out of her stomach and every thread of her being flushed with cold. 'His *son*?' she stuttered.

'Yes.' Alfgeir was looking straight at her. 'And then he left the king's longhouse and fell off the ledge.' His brow suggested impending thunder.

It's interesting how men can be dead set against killing unless it's them who are doing it. That thought wormed its way in ahead of something else that was niggling at her. *Something . . .*

Her hands were working on their own, touching the cold, clammy skin, feeling for wounds. She worked her way up the dead man's body, but it was clear his legs and arms had been damaged only by the landing; he'd not been fighting anyone, at least not recently. The silver ring on his forefinger was a little battered out of shape, but she thought that was just from long wear. But his head . . . it was in one piece but it felt uncomfortably loose in her hands. He must have broken his neck in the fall. She felt around to the back of his head and traced the bones down and – *yes. There.* She'd found the loose joints. Suppressing a small shudder, she turned her attention to his jaw, and—

Oh.

Helga looked up at Alfgeir. 'And nobody heard him scream.'

He looked at her, not hiding his mixture of suspicion and bemusement. He was used to being asked rather than told. 'No. Why?'

'Look at his throat.'

Alfgeir knelt down next to her. For a moment he was completely still: a giant carved from Asgard rock. When he looked at her, his eyes were calm, unreadable.

'Whoever found him would think he just fell,' the big man said.

'And landed on his back.' Helga studied the man King Eirik trusted the most. Somewhere in the back of her mind a small voice was suggesting that there might have been more subtle ways to get her point across, but she ignored it. 'Use your fingers – just here. Feel that? His neck is broken, but that's not from the fall. Look at the bruising.'

Alfgeir touched the man's throat again. There was a quiet to him, complete focus on the task. It didn't take him long to find it. He traced the damage, once, twice, then rose to his feet, more easily than she might have expected of a man of his bulk.

'He was hit,' Alfgeir said. 'So yes, I agree, it is reasonable to think that he might have been pushed. I'll tell the king.'

A thought snuck into her head. *You knew that already. You knew there was something wrong, but you needed me to tell you what it was.*

The big man sighed. 'He won't like it.'

Helga looked down at the dead man at their feet, no longer a breathing person, reduced to meat and bones and an empty face.

I don't expect Alvar Dal of the Dales liked it either.

Breki sat where Big Rolf had told him to at the back of the longhouse and surveyed the place. His hands still hurt like all hell and a pounding headache was not helping. He had slept in fits and starts, jolted awake by the pain at odd hours. When Rolf had woken him that morning, there'd been no hint of a joke about his sorry state – Rolf had just asked him how he felt and kindly offered to spoon-feed him mushed oats. He'd not seemed surprised by Breki's refusal. Thanks to the healer's bindings, he'd been able to feed himself, although just holding his wooden spoon had hurt more than he'd expected.

The North Wind herself had come to check on him too, even been solicitous in her own gruff way. She'd been muttering something about how 'pain was Ludin's way', and about how Breki getting hurt had been important – not much of it made sense, but the old ones didn't appear to be shamed by his failure, which was far better than he'd hoped for.

So no one else would share his shame. It was left for him to bear.

The longhouse had been cleared of most of last night's damage, with fresh soil tamped down over the tangible results of the evening's excesses. The wall panels had been flung open, allowing fresh summer air to replace the stinks of stale mead, piss and vomit. When he turned to the centre of the hall, Breki winced and blinked hard until the pain softened at the edges, but he could still hear echoes of the roar of the crowd. The throbbing of his left hand was almost drowning out the sounds of the king and Ingileif, who were droning on and on about some bridge—

Oh yes, *the bridge*. Big Rolf had been laying down his negotiating rules all the way to Uppsala, going on and on about the need to keep the king's men off-balance, and not being afraid of going in hard. He looked at the grizzled warriors sitting around the square table, frowning and carping at each other like fishwives. More than a few looked a little grey-faced after last night's events, and not a single one of them looked like they'd be going in hard at anything.

He didn't notice the tall woman from Ludin's delegation until she was nearly at Big Rolf's shoulder. Leaning in, she whispered a couple of quick words and a fist-sized bag passed from her to him. The old man glanced back, caught Breki's eye, and a quick, cheeky grin flashed across his face, disappearing just as suddenly as he turned back to the negotiations.

The contact had been broken just as quickly as it had been established: she had already turned and was walking straight out of the longhouse. Maybe she was Ludin's Big Rolf, Breki mused, and the thought entertained him for a moment – and then the doors opened and all the Southerners stepped in, walking across the floor at a brisk pace. None of them looked even the slightest the worse for wear after the night.

'Ludin!' King Eirik called, his voice cheerful, 'well met!'

'King Eirik,' the chieftain replied curtly, sitting in the middle of one side of the table. His men positioned themselves around him, the woman at his right hand and the swordsman on the other. Big Rolf had had some very descriptive things to say about Ludin on the way, but Breki had detected more than a little grudging respect in his words.

'We will finish our negotiations later,' Ingileif said suddenly.

The king looked bemused and the reedy Icelandic law-man next to him snorted.

Breki suddenly realised there was a person missing. Where was Alfgeir Bjorne?

The doors swung open again, and this time they slammed back against the walls on either side. Breki caught a quick exchange of glances between the North Wind and her advisor, who was looking highly annoyed. Ingileif looked far more settled; nothing much could move his chieftain.

The woman in charge of the Dalefolk stormed towards the negotiating table, a picture of fury, her men massed behind her, moving as one. Around the table, hands inched closer towards weapons, both visible and concealed.

King Eirik rose, palms down, appealing for calm. 'Well met—'

'Stuff your greeting,' she snapped.

The gaping hole beside King Eirik where Alfgeir Bjorne usually sat was suddenly very prominent. Some voices rose in protest, but there was steel in the king's voice when he barked, 'Hold your tongues! The leader of the Dalefolk has a right – and every reason – to speak.' Jorunn and her men had stopped a good ten paces away from the table. A moment later, he added, 'This is not Bluetooth's court.'

Breki could see people looking at each other and nodding, and there was the occasional smile too. He had the feeling that later on, Big Rolf would be asking him exactly what had happened just then.

'In fact,' the king continued, 'I wish she could have been reached sooner, but we did what we could.'

Behind the party from the Dales, Alfgeir Bjorne lurched into the hall.

Ludin of Skane looked bored. 'And is anyone going to tell us the source of all this noise and upset?'

'One of my men was killed last night,' Jorunn snapped. '*They* found him.'

'Oh,' Ludin said, and proceeded to study the rafters. The woman beside him leaned in and whispered something in his ear, quickly. There was the briefest suggestion of a shake of the head, but otherwise he looked more like an impatient child than an important warlord.

'How did it happen?' Ingileif rumbled.

'He was pushed off the hill,' Alfgeir rumbled back, and when his words were met with dull stares, he added, 'His throat was smashed. No doubt about it.'

'Not much honour in that,' Big Rolf remarked.

'NO honour!' Jorunn shouted. 'And *this* is how you want to start negotiations? *This* is how you show that you can be trusted? Are *these* your Guest's Rights, oh wise king? Water and welcoming speech should he find who comes to the feast. We come here because you guarantee our safety in your house!'

The scrawny Lawspeaker grimaced. 'Yes, yes, we know. But why are you shouting? There is nothing in the laws that says the king is responsible for drunken—'

'The king's purse will pay the blood-price.'

The Lawspeaker's head snapped to his right so fast that he almost broke his own neck. He stared at the king in utter disbelief. 'What? But you don't need to!'

'We take no responsibility for the death, which may even be an accident – but in order to show our cousins from the Dales that our goal is to unite rather than divide, we will meet the wergild.'

Breki had to stifle a laugh. The Lawspeaker was so furious that he had almost folded in on himself in his seat next to the king. But as Alfgeir made his way to Eirik's other side, he could see no sign of softening from the furious Dalefolk.

'If there is a killer on the loose, what else can we expect from the king?' Jorunn's words were now cold and clipped.

King Eirik did not waver. 'You can expect to be offered a seat at the table,' he said, and sat down again, as calmly as if he'd just finished negotiating over a few head of cattle.

At the opposite end of the table, the Daleswoman somehow managed to convey both fury and grace at the same time as she dropped to her seat, flanked by her men, who were all looking more than ready for a fight.

'What news of Harald?' Ludin's advisor interjected suddenly, like someone expecting to be answered, and answered well. 'That is why you called us here, isn't it?'

'It is,' King Eirik said. 'Word has reached me that he has whispered in my cousin Styrbjorn's ear and whipped him up into a frenzy of greed. He has, I hear, convinced Styrbjorn that he is entitled to all of the land under the feet of any of us.'

'And why is that our problem? He won't come north,' Big Rolf said. 'Not if he knows what's good for him.'

King Eirik smiled. 'You are right, of course: he will come straight for me and my house and the temple on the hill.'

Seeing the smug glances of his fellow travellers made Breki feel strangely embarrassed. Maybe it was because his hands hurt, or because he'd missed the lesson on cunning in negotiations, but he appeared to be the only one who could see that they were being led by the nose.

And sure enough, the king continued, 'However, there is a reason my dear cousin is named Styrbjorn the Strong, not Styrbjorn the Wise. He doesn't necessarily have any idea in his thick skull, especially not about what is and isn't good for him. So in a summer's time, after time to regroup, he'll be marching north, west or south, depending on what he fancies at the time, and plucking you like apples, one by one.'

There was silence for a moment, then he turned to Ludin. 'Do you want to sit at home for the rest of your life, unable to go raiding for fear of shadows on the horizon when your ship is too far out to sea?'

The old warlord showed little emotion, but there was a hint of a sneer on his face.

The king turned to the angry woman. 'Do you want to watch the Dales burn?'

She glared back at him.

Finally, Eirik turned to Ingileif. 'The men of the North are brave, but few. Do you want to count your crops, or your corpses?'

Voices erupted, and King Eirik let them.

The racket was making Breki's head thump again. To his left the woman in charge of the Dalefolk was shouting something about reparations and cheap tricks, and the swordsman from the south sitting opposite had leaped to his feet and was pointing at the Northmen. Big Rolf was up as well, and he too was barking about honour and negotiations. But Ludin of Skane just sat utterly still, watching and listening, as did the North Wind.

'Do you have proof?' the woman he thought he'd heard called Jorunn barked.

King Eirik looked coldly at her. 'Your wits are as sharp as any blade around this table and you are famous for hearing news on the wind that leads to your profit and others' loss. How much have you heard of Harald recently?'

'Nothing.' Jorunn's face was pinched; it was like her reply only just managed to escape.

The king's face suggested that was exactly the reply he'd expected. 'And Styrbjorn?'

Jorunn was being led to a conclusion and it was clear from her expression that she didn't like it. 'He was raiding in Anglia a year ago. I haven't heard anything about him since. But that doesn't prove that they are—'

'Styrbjorn is the new leader of the Jomsvikings.' Ludin sounded almost bored, like he had no interest in the fact he'd just dropped onto the table like a stone, or the effect it had on the council, but Breki couldn't quite believe his ears. The Jomsvikings were the stuff of legend: a whole town full of warriors for hire, true only to each other, working for the highest bidder, whoever that was. If the king's cousin really had risen to be their leader, that meant he was trouble. A lot of trouble. 'He fought Harald for a while last year, then they decided to join forces instead. Harald apparently gave him a hundred ships and his daughter to go with them.'

The mood around the table had twisted almost instantly as mistrust evaporated and disbelief changed to grim determination. Breki didn't know why they had all been ready to doubt the king, although he appeared to want the best for them, but everyone listened to Ludin.

He murmured to himself Big Rolf's oft-repeated words: *people were stupid, and Southerners doubly so.*

'Why did you not tell us this?' King Eirik looked like he was trying very hard to keep calm.

Ludin still looked utterly unfazed, but there was the merest hint of a smile on his face. 'You never asked. I assumed you knew.'

The king did not rise to the slight but instead turned to Jorunn and the North Wind. 'Now do you believe?'

'Let's talk,' the North Wind rumbled.

'I just . . . there's *something*. Something that bothers me.' Helga was sitting cross-legged by her table, watching the knife in her hand rise and fall rhythmically on the herbs almost without her volition.

'And what might that be?' In the corner Freysteinn stretched his long legs, then continued whittling.

She had been resistant to him being with her in the herb cabin at first, but he'd tucked himself away, quietly carving little figures while he observed her. The smell of the wood and the *snik-snak* of the knife had slowly become a source of comfort, so much so that now she felt his absence when he wasn't there. *I wonder what Hildigunnur would say? She'd probably make up some rude joke about a man with wood in his hand and then be delighted.* He had also, with an uncanny knack for knowing when he was and wasn't welcome to speak, started asking her about herbs and she found she had fallen into the role of teacher very easily.

At last she answered, 'The dead man today.'

'Mm. Tell me what you're thinking.'

That was another thing he did: when she was mulling something over, he encouraged her to talk. He listened and he asked questions. Having someone to talk to meant she hadn't felt the need to retreat into her own head for a long time.

'It's just . . . he looked so . . . peaceful. He looked like a big, sleeping child. But I can't help but think that he must have been terrified when he died.'

There was a silence from the corner, but she could tell he was listening intently.

'What did he look like?' he asked after a moment.

'He looked . . .' *Familiar.* The shock of it was like cold water in her veins. *The dead man had looked familiar – but why? How? She might have glimpsed him the day before, but this was different. She'd seen that face before.* It was hovering around the edges of her mind.

'. . . sad. I don't know.'

'Take your time to think about it. If you consider all the possibilities it will come to you,' he said. An all-too-recognisable note of honey crept into his voice. 'Other things may . . . come to you as well.' She glanced at him and was met by sparkling eyes and a suggestive wink. 'Something might come to you right now.' He rose – unfolded himself, gracefully – from the corner. The carving knife somehow vanished in his hands, as did the block of wood, and he was all suggestion and soft movement as he inched closer.

'No,' she said, and made her look say it louder. 'Not now.' At the flicker of disappointment on his face, more words tumbled out of her mouth. 'Later, though.' The smile on her face felt uncomfortable.

He leaned over and kissed her forehead. 'I am going to see Alfgeir. I will bring back information, and maybe some honey cakes.' There was nothing in his face to suggest that he had just been wanting to leap on her.

She smiled. 'I'll be here.'

Watching him leave, she felt like a weight had been lifted off her chest and annoyance flashed. *Why can't I ever anticipate how that man will make me feel at any given moment?*

'Curse them all,' she muttered. *Men. They were annoying, loud, full of themselves, dangerous and always bloody in her way.* And who the hell was the fallen man and why did he—?

There was a rapping on the door of the hut and a discreet, deep, '. . . hello?'

Another damn man, come to interrupt her work, her thoughts and her life. 'What?' she barked.

'Oh, nothing. Just come to look for some remedy.'

Her anger simmered down a little. Hildigunnur and the old rune-witch might have taught her wildly different things, but they had both been very clear on the fact that a healer had no right to withhold their skills from anyone, whether they liked it or not. Wisdom was like a sword: it had to be wielded wisely, or it would hurt everyone and yourself most of all. The cutting would have to wait.

'Coming,' she said, softer this time, more welcoming, and pushed herself to her feet. She spoke as she opened the door. 'So, what's wrong with you, then?'

The man standing in her yard looked old, but healthy. Long strands of grey hair hung down past his shoulders. He was leaning on a gnarly walking stick a good foot taller than he was. 'Oh, I don't know. Depends on who you ask,' the old man said, a sparkle in his eyes. 'I get these pains in my chest.'

'I see,' Helga said. 'Come in here and sit down. Let me take a look at you.' As the old man did as he was told she was dimly aware that the breeze she'd felt earlier had died down. The day was perfectly still, the forest was quiet. 'You look healthy enough,' she said, louder than she'd intended.

'I still get this pain,' the old man said. 'Here.' He took her hand and placed it gently upon his chest.

'That's your heart,' Helga said, 'and I can feel that it's beating just fine.'

'I worry,' the man said. 'In my family, we tend to die of the same things. Father and son.'

'I understand. Lift your arm. Does that hurt? And the other?'

'No, both fine.'

She put her hand back on his chest and told him, 'Take a deep breath for me.'

The bony chest rose and fell under her fingers. For reasons she couldn't explain, something about his presence was reassuring, almost like they'd met before.

She looked at the man and smiled. 'You're fine, you old donkey. You'll be around for a good many winters yet.'

'Thank you,' the old man said, the corners of his mouth lifting in return. He rose and explained, 'I just wanted to make sure. It's always better to know your kin is safe.'

Helga waved him goodbye and watched him with a frown as he hobbled down the path and disappeared behind the trees.

Moments after, the breeze carried the sounds of two heavy horses riding away.

Familiar. The word played over and over in her head until she was almost snarling in frustration. 'What is it? What are you trying to tell me?' she begged, but the answer wouldn't come and instead, she was left with an odd sensation, an itch she couldn't quite reach.

There was only one thing she could do. Pursing her lips, she gave a sharp whistle and moments later, Grundle's head appeared around the corner of the shed.

The mare looked at her.

'Yes,' Helga said, and when Grundle gave a distinct snort, added, 'But we're going for a ride and then there may be hay in town as well. And perhaps . . . an apple.'

Very soon after the forest was again echoing to the thunder of hooves heading away from Helga's farm.

'But does anyone actually know how many ships the Jomsvikings had last year?' Ludin's advisor leaned forward.

Breki thought she moved, talked and glared like a well-honed axe. If it was part of a chieftain's life to look people like that in the eye and negotiate, he thanked his fates that he was no sort of chieftain.

'I know the King of the Danes has long been fond of paying others to do his dirty work, but if the stories are true, a hundred ships from Harald will mean at least three thousand men. How many do you have, Eirik?'

'If we send out a summons we could raise five hundred within three days – but armed, ready and any use against the Jomsvikings here? At most a hundred.'

Ludin of Skane's snort was derisive. 'We have a large standing force on the south coast, with the ability to double that within two days – and in any case, we taught those puffed-up pups how to raid. I could have four hundred armed men here within three days' ride. How about you, old bear?'

'The North is our army,' Ingileif growled. 'We don't need to throw bodies on spears to win a war. The land will defend us.'

Ludin smiled like a fox. 'Good. Can you bring the land down here?'

Breki noticed the chieftain's massive hand sneaking onto Big Rolf's leg to calm him down. For the first time all trip, she straightened up in her seat. Leaning forward, she said to Ludin, 'If it comes to it, we will do what is needed.'

The chieftain from the south was still smiling, but Breki thought perhaps an edge had been knocked off and he looked like he might hold his tongue for a while. That was wise: the North Wind didn't say much, but her words carried weight.

'I say we take the battle to them,' Ludin said. 'We should head off now and sack Jomsborg.'

'Talk sense,' Alfgeir snarled. 'That would cost a lot of lives.'

'I'd rather burn their beds at night than wait in mine for them to do likewise,' Ludin spat back. 'They will be coming here to kill all of you – and you'd do, what? Wait and see? Gather information? See if you can hold them off till next summer?

Maybe you can find some particularly intimidating cows to throw at them.'

Breki wondered why King Eirik wasn't saying anything. The king was just leaning back, listening to the others argue.

'You'd need time,' Ingileif pointed out. 'Time and money.'

'You can find both,' Ludin said, 'if you find your spine first.'

Two of the Northmen went to rise, but before they'd gained their feet, Ingileif was motioning for them to sit.

'I thank you for your interest in my spine,' she rumbled amicably. 'If I ever grow tired of using it, I'll ram it up your—'

'Stuff it, both of you,' Jorunn broke in. 'Regardless of their strength, they won't attack without warning. They'll try to get something for nothing, either because they can or because they can't.'

Breki watched Ludin eyeing the young woman up like a fighting dog would. 'So you would wait, then?'

'I'd play for time while we sharpen our axes.'

This got a good response around the table, even from Ludin, who sniffed and admitted, 'That works . . . if you're right.'

Still the king held his tongue.

'And who would negotiate? You?' Big Rolf's voice was laced with contempt.

'Who else?' Jorunn said. 'After all, I would be happy to deal with any of you.' She glanced at the king's right-hand man, who glared back at her.

The doors crashed open, admitting a young man who ran towards the king; the look on his face caught the attention of the arguing parties, who all stopped their bickering.

Breki caught the quick glance between Alfgeir and Eirik, then the young man was by their side and whispering in the king's ear.

A moment later, King Eirik rose. 'Sails have been seen off the east coast. Styrbjorn is coming.'

Chapter 6

FIRE

There had to be something she'd missed. She needed to go back to Olver's farm and examine the body one more time . . . but she was already sure there was a connection between the boy who died in the forest and the man from the Dales who'd asked the wrong question at the wrong time.

Whoever killed the boy was in the King's Hall last night.

She urged Grundle to go faster, enjoying the speed and the feeling of the mare stretching out beneath her, the heat coming off her as she galloped. Helga allowed Grundle to set her own pace most of the time, but the thought of a killer in Uppsala was bringing back bad memories and too many questions. *Who was the boy and why did he have to die?* And perhaps even more importantly, *Who's next?* She couldn't remember the first time she had created a space in her mind to organise her thoughts, but through the years it had changed, from a storeroom like the one they'd had at Riverside, to a belt of pouches when she'd travelled with the Eastmen – easy to carry around, big enough to hold the things she needed to remember – to a place that was very similar to her herb shed. She readied it now, wiping clean its shelves and storage spaces in her imagination.

Ludin's old tunic was lying at her feet; for a moment she thought she could smell him: a cold scent of frozen blood on dead animals in winter. Her skin crawling, she poked it into a corner with the toe of her boot. *He likes to end lives.* The Southern lord would always be a suspect whenever anyone died near him. *We've been hunting.* He'd been leering when he said it.

The echo of Jorunn's voice shredding Thorgnyr's flimsy arguments drifted in behind her and she turned to the shelf to examine the exquisitely carved figurine of Loki that appeared to be staring at her and right through her. *She is a liar. A liar and a rat.* She'd seen the lovely face of Hildigunnur's daughter disfigured with fury. Jorunn could kill, she knew that. A weak boy and a drunken old man? Definitely.

'But why now?' she muttered. The walls didn't answer. 'Why at all?'

The man had been part of her travelling party and she could have killed him – or had him killed – at any point. Had she perhaps done away with him for the wergild? That was a possibility, and it would not be ruled out.

She turned again and stared at a wrestling belt, hanging like the lolling tongue of a giant wolf. Ludin again? No, that made no sense. She could feel his presence in her mind and that wasn't him. No, the man from the Dales, the bruiser – what was his name? Lars! The face of the brute came to her as she remembered him posturing in front of Freysteinn before he was folded up like a shift by . . . Alfgeir? She remembered the ease with which the king's right-hand man had closed in on his victims in the wrestling ring. If King Eirik wanted someone dead, Alfgeir would be the man.

Something nagged at her. Ludin, Lars, Alfgeir . . .

There had been four wrestlers, hadn't there?

Feeling the image of the herb store fading in her mind, Helga squeezed her eyes shut against the wind as the sensation of the galloping horse overwhelmed her, threatening to push away all clear thoughts. The image of an open face, square jaw and innocent blue eyes came to her.

The boy?

'No,' she muttered. The treeline rose up ahead, towering over her, a wide a ribbon of dark green blocking out the sky. 'Hardly – he was with me. He was in the longhouse the whole time.'

Breki watched those assembled in the King's Hall scramble into action, old rivalries vanishing like dew in the morning.

All eyes were on the king. 'Riders,' he snapped to Alfgeir. 'Send two to the north, three to the west and one to the south – and tell Nils in Rowan Glade to rouse his cousins. You know what to say. And send someone to find Styrbjorn. He will be coming through Husby.'

Without a word, Alfgeir rose and strode out of the longhouse.

The king looked around at the assembled negotiators. 'Are you with me?'

'Do we have a choice?' There was a hint of a challenge in Ludin's voice.

'Of course you do,' the king said, staring hard at the old man. 'You can be against me.'

All of a sudden, Breki became aware of the other men in the shadows of the longhouse. They'd been mostly standing still, minding their own business, occasionally bringing food . . . and they were all of fighting age and all armed. Ludin of Skane was outnumbered by four to one.

There was a moment of silence.

Then Alfgeir Bjorne's voice carried, barking orders outside – and whatever could have happened, didn't. Ludin snorted and shrugged. 'We are yours to command.'

King Eirik rose. 'Let's get ready for whatever awaits us, then.'

All around the table, the men rose with him.

As Breki got up, he found Big Rolf by his side. 'What's happening?'

'Brothers doing battle, as usual,' Rolf snapped, 'only this time we're caught up in the middle of it. Did you keep your eyes open, as I told you to?'

'Yes, but I don't know what I could have seen that you wouldn't have—'

'I'm not the only one around that table watching. They'd have seen who I was looking at.' Around them, men were moving towards the doors, which had been thrown wide open. The sunlight outside looked painfully bright. 'How did they react to the news? Ludin and Jorunn?'

'They both looked . . . surprised.'

'Too right,' Big Rolf muttered. 'But why?'

'I don't know. I don't even know what I'm looking for.'

'Say that we get the news, then say that one of them looks surprised and shocked and the other looks shifty. Which group do you want in front of you, where you can see them? And which one do you want at your back?'

Breki's eyes widened. 'Oh. I see.'

As they stepped outside, the noise of Uppsala assaulted them from all sides. It sounded like a good half of all the inhabitants were shouting at the other, and all the while, clanking metal was interspersed with whinnying horses and crying children.

Breki flinched. 'Is this what war sounds like?'

Big Rolf stopped and looked up at him. 'No, boy,' he said at last. 'There's usually a lot more screaming.'

The forest was oddly silent and Grundle kept tossing her head, snorting her objections. They could keep up a reasonable speed in amongst the trees, but there was a sense of *obstruction*, a sense of being hemmed in, that made it hard to concentrate.

'Ssh, girl,' Helga whispered, leaning forward to stroke the mare's neck. 'It's fine. We're just going to go and ask questions of the dead.'

Who killed you, boy?

And why?

And how do you know the fallen man?

She squeezed her eyes shut. There were too many questions, and the dead weren't likely to offer any answers. Instead, she looked around, happy to notice signs of the constant battle to tame the forest. Here a tree of manageable size had been cut, there a bit of bush had been picked clean. She leaned over Grundle's neck and whispered, 'We're getting closer, girl.' The horse ignored her and kept to the path.

Helga smiled. There was something comforting in the horse's presence – the size of her, the warmth, the different ways in which she showed her moods. Rays of sunlight were starting to break through the leaf cover as the trees thinned out on both sides. The horse picked up speed again and at last Helga could see Olver's farm in the distance. As they left the forest, she kicked her heels gently into Grundle's side, urging more speed, calling encouragement as she did so.

The horse obliged and they thundered across the tilled field together. Helga closed her eyes and let the wind blow all worries out of her head. They closed the distance quickly and before long she was in Olver's yard and dismounting before the old farmer, who got up from a well-worn stump, brandishing a half-sharpened scythe.

'Helga! Well met, girl. What brings you?'

'Well met, Olver. Have you burned the body yet?'

He looked guilty. 'We were going to do it today. We would have done it yesterday, but there hasn't been time – a fox scattered our chickens and—'

Helga smiled at him. 'Good. Can I see him?'

Frowning, confused by the sudden turn, he asked, 'See him? Why? He's still dead.'

'I just need to check something.'

Olver shrugged. 'Suit yourself. We laid him by the woodshed. He's under the cloth.' He gestured towards a small wooden building at the back of the farmyard.

Helga smiled again, thinking, *It's strange how just dragging the sides of your mouth upwards makes people relax.* 'Thank you.'

'Shout if you want me. I've got things to be getting on with. Hugin will be back from the fields soon if you need help.' With that he turned around, headed back towards his seat and picked up the sharpening stone.

The boy was laid out by Olver's stacks of drying timber, a shapeless lump under a large square of rough sackcloth weighed down at the corners by heavy stones. *We'll all end under the cloth sooner or later*, Helga thought grimly. Gritting her teeth, she knelt down – slowly – and pulled the cloth to one side. For the blink of an eye she saw the face of Karl Unnthorsson, the first dead body she'd ever seen, sliced up by his brother in his father's house.

It was the smell that brought her back.

There was a *wrongness* about it, a warmth in the escaping air that smelled a little like someone making soup out of bad ingredients. The boy's appearance had not improved any, but Helga ignored the sallow, waxy skin and the glassy eyes.

'What more can you tell me?' she muttered, but the boy remained resolutely silent – and annoyance flared in her. *You can't hide from me.*

Glancing over her shoulder to make sure no one could see what she was about to do, she leaned close and let her hands roam over the body. The feel of him, cold and clammy and soft, made it hard to resist yanking her hand away, but she bit down on her nausea and continued searching. No one would consider her touching the dead body like this to be normal, or a good thing; if Olver or his son caught her, they might think ill and speak worse of her, so there was no time to waste – and to add to her troubles, she thought she could hear a horse in the distance, and it was closing fast. However, the boy had nothing, no possessions, no markings . . . he was just a boy like any other boy, dressed in worn, utilitarian clothes, not carrying anything.

Except . . . what was that?

A lump.

There was something round and metallic by his left hip.

The horse was in the yard now. Olver had been joined by his son; she could hear them talking.

Quick as a flash Helga whipped out her knife and cut a small hole in the boy's trousers. She could feel the point of her knife carving into flesh and cursed herself for being clumsy, but—

There! I was right: metal. She stuck her finger into the hole and felt the hard ridge of something. Behind her, she heard Olver telling his son to go and check on their visitor. She gave a swift tug and there was a flash of silver in the sunlight – *a ring!* Trying hard not to hiss in frustration, she hid her new-found treasure, eased the knife into its sheath and tugged the boy's tunic back into place. Helga had just had time to straighten herself before Hugin appeared, looking slightly uncertain.

He stood and stared at her before asking, diffidently, 'Do you need, uh, help?'

Fighting a sudden urge to giggle, she kept her face solemn and serious as she said, 'Thank you, but I think I have seen what I needed to see.' As she rose, she enjoyed the fact that the boy took half a step back. His half-shuffle, half-side-step alongside her as she went to grab Grundle's reins was equally amusing.

As Grundle started moving under her, picking up speed with every step, she looked back and waved to the two men, standing there side by side, young and old, hewn from the same rock, watching her ride away. *Father and son.*

She thought of her adoptive mother, Hildigunnur, and her daughter, the woman who was even now in Uppsala, negotiating for the Dalefolk. What would her mother have done if Jorunn went missing? *Anything.* So where had the boy been, then?

'It's the same questions,' she snapped into the wind. 'It's the same bloody questions: why, what, who? That's all I have and I know nothing about the damn boy: nothing at all.' The forest had swallowed her now, the treeline stretching out on either side of her, filling her eyes with browns and greens of every shade, while she tried to fend off the insistent voice in her head cursing her own stupidity for not being to work out things that ought to be so simple.

The boy had to have come from *somewhere* – so where was that?

If she was going to have any hope of solving this mystery, she'd have to start afresh, go back to the beginning, when she first saw the body. The memory of that pallid face and accusing look kept her focused on her purpose.

She imagined the scene in her head: Olver and his son had found the pale, pudgy boy in the copse, but there was no blood where they'd found him, and they thought he'd been in the river, so that couldn't be where he'd been bashed.

'Where's the bloody river?' she said out loud, searching for memories of the feel of the landscape, the colours around the path the boy had taken them to find the body, the smells – and finally, the sounds.

There. She focused, and pinpointed the sounds of water, running happily.

Slowing Grundle to a walk so she wouldn't miss anything, they picked their way through the trees until they were standing on a slight ridge looking down on the river. From here, it didn't look like much – it was just three or four feet wide, maybe, and she didn't think it would reach much past waist-height on a man.

That's still enough to carry an unconscious body, though. She dismounted, wondering if she was standing up- or downriver, and after a moment or two, decided to go against the flow. Ignoring Grundle's snorted protests, she grabbed the reins and started walking as briskly as the trees would allow, scanning the surroundings for anything that shouldn't be there.

Her stomach recognised the site where they'd found the body before her eyes did. For an eyeblink she thought she could see herself crouched over the lifeless form on the forest floor, Freysteinn hanging back, watching from a distance, tense and concerned.

But there was nothing there. Without the body, the riders and the fear, the copse was just another part of the forest.

'But I'm on the right track,' she muttered to Grundle and walked resolutely past the point where she'd watched a young man die and been unable to do anything to stop it. She willed the forest to give up its secrets, to tell her what had happened, where he'd died, but the trees were silent and as she moved further upstream, her hopes dwindled. The sheer weight of the woods settled on her, the quiet strangling any hopes of a response.

She almost missed the stones.

They were tucked away nicely behind three thick tree trunks, a circle dug in to hide any blaze from prying eyes, but it was clear as day: this had been a campsite, probably for a couple of nights. The ashes were undisturbed and when she bent down and sniffed deeply, there were no strong odours; no one had lit a fire there for at least three days.

'Stay, girl,' she said to Grundle, who looked at her, then immediately wandered off in search of grass.

She turned her attention to the circle and noticed a clear gap where one of the stones had been removed. There was a dark patch on the one next to it. She knelt down and touched the mark, which was dry, like a thin coating of resin.

It was also flaky to the touch.

Blood.

She stood up, almost in a trance. 'He stood . . .' She looked at the fire circle and imagined the body as she'd first seen it. *Where would his feet have been?* Staring at the ground, she saw nothing, until—

'Yes!' she cried, and laughed when Grundle whinnied in response. 'No, not you, idiot horse. But look, I've found something.' She walked across the little clearing, then got down on her knees so she could examine the faintest of footsteps, two pairs, different sizes, and an indentation where she thought the boy's elbow might have hit the ground. In her mind she could actually see his body falling.

She winced at the sound when his head hit the stone.

She watched the shadow-clad attacker reach down and wrench the second lump of rock free.

She felt the pull of cloth tightening as the arm rose. Moments later, it was over.

The boy's head was lolling to one side. The attacker grabbed handfuls of his tunic and dragged him upright, then, supporting the boy's weight, started to propel him towards the river. Still in her trance, Helga glanced down at the footsteps leading away: two heavy steps, and a line made by the boy's heels. In her mind, she walked with them down to the bank and stood there, watching as the attacker pushed the boy in the river.

The body bobbed there for a moment, then floated gently away.

Grundle ambled over and nudged Helga, who blinked and found herself alone in the forest, staring at two stones in the river, at the light flashing on the sparkling water, dancing in between the rocks, bouncing up and down. Up and down. Side to side with the stream. Up again.

It wasn't the light. There was something there.

Heart thumping, Helga crouched down and stared into the water. A leather thong was wedged in between the stones, but the metal medallion hanging from it was twisting in the current; that was what had been catching the light. It was about the size of a thumb, and when it spun front side out it sparkled silver. She reached into the water, a little shocked at the cold, grabbed the leather and carefully dislodged it from its anchor.

She wiped the amulet dry on her shirt, then examined it. As she stared at the carved symbol on one side, she realised she'd seen it before, and recently. For a moment, Helga felt like the cold river was flowing in her veins. Jorunn's face floated before her eyes, looking at her like she was nothing – no, less than nothing. The symbol was on the side of her cart.

Then she remembered the ring she'd found in the boy's pocket. It was just a narrow silver band carved with a simple pattern, the sort worn by any number of people . . . and by Alvar Dal, on his oft-broken forefinger.

That settled it: the boy had been one of the Dalefolk, and the other victim, Alvar, had to be his father – but had he been one of Jorunn's men? And if he was, why then was he in the forest to the east when Jorunn's party came from the west? New questions were racing headlong through her mind.

She might not like it, but it was all too clear which camp she would find the answers in.

The horses stomped and shifted, tossing their heads, pushing and generally trying to carve out space for themselves in a crowded field. The Northmen gathered together, all fifteen of them, sitting tall and proud on their mounts. All pretence of harmless trade had been discarded: now every man exuded as much threat as they could. On their left, Ludin of Skane's group waited dully in the manner of the lifetime soldier, conserving energy best spent in actual battle. Jorunn, sitting at the head of her delegation, was flanked by her hard-faced grey-haired captain.

They all turned when the king rode forth. His horse was a magnificent, muscular beast, snorting and baring its teeth, pawing at the air, clearly raring for battle. King Eirik sat tall, his well-made, well-used mail shirt catching the light. At his side was his favourite hand-axe, in a lavishly tooled leather scabbard.

By his side was Alfgeir Bjorne, the bulk of him making his favourite mare look like a toy horse.

'The gathered host brings pride to your regions.' The young king's strong voice cut through the babble and everyone fell silent.

'However, we will not ride out just yet.' Looks were exchanged, but no one said a thing. 'I will have my riders back before we go – I want to meet Styrbjorn head-on, and in the right place, so best we all dismount and wait.' Looking around, he added, 'But don't get too comfortable. Valhalla will call us soon enough.'

Beside him, Alfgeir landed lightly on the ground. 'Food will be brought, and hay for the horses,' he growled.

Around them the men from the south, west and north got off their mounts. Necks were cracked, shoulders stretched and knees bent.

Freysteinn approached Alfgeir and asked, 'How can I help?'

'We'll need riders. Is your horse fast?'

'Fast as anything,' he said, smiling.

'You might need it.' There was no mirth in Alfgeir's voice.

'What's the plan?'

'We ride out against Styrbjorn and stop him in the woods where we can use the cover. Depending on what we learn, we'll then fall back and defend Uppsala. It'll give Thorgnyr enough time to organise our defences.'

Freysteinn looked past Alfgeir Bjorne at the Lawspeaker, who was standing halfway up the hill arguing with a handful of men. 'We will need a bit of luck.'

'Thorgnyr is a good man. He will do what needs to be done.'

There was a hint of a smile on his face that suggested he knew full well how much the Lawspeaker was going to hate this task.

'I will keep an eye out and once you ride, I will follow,' Freysteinn said. 'My horse flies like a greased lie, so you need not worry.'

'I'll stop worrying when I'm dead.' A shouted conversation caught Alfgeir's attention. He turned his head to see what was happening and moments later, went striding off towards the edge of the field where one of the Northmen had apparently strayed too close to the Dalefolk.

Freysteinn watched for a few moments as Alfgeir weighed in, barking at both men until they backed down, and smiled. He mounted gracefully, then bent close to his horse's ear and whispered, 'I've talked you up some, boy. Now go!' A sharp kick to the sides sent the animal lurching forward, but he quickly picked up speed and soon enough the field was out of earshot. Freysteinn didn't let up but drove the beast on towards the edge of the forest. The trees grew closer; the line of green and brown became a looming presence and soon enough the forest swallowed him. The path he was following wound its way around big trees and across streams, but Freysteinn didn't let the horse slacken until it slowed down in anticipation of the final bend in the road.

Only then did he rein it in, and a moment later he was jumping off, landing softly and yelling, 'Helga!'

But no one answered.

Even with Grundle's hooves beating a steady, heavy rhythm on the grass, Helga could almost hear the amulet on the leather strip whispering secrets at her from where it nestled, tucked away in the folds of her shirt. She just needed to get home, get her mind settled and plan what she was going to ask the Dalefolk, then everything would fall into place. Who would her mother have selected? Jorunn? She snorted and instantly dismissed the idea. No, she would not go to Jorunn, daughter of Unnthor, and offer any sort of information. The brawler, Lars? No. There had been a lot of malice and no compassion in his eyes. In her mind she brought up the face of the grey-haired man with the grey beard. There was something about him that suggested he could be useful: he looked like someone who might be kept talking until something slipped out. The thought of getting some answers to the questions clawing at her filled her with excitement. She thought about the things she'd brewed for the sick to take pain away and now she waited for the same blissful release of finding out – well, if not what had happened to the boy and why, then at least who he had been.

The questions filling her head offered themselves up to be asked when she met the captain of Jorunn's guard and she was right in the middle of discarding the bad ones and polishing the good ones when she felt Grundle picking up speed. Looking around, she recognised the shapes of the trees, the curves of the path.

'Nearly home,' she murmured, and when Grundle tossed her head and snorted, 'What?' Rounding the bend, she saw Freysteinn's horse standing in the yard. *Why is he here? He's not supposed to be.* He had a knack for knowing where she was and when she'd be home. She could not remember him ever waiting for her.

Something felt . . . *wrong*.

Where was he?

She dismounted quickly, just as he emerged from the house.

'There you are,' he said, flashing a smile at her. *Loki take your hide . . .* She could feel her carefully assembled questions slipping through her fingers. Suddenly the curve of his neck was much more interesting, the width of his shoulders, his hands . . .

Stop it! She became aware that she hadn't spoken yet. 'Yes. Here I am. And so are you.' *What?* She was suddenly furious. He had reduced her from a truth hunter to a half-wit. 'What do you want?' Somewhere in her head a thought appeared, something different. Dimly aware that she'd just snapped at him, she pushed it away and tried to regain control.

If he thought her sharp, he didn't show it. 'I just came to . . . um . . .' Freysteinn's gaze wavered and he looked at his feet.

He never hesitates. She could not name the feeling, but she could taste it, bitter and cold. What was going on? She watched him take a deep breath and when he looked up at her again, her heart leaped.

'Styrbjorn has landed. I will have to go out with Alfgeir, run messages for the king.'

For a moment she couldn't speak. In her mind she saw slashed, bleeding and battered bodies, lying broken and lifeless. She saw him discarded on the ground, cold and still and gone.

The words burst out of her. 'I found the place where the boy got killed.'

He frowned. 'What?'

'The boy – the boy by the river.'

'That was yesterday.' His eyes narrowed. 'I remember – I was there.'

Mention of the boy seems to have angered him. Quick – explain. Her heart thumping, she pushed the rest of the words out. 'No, that wasn't where he died, that was where he ended up – he floated down the river. He died further up. I found his campsite.' *Please, understand me – understand that I must have answers—*

But his face had grown hard and cold. 'Good. Maybe you can tell me about it if I come back.'

'What do you mean, "if"?' she snapped.

'I might catch an axe in the skull tonight, Helga – I might never see you again!'

The sudden explosion, the fury of him, made her take two steps back. '. . . no,' she said, and the feeling grew in her like a wave. 'No.'

And she was her mother, and every woman who had ever sent a man to sea, and she would be obeyed. She looked him straight in the eye and said firmly, 'You will get on your horse and you will ride hard and ride wise, and if you so much as see a blade, let alone catch one, I will find you and bring you back from the dead if I have to, just so I can flay you for your stupidity and wear your skin as a tunic. One way or another, you are keeping me warm this winter. Do you hear my words?'

She came back to herself then and felt for a moment that she saw into the heart of him.

He stared at her with something that looked like fear and happiness at the same time. 'My mother told me never to mix my limbs with a Finn-witch.'

'Well, then your mother was no less of a fool than you are. I am not of the Finns.'

'But you do not deny that you are a witch?'

Somewhere, faintly, at the back of her head, Hildigunnur was smirking. 'Why don't you disobey me and find out.'

Her words brought the familiar sparkle back to his eye. 'You have a way of making a man wish for long winter nights.' With that he strode past her, close enough for her to catch his scent, mounted swiftly and turned his horse around. He rode out at a gallop, one hand uplifted in farewell.

The echoes of a sharp cry drifted through the trees and then there was silence.

Breathe. The familiar smells of pine, herbs and soil settled her. *Breathe.* For a moment, she imagined that she could smell wolfs-bane. *Breathe.* Grundle had already taken herself off to where they kept the brushes.

Helga allowed her body to sink into the rhythms of the things that had to get done. If everyone was moving out, they would need poultices, drenches and bandages. It might not pay well, but it couldn't hurt her cause to help Eirik. *As long as we win.*

As she swept the brush firmly but gently over the horse's flanks, whispering soothing sounds to her, Helga turned inward and looked again at her questions. She conjured the face of Jor-unn's grey-haired captain as she nudged this and pushed that until slowly her thoughts started taking shape again and she was somewhat reassured.

Once Grundle was groomed to the horse's satisfaction, she moved into the herb shed. She still felt a little out of sorts, she realised, and suddenly couldn't remember where she'd left the things she needed. She had to do some rearranging, making sure that the dangerous herbs were back where they belonged. It was unlike her to not put things away in the right place; if that was where her mind was at, she'd need to be careful when matching wits with the Dalefolk.

After all, there was a killer out there.

'You haven't answered my question.' Drifa stepped into the sunlight, casting a shadow on the kneeling figure.

'Maybe I don't want to.' Ludin of Skane pulled on his thick boots and set to tying up the leather straps, ignoring his advisor.

'Is this the right thing to do?'

He looked up at her. 'Is anything?'

Through the tent they could hear the sounds of shouted orders and the forced joy in the replies of men preparing for a battle they didn't want.

'The Jomsvikings are tough as they come and Styrbjorn is downright vicious. Do you remember the time we found the village he'd—'

'Yes.'

'And so why are we—?'

The old man looked at her. 'Because all that we say about Styrbjorn, the world has said about me twice over.' He sighed and halted his preparations. 'We side with the king because we have to. He needs us – but we need him too.' His voice was soft. 'I am old, Drifa, old and tired. An outside threat—'

'— like Styrbjorn?'

'Yes, like Styrbjorn – that is useful to us. Anything that makes people wary. It will bind our alliance together. The other option – to run with Harald's pit-hounds – is not a good choice. Those who pay for the blade fear it the most, and I know Bluetooth's ilk: he would not wait long until he'd set them on us anyway, and then we'd have nothing, no friends, no blades and no land. No, the only way forward is to stand with Eirik – but it must appear to be an uneasy alliance.'

Drifa looked at him quizzically. 'Why?'

'Because if we are the sharp end of Eirik's army, others will fear us, and if he remembers that fear, he will give us respect. Respect buys time, enough for me to die an old man and for the future of Skane to be someone else's problem.' Ludin grabbed his axe, a thing of black iron menace with a well-worn handle. 'You are sharp as the frozen edge, Drifa, but you still need to learn.' Standing up, Ludin twisted, cracked and flexed his joints before turning back to his right-hand woman. 'Know what you want – and do anything to make it happen.'

With that he ducked under the hide tent flap and disappeared.

The trees were showing faint tinges of gold and shadow by the time Helga saddled Grundle again, this time for the ride into Uppsala. She could feel the weight of the bags on her hip, stuffed with as much shaved juniper root, goatweed and ribwort as she could muster. Thin-spun wool soaked in mayweed juice was rolled up and tied, ready to wrap around nasty cuts. 'Do you think they'll want me to go with them?' she asked, absentmindedly.

When Grundle snorted in reply, she laughed. 'How could you

know?' She leaned over and stroked the warm muzzle. 'You don't worry too much about us, all told, do you?'

The horse snorted again, impatiently: the saddle was on and that meant *run*.

'Yes, yes,' she muttered, 'I should listen to you in all things. Then maybe my stores wouldn't have run so low.' She grimaced. When she'd gone in to fill her bags, she'd found she was almost out of ground ivy and wormwood, and low in burdock and vervein too. She was still bothered about leaving the wolfsbane bag in the wrong place as well. *What would Hildigunnur have said?* She could remember all too clearly the cold look on her mother's face when orders weren't followed precisely. And as if that wasn't enough, the soft flesh above her hip had suddenly started aching in memory of the Eastman witch's bony fingers. They would lash out like cat's claws, raking, prodding or pinching, depending on what Groa thought she had done wrong.

I was busy!

She mounted smoothly, cursing herself for having make-believe arguments with women long gone from her life. But it was true, she *had* been busy, ever since she'd first seen Freysteinn, when it had suddenly become harder to keep her mind on the work, the slow grind of finding the good herb patches, the cutting, drying and sorting, the planting and harvesting in her own herb garden. She thought of him now, the way he made her feel, and as the familiar trees fell back behind her and the plains below Uppsala opened up before her, she suddenly felt like she could see him – see him with her – from a distance.

He's turned my head good and proper, she admitted to herself, then, 'You are Loki's child and no mistake,' she said to the wind whipping around her ears. Like a fool, she had allowed a man to become the most important thing in her life.

But no more.

She would fight to keep a clear head and push Freysteinn away until she had found the boy's killer.

Out of habit she looked up, searching for the sparkling chains on the temple, but they were not the only things catching the sun today.

A meadow of spears, helmets and shields had sprouted in the field where she'd pitched her wagon only yesterday. *They're ready to go – I almost missed them. Now, be calm.* She pushed aside the desire to urge Grundle into a gallop and draw attention to her arrival, instead slowing down a bit and looking around.

The men of Uppsala were unfamiliar in battered helmets and old mail shirts, except for the large frame of Alfgeir Bjorne, stalking between groups, stopping here and there to pull, push or bash someone into shape. She caught a glimpse of Ludin and his men, in the middle of the crowd, looking bored. *That is probably the best thing they can bring to this gathering: calm.* The Dalefolk were clustered tightly to one side, and all eyes were trained on Jorunn.

There would be no way to get to her greybeard captain, not now.

'Everything is going the way of Odin's eye,' she muttered, slowing Grundle further and cursing herself for not having gone straight to town. *Why did I go home? It was almost as if I knew that he was there . . .*

The Northmen were sprawled over a large area. She could see

some of them were fussing over a covered wagon while others were busying themselves sharpening blades, sending the scrape of stone on metal whistling through the air. On a hunch, Helga guided Grundle towards their horses, where she had spotted the young wrestler preparing the animals as best he could with one arm broken and the other sprained. He saw her coming and she raised a hand and smiled, happy to note that his cheeks coloured ever so slightly in response.

'Well met, Breki,' she called, dismounting beside him.

'Well met, Healer.' After a brief pause, he added, 'Thank you.' Casting a glance at her lathered horse, he handed her his brush.

'I'm Helga. And I'm glad to help. How are the hands?'

'They hurt like—'

'Being bitten by a badger on the arse?'

He smiled awkwardly. 'Maybe not what I was going to say, but it sounds about right.'

'They are going to heal, I promise, and quickly.'

He gestured at the assembled men. 'Not quickly enough, though.'

Helga's scalp tingled. She'd seen Hildigunnur pouncing, getting people to talk: here was the opening she needed.

'This?' she said, with a confidence she didn't feel. 'This will be over before you know it. Styrbjorn will show up, Eirik will negotiate and the whole thing will disappear. I'm willing to bet that they'd even hold off on the fighting until you can participate, if you asked them nicely.' She smiled, to show him she was on his side.

The boy frowned for a moment, but then whatever he was

thinking about went the right way. 'It's just stupid,' he said gloomily.

'I know,' Helga said.

'If he'd known about Styrbjorn, do you think Ludin would still have—?'

'I don't know him, but I don't think that one thinks like we do. He might have tried to do even worse in order to get himself ready for the fight.'

You got off lightly, Northman-child. You need to understand that fight means pain and there is no glory. Please understand this. There are so many like Ludin of Skane out there. The eyes of the dead boy were there again, staring blankly at her.

Breki grimaced. 'I . . . well, I guess I'm happy he's on our side.'

'That's true. Be glad of what you have.'

'Are you the healer?' The voice startled them both and they turned to see Lars, the Dalefolk bruiser. He'd had stopped a good ten yards away, but he was still a formidable presence. Helga saw Breki tense up immediately, clench his fists and remember – quite painfully – that he was healing broken bones. *He'd try to protect me with one hand. One of Tyr's chosen, this one.* She could feel the weight of the rune-knife by her hip, but she didn't feel like she was in danger. *Not yet, at any rate.*

'Yes,' she said, smiling. 'Why do you ask, friend?'

He looked a bit taken aback by this. 'I need burdock – chopped in spring, if you have it. For my joints,' he added, almost sheepishly. 'I'd like to have a feel of the leaves – I pick some myself, back home.'

She studied the big man in front of her. *You look like someone who's been kicked by the world since your first day born. No wonder your joints hurt.* The idea of his stubby, fat fingers plucking dainty herbs struck her as funny, which was an odd thought to have, standing in a field full of warriors. She patted Grundle and asked Breki, 'Are you happy to look after her?'

He grunted curtly and as he resumed his grooming, Grundle neighed and turned her tail towards Helga with determined petulance.

Oh, stop it. I am not abandoning you. And besides, you'll get better service from one of his hands than two of mine.

Walking towards Lars, knowing exactly what she had with her, she made a show of thinking. 'Um . . . burdock . . . I don't have any on me, but what I do have' – she patted the bags at her hips, left, then right – 'is mayweed, and thyme, for taste. Any good?'

'Hm.' He fell in beside her, but half a step behind. 'It's not what I wanted. It stinks like horse-crotch.'

A strange comparison, big man . . . But she resisted the impulse to make a rude joke. *You don't loose an arrow after every fowl.* 'I've dried and aired it and soaked it in honey.'

'Huh.' Somehow, although she wasn't sure how, that one grunt suggested that he was impressed. 'Sometimes it turns your skin itchy,' he added.

She thought about that for a moment, then told him, 'You're from the Dales, aren't you. It does depend on what you eat, I think. I travelled through there a while back and I rarely saw anyone eating fish. If you eat fish, the mayweed won't hurt your skin.'

'Fish?' The question was born somewhere deep in his belly and hardly made it up and out of him. 'Do you think so?'

'We eat a lot of fish here. I use it all the time and hardly ever see any trouble.'

'Huh.' A pause, and then he admitted, 'That would make life easier, because burdock is not easy to find this time of year.'

'You'd be reliant on stores,' Helga remarked.

'Or have to carry some of my own – which I generally do, but I used it all up.'

'And there we are,' she added cheerily. 'Mayweed and thyme?'

The big man grinned. 'You can talk, I'll give you that.'

It didn't take Helga long to make up the package for him, then they continued towards the mustered warriors. They had walked a few steps in silence when Helga noticed a fresh cut on the bruiser's cheek. 'Want some salve for that, while we're haggling?'

The big man sounded oddly embarrassed. 'Nah, I'll leave it to sting for a bit.'

'Why?'

'It'll remind me to watch my step.' When he caught Helga looking at him, he added, 'Got into a bit of an argument with Ludin's woman.'

'Who – Drifa?'

He grunted. 'Probably. Tall, blonde, sharp as a blade in the night. I asked her if she had any herbs but something went wrong somewhere and before I knew it she'd proper smashed my face. I wasn't going to do anything, but Gunnar of Skar was there and I think he felt he had to make some noise.'

Helga offered a non-committal 'Mm.' She'd let Lars get the words out.

He turned towards her and stuck his hand down the side of

his tunic. After a little bit of rooting around, he brought out a piece of silver that appeared to have been hacked off something. 'Here. I have a feeling you'll get more use out of this than I will.' She stared at the metal for long enough that she didn't notice his massive hand closing surprisingly gently around her wrist and pressing the piece into her palm. It was worth at least ten times what she'd given him.

'Thank you for listening to me,' he muttered. Then, after a moment's thought, 'I'm Lars.'

'Helga,' she offered in reply, thinking, *Thank you, Lars*. He'd clearly decided that she liked him and cared for him, which was just what she'd wanted. The silver . . . she would find a use for that too, no doubt.

'Well met.' Out of habit, she read his face. *And . . . here it comes.*

'. . . wait. You're the one who came to the wagon.'

What would this one want to hear, and how? She settled on a combination of curiosity, dim wits and innocence. 'What do you mean?'

Like a dog with a bone, he worried at it. 'You came and argued with her – you told her all our goods were overpriced!'

He's smiling. That's interesting. 'Oh, *that*. Well, yes, that was me.' Talk less, Hildigunnur's voice whispered in the back of her head. Let him fill in the gaps.

'She didn't like that,' Lars went on, his tone confiding. 'She doesn't like people speaking up.'

'Doesn't she?'

'No, she strikes that right down. Her and that tree-coloured bastard shadow of hers. That one doesn't even blink.'

'She must have been annoyed when the man fell, though?'

'Poor old Alvar. He was on our pots and he drove the wagon. Kept talking about his boy who'd gone to seek his fortune at the king's court – all he wanted was to find the kid and bring him home. I don't know if she even knew his name. She was angry for about one eye-blink, then she was feeling her way around how to use it. She'd do anything to get an advantage, that one.'

Their walk had been as slow as Helga could make it, but they were nearing the camp of the Dalefolk. *I've just got a couple of questions left.* 'What kind of advantage?' She wanted to make it sound like idle curiosity, nothing more.

'Trade deals, I think,' Lars muttered, sounding a lot less certain. 'She might get a part of what she negotiates – what goes east from us and what goes west from the king. We were hired to protect her, make sure no one tried anything stupid. And you are right.'

'About what?'

'The wagon: it's just full of shit we picked up on the way, not worth half what she's trading it for. She's a talker, that one. A lot like you, in fact.'

More and less than you'll ever know.

Still keeping most of her attention on Lars, she scanned the area out of the corner of her eye, searching for Jorunn, but she was nowhere to be seen.

'So we are agreed.' King Eirik's words rang with finality and the grim faces around the table nodded. 'My men will ride up ahead. Ludin will take the left flank. Ingileif, your lot gets the right side. Jorunn—'

'I guard the rear. But take Nazreen with you up front. He will follow your lead and he is easily the equal of any six men I've ever met.'

Ludin snorted at this, but Alfgeir leaned in and whispered something in King Eirik's ear.

'Very well,' the king said, 'he'll ride beside Alfgeir. And now it's time to go and meet our kin and see what they want.'

There was a clatter of metal as Ludin and Ingileif got up and left, Jorunn following after a beat. Without a word, Alfgeir passed Eirik a big bull-horn and the two men walked towards the doors of the King's Hall.

'I wonder what gifts my cousin is bringing us,' Eirik said as he stepped over the threshold.

Alfgeir snorted. 'If he's anything like he was when he was younger, he'll have packed nothing but trouble.'

King Eirik frowned and looked out over Uppsala. The temple cast its long shadow over the houses. Out on the trading field, he could see the massed men. 'How many do we have?'

'All told, about two hundred and twenty, with another hundred riding with Fenrir on their heels to get here in time.'

King Eirik let out a soft hiss. 'I see,' he said finally. 'So we'll have to move fast.'

'Where do you want to go?'

'Vasby – because if he gets to the woods before us, we're all dead. Right. Let's do it.'

King Eirik drew a deep breath and blew his horn.

*

By the time King Eirik's riders got to Vasby, they were cloaked in shadow. The trees rising up to meet them like a black wall were already blocking out the bluish-grey of the fading sky. A half-step behind the front, Alfgeir broke from a small group and rode up to where the king was leading the way.

'The riders are all back. They've seen Styrbjorn – he's definitely going to be coming through here.'

'That's fortunate,' King Eirik remarked dryly. 'If he does choose any of the other routes, there will be no home to go home to.'

'So how did you know he'd go this way?'

'Because it's straight and quick: it is the strong man's path.' King Eirik paused, then added, 'Also, there's no thinking involved.'

Around them, the king's warriors were slowing their horses down to a careful walk as the forest swallowed them. 'Have the men been informed?'

'They have.'

'Good,' the king said. He dismounted, weapons jangling. 'Give the command.'

But that wasn't necessary; the men behind them were already on the ground. A handful dropped back to secure the horses while the rest silently followed the king on foot into the fading light. Through the trees the shadows were drifting, disappearing, then reappearing, deeper and darker.

'Not bad,' King Eirik muttered. 'Do you think he'll buy it?'

Alfgeir Bjorne didn't answer.

The army of the Svear kept inching towards the clearing. Where the trees thinned out up ahead they could see glimpses of sky.

No one spoke, just *step . . . step . . . step.*

As agreed, they slowed down and spread out before they entered a clearing the size of a small lake. The trees rose tall on both sides, looking like jagged black cliffs. Across from the clearing a gap in the treeline suggested a similar exit. A trodden path crossed the open ground.

King Eirik looked around in the gloom and found the faces of Ludin and his swordsman on the left. On the right was Alfgeir, towering over Jorunn's dark-skinned man and the North Wind.

They all stepped forward together into the clearing.

'And how many men do you think he'll think we have?' Ludin said dryly.

'Enough,' Eirik said.

The old warlord didn't answer.

'If the riders are right, he shouldn't be far away,' Alfgeir said. 'Won't be long n—'

The dark-skinned man pointed across the clearing, a lazy movement, like he'd seen something mildly interesting in passing.

One man stepped out into the clearing on the other side.

'Hel's teeth,' Big Rolf hissed.

Behind the first figure, more stepped forward. There were at least twenty of them. Beside them came another twenty. And another.

'Styrbjorn does not appear to feel the need to hide,' Ingileif remarked.

'Here we go,' Eirik muttered. Then he cupped his hands around his mouth and shouted, 'Cousin! We come to talk.'

The only response from the other side was more and yet more men, stepping calmly into the clearing alongside their fellows.

'We're going to have to go for it,' Alfgeir said.

'I know.'

The king moved forward, his chosen men following him: two steps, three steps ... five ... Nobody said anything when the figure at the head of the opposing army started walking towards Eirik, but there was more than one silent sigh of relief. The figure was flanked by two men.

At Alfgeir's side the dark-skinned man nudged him, gestured. There was a shared look.

'No.' Alfgeir shook his head, raising one arm then forcing it down with a meaty hand. 'No fight. Just' – he mimed – 'talk.' The shorter man gave him a bemused look, then shrugged and continued walking.

Midway through the clearing the king stopped, and his men stopped beside him. All hands stayed off hilts and clearly visible as they waited for Styrbjorn the Strong.

The king's cousin took his time, at last coming to a halt a polite axe-and-a-half away from the king. It was easy to see where the nickname came from. The mercenary captain was easily half again as broad as Eirik, with powerful shoulders and a heavy frame. Dark hair and a thick black beard gave him a sinister look. The men beside him had the same build, born of rowing ships and bashing heads.

'Well met, Cousin.'

There was no response.

After a moment, Eirik said, 'We do not wish to raise blades against our family, but you come with war-men at your back. What do you want?'

Cold looks were exchanged, but still there was no response.

'The Svear are mighty when they stand together, Cousin. I have Ludin and the North Wind at my side. Join us, and together we can sweep Bluetooth across his flat sands and into the sea, where he belongs.'

Slowly, Styrbjorn's arm rose, palm flat, fingers spread out.

Then it fell, hard.

For a moment, nothing happened.

Then flames rose in the woods, outlining Styrbjorn's army in silhouette. A mass of mercenaries stepped forward simultaneously into the clearing. Spears drew black lines on fire held high.

Styrbjorn the Strong smiled.

'No.'

Chapter 7

FIGHT

Nightfall brought flames to Uppsala. Some people lit fires outside their cabins; others raised torch-poles. No one wanted to sleep until news came of the king's journey. A large bonfire, visible from a vast distance, was lit atop the hill.

Come home, Helga thought. *Come home, you idiot.* She'd waited for a while after the warriors left and managed to tease a little more conversation out of young Breki, but there was only so much he could tell her about the north. Poor boy. This was probably a bit more adventure than he had bargained for.

After that, she'd walked among the people and listened to their concerns, told them stories, some she could remember and others she made up, asked about relatives and other news, doing it all to keep their minds off what might happen . . . and what might not. More information about Styrbjorn's whereabouts filtered in, along with a steady stream of farming families from the south – the young and the strong had saddled up and gone straight back out to join with the fighters while the women, children and the elderly sought shelter in the town. The King's Hall was already full of refugees, which was keeping King Eirik's household busy. She'd even seen Hertha and Ida, in passing. They both looked tired and scared, but they'd greeted her with smiles.

The latest information was that the mercenary army was marching straight and true towards Uppsala; it wasn't going even an inch out of its way to sack and burn ... *yet*. Needless to say, this information wasn't making people feel any better.

Now Helga kept to the shadows.

If you want to see in the dark, stay away from the fire.

'Yes, Mother,' Helga muttered. The temptation to go and stand by the bright, warm flames out of spite was strong, but she had to admit that Hildigunnur was right. She always was. The light from the fires would comfort her all the while it was blinding her, and the heat would lull her to sleep. The flames were meant as a beacon, so someone had to stand watch in the darkness to make sure it guided the right men home.

'Rider!'

The call went out moments before she spotted him herself, far out on the plain: a tiny speck of darkness separated from the tree line and headed towards Uppsala at great speed.

Helga's heart leaped and her stomach lurched, her body knowing before her mind did.

It was him.

She forced herself to stay still for a moment, to get a proper look at the little black dot on the moon-washed flatland and estimate where he'd arrive.

There. Got him.

She walked away from her viewing spot in the shadow of the

temple and made her way calmly down the hill – until her foot slipped and an image slammed into her head: the peaceful corpse of a fallen man, staring blankly up at her, and suddenly she felt him on her like a weight, his stilled face crushing her chest, and she started running away from the dead people in her head and towards Freysteinn, towards safety.

Tears welled up behind her eyes and she clenched her jaw shut. 'Enough, you stupid—' she started hissing at herself in anger and disgust. She didn't finish the sentence but instead stopped in the dark and pressed her balled fists into her eyes. Fear rippled through her – the night, the fight, the unknown – and clashed with relief as certainty swelled in her. *He was alive.*

She remembered the searing heat of him, the scary strength of his embrace, and yet still she kept sobbing. At last, forcing herself to breathe, she muttered, 'Eir guide my hand.' As her thumping heart slowed down, she repeated it, again and again, until the tears had sunk back down into her throat and at last dissipated. She could feel the weight of the runestones around her neck – it was soothing, like bare feet on soil. As she found calm she could hear the whispered wheeze of Groa, the old witch: *Call for Eir and she will take care of you.*

'You bastard,' she muttered. *How could one man turn her head so badly?* 'I promised,' she told him. 'I have to find the killer, so get out of my head. Just for now,' she added, almost apologetically, and got immediately angry with herself. 'Who am I talking to?' she spat. In the darkness she could hear the calls of 'Rider! Rider!' bouncing around the hill. Now everyone else had seen him as well and it would be impossible to get to him.

She ran.

Briefly, she considered the possibility that she might be wrong; it might not be him after all. *Maybe it's someone else? Maybe he fell off his horse and cracked his head?* The memory of the campsite by the river popped into her head again and she shook it away, snorting like an angry mare. 'You'd better have some good news.' She bit off each word as she picked up speed, running down the hill as fast as she dared. Here and there firelight danced into her path, making her visible for an eye-blink as she went charging past the inviting circles of heat.

She had to know that he was safe. *Had to.*

The way he sat his horse in the middle of the throng was almost contemptuous. He was out of breath, wild-eyed and fierce. Steam rising from both horse and rider was lit by a handful of torches from below. 'Styrbjorn is coming,' Freysteinn repeated. Over a rising chorus of questions, he continued, 'They met him at Vasby and offered to talk, but he will not agree to anything but the blade. King Eirik will set up camp on our side of Fyris Fields. He will meet his cousin in the morning. He says everyone should bank their fires, pack what they need and be ready to run far and run fast at the first sign of trouble.'

'How will we know?' an old woman shouted.

Freysteinn looked down on her. 'The king will send a rider. If you see an army – run.' *He looks like he's done nothing else in his life. He is a commander.* She felt oddly proud of him, like he was her personal achievement. The people of Uppsala didn't appear to share her view, however; they didn't have any more questions, just the occasional muttered curse as they pushed past him.

Should I be going too? She turned the question over in her mind, came to a conclusion and stood her ground.

As the people left with their torches, the darkness crept over them. She knew he'd seen her, but he was clearly going to play the role of stand-in chieftain to the end. Only when the last person had gone did he dismount.

'You're here,' he said softly.

'You came back.'

'You are worth coming back for.' He was near her now, all heat and sweat and smell of horse.

Deep breath. Clear your head.

'But I have to go to the camp.'

'I'm coming with you.' The words were spoken before she even knew she'd thought them, but they were right. There was no way they would be separated from now on.

He paused for a moment. She could feel his eyes on her, but with the moon behind him she could not see them clearly, or figure out what he was thinking. *Always look at the face*, a memory whispered at her. *See what's inside. Look at the face and you'll know who they are.*

Finally, he spoke. 'I guess you are.' There was a hint of amusement in his voice. 'Where is that tempestuous old nag of yours tied up?'

'You will watch your mouth or I'll stuff a pine cone in it when you sleep.'

He reached for her and his hand was warm on her shoulder.

There was tension in his grip, but he said nothing, only pulled her close and closer still, and for a moment everything else melted away, everything except the smell of burning pitch lingering in the air, mixing with the cold night air and the warmth of him.

Finally, head buried in her hair, he whispered 'We have to go.'

The only sound during their night ride was the thunder of hooves. *Eight hooves*, she thought, and a memory scratched at her somewhere. She looked up to see the stations of the gods blazing above her: the burning embers from Muspelheim. Somewhere up there, Odin might be looking down on the two of them, racing through the night to get to the king. *And what would he think?*

The rune-stones around her neck suddenly felt a little heavier.

But Grundle was moving under her like a rhythmic dream and the *thud-thud-thud* was perfectly echoing her heartbeat and for a moment nothing existed except her and him and the horses and the night.

And the questions.

She bit down hard in frustration. Like a bad smell, the questions crept in and wouldn't leave her alone. Why did the father and son have to die? What did they know? And who killed them?

'Helga!' Freysteinn was pointing at something. She followed the line and saw – *yes, there!* – a thick line of black, breaking the dark outline of the ground. The king's camp.

She waved to indicate that she'd seen the target, then leaning forward, she pressed her heels into Grundle's sides and murmured. 'Come on, girl. Let's show him how it's done, shall we?'

The joyful straining under her filled her heart. This was life, racing horses at midnight. For a moment she thought she could feel the vibrations of his mount, step in step with hers, trailing her, and they were one and the same, two halves of the same whole, thundering through the darkness on Sleipnir himself.

It was only thanks to Freysteinn that she avoided a stomach full of barbed metal.

He somehow managed to squeeze an extra ounce of energy out of his horse, inching ahead of her and holding his hand up while shouting, 'Whoooa!'

Grundle responded, slowing reluctantly, and only then did Helga see the shadows of the armed men, a lot later than she should have, but they had already recognised Freysteinn's voice and had lowered the points of their spears.

'Are you going to stab your friends?' His command had a tense note of anger – or fear.

'Go to the king,' came the reply. She didn't recognise the men – *Northerners?* – but they had not been moved in the slightest by Freysteinn. *So he doesn't command everyone just yet, then.*

She walked Grundle forward, unable to think of anything to say. As the shadows on the ground transformed into more soldiers Freysteinn looked *changed*, somehow. Gazing around, she couldn't blame him: everywhere she saw fear and fury: in the set of the men's shoulders, the way they carried their weapons. She was suddenly a lot less clear on the chances of King Eirik beating his cousin.

Cutting through the muted sounds of hooves on soft grass,

they could hear shouting from a gathered group ahead of them. She urged Grundle to catch Freysteinn, but he wasn't showing any urgency now.

'What's happening?' she whispered.

'Don't know,' he said, peering around. 'Sounds like someone is angry.'

That's not a lie. Someone spoke – no, *screamed* – and then she recognised a deep rumble, but she couldn't make out the words. 'That's Alfgeir,' she said.

'Mm.'

'So the king must be near.'

'Probably.' If anything, he slowed down.

What's going on?

'LET ME GO!' Something was definitely happening in the group up ahead, because men and horses alike had taken a few steps backwards.

'Is that . . . Ludin?' Helga asked.

Freysteinn didn't reply but dismounted and held the reins of his horse in one hand. Helga did the same. Sounds of scuffling and straining could be heard from the group, but there were still too many bodies in the way and it was impossible to see what was happening.

'We will not.' The big man's voice rang out, half communication and half proclamation. 'Your blood is up.'

'Too fucking right it is!' Ludin roared. 'You will pay for this!' He continued shouting, but now the words were lost in grunts and fury. Helga watched Freysteinn wordlessly hand the reins of his horse to one of Alfgeir's boys and start pushing past to get to the centre. She knew he needed to relay news of the town, but it still hurt a little that he'd just left her.

She found herself standing next to a rider she didn't know. He glanced at her, but if he was surprised to see a woman there, he did not show it.

He's afraid. 'What happened?'

'After Styrbjorn, Ludin's Drifa was stabbed in the forest somewhere. She was left for dead.'

The night felt a lot colder. *The killer must have gone with them.* 'Is she—?'

'Somehow managed to drag herself onto a horse. She's a tough one, is Drifa. We only just found her in time – she's alive still, but only just. Ludin has promised to kill every single man here who has ever held a knife – it took Alfgeir and three big lads to tie him up.' The rider paused for a moment, then said quietly, 'Makes you think about the stories they tell of him. I've never seen anything like it.'

'Thank you.' Helga was moving forward before she had time to think, already squeezing her way into the middle of the group. *A woman is hurt and I am needed.* The men were warm and heavy around her, like farm animals, but they weren't trying to stop her and it was easy enough to slip past them. A circle had formed around Alfgeir and Ludin. When she saw the Southern chieftain, Helga almost stepped back into the anonymous safety of the crowd. Even though he was solidly tied up with four rounds of thick rope, there was absolute and unquestioning murder in every bit of him. He was flanked by two of Alfgeir's bigger boys, one of whom was clearly favouring his right leg. *The way someone would if someone else had just planted a booted heel on top of it, hard.* The other was bleeding freely from a gash on his forehead. A third strongman stood a few steps away, ready to spring forward if Ludin of Skane made a move. Well, another move. Gunnar of Skar stood by Alfgeir, looking concerned. *Here they are, all these big men, and nobody knows what to do.*

Alfgeir held his massive hands up for calm. 'We don't know—'

'Like fuck we don't,' Ludin snarled.

'It could have been one of Styrbjorn's—'

'You know it wasn't. It was someone here, some white-bellied little shit' – he turned to glare at the crowd, and the pure heat of his hatred made even the most seasoned warriors step back – 'and I will find you, and I will gut you like a fish.'

Helga had only the blink of an eye to figure out what she was doing, but it wasn't needed because her feet had already taken her into the circle, almost within range of the furious Ludin. She scanned the faces and saw a mixture of surprise and disbelief. *Good.* 'Where is she?' she snapped. For a heartbeat she wanted to whip her head round and find her mother in the crowd, because that voice was Hildigunnur through and through.

Well. If that's what we're doing, best do it properly. She sent a lightning-quick thought to the woman who had taught her, turned to Alfgeir and put all the command she could muster into her voice. 'Take me to her.' *This is the moment. Either it goes, or it really doesn't.* She did not wait for the big man's response, because she'd learned some things from the man she'd come to think of as her father too. A hunter waited patiently, but when the moment was there, they shot to kill.

She turned to Ludin and looked him straight in the face. The intensity, the fury of him caught her like a blast of heat from a forge and she willed herself to make him see that he had no power to hurt her.

Make them doubt themselves. Make them wonder. Give them not an inch. She put the cold of winter's shadow in her voice. 'You're wasting time.'

Ludin scowled at her. 'Ask them,' he spat.

Helga turned and looked at Alfgeir, voicing a silent question.

'I'll take you there.' Ludin's swordsman had reached her and now he took her by the arm, almost pulling her off her feet in his eagerness to get her out of the circle. The last thing Helga saw was Freysteinn watching her leave, his face immovable in the half-light. For some reason that stung. *I thought you'd be impressed.* The thought was there, then gone before she could look at it, replaced by the urgency of a badly injured woman lying somewhere in the darkness. *You're not done, girl.*

'Tell me everything,' she ordered Gunnar of Skar, her words short and sharp.

'We were going through the forest,' he started immediately, sounding far more subdued than she'd heard him before. 'Styrbjorn had his men light a fire behind them so they couldn't go back, so we had no choice but to retreat. Our groups got mixed up and somehow Drifa must have got separated from us. Not that we worried, because we all know she can look after herself . . .' His voice trailed away.

Helga focused his attention again. 'What are her injuries?'

'She took a knife to the throat. Whoever did it must have come up behind her, and fast – but they botched it.'

Her heart thumping in her chest, trying to sound calm, Helga asked, 'How?'

'They went in too shallow and didn't rip through the windpipe.'

She was suddenly uncomfortably aware of the man dragging her through the darkness, talking about how to take lives as casually as a blacksmith complaining about an apprentice. *The life of his friend, at that.* 'So it's, what? A cut?'

'It's a deep one, at that, but I wouldn't be surprised if she'd dropped down immediately and made far too much of it. Played dead, you know.'

'Why—?'

'Because that's what I taught her.' Gunnar's voice had suddenly gone cold. 'And when she comes back to us I will have her tell me who did this to her, and I will get to them before Ludin does, and I will cut them.'

Helga was thankful for the dark. He was a named man, deadlier than most, and she could hear the murder in him, but she doubted that he'd want to see what little effect his threats had. She could almost hear Hildigunnur: *When men are afraid, they threaten. When you are afraid, get things done. The thing you fear doesn't care about words.*

'We're here,' Gunnar announced.

'Here' turned out to be a hastily erected lean-to. Helga crawled in and sat next to the still shape under the blanket. She breathed out, but she couldn't quite keep away the smell of fresh blood. *A deep one indeed.* 'Light?'

187

'Wait,' Gunnar said, vanishing into the gloom.

Touch. Softly – ever so softly – Helga reached out and touched the woman, who was *cold. Too cold.* Running a quick mental inventory, she felt for the bag at her hip and pulled out the wormwood. First thing to do was to stop the flow. Grabbing just a pinch of leaves, she chewed them to a paste in her mouth, grimacing at the bitter taste. 'You can't carry much in a leaky jug,' she muttered. How many times had she heard Hildigunnur say that? She'd stopped counting after the first ten days, instead training herself just to chew to the right consistency until it became something she did without thinking.

She tested the paste, squeezing it between thumb and forefinger. Almost ready. Willing herself to slow down, not to rush but to go at the right speed for the cure, she thought about the old crone who had patched up the boys who'd been fighting over her. Those bony hands moved fast, but they'd never hurried. Just like Hildigunnur, she did the right things in the right order.

Stop the flow. That was always first.

'Is she going to survive?'

The sound of Freysteinn's voice balanced the surprise, but only just. She managed to catch the yelp before it escaped. 'I don't know. I just got here.' Her voice sounded hard. Brittle. 'You startled me.'

'Forgive me. I thought you heard me.'

I damn well didn't. 'I can tell you in a moment.'

Freysteinn leaned in and touched her arm. 'If she is in your hands she has the best chance possible. I think—'

'Well met . . . ?' Gunnar's question was at least part challenge. He was close, too. *Close enough to strike.* He held a small torch in his left hand, hidden behind a buckler. Shadows flickered on his face and hid his right-hand side.

'Freysteinn. I ride for Alfgeir.'

There was no response.

'He's with me,' Helga added quickly, and now she could sense Gunnar shifting ever so slightly and leaning in, casting light on Drifa's body. There was a slight twist of the torso – maybe like someone sheathing a long blade hidden behind their back – and then he was kneeling next to her, closer than Freysteinn. The quiet coming from her lover's direction was almost tangible, but she couldn't spare it a thought, for she had things to do.

Her skin is like wet ice, which is not good. 'Shine the light on the wound. What's this?'

The flame illuminated a rich dark blue scarf of some sort, wrapped around the woman's neck.

'My cape.'

She had a fleeting image of Gunnar striding across to her bench in the longhouse, his richly embroidered cape slung over his shoulder.

'I cut a strip off it – I had to stop the flow.'

That deserved praise. He may have saved her life. 'You did well.' *And now I have to be very careful indeed.* Pushing the paste to one side in her mouth, she wet her fingers and nudged them under the horrifyingly expensive bandage, inching it away to avoid doing more damage. *There.* The cloth moved under her fingertips as she pushed – and then it gave way and she remembered the cloth she'd cut away from the first dead body she'd ever seen and for a moment the wound was all wounds—

And then the gash was revealed in all its gore.

'See? Whoever did this was in a hurry. Or sloppy.'

She breathed in deeply again, telling herself firmly, *Back to the task.* The wound was a gaping mouth below Drifa's chin, a thumb's-width and dark with barely clotted blood. 'Sharp knife,' she muttered. 'Thick blade. Some force on it, too.'

'A killer's weapon,' Gunnar said, 'short, probably, and easy to hide – but whoever wielded it should have done so again, to make sure.'

And then we wouldn't be here. Helga's fingers were in her mouth. She could taste the cold from Drifa's skin and the smell of the blood mixed with the faintest taste on her fingertips. The paste, a thumb-sized ball, was dark green on her fingers. This part of it always felt a little bit . . . disconnected. She watched herself spread the paste smoothly across Drifa's throat. Hildigunnur had explained how it worked, that it would stick the blood together with the skin and form a barrier so the heat couldn't escape.

She often thought about her mother's teachings, and the ramblings of the old crone too, using them to distract herself when she needed her hands to think – and now they were re-folding and wrapping the ribbon of cape gently around Drifa's neck.

She sat back on her heels and breathed out deeply. 'She is weak and will need help – but if we get out of this' – she gestured around them – 'she will live.'

Torchlight flickered on a relieved smile. 'Thank you,' Gunnar murmured.

Beside her, Freysteinn rose, and without thinking, she followed.

The swordsman stayed kneeling by Drifa's body. His stillness was unnerving.

'There is one other thing,' he said just as Helga was turning to walk away.

'What?'

Working tenderly, he pried open Drifa's clenched fist. 'After she was attacked, she carved this. I tried to clean it up.' The emotion caught in his voice for a moment, then disappeared. He brought the torch closer to illuminate three blood-crusted lines in the woman's palm. 'Do you know it?'

'I'm not sure. Let me see.' Kneeling down again, Helga's mind raced. *Which one is it?* And then the next thought: *She carved this while she thought she was bleeding to death.* 'It's hard to tell.'

'Try harder.' Gunnar's words fell heavily.

'She just said she didn't know.'

It was sweet of Freysteinn to step in to protect her, but he hadn't been listening. Neither of them had.

I said it was hard to tell.

I didn't say I didn't know.

The torchlight turned out to be less necessary for finding their way back to the main camp. It was easiest to listen for Alfgeir's voice, booming over an argument that involved at least another six people.

'—there is no point!'

'We're going to get carved up—'

'—and then Styrbjorn barred their houses and burned them all—'

'The king commands you: *be silent!*'

When they were near enough, Helga could see the king's right-hand man was squaring up to two separate groups. Beside her, Gunnar muttered some sharp curses and dashed away to align himself next to one of them.

'So that's Ludin, then,' she whispered to Freysteinn.

'Yes. This isn't going well,' he whispered back. 'The Dalefolk are off too, it looks like.'

The brief moment of silence was broken by Ludin. 'But you're not the king. And the king isn't here.' When Alfgeir hesitated, the old warlord continued, 'No – his Majesty ran off on a fast horse, did he not? Into the darkness. And you're saying we shouldn't do the same?'

This unleashed a wave of murmurs and half-spoken conversations. The single torch cast light on the angry faces.

Helga turned to Freysteinn. 'How will Alfgeir—?'

'Sssh.'

Anger flared in her. *Listen to me!* She could take this from men she didn't care about, but from him? While she thought this, the pause stretched – and stretched – and then Alfgeir spoke. This time, the words were not bellowed. 'The king did not ride off alone. He will be back before sunrise. And when he comes back – what shall I tell him? That Ludin of Skane ran away from a fight he could have won?'

More noise. *Why is it that men can't ever take turns to talk?* Beside her, Freysteinn was taut as a hunting cat listening for mice.

'Ludin can't back down,' he hissed. 'He'll leave. He never backs down.'

'I think you're wrong.'

'What?'

It was almost as if he'd forgotten that I'm here. 'I think you're wrong. I think Ludin will stay. For Drifa, if nothing else.'

A brief silence, then, 'And wouldn't that be a hell of a thing.'

Warmth flooded her heart. *He's back.* He sounded like *him* again – like sunshine on a summer's day. She felt like she'd said something clever and funny, and just when she was getting ready to savour the feeling, the image of a blood-crusted rune carved in a palm came back to her.

Nauth. The rune of need.

Thoughts swirled in her head as Drifa's face reappeared in her mind, animated and sparkly. She'd taken an instant liking to the woman, feeling like she was the older sister she'd never had, swooping in to save Helga from Gunnar's inane prattling. The swordsman had looked a ridiculous figure in the King's Hall that evening. *Just like a wolf in a dress.* The night before battle was another matter entirely: this was his world and he was at home in it. She tried to remember the conversation from the longhouse, but she could also feel the warmth of Freysteinn, moving closer – and then a strong, wiry arm was around her shoulder, pulling her in, and she marvelled at the weight and the heat and the touch and the smell of him. A tingle of familiar sensation snaked its way down towards the pit of her stomach and she barely suppressed a leer. *Not now.* That being said, no one would be able to see them in the dark, and they might not get another chance for a while . . . Her hand rested on his thigh. She moved it, ever so slightly.

'. . . what's this?' he muttered in her ear.

She squeezed a little harder, feeling him almost leap in her hand. 'You know full well what it is, *rider*.'

Feeling the heat rise within her like a free fire, she grabbed a handful of his hair and pulled him in towards her.

There were no birds singing at dawn. Instead, Helga was awoken by the cold in her bones, mixing with a particularly unpleasant scraping sound. Thinking back, she vaguely remembered rolling onto a rug that Freysteinn had found somewhere in the night and snuggling into his warmth, feeling sleepy and contented. Then she remembered what happened before that, and smiled drowsily. But the sound wasn't going away: a rhythmical, high-pitched thing, slicing through her to the bone.

'What is that?' she muttered.

Freysteinn lay beside her, completely still. 'Styrbjorn's men.'

She sat bolt upright. 'Where?'

But Freysteinn didn't move. 'They're sharpening their blades.'

The sound set her whole body on edge. It made her jaw clench and forced her teeth together. She felt alone and vulnerable and scared. *They are already fighting us – and winning. You have to admire the skill of it.* For a moment she thought of laying back down with him, pulling up the furs and hiding, but it was too late. The cold air on her shoulder had woken her. She rose.

He didn't say anything, but she could feel his eyes on her. Moments later, he was getting to his feet as well, faster than she had.

'Helga?' She didn't recognise the voice. The man had approached from behind and stopped a reasonable distance away. When she nodded, he continued. 'Could you come with me?'

'Why?'

'Alfgeir needs you to come and take a look at something.' She had a moment to register that the gentle cloud of breath was moving before she realised that she was as well, walking behind the messenger who had already taken off. So no time to waste. She glanced at Freysteinn, whose raised eyebrows offered a question.

She shook her head. *Too slow, rider.*

As she walked through the camp, her spirits sank. *It looked a lot better in the dark.* There were no tents to speak of. Tired, haggard men were dragging themselves up off the ground. She could tell the more battle-hardened of them were the ones seeing to their weapons with movements that were still more sleep than thought. Others looked sick with worry. And still the sound of sharpening blades still sliced through the air.

Scree-schlik.

Scree-schlik.

They were past the main body of men before she spotted Alfgeir's hulking frame. He was kneeling down and she sighed. *Another body, then. Why couldn't he have stubbed his toe or something?* She thought again of the rune in Drifa's hand. *Need.* But whose need? Need for what? Then she noticed that Alfgeir wasn't alone. There was someone else with him, a slim man, nowhere near his size – no . . .

A woman.

Jorunn.

At that moment she understood Grundle when she urged the

mare to jump a brook she didn't want to, as she went hurtling towards the point when she had to take off, wanting nothing more than to dig her hooves in and reverse.

She could see Jorunn's snarling face and the point of the knife when she was caught in the hut with her foster-brother Einar. *I nearly died that night.* She'd not allowed herself to think about it much, for her plan to draw out her foster-brother's killer had worked all too well then.

And now she was here, within striking range of Alfgeir and Jorunn, two people who had definitely killed before, kneeling over a dead body.

Alfgeir looked up at her. 'They found you. Good.' Then he stepped aside with respect. Jorunn grudgingly mirrored the gesture and at last Helga could see what they had been covering.

Lars Larkwood, Jorunn's man, laid out straight, stiff, pale and very dead.

With all the life gone out of him, he looked less like a man and more like a fallen tree.

Alfgeir and Jorunn both looked at her. Neither of them spoke, but it was clear what she was supposed to do. She sat next to Lars and studied him.

No cuts, no wounds, no blood. She touched his head, feeling for the skull through thick hair. *No shortage of lumps and bumps, but none new.* There was a hint of a scent, though. Leaning close to his mouth, she sniffed. Yes, definitely something. She reached down and pried open his mouth. A late meal of mead and meat blended together to offer the smell of a gently rotting carcase, but there was another note in there as well.

Juniper root.

And if she could smell it on his breath, there had to have been a lot of it.

Enough to hide something else.

His lips were a deep shade of blue and his neck veins were bulging.

She looked up at Alfgeir and Jorunn. 'He was poisoned.'

Jorunn's jaw clenched in fury. 'I knew it,' she hissed. 'That *bastard*—'

'Let's not be hasty,' Alfgeir said, looking miserable. For a moment, Helga felt for him. Facing a daughter of Riverside in full fury was not for everyone.

'Oh, you're wrong, old bear,' she snapped. 'We'll be as hasty as we want.'

'You don't know that it was him.'

'Then who else? No, this gets called out, and right now.' She was up on her feet and off before Alfgeir had risen halfway.

'Jorunn – wait,' he shouted, but she didn't even look his way; all he got was an angrily dismissive arm-wave.

Alfgeir rose quickly and went charging after Jorunn. A hastily cast look suggested to Helga that she should be following. Having seen Jorunn at full speed, Helga knew she wouldn't be able to keep up, and it turned out keeping pace with Alfgeir Bjorne proved to be surprisingly hard too.

By the time they'd caught up to Jorunn she had roused her entire camp and was on her way to meet Ludin of Skane.

'Jorunn, *listen*.' Alfgeir's voice was pleading, but all he got was that upraised hand, palm forward, again, and no break in her speed. The Dalefolk were swept along in her wake.

'Ludin of Skane, Bed-burner and Child-slayer! Stand up and be counted!' Jorunn's voice rang out, loud and clear.

Well, if he didn't hear that, he's dead too.

The grey-haired captain, Jorunn's ever-present dark-skinned shadow and the rest of her brutes had lined up behind her, but they could have taken their time for it was a while before there was any movement in the Southerners' camp.

Eventually Ludin emerged from a tent, fully dressed. *And armed*, Helga noted. She remembered watching an accident happen once: two horses had been passing when one of them lost its footing and slid down an embankment, falling over to land on its rider.

It had all happened surprisingly slowly and yet no one had been able to do anything to stop it.

Ludin of Skane sauntered up to meet the Westerners. There was no tiredness in his body, only the weary resignation of someone who has been in thousands of fights and is about to add one more to the tally. 'What do you want?'

'You avenged the attack on your advisor, but you chose the wrong target. I proclaim you a law-breaker and a coward.' Jorunn was somehow managing to keep her fury from erupting and what came out instead was, word by word, a performance worthy of the sharpest Lawspeaker. 'I demand wergild for our slain fellow.'

'Demand all you like.' Ludin spat. 'Wasn't me. I'd have sliced him up. And if you had half the wit you pretend to, you should be shrieking at the king. This is all his doing.'

Alfgeir took a step forward, seeming to grow in size as he did so, but he too stopped short of attacking. 'That is horseshit, Ludin, and you know it. This is the work of Bluetooth.'

'I haven't seen old Bluetooth for a while now.' Ludin looked around, as if he was expecting the King of the Danes to stroll into camp. Then he hocked and spat again. Behind him, the men of the Southlands were emerging, all dressed, all armed. 'And the same goes for our so-called king.'

A crowd was gathering around them. Most of the men of Uppsala were lining up behind Alfgeir, but a fair few were keeping their distance.

Too many of them agree with Ludin, Helga thought. The realisation was unpleasant.

Jorunn broke the silence. 'Do you deny that you are responsible for the death of Lars Larkwood?'

Helga watched her carefully. Either she was very nearly too furious to contain herself, or she was giving a fantastic performance.

'I grow weary of this.' Ludin stepped forward. Like a waft of smoke, the dark-skinned man drifted in front of Jorunn and stared straight at the chieftain. A moment – and then Ludin looked at Alfgeir. 'Are you the king now, Alfgeir? Are you going to do anything about this?'

Alfgeir stood there, rigid, but did not answer.

'Come now, people. Fight the enemy, not each other.' The North Wind's voice rumbled in from the side and now Helga noticed the Northmen had silently gathered into a small wedge, ready to rush in and separate fighting groups.

'I'm not fighting anything or anyone,' Ludin said, sounding

bored again. 'and you can have your skalds sing of that, if you will – how King Eirik's alliance was so *limp'* – he looked at Alf-geir – 'that it robbed Ludin of his taste for a scrap.' He stood up straight, in mockery of a royal bearing. 'We wish the people of Uppsala all the best in the coming battle, and hope that they will not grow weary of hearing the screams of their mothers.'

'If he's leaving, so are we,' Jorunn snapped. 'We will not be forced to fight a lost cause.'

'The soft lands of the south yield nothing but cowards,' the North Wind growled. 'We will stand and fight, and we will remember who ran away.'

'You won't remember for long,' Ludin snapped back.

What is happening? Helga felt the words leave her before she was entirely sure what she was asking. 'Did anybody else feel that?'

The furious council members looked for all the world like galloping horses asked to suddenly change direction. Ludin sput-tered and Jorunn shot her a deadly glare, but the North Wind was quickest. 'What?'

'The ground – it's shaking.'

Silence spread around the circle, followed by wary glances. *Now they feel it too.*

A calm descended on Ludin, who pivoted towards the enemy position and started snapping short, clear orders.

Jorunn's captain was issuing orders of his own.

The Northmen had formed a circle around the North Wind and were scanning the horizon. The only person who looked completely unworried was Jorunn's dark-skinned guard.

'Take your hands off your weapons, you idiots,' Alfgeir's voice boomed. 'You're not under attack.'

General confusion spread, until someone shouted and pointed at something behind them.

A thin brown stripe on the horizon was growing bigger, and with it came a faint sound carried on the wind.

Cattle—

A herd of cattle.

No – more.

A lot more.

And there, in front of a herd of cattle the likes of which Helga could never have conceived, rode King Eirik. He sat his horse, looking down on the herd, communicating in shouts and pointed commands to a handful of other men on horseback. Slowly but surely the herd came to a halt a few hundred yards away from them, accompanied by murmurs of disbelief from the assembled men. The king covered the distance between them in no time, leaping to the ground before the horse had even stopped.

He scanned the assembled group.

'King Eirik, we demand—' Jorunn started up, but he silenced her with a glance.

'Tonight we will dine in my hall and we will settle scores old and new. Now, however, we have work to do. Jorunn, Ingileif and Ludin, give me all your men and every last bit of your best rope.'

Chapter 8

SUNRISE

It took Helga a while to comprehend what was happening in front of her.

To the background cacophony of sharpening blades shrilling out across the fields, warriors from all corners of the land of the Svear were working together to push, pull and cajole indignant cows into line, looping ropes around their forelegs and their thick bellies to link them.

The first pair looked a little awkward, bound together like some two-headed freak, and when another two had been lashed to either side, the animals lowed in protest – but they did not move. Soon after, two had become ten, standing side by side and all facing towards the Jomsvikings.

'More, faster!' King Eirik barked.

In front of her, Alfgeir was pulling gently on the nose-ring of a big bull who already looked furious, trying to move it into place alongside the others. Ten became twenty, and still the cows kept coming. A second wave of workers were working on tightening the ropes, all the while keeping up a steady stream of soothing murmurs.

'Spears!' Ludin commanded from somewhere out of Helga's sight. A gaunt man came running almost immediately with a bundle of throwing spears, which Ludin's men proceeded to jab under the tightened ropes, point outwards. Twenty became forty.

'It's a wall,' Freysteinn whispered by her side.

'Except this one has spikes and legs,' Helga replied, without looking at him.

'The king is wise,' Freysteinn muttered.

Wise in the ways of murder.

As the wall grew, so did the noise from the enemy camp, and the tension rose among the men. The Jomsvikings were now chanting to Tyr, the god of war, in rhythm with the scrape of their sharpening stones.

Then, all of a sudden, the noise from the other side stopped.

'Faster!' Alfgeir hissed. All around him cows were being hurried into place and tied into the end of the line.

Across the field they could see smoke, and then fire.

In a daze, Helga watched Ludin sprint to King Eirik and start an animated conversation, but the king held up his hand to stop him. 'Faster!' he shouted over the men's heads, and only then did he lean in to exchange quick words with the chieftain of the south.

When Ludin turned away he had the most hideous smile on his face.

What is this?

Helga felt like she was swimming in a dream. She stood and watched while everything happened around her: everyone knew and understood their purpose except her. Freysteinn stood with her, and she loved him for that. He felt like the only solid thing in this strange, nightmarish world.

The Jomsvikings had already covered a quarter of the distance between them. Their torches could be clearly seen.

'Everyone behind the animals!' Alfgeir cried, but he didn't need to tell the fighters twice. Within moments two groups had formed: Ludin and the North Wind on one side of the living wall, the king and Jorunn on the other.

'Wait!' King Eirik raised his axe.

Only when Styrbjorn's army had crossed halfway to their position did the axe fall.

The horsemen who had ridden with the king were now patrolling up and down the line, prodding the cows into movement. The sounds of protest grew quickly as the animals pushed to be free of the constraints and each other – but all they accomplished was to pull each other along.

Helga's blood ran cold when she saw the panic set in, spreading from the centre of the wall, and within moments the ground was shaking under her feet as eighty or more cows lashed together ran at full speed towards the mercenaries. Behind them and to the side, the Svear sprinted as fast and as silently as they could.

The Jomsvikings showed no signs of slowing down until they were only three hundred paces away from King Eirik's wall of fury, then some of them hesitated, but over the roar of the stampede Helga thought she could hear someone shouting for a charge.

The impact was horrifying. The torches were driving the animals into a frenzy – but none of them could go backwards, so they started pounding straight through Styrbjorn's army. Screams of battle quickly turned to screams of rage, and then cries of pain. Those few mercenaries who managed to get out of each other's way and escape to the side were hacked down without mercy by King Eirik and his men.

From their position a hundred and fifty yards away, Helga and Freysteinn watched in silence. She'd been grateful when he'd first returned, pleased Alfgeir had ordered him to stay behind, ready to ride like his horse was Sleipnir itself to warn Uppsala if the battle turned, but now she just felt numb. The odd man-high spray of vein-blood now and then caught Helga's eye and a dying cry pierced her ears, but the Battle – or more properly, Slaughter – of Fyris Fields was over surprisingly quickly.

There had been no injuries to speak of on their side.

Helga had not been allowed onto the battlefield until Eirik, Alfgeir and a handful of others, armed with spears, had gone before and fed the crows. Those sharp jabs downwards ensured that there would be fertile soil in Fyris Fields for many years to come.

Don't think about it, she told herself. She knew better than most how the human body broke – but that didn't mean she enjoyed seeing so many of them cut and bruised and smashed and trampled. *They came against us – and they would have done worse to us.* Yes. Let's say they would have. More time had been spent ending the suffering of the most injured animals, followed by quick and efficient butchering. After all, a winning army had earned a feast.

Pushing aside the sounds of Fyris Fields in her head, she tried instead to listen to the noise of triumphant Uppsala. The return of King Eirik's army had been loudly joyous: the racket of women crying in joy, laughter, old people shouting. Most of the men participated, quickly inventing heroic deeds that grew in the retelling, and the sun even broke the clouds to shine down on them.

Standing in the stirrups, King Eirik held his axe aloft and banged it on his shield boss until the roars slowly died away. 'Today, the Svear stood together!' he shouted. Yells of approbation from the crowd. 'The King's Council met, and together we vanquished those who would threaten our lives and steal our lands!' Cheers, mixed with boos directed at the king's cousin. Styrbjorn the Strong was standing proudly by Alfgeir's side. The left side of his face was covered in dried blood from a nasty cut to his head and thick rope was wrapped around him a respectful number of times.

You won, yes – but you're not taking any chances. Sensible king, Helga thought.

'And now we celebrate our cousins from the south, north and west with a feast!' Further roars as the king's men rolled out barrels of mead.

Standing next to her, Freysteinn muttered, 'He's certainly free with his mead, is our king.'

'They were afraid,' Helga said, 'and now they are happy. Why aren't you?'

He turned to her and smiled. It was a tired smile. 'I don't think this was King Harald's last effort.'

'Of course not.' She found herself getting annoyed. 'But right now we are not being slaughtered by mercenaries, and right now we are winning.'

'You're right.' He leaned in and kissed her cheek, but it felt wrong. *He's exhausted, that's why.* She squeezed him back and resolved to follow her own advice and enjoy the moment.

A tall man with a square-jawed, youthful face had appeared next to the king and Alfgeir. A shock of white coloured a sweep of blond hair. Someone had mentioned an Icelandic skald coming, but with everything that had been going on she'd completely forgotten about him.

Handsome enough, Helga thought, *for a lack-beard.*

The crowd was getting excited. 'Bragi the skald!' someone shouted, and the rest took up the cry. 'Bragi the skald!'

'Do you wish to hear what the gods think of King Eirik?' The Icelander's voice boomed out over the field.

The people of Uppsala roared their approval.

He cleared his throat.

> 'Council-caller
> Rule-maker, shield-biter
> Odin's eye found
> On him resting
> Wise King Eirik
>
> Foul kin coming
> Few in number
> Were the Svear
> All would follow
> Wise King Eirik

From the south
Ludin stood,
Widow-maker
By his side
Roared the North Wind,
Fierce and strong
With them rode
Unnthor's daughter
Claw of Cunning
Sharp and biting.

Fyris Field
Flooded, red
Growing fat
With Odin's harvest
Styrbjorn's hopes
Gored on the horns
Of Eirik the Victorious!

The crowds cheered, and Alfgeir the loudest. 'All hail Eirik the Victorious!'

Helga looked over at Freysteinn, who forced a smile. 'All hail,' he echoed.

A warm feeling washed over her: she wanted to protect him, to heal him. When she spoke, she was not surprised to hear a fair amount of her mother's voice. 'Right. You're coming with me and you're having food and sleep.' When he started to protest she silenced him with a firm glance. 'No. Home, food, sleep. The council will finish its business and we will let it.' To her surprise he let her lead him away.

Maybe this dog can be trained after all.

The midday heat woke them both. Helga's cabin was stifling and she found she was sweating. Freysteinn lay next to her, awake but looking drained.

'Better?' she said, softly.

'Much.' He sat up. 'It's warm.'

'You are wise,' she said in mock seriousness.

'In some things,' he replied, a hint of sparkle in his eye.

She stretched, enjoying the feeling of soreness in her muscles, less of an ache and more of a confirmation that she had *done things*. 'Shall we go and see whether the king is ready for a proper celebration?'

He rose with her and they dressed in companionable silence. Outside, the horses were waiting for them, grazing contentedly in the shade.

They were in the saddles and riding at not much more than a trot before he spoke again. 'I hope they have settled the issue with Ludin.'

'Yes.' Helga's stomach sank. *How could I have forgotten about that?* As that particular pebble hit the water, rings started to spread: Jorunn shouting at Ludin because Lars was dead. Lars was dead because Drifa was attacked. Drifa was attacked because she asked questions about the dead cook. The cook was dead because he wondered about his son. And a boy had died in old Olver's arms with an accusatory look on his face.

And still she had no idea who, or why.

She could feel her shoulders tense and her teeth grit and she cursed Freysteinn well and truly. *It was good, just now! Why did you have to make me think about the murders?* But once she had started, there was no stopping it and her mind started worrying at the problem like a dog at a bone. As the fields fell away behind her, she wondered what she had seen or heard that held the key. Freysteinn was lost in his own thoughts, so she forced herself out of irritation and made her mind drift to her storeroom.

It was a mess: Ludin's axe and Jorunn's cape. Leather bracers decorated with the unknowable scribbles of the dark-skinned man. The bear-claw necklace of the North Wind – and even a huge wrestling belt that could only belong to Alfgeir Bjorne.

Everyone is a suspect.

She slammed the door in annoyance and thought everything away, then opening it again, she looked upon an empty room. *That's better. Now – why am I here?* Turning to the door, she pulled out her rune-knife and carved a symbol for the last person attacked, tracing her way backwards. Lars because of Drifa. Drifa because of the cook. The cook because of the boy . . . It all came back to the boy in the river. *I cannot find out, from what I know, who did it. So why?*

Why was he lurking in the woods outside Uppsala?

She drew a line with the point of the knife, enjoying the sensation of wood giving way to metal.

A rock to the head.

The attacker would have had to be nice and close for that. He died in the clearing – and there were no signs of a fight, no signs of arms being raised to ward off blows.

He thought the murderer was his friend.

It wasn't much, but it made her feel warmer, somehow. A faint memory scratched at the back of her head. Something about sons seeking glory . . .

. . . and then she remembered: *My son left to seek his glory. His fortune at the king's court.*

King . . . Eirik? No, she would have recognised the boy, especially if he'd been looking to hang around in Uppsala. And if it wasn't Eirik, she could think of only one other king. What if—?

'Why is everything so quiet?' Freysteinn pointed to their left.

Blinking her way back to the present, Helga shook her head free of thoughts and peered where he was pointing. Uppsala looked . . . normal. There were no songs, no sounds of revelry. 'I don't know,' she said.

Without warning, Freysteinn spurred his horse and set off at a gallop towards the town.

Helga lurched in the saddle as Grundle whinnied, gladly taking up the challenge, and bolted after him.

She caught up with Freysteinn just inside the doors of King Eirik's longhouse. He'd dismounted before the horse had even slowed down to half speed and set off at a run up the hill towards the King's Hall. She grabbed his reins and secured both horses. She didn't like to admit it, but his strange reaction to what had appeared to her to be completely ordinary had unnerved her. There were any number of reasons for pushing hard to get back, but a lack of celebration wasn't one.

An unsettling realisation hit her. *I don't know what he's thinking.*

And there was no asking him now. She just about remembered to look around and take in her surroundings, noting a depressingly familiar smell, before her attention was drawn to the king.

He was sitting with Alfgeir and Thorgnyr around the long table with some of his most trusted warriors. The North Wind was there with a few of her closest, and Jorunn had her captain of guards and the dark-skinned man beside her. Ludin looked utterly bored, but he had his swordsman by his side, along with a gaunt young man who was scanning the room like a trapped dog.

'Helga! And Freysteinn. Come here.'

Of course she had spoken to the king before, but her name didn't feel familiar coming from his mouth like that. *Why does he need us?* She walked towards the table, just behind Freysteinn. *He's not looking at me. He doesn't care.* The thought stayed for a moment, then buzzed off like a bee in spring. She found herself quite suddenly at the edge of the table, uncomfortably aware of the number of eyes on her, appraising, evaluating. *Like I'm a broodmare in heat.* She felt herself twist up inside. Any number of possible options whirled through her head, with her responses to each becoming sharper and sharper.

'Well met,' the king said.

'Well met.' Freysteinn sounded somehow both subdued and tense. *What is he worrying about?*

'Since this morning,' the king said, 'Styrbjorn has decided to share information with us.'

As a wave of cold smiles and hard glances spread around the table, Helga put a name to the odour she'd caught when she'd walked into the longhouse. *Blood.*

As if in response to his name, a low moan came from what she'd thought was a pile of furs cast away in the corner. Three of Alfgeir's bigger lads were standing over the vanquished mercenary leader and the moment he made a noise, one of them kicked him in the stomach.

The king looked at Freysteinn. 'And we think you're right.'

Right about what? Helga didn't understand what was happening. She didn't like not knowing what was going on.

Freysteinn looked unmoved by their compliments. 'Has he confirmed it?'

'He's said a fair few things, most of them to do with pigs, goats and our mothers,' Alfgeir said. 'But he has only recently agreed to tell us what we need to know.'

'Apparently King Harald promised him fifty ships full of hard bastards,' the North Wind chipped in.

'Which never showed up.' Ludin's smirk threatened to rip his head in two.

They are enjoying themselves. They think they've won. And that was sort of true – but something about it felt wrong. There were too many people in the room and too much conversation. She had a brief pang of longing to be out of this place, just her and Grundle racing across the plain, then her mother's whispered voice made her pay attention: *Men talk, women listen. Men rule, women decide.*

'Can we trust him?' Jorunn sounded cold, calculating, weighing options and information like pieces of amber.

What a stupid fucking question. Helga felt doubly annoyed. What kind of nonsense was this? Of course they couldn't. They were being so *slow*. They were all too busy taking their time to chew over their own importance. She found herself getting frustrated.

'No further than we can throw him.' King Eirik's voice suggested that the exact distance might very well be established in the near future.

'If only we knew what King Harald was thinking . . .' The sentence died on Freysteinn's lips.

Alfgeir glanced at the king. 'Sit,' the big man rumbled, clearing space on a bench and motioning for them both to take a seat. As they did, King Eirik nodded to the chieftains, who turned and spoke to their own men. Within moments, most of them had silently left the longhouse.

This is an odd collection, Helga thought, looking at the young wrestler and the short Northerner flanking the old bear. Jorunn's captain had departed, looking none too pleased, but the dark-skinned man remained. Gunnar had left Ludin's side, leaving the gaunt, pockmarked man, who was probably younger than he looked, but with the haunted eyes of someone who had seen and done bad things.

'We have thought about this,' King Eirik said, 'and I think we'll have to find out.'

The daylight stung her eyes. The past few days lay on her shoulders like a double wolf pelt, pulling her down, and her mind felt woollen. *Not now!* She tried desperately to think of the sharp edge of a knife, but there was no hiding that she felt more like a mallet. *Or a nice, big rock, held in a fist.*

They stood outside, all seven of them: Big Rolf, the wrestler

Breki, Jorunn, the dark-skinned man whose name – *Nazreen* – felt like a blade in the dark on her tongue, and Ludin's man, who'd introduced himself as Haki and said nothing else.

And then there was Freysteinn, and her.

'We'll need two carts.' Jorunn's voice was clipped and commanding. Helga felt her hackles rise and fought down her immediate response. *Get them yourself, bitch.*

'I can provide,' Freysteinn replied.

Jorunn turned to the Northmen. 'What did your chieftain say about supplies?'

'Ambers, herbs and furs,' the short man said. 'Courtesy of the king.' His voice was laced with badly concealed contempt.

So I'm not the only one who thinks this is a very, very bad idea. Good.

Freysteinn started down the hill. Helga looked around the group of people she didn't know and before she'd realised, her feet had decided for her and started after him. 'Wait,' she hissed.

He looked over his shoulder at her, smiled and slowed down. 'Come on then.' There was a twinkle in his eye. 'We've got things to do.'

She caught up and for a moment couldn't decide which question to start with – but she couldn't stop herself blurting out, 'This is the most half-witted idea I've ever heard. Why are we going to Hedeby? Straight into King Harald's spears?'

Freysteinn's smile was almost indulgent. 'Why would he have his spears out? He won't suspect us of anything at all. We'll just be traders.'

'That's a sack of pig-shit and you know it. Everyone there will know Jorunn—'

'—as a trader,' he finished for her. 'Someone who frequently travels – to Uppsala, to Hedeby, to wherever she likes.'

'And what will we be on this trip?'

Freysteinn kept walking, moving towards the stables. 'You'll be you: a dealer in herbs. Ludin's Hel-spawn will be our guard. The old-beard will be the grumbling cook every trade cart has, for reasons I've never understood, and *Nazreen* will follow Jorunn around like a creepy shadow and make people want to not ask about whatever he is.'

'And you?' For some reason, his smug, ready answers were becoming deeply irritating.

'I'll be the handsome driver,' he replied, grinning as he ducked into the stables.

I'll tell you where you can stick your reins. She scowled at the doorway he'd disappeared through, wondering why he was altogether too happy about this. For a brief moment she wondered if he'd set his sights on Jorunn, then dismissed that thought out of hand. She'd told him about Jorunn: he knew the woman was a liar and a murderer . . . and now she was being forced to share the same carts, by order of the king.

Helga felt suddenly dizzy with the speed of events. One sunrise ago, Uppsala had stood on the brink of being razed to the ground by a great horde of brutal, bloodthirsty warriors. Now the Jomsvikings had been defeated and their fierce captain was roped up in the King's Hall, no doubt to be ransomed back to the other side of his family – after a comprehensive beating, of course. And still there was something that was nagging at her, scratching at the back of her mind like a hungry rat.

They'd stopped searching for the murderer. They'd clearly all just decided that it was down to King Harald, but why would Styrbjorn's man – or men – have been killing people at random? Why would they have stripped the boy of everything that might identify him? Why would they have snuck into the heart of enemy territory, just to murder a cook? Especially before the attack, when being caught might have given the whole game away? None of this made any sense.

So they were wrong – and Freysteinn was happy to be wrong.

Don't worry. You can just go to the king and explain that you have a vague idea that there was a spy for King Harald in the middle of the council who had nothing to do with Styrbjorn and . . .

She couldn't even finish the sentence. She felt sick – worse, she was sick and angry at the same time. The king was proudly wrong and Freysteinn was proudly smug and this whole mission was stupid and everything was more than a little sour.

The doors opened and Freysteinn emerged, leading an utterly boring, stolid-looking gelding. *That's the king of all carthorses,* she thought, then chided herself. *Things might not be going to your liking, but you cannot take it out on a horse.* 'No matter how stupid it looks,' she muttered, taking care to turn away from Freysteinn as she spoke.

'Our brave troops will charge at the evil in the west from atop this brave steed,' Freysteinn said, smiling.

Yes, you're still pretty, but you're also very annoying. Everything is. 'I'll go and see what I can rustle up to trade,' she said. As she turned away, she thought she saw a shadow of something on his face, but she didn't care. *I'm not going to stay here and suffer your chirping.*

A surge of spite gave a spring to her step that she really didn't feel. She held her head high as she walked away, back down the hill to where she'd tethered Grundle.

It didn't last long.

Like her own personal raincloud, the strain of the last few days overtook her and with it came the questions, all swirling around and melting into one:

WHY?

'I – don't – KNOW!' She clamped her jaw shut so hard it felt like she'd never speak again and discovered biting down felt *good*. All she needed was a good, thick bone to bite through. Her blood felt boiling hot, then freezing cold. Fury washed over her in waves and she could feel hot tears pressing at the backs of her eyes.

And then she saw him again, the boy, sodden and bluish from the river, staring at her with accusing eyes just before the last of his life drained out of him. He wasn't from Uppsala, and neither was his father.

He was different.

Different because . . .

She grasped for the answer. There'd seemed to be almost a look of warning on his face. Helga was only dimly aware that she was barging past people she knew, ignoring hails, almost bowling over a white-hair, and when her hand finally closed on Grundle's reins, it was trembling. Her head was swimming with details – the crushed throat of the fallen man, the death of Lars – and still nothing made sense. Feeling the warmth of the animal and the familiar smells helped some, but not enough.

I need to get away.

She vaulted onto the horse's back, feeling a little pang of happiness when Grundle offered one of her ill-tempered and long-suffering snorts. 'I know,' she muttered, patting the mare's neck, 'but there's grass at home as well, and it's sweeter there.' A toss of the mane suggested that Grundle had definite opinions on this that were not necessarily in her favour, but she obeyed.

'Wait.'

The voice was dry, harsh with age and used to being heard. Almost against her will, Helga found that her instincts had already stopped her and were suggesting she do as she was told. Looking down, she had to fight to suppress a smile.

Crones. They'll be the death of me.

'You look well, Ida.'

The old woman stood defiant, like a stubbornly territorial chicken, and stared up at Helga like their heights were quite reversed. 'Of course I do,' she said tersely. 'I've been eating.'

'Good.' *Have you been overthrowing King Harald? Because that's what I need to go do now, apparently.* But she didn't voice her thoughts because the old woman's eyes were still trained on her with intensity. There was more to come.

'You're still wondering, aren't you?'

Grundle snorted under her. Grass here was preferable, it appeared, and grass at home might be acceptable, but this chatter was not. 'About what?'

'Whether I am all alone, and whether I'm going to get my head chopped off.'

Whether you are all alone . . . Helga's spine tingled. '. . . yes. Yes, I do wonder.'

'They think the fox takes the chickens. But I'll tell you something.' The old woman grinned, revealing a mouth full of surprisingly sharp teeth. 'It's not. Sometimes the chicken takes the chickens. Your worst enemy might be right next to you.' Snapping her mouth shut, she giggled, turned sharply and surged off.

Helga watched her go, not entirely sure what to think. In a half-daze she reminded herself to visit Hertha with new medicines for the mad old woman. *Sometimes the chicken takes the chickens.*

Almost as if the very thought had summoned her, the farmwife walked into view, concern on her face. 'Was she bothering you?'

'What?' It took Helga a moment to catch up. 'Oh, Ida? No, not at all. She was just giving me a lecture on the finer points of chickens.'

Hertha rolled her eyes, *What can you do?* and Helga added kindly, 'She looks much better, though.'

'Oh, yes. She helps around the farm now. She's still a little too keen on the chickens for Nils' liking, mind, but you've saved her neck, girl.'

Helga smiled. 'Love and food has saved her neck. That's all your doing.'

The big woman smiled back, almost a little awkwardly. 'The kids ask after you.'

'I'll be sure to swing by soon.' *If I ever come back from Hedeby,* she didn't add.

'They get very excited when we get visitors. Well, except for that strange boy who came to ask about the council. They didn't much take to him.'

Suddenly Helga felt like she could taste cold in her blood. 'What boy?' she stammered, failing entirely in her attempt to sound casual. She tried to cover up her halting voice with a hasty smile.

If Hertha noticed anything amiss, she didn't show it. 'Reddish hair, pale face. West coast accent.'

'Oh,' Helga said. 'Strange.' *Keep her talking!* she hissed at herself. 'Must have been a ... um ... a traveller, I guess. What did he want?'

The big woman screwed up her face in recollection. 'Darned if I know. It was all a bit odd: he started out perfectly normal, but then he started getting a bit nervous – I've no idea why; it wasn't like he was asking anything secret, after all. He just wanted to know if we would be going to the council, who'd be coming. The more questions he asked, the quicker he spoke. He said "we" once or twice, so I asked about travelling companions, but he made some strange excuse and practically ran away. I hope he found whatever it was he was looking for.'

Helga's head was buzzing. 'I'm sure he did.' *Well, he found something, all right, although I doubt that was what he was actually looking for.* 'But I mustn't keep you – best go and find your big chicken.' She gave Hertha a beaming smile. 'I have to get going too.'

The farmwife moved closer and took Helga's hand in her big, callused hands. 'Look after yourself, girl. We like you.' With that, she turned and strode off in search of her mad old auntie.

It took Helga a while to get her senses together enough to realise that her hips were swaying to Grundle's gentle walk. The horse hadn't bothered waiting for any order; after all, Helga had already said they were going home. 'At least one of us has some sense,' she muttered, and the horse whickered in approval.

Drifa, Alvar, Lars and the boy: they'd all been asking questions – and they'd all found answers, after a fashion.

'More answers than I can manage,' Helga said bitterly. She managed a brief smile when Grundle snorted in agreement. As they travelled together towards home, one phrase played on her mind.

Travelling companions.

'She's . . .' Breki muttered under his breath.

'About as pleasant as an axe to the face?' Big Rolf replied, and when the boy nodded, he laughed. 'True, but she's on our side and that's where you want people like that.' They were far enough away for Jorunn not to have noticed them as she continued ordering and pushing people about, generally snapping at them to do her bidding. Her men had finished loading up the cart and equipping the two carthorses with plausible, not-too-ornate rugs and saddlebags.

Big Rolf looked at Breki. 'It's a shame you can't go, boy. You wanted adventure. But I don't think this one would be to your liking.'

'Mm,' Breki muttered, 'there's no denying that.'

It didn't take Jorunn long to get the carts loaded and the workers dismissed and soon there were only six of them left. 'Right,' she said, her words weighted with the expectation of someone who is usually instantly obeyed. 'What are we waiting for?'

'Helga.' Breki felt the name leave his mouth before he'd had time to think about it.

'Hm,' Jorunn replied, 'yes.' She turned to the messenger the king had sent. 'Where is she?'

'She rode for home to fetch things to trade.'

It was hard to tell what Jorunn was thinking just from looking at her face, Breki found, but her voice was flat when she said, 'I see.'

Out of the corner of his eye, Breki thought he might have seen Big Rolf hide a smirk.

'Look, there she is,' the king's man said, pointing to the east, and he must have had really good eyes because it was a good few moments before Breki could make out the lone rider approaching. They all watched as the dot became a smudge, then a figure, then the young woman with the long dark hair. She dismounted gracefully and patted her mare fondly on the neck.

'You took your time,' Jorunn said flatly.

'I thought a party of six was a bit too big to account for whatever's on those carts,' Helga replied. She unhooked a large sack from her saddle and slung it onto the amber cart. 'So I brought some more.'

Breki couldn't help but glance at Big Rolf, who managed in one look to say that yes, he'd seen the exchange and no, he really shouldn't say anything and yes, they'd talk about it later and yes, he should stop gawping like a moon calf.

If they had been two men, he'd be expecting to break up a fight, but somehow the kindling between the two women didn't catch fire – not this time, at least. Instead, Helga got back into the saddle and guided her mare to one side. Two serviceable mounts had been provided for the dark-skinned man and the scary one from Ludin's party, but Big Rolf clambered up onto the cart with an easy joke about being old and bored of horses.

Suddenly it was time. They were ready to ride out.

The cold, sinking feeling in Breki's stomach was quite at odds with the heat of the summer sun. As the carthorses slowly got going, the group nudged forward, then settled into a steady, relaxed pace. Breki looked up over his shoulder at the god-house, towering over them, impossibly huge, with its golden chains glinting in the sun, then turned back to the carts heading towards the treeline.

He kept watching for a long while after they disappeared.

'Be safe,' he muttered, still cold. 'Be safe, old man.'

Not long after the trading party spies had set off for Hedeby, Ingileif's men started loading up the last of their horses. The North Wind was watching her men readying mounts, checking saddles and distributing supplies in sacks when Eldar approached her.

'There's . . . a problem,' he started bluntly.

She didn't need to ask. 'Take me to her.'

They walked together to the covered cart that had been positioned well back from the edge of their camp. Eldar politely leaned in and pulled aside the heavy cloth flap for Ingileif, but stayed outside and turned his back on the cart, almost as if guarding the occupants from disturbance.

The air inside was thick and smelled faintly of burning wood. The woman, who wasn't much bigger than a child, was sitting in the back corner, like she'd been trying to push herself away from the scattering of bones in the middle. She looked up at the North Wind and croaked, 'The wolf is still howling. The paw is soft, but the claw is sharp.'

Ingileif looked at her, then the bones. Her smile was tired. 'Oh, that's hardly new, Vala.'

'The wolf – the wolf will kill again. It will kill again.' She wrapped her bony arms around herself like a protective cage. 'It will hunt long and kill.'

Ingileif reached in and stroked her fine white hair tenderly. 'Sleep,' she murmured. 'We'll be moving soon. You'll see the hills and the trees and then everything will smell right. Would you like that?'

Cloudy eyes blinked at the Chieftain of the North and the crone nodded.

'Good,' Ingileif rumbled. She scooped up the bones in the leather patch they were scattered across, tied it up into a pouch and deposited it in the far corner of the cart.

'The bones are covered. The gate is closed. Rest now, Vala,' she ordered, but without looking to see if her orders were obeyed, she ducked back out.

Frowning, she stared at the spot in the treeline where she'd last seen the trading caravan.

Chapter 9

JOURNEY

Helga looked at the horses, plodding stolidly on. *You don't care, do you?* The two mares had doubtless been pulling carts all their lives; at any rate, they appeared to be utterly unconcerned by the fact that these particular wagons were headed straight for the coast, where they'd somehow manage to find and board a boat to sail for the land of the Danes and from that foreign shore, to make for Hedeby.

Helga was uneasy about the journey herself, and not just because she thought the whole idea of trying to spy on King Harald was crazy. But she had to admit to also being a little intrigued. She'd often heard about Hedeby in travellers' tales. People she'd met who'd been there generally wore it as a badge pinning a cloak of understatements. *Sure there are a lot of people there, but you know, you get used to it. King Harald is a fair ruler, really. He just wants people to do what they're told. The mercenaries are rough, but they keep to themselves. The smell—* They usually cracked when it came to talking about the stench of the place.

And now she was going to find out for herself. She patted

Grundle's neck absentmindedly and the horse snorted in response; she was already bored with the slow pace. There was nothing intoxicating about cart-speed, and there was no hope of using scouting ahead as an excuse to get away, either, not when Jorunn had ordered everyone to stay in a tight line, with her man Nazreen up ahead with her and Haki bringing up the rear. Big Rolf and Freysteinn were driving the carts and Helga had just been told to 'stay close'. *Out of the way of the men,* a voice in the back of her head added coldly.

Jorunn had appointed herself the leader of the mission from the first moment and none of the men had dared to disagree. Despite herself, Helga had a certain amount of admiration for the pure *edge* on the woman. She could silence a group of hard-bitten warriors with just one look. *But after all, men are the easier opponents.* Some of her own conquests drifted up from where she kept those memories and the corners of her mouth rose, unbidden.

'What's so funny?'

Startled back into the real world, Helga glanced over at Freysteinn, who looked very comfortable flicking the reins and pretending his cart needed any sort of driver's care when she had no doubt the carthorse could manage perfectly well without him.

His steady gaze made her a little nervous. *How long have you been watching me?* 'Nothing,' she said. 'Just remembered a funny rhyme.'

'And you're keeping it for yourself? On the road? That's not right, is it?'

She kept the smile fixed and her eyes twinkling. *And this right here is why we don't lie.* 'Of course not.' *Something funny. Come on!* But nothing came. 'You may have heard this one.' *Mother, come on, help me.*

And then she remembered.

'Cows will moo and sheep will shit and critters will be
   counted –
But make sure you get off the horse before the mare gets
   mounted.'

He leered at her, his eyes bright with suggestion. 'Hadn't heard that one,' he said. 'Some good advice, there.' He was about to say something more when they both caught a sudden movement from up front: Nazreen's hand had shot up, palm out. He didn't need language for that; the message was clear. *Shut up.*

A flash of annoyance crossed Freysteinn's face. 'Little shit,' he muttered. 'He may be a fighter, but he knows nothing about being in charge.'

There was an unpleasant edge to her lover that she hadn't seen before and it made her feel a little sick to her stomach. His cheerfulness had vanished and while it had been annoying, it was preferable to whatever this was.

She stared at Nazreen, then looked back at Freysteinn, her spine tingling, although she couldn't yet tell if it was good or bad. '*She* trusts him, though.'

'Can't imagine why.'

The decision was right there in front of her . . . And this was a game she knew. She felt bad for a moment, but . . . *He should have asked how I felt. He should have asked what I wanted.* 'Neither can I. I think you should be up at the front, at least.'

'Yeah,' Freysteinn mumbled. *Like men do when they are just agreeing with themselves,* she thought.

'Maybe—' She left the idea floating for just long enough, like a hook in the water, waiting for a bite.

'We should be going faster.'

And there it was. 'Mm,' she said, pinching her lips together to avoid smiling. A dark thrill coursed through her as she saw the tension build in him. It started in his hips and his lower back and spread to the arms and legs slowly, like a disease. *Now all we need is timing . . .* Something told her to hold back, and she listened, saying nothing, just glancing sideways, innocently, at Freysteinn.

Who was now looking like a bottled thundercloud.

Helga allowed herself a small inwards smile as they rode on in silence. The seed had been planted and watered. He'd been delighted by this little adventure and convinced that it'd be fun – but not once had he thought to ask her for her opinion, or advice.

Let's find out how smart you are when you're in the driving seat, cart-boy.

The tall trees enclosing the fields around Uppsala eventually gave way to gently rolling fields. After that the road wound through a denser forest of towering pines and thick yew trees, until the low, hunched shapes with needles so dark as to be almost black, punctuated by bright red berries warning of danger, suddenly opened up to reveal a lake as wide as the eye could see.

Helga remembered arriving at the other side of that lake a few years back, thinking that she'd reached the sea and somehow missed the biggest town in Svealand. She'd known nothing then. *And do you feel you know much now?* The question had more than a hint of her mother's voice gently telling her she was being an idiot, but in any case, she lost the answer in the steady thud of hooves on hard ground.

The lake changed beside them as they followed the waterline south. Jorunn went on ahead, clearly trusting no one else to scout for her, and returned to announce that the ferryman, having heard of Styrbjorn's advance, had found a very urgent reason to visit relatives in the north. Eventually, even the near-endless water disappeared behind them and they were once again swallowed up by trees. Above them, the sun started its slow sinking towards the edge of the world, vanishing just as they reached the edge of the forest.

'Camp.' Jorunn's command was short and sharp.

'What – here?' Big Rolf's bushy eyebrows almost knotted together in the middle.

'The copse,' Jorunn snapped, pointing to a covered depression in the ground no one else had noticed about a hundred paces away. 'There's cover from the wind, trees at our back, sightlines, easy to guard. More questions?'

There weren't.

As the carts turned towards the destination, Helga caught a glance of Big Rolf's face. The North Wind's advisor looked like he'd been carved out of stone. *If you hit a bump in the road, you'll bite your tongue off.* She wondered why she was finding it so satisfying, watching Jorunn whipping the men around her. She remembered those fateful days at Riverside and how the woman's lying and scheming had sickened her and asked herself what had changed.

Maybe it's me.

Dismounting, she breathed in through her nose and caught the smell of forest, sun-warmed bark, resinous sap and pine needles. She led Grundle to a patch of long grass and looped the reins loosely around a nearby branch. She had a vague awareness that behind her, the camp was being set up without much in the way of barking of orders from anyone. As the mare settled down to graze, Helga pulled out a brush and started the long, even strokes along her flanks.

The smell of Grundle mixed in with the cooling air, which made her think of summer nights with Hildigunnur, listening to her foster-mother talk about the world, or at least her view of it. A man's place was to fight his corner and stand his ground, take what life gave him and share it with his family and friends. A woman's place . . . was to find herself a good man, then spend her life whispering in his ear so he did what she wanted him to do.

'Men rule, women decide,' she mouthed, hearing the words as if they were being muttered by another voice from long ago. Grundle whickered and turned her head. 'No, not you. You're a horse,' Helga said softly, getting a gentle nudge in return before Grundle returned to the much more interesting subject of grass. 'You rule and decide, and allow me to hold the reins so I feel important.'

Helga looked over at the camp. Jorunn, standing a little way apart from the men and observing them, was an achingly similar figure to Hildigunnur. *It must have been strange to see one's own daughter become a grown woman.* 'And a murdering liar,' she added, and the venom in her voice surprised her. But on the other hand, like Grundle, Jorunn was also trying to both decide and rule, and that was exciting to watch.

For no reason she could fathom, Helga suddenly found herself getting angry. 'She has no business looking like my mother,' she muttered through gritted teeth. 'No business at all.' She remembered all too clearly being the only child on the farm, and then losing it all when Hildigunnur's real children came back. She would never forget that rush of pain, of being a cuckoo in the nest, an unwanted stepchild, when she saw Jorunn standing next to her blood-mother. They looked so alike. It was sometimes hard to remember that the woman in charge of their crazy expedition to spy on King Harald was the same woman who had murdered her own brother and threatened to gut Helga like a fish. And because they looked so alike, it was also hard to remember that the woman she was looking at was *not* her mother, the person who'd taught her everything she knew, who'd brought her up with love, wisdom and filthy jokes.

'Stupid,' she muttered, mostly at the feeling in her chest.

As she worked meticulously to rub down the mare's coat, she studied the men. They hadn't traded four words between them before now and yet they were working together as if they'd never done anything else. Short commands were exchanged and batted back with the occasional question. The horses were tethered and tended to, wagons secured and covered, lean-tos erected. She spotted Haki, who'd conjured up a bow and arrows from somewhere, disappearing into the forest with Freysteinn, who was carrying a hand-axe and a sack.

Big Rolf went off in another direction with a battered old pot in one hand.

Nazreen exchanged words with Jorunn, then rode off towards the setting sun at quite some speed.

The forest suddenly felt very quiet indeed.

Helga switched to Grundle's other side, where it turned out she could watch Jorunn without being seen. She was surprised to see that as soon as the men were out of sight, Jorunn, wincing, hunched over, as if to relieve pain in her stomach.

'You're good and done,' Helga muttered to the horse as she felt in her herb pouch for the right quality of leaf – *there, yes, that's you.* She straightened her back as she walked towards Jorunn. The look she got was not inviting, but she found she didn't care. This was different: she was on familiar ground.

'Here.' She handed three leaves to Jorunn. 'Chew this.'

Jorunn was about to say something when another cramp hit her and instead she gritted her teeth and hissed.

'If you do this now, the pain goes away before they come back.'

Jorunn's face was set in a scowl for what felt like an eternity before she found her words. 'What is it?'

'Dried juniper leaves in honey.'

'Honey?'

'Tastes like moose-arse otherwise.'

A half-snorted laugh. Jorunn's fingers felt cold, brushing against her palm. Moments later she was chewing. 'Mm, you're not wrong there. The honey is good – but there is a definite flavour of arse at the back.'

Helga nodded, but said nothing. Now that she had time to think about what she'd just done, she realised she had no idea what to say next. The last time they'd been this close, Jorunn had fully intended to stab her in the gut, blame the stable-hand and leave her to die.

So let's wait.

Jorunn's eyes were closed as she chewed, but moment by moment Helga could see the leaves take hold. She'd tried to explain to Freysteinn once how watching someone start to feel better made her feel a bit like watching them fall asleep – or in this case, seeing every muscle in their body relax as the pain went away. He'd said something nice – he always did – but she'd not had the sense that he'd understood her. Now she was standing in front of a woman who had murdered her own brother, someone who had broken her – *no, their* – mother's heart, and yet it still felt good to be able to take the pain away.

'Better?'

'Oh, much,' Jorunn replied almost huskily, and then she added, 'I hate it.'

'Yeah, me too. I don't think anyone likes it.'

Jorunn opened her eyes. The harshness was gone, along with the commanding fury, leaving something that Helga didn't recognise. 'I think if it happened to them they'd be at war with everything.'

Helga shrugged. 'Men rule—'

'—women decide.'

The silence between them was thick.

'How could you do it?' Helga felt her heartbeat slow and the blood harden in her veins. The words were out there now and there was no taking them back.

Jorunn looked at her like she was seeing her for the first time – and then something gave way. 'I don't know,' she said, her voice flat. 'I was so . . . *angry*, all the time. Nothing moved fast enough. I wanted to be rich, but I didn't want to wait for it. In that way, I wasn't so different from my dear brother.'

You actually regret it. The certainty hit Helga hard. Jorunn suddenly looked tired; tired and sad. 'I had this half-baked scheme to charm the gold out of our father, but that didn't amount to much, not once Bjorn killed Karl. I was acting without planning, and I have never been very good at that.'

Steady, now. Helga clenched her fist, once – twice – three times, the last time so hard that she felt her hand might break. *What was going on?* Jorunn's words had gone straight to her cheeks; Helga thought if she touched her face, she'd be warm to the touch.

She looked at the woman who looked exactly like Hildigunnur.

'. . . thank you.'

That was unexpected. 'I . . . uh . . . for what?'

'For making me say what I did and forcing us away from Riverside. Apart from anything else, it was devious.' There was the smallest glint of a smile on Jorunn's face. 'The old hag taught you well.'

'I got lucky.' The words tumbled out.

'Maybe,' Jorunn said, 'but it made me go my own way, apart

from Sigmar. I went down south, where being a woman could be a real advantage in trading.'

'Why?'

'Because they made their deals while staring at my tits,' Jorunn said, 'and as it turned out, that didn't really help them think.'

Helga was filled with a deep yearning for her mother, to see that twinkle in her eye as she shared a dirty joke . . .

'I imagine you've used your own charms once or twice.'

Helga looked up and met Jorunn's eyes. 'Me? Never.'

Jorunn chuckled. 'You've not made your fortune on lies, that much is certain. I reckon—'

They both heard the snap of twigs in the forest: someone was coming towards them and they didn't care if anyone heard their approach.

Without thinking, Helga found her hand on the rune-knife. Beside her, Jorunn's stance had also shifted subtly, but there was no sign of fear. *You've been in a fight or two.* Helga felt a little bit safer.

Moments after, the rangy form of Haki became visible between the trees. He was carrying the body of something big over his shoulder – a bird of some sort.

Jorunn relaxed slightly, but kept her eyes fixed on him. 'Well met!' she called.

'Well met,' Haki replied, the words only just short of a grunt. He crouched and proceeded to pluck the goose with fast and brutal movements.

The wound where the arrow had ripped through the chest was clearly visible. *One shot. Must have surprised the shit out of the bird*, Helga thought. However little attention Haki paid to them, though, his mere presence was enough to turn Jorunn once more into the leader of men. Her walls were up and without a word, she busied herself counting and re-counting the goods in the wagons.

Guess that leaves me talking to the horses. Moving over to where the carthorses were lazily grazing, Helga busied herself grooming the animals, which was comforting work; she could let her mind wander. She thought of Jorunn, what had just happened between them and how it had happened . . . the grimace of pain that had eased off with the leaves; the emotion on her face as she talked about those fateful nights at their parents' farm.

She looks so much like her mother. It was almost enough to erase the fact that Jorunn was a murderer.

But there it was again: the face of the dead boy, staring accusingly at her. Anger flared and she wanted to scream, *I don't know!* She had been so busy being furious with Freysteinn that the questions had left her mostly alone . . . but now that he was gone they'd started creeping back. Why would some unnamed man of Styrbjorn's kill the boy? And why would they sneak into Uppsala to kill only a fat cook? None of it added up to anything that made sense. And if it didn't, well, why was King Eirik sending them all away to spy on Harald Bluetooth?

Her brush strokes slowed just as the horse's head perked up. When she paused and let the world in, she could feel, very faintly, the thump of hooves.

Someone was coming their way, and fast.

She looked back at the camp and saw white down drifting to land on the half-plucked carcase of the abandoned bird. Haki was nowhere to be seen, and neither was his bow. Jorunn, on the other hand, was standing in the middle of the camp, head held high.

The bait . . . and the hunter.

Helga's heart started thumping. There was something about Jorunn's defiant stance that terrified her. *She expects trouble.* Now the rider was easy to hear, but still hard to place; with the echoes bouncing off the trees, it sounded like the horse was coming from three different directions at once. *Or there are three riders.* Helga pushed that thought away and very calmly forced her hands to take hold of the carthorse's reins. There was no time to saddle the animal, but she'd be able to get away quickly. A burst of shame hit her in the stomach. *So that's how it is, is it? Running away? Is that how we treat our . . .* the word drifted through her mind and settled on her tongue *. . . our sister?* It tasted unfamiliar.

She watched, half in a daze, as the reins dropped from her hand, then she walked over to stand next to Jorunn. It felt like she was walking up-river against the current.

The command was short and sharp. 'Whoever is coming, follow my lead. Stand tall and show no fear.'

The thundering of the hooves had stopped bouncing around: the rider was coming straight from the east, following in their tracks.

'There.' The blurred shape of horse and rider were drifting into vision.

'Saw him.'

Jorunn was right: it definitely was a man, and a big one, at that. Something tickled at the back of Helga's head. 'I think—'

The briefest movement of a hand and she stopped talking again. Her fear had changed, though; she was no longer afraid for their lives but she was worried about the rider. There was something familiar about him . . .

Up ahead, the shape slowed down and became a lathered horse and large man, well balanced but clearly favouring his left side. An oak of a man . . . or . . . ?

It is him. 'Don't shoot!' After the tense silence Helga's voice sounded loud and shrill and she could feel the side-eyed glare of Jorunn burning a hole in her head. 'It's one of the Northmen,' she said quickly. 'The boy wrestler.'

The arrow's flight sounded like an indrawn breath – and then it thwacked into the trunk of a tree, several paces away from the boy's head. The horse reared but Breki calmed him down quickly and efficiently. He looked down at Jorunn, then raised his right hand and showed it, palm out. Wincing, he dragged up the second one as well.

'Well met.' Jorunn hadn't budged an inch. Behind her, Haki ghosted out of the woods, a new arrow leisurely nocked.

'Well met,' Breki said. 'May I dismount?'

'You may. Word from King Eirik?'

'Nothing of note,' Breki said, grunting as he landed heavily. 'He and Ingileif talked after you'd left and they decided that I should join the caravan.'

'Did they, now.' She inclined her head by way of permission.

As Breki silently walked his horse over to where the others were tethered, Haki sat back down by the half-plucked bird. Helga noticed his bow and arrows were still within easy reach, even though Jorunn had started rummaging in one of the carts, completely ignoring the newcomer.

Helga drifted back to the horses herself and resumed grooming the carthorse, finding herself conveniently near enough to be able to talk quietly to Breki without being overheard.

'How are the hands doing?'

Without looking at her, he replied, 'Hurts like I'm Fenrir's chew-toy.'

'Good,' she said, and noted the stifled chuckle. 'Well, maybe not quite what I meant, but it shows they're healing. It would be a lot worse if either felt dead or numb.'

'I'd rather have them not hurt at all, if you don't mind. He grinned shyly, then admitted, 'I guess they are a little less sore than yesterday. This one especially.' He held up the sprained wrist, which was a lot less swollen than it had been.

They fell silent again. Helga was enjoying the warmth and weight and the small sounds of the horses; not for the first time she wished that more people were like animals. She forgot herself in the long, firm strokes, bringing a shine to the beast's coat, until Jorunn's voice rang out behind her.

'Any luck?'

'A little.'

Hearing Freysteinn's voice, Helga couldn't stop herself looking over her shoulder. Even in the fading light she could make out the darker silhouette of her lover, a bundle of something on his shoulder, emerging from the forest. At almost the same time, Big Rolf appeared from the opposite direction, lugging something heavy. As they both got to the centre of the clearing, Freysteinn dumped his firewood in a heap and knelt down to stack it properly so he could start the fire. The Northerner worked silently beside him; Helga wasn't sure if he'd noticed Breki's arrival, for he gave no sign of it.

Soon enough an amber glow appeared, growing steadily until tongues of flame were licking upwards.

Big Rolf walked to one of the carts and unhooked the large iron cauldron, which he suspended over the fire, announcing to no one in particular, 'Pot's on.'

Then at last he looked over at the horses. 'Well met, boy. Took your time, didn't you?'

Breki smiled, and Helga could see the affection on his face. 'I thought I'd enjoy the time being away from your smelly old arse.'

'I'm surprised you found us, seeing as you couldn't find your way from under your mother's dress a couple of summers ago,' Big Rolf replied.

'That is true enough,' Breki said, still grooming his horse, 'But unlike you, I continued growing after eight summers.'

This brought a chortle from Big Rolf and smiles from Haki and Freysteinn, who'd been enjoying the exchange.

'Huh,' Big Rolf said, 'I'll have to hack your legs off in your sleep for that one, boy. Can't have you looking down on your elders.'

'At least you're smart enough to wait until he lies down,' Freysteinn chimed in.

Big Rolf put on a voice of mock outrage. 'Oh, so it's everyone pick on poor old Rolf now, is it? Who's next? The brown-skin?' He looked around. 'Where's he gone to, then?' When there was no answer, he turned to Jorunn. 'Where's your warrior gone? Have I gained what you have lost?'

She's alone. The realisation hit Helga like a hard punch to the stomach.

Hildigunnur had never stopped telling her to imagine what it was like to walk in someone else's tracks, and now Helga was getting a full helping of being in Jorunn's boots, she rather wished she wasn't. Big Rolf's words had had just the right amount of challenge to them: not enough to act on, but more than enough to chip away at her right to command. And there she stood, completely without friends – but if Jorunn was at all bothered, she didn't show it.

'If you count your broke-paw bear cub as a warrior, then I guess that's true.' An artful pause. 'But that would also suggest that you think the two of you can best me.'

Helga had to fight hard to keep from smirking. *Play and counter-play.* Jorunn had shown herself to be a strong Tafl player the last time Helga had met her, five years ago, and since then she'd been surviving on her wits. Now Big Rolf had put himself in position: either he had to take the full step up, or—

'Of course not. I am an old man and you are at least half Finn-witch.'

'And the other half of me is hill-troll. Remember that.'

Helga couldn't but admire the perfect weighting of joke and threat in Jorunn's reply.

The faint sound of drumming hooves from the direction of the sunset drew everyone's attention away from the old man, but it was only Nazreen, coming out from the cover of the trees.

Say whatever you want about him, but that man can ride, Helga thought, admiring the sight. It was hard to distinguish horse and rider, so thoroughly unified were they in their rhythm. She felt a brief tingling sensation and instantly slapped it down. *No. Absolutely not. No thinking about anything like that.* Instead, she turned her attention to Freysteinn, hoping for some distraction.

What she got instead was a faint, shadowy sense of satisfaction from within.

Freysteinn was so busy tending to a cook-fire that really didn't need tending that it would have been less obvious what he was thinking if he'd climbed up a tree and screamed it. 'Never underestimate the power of the whispered word,' her mother always said, and here was the proof: not only was he studiously ignoring Nazreen, but he had apparently lost all his joy in the journey.

Nazreen dismounted right next to Jorunn, landing with enviable softness and immediately giving his report in his harsh, scratchy language. Two – three? – sentences in, Jorunn spoke, just a word, and he stopped immediately.

Helga's heartbeat quickened ever so slightly as she realised he was walking towards her. A thrill coursed through her. She determined she would not look at Freysteinn and instead, she focused on the horse, patting the animal's thick neck and murmuring the final soothing words. She got a snort in return. She didn't need to look up to see Nazreen's big brown eyes regarding her; she felt . . . studied. Measured.

Play this right, girl. She smiled at him – *just so* – and gestured to take his reins. His brow furrowed for a moment, then he understood and smiling, shook his head. She smiled back, silently offering him the brush and he inclined his head slowly, gracefully. *Yes, thank you.*

And now for the final twist . . . Her hand grazed his as she handed it over. His skin felt firm, warm and soft—

Helga slammed a heavy stone on the first three thoughts that followed and instead, she smiled again, this time looking him straight in the eyes. His lips lifted a touch in return, then he turned to the horse and started rubbing the beast down.

Bait, set . . .

As Helga turned away, she made sure to glance across at Freysteinn. The uncomfortable shade of red on his face suggested that he had definitely seen the exchange.

. . . trap.

You should have listened to me when you had the chance.

The glow of the fire softened everything. Breki leaned back, enjoying the feel of a full stomach. 'That stew was good.'

'I know,' Big Rolf grunted in reply. Across the fire from them, Jorunn sat up and muttered something to the brown-skinned man. Over to the side, Freysteinn was busy telling a story to Helga and Haki that appeared to involve something about a man and a wolverine in a bag.

'Why are you here?' Big Rolf's voice was quiet, but there was a hardness to the question that made Breki flinch.

'The North Wind told me to come.'

'When?'

'Just before I got here.'

'No,' the old man hissed, 'when did she tell you that you had to leave?'

'We were about to go home, and then she was called away. I think she went to talk to Vala. It was after that. She said that you could probably use some company.'

Big Rolf cursed under his breath.

'Why?'

A gust of wind caught the embers of the fire, sending up a whirl of sparks. The old man took a deep breath. 'It could mean any number of things,' he said slowly, 'and none of them are good.'

There was a peal of laughter from Freysteinn's corner, then Jorunn interrupted. Surveying the small group, she announced, 'While we still have time on our side, it might be wise to share a couple of stories.'

Big Rolf's interest immediately perked up. 'I like the sound of that. What have you got, Finn-witch?'

'If this wasn't what it was, Son of Dwarves' – Big Rolf chuckled – 'I'd give you the honour of going first – seeing as you have less time left in this world than we do.' Seasoned with a smile, this got an appreciative head-nod from Jorunn's captive audience. 'But maybe there are things we should be aware of. So if no one complains, I'd like to start.'

The old man smiled. 'I don't see anyone lifting so much as a finger. The word is yours.'

Helga watched as Jorunn *grew*, somehow, almost as if she had walked through a door and come out a different woman.

'Trading takes you to strange places,' she began, 'and you see and hear some strange things. How many of you had heard of King Harald before this?'

All but one hand rose. Nazreen remained motionless, but he was clearly listening closely.

'And how many of you have seen him, in the flesh?'

The hands sank down again.

We know nothing – and she's holding it up in front of us so we understand that.

'I have. One summer ago I was forced to go to Hedeby. I don't like it – it's too big, too many traders, not enough space – and then there is Harald himself. When I arrived he was away, so I did what I needed to do and was about to head south when word came that the king was returning from bashing the Angles, so I decided to hang about for a bit. I had a couple of expensive things in the cart I'd not been able to shift and we all know big men tend to get a little loose with their purse if they've been lucky on the raids.

'Of course, I wasn't the only one awaiting King Harald's arrival. It hadn't been a good summer – too much rain, too much wind, too little sun – and what hadn't rotted in the ground was late to harvest and of poor quality, so Harald's Godsman was intent on getting some significant sacrifices. Even before the sails had been spotted he was talking about how they'd need to give three or four thralls, at the very least, and preferably Greymane, Harald's favourite horse, to show the gods how serious they were. The Godsman, Troels was his name, was a powerful man: he was tall, with broad shoulders and long blond hair. He knew his horses and he knew his gods. Nobody said anything, but there was a tension about the place . . . which is not necessarily bad for trade.' Jorunn smirked.

'The king sailed with eight ships – a small band, but they were all hard men. Less than half a day after, the first sail was spotted and by mid-afternoon, the men were stepping onto Dane-soil. The women were jubilant: the men were loaded with gold and they'd brought home half a ship's worth of thralls to boot. It sounded as if their time a-Viking was as good as any raider's drunken boasts, which is saying something.

And then I saw Harald Bluetooth, and it became clear why he only needed a few men to carry much home.'

'Why is that?' Breki asked, almost breathless with excitement. He'd been hanging on Jorunn's words from the start of the tale. 'Is he fearsome?'

Jorunn smiled, and there was a bit of mystery in her features. 'Oh yes, he is,' she almost purred. 'Like I said, trading takes a person to strange places, where they see strange things. And I have never seen a man who made my blood run colder than King Harald Bluetooth did.'

Helga felt the intensity of Jorunn's stare for a moment – and then it was gone and the skald in her returned to the audience held captive by her words. It was no longer than an eye-blink, but the message was clear. *You knew my father. You knew my brothers. You know what dangerous men look like.*

'The king was in the midst of the throng. He didn't shout. He didn't gesture. He certainly didn't roar or thump his chest. And without him having to say a word or use his fists or boots, the crowds parted for him.'

She stopped and added wryly, 'They didn't part for Troels, at least not willingly. I was near enough to see the Godsman elbowing his way towards the king, although I couldn't hear what was said, at least, not at first. It was clear he was asking for his sacrifices, but it looked like the king was just ignoring him, because even while Troels was still talking, he'd turned away and was talking to a couple of men. But the Godsman must've been an even braver man than he looked, because he stepped right in front of Harald.'

She took a breath, almost as if shocked herself at what she was about to reveal, and Helga admired her artistry. It took real talent to get people hooked on your story like that.

After a heart-beat, Jorunn continued, 'At that moment it seemed like everybody around them suddenly forgot what they'd been talking about, all except for Troels, who raised his voice to make sure the king was paying attention to him. He spoke about the abysmal harvest – and he was right, it had been dreadful, and it was going to mean real hardship for a great many people come the winter – and said that it was crucial that they take six thralls—'

'*Six?*' Big Rolf exclaimed, looking aghast. 'But that is just stupid—'

'Of course it is,' Jorunn agreed. 'Even if you believe that you should waste perfectly good thralls like that and you have the thralls to spare, six would be outrageous. It was a push for power.

'And the king said no.

'He didn't raise his voice, but everyone heard.

'Troels didn't like it and he was almost shouting – I doubt there was a man or woman or child in Hedeby who couldn't hear him – when he told the king that the gods would be furious with him. For some reason King Harald started smiling, although I couldn't see what was funny about being shouted at by an angry Godsman, but it sure riled him and he was in the middle of that old verse about listening to the thunder, waving his hands about, when there was a brief flash of light, as if the sun had caught on something – and then there was a lot of screaming and Troels sank to the ground.

'It happened so quickly: the gods might have been alive in his head, but Troels was very dead. The king had shoved one of the White Christ's spiky-ended crosses into his eye, so hard that I was surprised it hadn't come out the other side.'

She paused and looked round the circle. 'King Harald just turned and walked away, his chosen men hard on his heels. He didn't say a word. But you know, bad as that was, it almost wasn't the worst thing. That was a boy of maybe seven summers who ran up and dropped to his knees by the body. For a moment I thought maybe he was kin to the Godsman, maybe he was grieving – until he put his foot on Troels' face, grabbed the cross and yanked hard until at last it came loose with this horrible wet, sucking sound.

'The little bastard saw me watching and stuck out his tongue. "Loot is loot," he said. "And loot belongs to Father." Then he ran along after the king. They call him the Brat Prince, apparently. Sweyn is his name.'

Jorunn dropped her eyes and let the silence grow before saying quietly, 'I left Hedeby very quickly after that.'

Helga looked around at Jorunn's audience. Some were staring at her and Breki's mouth hung open.

A good story, well told.

'I'd not heard that one,' Big Rolf said. 'I didn't know he'd abandoned the gods.'

'King Harald will deal swiftly with anything that doesn't benefit him,' Jorunn said. 'He does not like the unexpected, and he does not like it when his men make their own decisions. That's worth remembering.'

The serious faces of the men around the fire suggested that they were unlikely to forget.

Night softly turned to day, heralded by the piercing bird calls amongst the trees. The warmth of Freysteinn's body countered the cold of the ground seeping into Helga's bones. She was missing her bed like a dear departed friend, thinking bitterly, *Of course it was Loki who invented sleeping outside.*

'Awake?' Freysteinn whispered.

'Mm.'

'Get up?'

'Mff.' Words would come later. Just now, the heat of his skin was the only good thing in the world and she wished to hold onto it for just a little longer. She just needed him to not speak, not remind her of—

Too late. The events of the past days came flooding back to her – the way he'd stormed into the longhouse, how happy he'd been when the king had ordered the journey, how little he had thought of her or talked to her, about anything – and suddenly she wasn't reliant on him for heat any more. Sighing, she rolled out from underneath the blanket and went to see to the horses. She did not look back.

Grundle greeted her with a head-toss, as if to ask her where she'd been, and Helga stepped in close, stroked the strong neck and muttered, 'At least you won't let me down.'

It was only when Grundle snorted that she realised she wasn't alone. She'd not noticed Nazreen, grooming his own mount with absentminded detachment. He looked over at her and she smiled at him. *I can see why Jorunn keeps him close.* There was a peculiar grace to the man, an effortlessness. Freysteinn had something of the same thing, but his was much more bound up in muscle and forward motion. Nazreen *flowed*, somehow.

Grundle gently butted her hip, as if to say, *Stop looking!* and Helga obeyed, biting her lip gently to help her snap out of it. *Doesn't hurt to look*, she argued with the voice in her head – the one that sounded suspiciously like her mother. She looked at the horse. 'Just so we're clear,' she whispered gently, 'you are not a shape-shifted version of Hildigunnur, are you?'

The horse shook her head and nuzzled her.

'No, of course not. You'd already have kicked me from here to the sea for being daft if you were.' She looked up, laughing at herself, and straight into the brown eyes of Nazreen. Her breath caught in her throat. He'd walked over to them without either of them noticing. Smiling calmly, he gestured towards Grundle.

'Yes – yes, of course,' Helga stammered, handing him the brush.

He took it from her and moved in front of the mare. Grundle looked at him, stiffened up and snorted, hard. Helga immediately stepped towards him, but stopped when Nazreen spoke to the horse in his tongue. The words sounded like a question and she could almost see Grundle pause.

He repeated the phrase, softer this time, and while Helga didn't understand the words, she could feel the cadence, the poetry.

This time Grundle tossed her head and snorted again, but this was different – it was a communication, almost.

Nazreen kept his eyes trained on the mare and moved to her side, slowly and calmly, then started brushing her in a circular motion, just the way she liked it, smoothly but firmly. Helga could see the tension disappearing from the curved back like dew vanishing before the sun.

Something about the communication between man and beast was absolutely compelling to watch. *She accepted him almost instantly.* She had just started thinking about that when a voice interrupted her.

'Good morning!'

Her shoulders immediately clenched, even before she'd had time to understand the words or recognise the forced cheerfulness in Freysteinn's voice. After a moment she'd worked out why she'd had such a visceral reaction to a simple greeting: he sounded like someone trying – not very well – to contain his anger.

'It is,' she stammered. She dimly registered that Nazreen had slowed his strokes. Freysteinn was close to her – suddenly too close – and she wanted to push him away, but she didn't.

'I see you've hired a horse-boy.'

Suddenly her idea of winding him up and setting him on Nazreen felt stupid. She had wanted him to suffer a little because of how he had treated her, how he had ignored her and made her feel like he didn't care – but it had gone too far. He was clearly hurt and angry. She smoothed her voice as much as possible, hoping to calm him down. 'He asked to groom her. I didn't see the harm.'

Freysteinn looked taken aback. 'Are you kidding? That bloody nag will take his shit-coloured hand off!'

And just like that, her guilt vanished. He was being an arse, and to her horse to boot. 'She looks like she doesn't mind the attention at all.' She looked him straight in the eye, chin up. *Yes, that was exactly what I meant.*

Just as he was about to snap something back, a soft voice interrupted them. 'She is beautiful horse. Very wise.'

The shock knocked the wind right out of Freysteinn. He turned, incredulous, to Nazreen. 'W— What did you say?'

Nazreen gave them a fleeting look, then went back to Grundle. 'This horse. She is beautiful. Wise.'

'Do you understand me?' Freysteinn demanded.

'Yes.' Nazreen was still studying the horse.

'How the—?' Words seemed to collide in Freysteinn's mouth. 'You lying little—'

Nazreen raised his eyes and told him sternly, 'I do not lie.'

'You never told us you understood!'

'Ah.' He smiled again. Like an uncle speaking to a demanding child, he replied, 'You never asked.'

'Fucking—'

'—lot to do this morning,' Jorunn broke in, and Helga could see Freysteinn hadn't noticed her standing by the carts, watching them. Smiling, Jorunn added, 'And you can calm down. He understands some, but not a lot.'

This did nothing to remove the scowl from his face.

'And if you've got time to get all hot and bothered about that, you've got time to ready the carthorses.'

Beside her, Helga could feel Freysteinn push away. She watched silently as he strode furiously towards the other horses, tethered together near the carts.

Now her head was a little clearer, Helga felt suddenly dizzy. *He understands.*

A moment, and then—

Of course he does. The realisation of the power of Jorunn's weapon hit her full on. She could leave Nazreen anywhere, looking different, playing the mute foreigner and reporting *everything* back. *Oh, Hildigunnur would have loved this.*

She turned to check on Freysteinn, who was busy tacking up the horses. Jorunn inched closer to him, and there it was: a question, followed by a response. Helga waited. Yep, here came the inevitable sharp retort, then the chuckle, the shared laughter. This was what Hildigunnur had taught them: the way to lead. *Get them with jokes and surprises, ask for their opinions where the answers were already given and tell them they were crucial to the success of whatever needed to be done.* Her father would have done the same with a heavy look and a growl, but women had to rule differently.

For what it's worth, Freysteinn looks well and truly ruled.

The exchange had not been missed by the Northmen, who were also up and tending to their morning tasks.

A little later, Haki drifted in from the forest and threw a bundle of pheasants into the foremost cart.

Before long, the caravan was moving again.

The emotions of the morning soon gave way to the monotony of the road. Helga found herself lulled by the rhythm of the horse moving under her. The surprise of Nazreen's revelation still lingered. *You never asked.* She smiled at the simplicity of it.

You never asked.

And that turned her mind back to her growing list of unanswered questions. *Why?* The boy – argument, robbery, whatever. Fair enough. But why then the father? And after that? How was Drifa connected? Or Lars? They were all there to . . .

. . . attend the council.

And if the council was shattered, and King Eirik's allies were scattered to the winds . . . who would benefit the most?

I'm going to need a bigger storeroom.

The thought was so ridiculous that she had to stifle a panicked laugh. Then she turned her attention to the shelves. She put Alfgeir Bjorne's wrestling belt on one. With a fractured council, the king's man would be more important than ever when it came to making deals, connecting people, sorting arguments: being the hand that held and wielded the king's power.

On the next she placed Jorunn's cape. Weakness was opportunity, and if the king was weakened there would be opportunities a-plenty for squeezing his coffers. As an afterthought, she placed Nazreen's boots underneath, because she very much doubted that Jorunn did her own dirty work very often.

She could feel Ludin of Skane's cold eyes on her neck. Surely he would not have nearly killed his trusted friend? *'Nearly' being the key word here.* She thought of Gunnar the swordsman, and how coldly and clearly he had described the attack on Drifa, and in such detail. Could he have . . . ? No, that didn't feel right. There was little guile to the man. But there would have been eyes on Ludin at all times, so maybe he would have sent a . . .

She glanced at Haki. He looked completely relaxed as he rode, rocking gently in the saddle. It was all too easy to imagine him dispassionately smashing someone's head in with a rock. The bow and arrow went on the shelf next to Nazreen's boots.

That left . . .

'Helga,' Freysteinn whispered. The anger in his voice had been replaced by urgency. 'Listen.'

Studying him, she couldn't help but notice that he sounded worried, even afraid. 'What is it?'

'Helga, I have been too busy talking and I have not listened to you as I should. You are right – the murders? It makes no sense that Styrbjorn is behind them.'

A wave of happiness swelled in her and she loved him. He was so beautiful, so proud and strong – and this was him apologising. He had realised what he'd done.

'I think whoever did it wanted to unseat the council and create havoc,' she whispered back. 'And I think they had nothing to do with Styrbjorn appearing.'

There was the briefest flicker of hesitation.

He's listening to me. He's actually thinking about what I have just said.

'That makes sense.' He glanced over at the carts. 'Did you see his face when the boy caught up?'

Big Rolf? Who else could he mean? Helga frowned. No one. 'He didn't look too happy,' she admitted slowly.

'No, he didn't. The boy said something about being sent by Ingileif, didn't he? I reckon the wily old bear figured out that the killer had left Uppsala and is on this caravan. Maybe she thought Big Rolf could find them – or maybe she knew all along that Big Rolf was the killer and she sent Breki to warn him before he got found out.'

Think, girl, think! She added up the murders. Big Rolf had certainly been near enough for all of them. And there was no love lost between the Northmen and the king, that was a fact. But there was *something* . . .

'Are you sure?' Something was nagging at her, but she couldn't yet place it.

Freysteinn looked embarrassed. 'No, I'm really not . . . but I am not as good at this as you are.'

She could feel her cheeks getting warm and warned herself sternly, *Stop it, girl: keep your head.* 'We will pretend that nothing has changed and keep our ears open,' she decided. 'I will talk to the boy, see what he knows.'

He looks so relieved. And she realised that she felt relieved, too. She was no longer alone in worrying about the murders, and he needed her to make sense of it all. She looked at the back of Big Rolf's head, feeling a little bit uneasy – but that was just fear. Big Rolf had no idea that they were on to him. They could watch him and set their trap.

Haki was not the only one who could hunt.

Chapter 10

QUESTIONS

They didn't need the noisy seagulls circling overhead to tell them they were close; they could all smell the salty air and the promise of sea. About time, too. The days had felt almost endless. Nobody had offered any conversation and even Jorunn had given up on trying to get them to share stories or experiences. Haki had a frankly uncomfortable knack for immediately disappearing into the woods and killing something whenever they stopped, and the number of words he had spoken in total could probably be counted on one hand. Nazreen scouted ahead, regular as the sun and the moon, and kept himself mostly to himself.

And our prey hasn't given anything away at all.

It was Big Rolf who, after Jorunn, had tried the hardest to get people talking to each other, but even his jokes had been running dry after a while and so the caravan had been just marking the time in hoofbeats and silence. When they passed Gefjon's Lake, even the seasoned travellers had gawped, taken aback by the sheer size of it. But nothing out of the way had happened there, or anywhere. They'd just plodded on.

And so, we hunt. Helga nudged Grundle up to Freysteinn's cart. Three days in, the driver's plank was clearly feeling a lot less friendly to his backside. She gestured at the seagulls and asked pointedly, 'What happens now?'

'We get on the boat.'

'And then?'

'We keep prodding. If we get near Hedeby and he still hasn't given anything away . . .'

She waited, but there was no follow-up. 'We'd have to turn and run, wouldn't we?'

He looked uncomfortable with this. 'Maybe . . . but we might be wrong. What if it was Styrbjorn all along? We need to get to King Harald.' He saw her face and his tone changed. 'I'm sorry – I just don't know. That's why I told you . . . I hoped you would make it all make sense, the way you do.'

But I can't do that if I don't have anything to go on, can I? She liked his reliance on her, but it was also frustrating.

'He has been very careful to do nothing out of the ordinary – and it is not as if we can just ask him.'

Her own words took a while to sink in, but when they did, the question formed in her mind and would not be erased.

And why not?

Slowing Grundle a little, she allowed the cart to move ahead of her. Reaching into a pouch on her belt, she pulled out a square tile about the size of her fingernail. Within moments the knife was in her hand and with a couple of deft flicks she carved a rune.

Nauth. Need.

Her fist closed around the tile and she touched her index finger to her mouth.

'I need to know if he is telling the truth,' she whispered.

Above her head, something large and black beat its wings and took flight from an unseen branch.

'It's big.'

Haki's first words for three days took them all by surprise. An impromptu camp had been set up on the shore as they waited for the ferryboat. The horses were grazing contentedly in the shade of a big rock while the caravan party slumped among the stones. Haki walked up and sat on the highest point, staring out to sea.

'Can't argue with that,' Big Rolf replied.

The expanse of rich blue stretching on for ever made Helga dizzy and a little bit uncomfortable. The big lake had been an impressive sight, but even that had had the suggestion of trees in the distance, a hint of an end. This just went on and on and on . . .

And under it all lies the coiled strength of the wyrm, holding the world together. For a moment she fancied she could see the dark green glitter of scales. 'Will the ferryboat be here today?' She cringed at the sound of her own voice – she sounded squeaky and nervous, but none of the others appeared to have noticed. Her palm felt sweaty around the carved rune.

'Every day.' Nazreen sounded hesitant but careful.

We've run out of time.

Think, girl. Think! Trying her hardest to look leisurely, she ambled over to where Rolf was lounging on a flat rock. He too was staring down at the sea but he looked calm and settled.

Now to leap. Helga sat down and gazed at the line where sea met sky. 'You have to hand it to him,' she said, pointing at Haki. *Give him time to think, to wonder . . . and then—*

'He is a proper skald.'

Big Rolf chuckled. 'Yes indeed. I can envision it now – "The Ballad of the Sea", by the famous Haki Wordmaster.' He cleared his throat. 'Sea – I saw it, Blue and splashy—'

'Water make go bashy-bashy,' Helga continued.

Rolf rose to the challenge. 'Wish for words, it plagued me so—' He looked expectantly at Helga.

'I used the only two I know.'

'Hah!' Rolf's genuine laugh made Helga smile.

Then she glanced up at Haki, perched on his point above them, studying them both, like a bird of prey coolly sizing up his victims. When he spoke, his voice was serious and weighty.

'Fared I the whale-path
West for winning
Gold and tears
Of foes' women.
Once for the learning,
Twice for my scars,
Thrice for slaying
Weaker skalds.'

From a nearby rock, Freysteinn whooped. 'That's you told, claybashers! Turns out the mute has a voice.'

Big Rolf turned to peer at him. 'Thank you, Haki. We have been shown our rightful place—'

'— which is clearly beneath you,' Helga continued.

Haki shrugged and looked away, back out to sea.

'Cheerful,' Helga said.

'Mm. But you have to admit, unlike us, he is a proper skald.' The timing and the twinkle in the old man's eye made Helga smirk.

'You're not wrong there.' Inside her head, the voice of her mother urged her on. *This is good. He's listening. You've shared a joke. Go!* But there was something else holding her back, so instead, she followed her father's way and just sat quietly. The morning sun caressing their backs cast a net of diamonds on the water. The lapping of waves at the base of the rocks was gentle, like the prattling of babes, and the occasional caw of a seagull in the distance faded quickly.

Helga contrasted the water with its many colours and hues with the dark blue rocky coast. Further out there was a strand of lighter blue where a stream cut through and above the heavy weight of dark green. There were stripes of black where the light couldn't reach.

'It *is* big, isn't it?'

'It is,' she said quietly. *Don't look at him.*

'Spent much time near the sea?'

'No. I grew up in the valleys. This is my first time.'

'Mm.' There was a brief silence. 'I sailed a little, once.'

'Where did you go?'

'Here and there,' Big Rolf said.

'And would you perhaps sometimes come back with slightly more than you left with?'

'Perhaps,' the old man said, a smile in his voice.

Helga's heart beat faster. *Here's a chance.* She touched the ridge of the rune. *Tell me.* 'Sometimes people forget their things.'

'They do.'

'And on occasion they have to be helped to forget.'

Big Rolf made a discontented half-growl. 'On occasion, yes. I was never at the front of . . . *that*.'

Like a hunter, Helga held still. *Give them time and silence . . .*

'They talk a lot about honour, but I don't see the glory in butchery,' he said quietly.

'Mm.' *Keep talking, old man.*

'Outwit your opponent. Negotiate. Barter. Position your argument. You can – and should – stand your ground if you must, but to fall on defenceless, terrified villagers in the dead of night? No, that's not for me.'

Careful, now. 'I bet they didn't all agree with that.'

A cold laugh. 'Oh no, they surely didn't. I usually stayed back and watched the boats or the horses – and I got called all names under the sun for it. And there is only one reason why I can bear it.'

'Why?'

'Because *they* are all dead by now.'

'Sail.' Haki's voice hadn't changed tone at all, but there was no denying it: there was a sail on the horizon.

Quick! 'Grim work, raiding.'

Big Rolf looked at her then. 'And what would you know of grim work?'

'My father – my foster-father – was named Unnthor Reginsson.'

The old man's eyes narrowed and the intensity of his gaze doubled. Helga felt the colour in her cheeks rise.

'Is this true?' He didn't wait for an answer but glanced at Jorunn, standing on the stony beach with one hand shading her eyes as she watched the progress of the sail. 'Same as . . . ?'

'Yes.'

Big Rolf looked away and whistled quietly. 'You'd know, then.' Turning back to her, he suddenly looked more tired, like something had drained out of him. 'I just had no stomach for it. All the blood. The screaming.' His eyes drifted as if in search of a memory and for a moment it looked like he was somewhere else, far away in time. 'That was for others, men who knew what they were doing.'

Careful. Helga realised that she'd forgotten to breathe at some point and exhaled slowly. 'Whoever did for the people in our camp . . .'

'. . . also knew what they were doing,' Big Rolf added darkly.

Right, fish. On the hook you go. Helga inched her eyebrows up a fraction to what she imagined was her most convincing face of overwhelmed innocence. 'King Eirik said that Styrbjorn—'

Big Rolf scoffed. 'The king knew full well that Alfgeir beat that out of him. He had to say something to calm the people and break up the council. It didn't matter whether it was true or not.' The old man eyed her, frowning. 'And I don't think you believe it either.'

Her heart thumping, thinking what to say next, Helga was

interrupted by movement in the corner of her eye catching her attention. Haki was rising to his feet with quiet purpose.

Too late. But I have learned a lot.

'Time to go,' she said, gently.

'What? Yes,' Big Rolf said, tumbling back down to the present from wherever he had been a moment ago. Around them, the other travellers were all busy rounding up horses and lashing down carts. The sail that had been just a dot on the horizon was now the size of a thumbnail and closing fast. Helga climbed down from the rocks to where Grundle stood waiting for her and peered around, looking for Freysteinn. She paused a moment, turning back to the sea to check on the sail, and then understood: the vessel was heading for a sandy beach a little bit further up the coast.

She caught up with Freysteinn around halfway towards the landing site.

'Well?' he muttered.

'Well what?'

'What do you think?'

She closed her eyes and allowed the impressions of Rolf to flow back to her. His eyes, his voice, the tension in his muscles. Nothing suggested hidden malice, not then, nor earlier. She thought about all the traders who had wanted to fleece her, how their faces would twist, their mouth twitch or their eyes narrow or shine when they thought they were being clever. Most traders had their little tells, even if they didn't know it. She had no doubt Big Rolf had his secrets, but he'd shown no sign of hiding anything when they'd been talking about the murders. If he was a liar, he was by far the best she'd ever encountered. *And knowing that will be a great help when he slits our throats in the night . . .*

She thumbed the rune in her hand. It felt warm to the touch, like the remains of a smouldering fire.

But she wasn't quite prepared to be definite, not yet.

'I . . . don't know.' The admission felt sour in her mouth, and for a moment she was afraid that Freysteinn would be either angry or disappointed.

Oddly, he appeared to be almost happy. 'Don't worry. I think you'll definitely find our murderer soon.' He smiled at her, which went some way towards helping her mood. *He means it. He really believes in me – and he's right, I will. I will find him – or them.*

The travellers lined up the horses and carts on the beach, ready to board. As the ferryboat closed in, Helga felt herself tense up. It looked so . . . *big.* Glancing over at Big Rolf, she couldn't help but think about how short he was in comparison. How was the old man going to get on board? He'd struggle to reach—

An image of Drifa's wound entered her mind unbidden.

He'd struggle to reach.

'She sits well in the water,' Big Rolf remarked.

'It's a bucket.' Haki spat contemptuously.

'It'll do.' Head held high, Jorunn did not look at all like someone heading into the lair of a dangerous enemy.

Biting the inside of her cheek to keep all her thoughts at bay, Helga followed.

'What's wrong?' Freysteinn's face was a picture of concern.

'Nothing.' *Everything.* Helga's stomach felt like it contained a mouse being batted around by a particularly cruel cat. There was a definite stench coming from somewhere in the bowels of the damned boat and she could feel the bile rising in her throat. 'I'm just – thinking.' *About depositing my insides on your face.*

She could feel his hand on her knee. It was warm and reassuring and it did no good whatsoever for the sour taste in her mouth.

'Just try to relax.'

His face was open and earnest and she wanted to plant a fist in it. There was *nothing* about this which was making her feel even slightly like relaxing.

When the ferryboat had landed, the boatman and Jorunn, who clearly knew each other, had been quick to negotiate passage. A sinewy horse-boy took charge of the animals and had them all tethered to a tall post set into the middle of the deck before the last man was on board. He was clearly used to horses, because they all followed his gentle muttering voice and stood placidly, ignoring the loading of the carts, which was considerably more time-consuming. Under Big Rolf's guidance, the men had already taken the wheels off the carts and after they'd carried those on board as well, they'd been made to restack them several times, grumbling loudly, until Rolf was satisfied they'd properly balanced the load.

Helga, standing quietly by and watching, hoped fervently that nobody would ask her the question, but the gods must have had their attention elsewhere.

Big Rolf leaned over. 'Sailed much?'

Fuck.

'Yes,' she lied, and wondered why for a moment, especially as she'd already told him she'd been raised in the valleys. Then she glanced at Jorunn, who was standing at one end of the ferryboat, looking straight ahead, and she saw the shadow of Unnthor Reginsson, trading in death and destruction.

Show no weakness. Men rule, women decide.

'I've done my share.'

The old man nodded sagely. His voice was kind. 'You've no doubt had to tell green-faced children to find a rhythm and roll with the waves yourself then.'

Vomit rose in her and she fought back a cough; even so, a thin burning line of sour spittle found its way up past the barrier and into her nose.

'Yes,' she said tartly.

'Not sure about the stew last night,' Big Rolf said conversationally. 'That scrawny wood-hen Haki brought down? I reckon it was tasting a little strange. Just so you know. I was feeling a bit . . .' He paused, patting his taut belly. '. . . well, tender before we got to the beach.' He didn't wait for her reply but ploughed on, 'I'm hoping it will keep until we land, but if not, expect me to be asking the boy to help me season the waves some.' Chuckling at his own joke, he turned away and looked ahead.

It was only when she'd forced the bile back down that she replayed his words in her head and realised what he had been saying. She found herself more thankful than she wanted to be. They had been sailing for long enough that the coast behind them had diminished into a thin blue line. She allowed herself to imagine that she could see the beginnings of a coastline up ahead – until the wave they'd been cresting disappeared under them and she found her stomach lurching again, offering a dull, broad discomfort to contrast with the pain of her fingers digging into the beam she was sitting on.

This is it. I will die. My insides will die, and the rest of me will follow, slowly and painfully. I will not survive this. She looked at the back of Freysteinn's head. *And if he turns and smiles at me one more time and suggests that I am weak but it will be fine in the end, neither will he.*

A fat drop of spray landed on her face and she reached to wipe it off. *But my hands are dry.* The thought registered just as she touched the spot of sticky wetness on her face and she looked up, expecting to see a gull.

Instead, a raven swerved away, cawing on the wind in what sounded suspiciously like laughter.

The realisation of what had happened hit her and white-hot rage exploded in her chest. The cloying smell of the birdshit reached her nostrils and tears of rage mixed with the swelling nausea just as Freysteinn turned around.

That look.

For a moment – half a heartbeat, surely no more – something flashed in his eyes. Then a mask of concern slid over his face, almost impossibly quickly. He mouthed an 'Oh!', then without words conjured up a rag from somewhere up his sleeve and passed it to her, inching closer so no one needed to see her wiping the birdshit off her face. Her heart thumping in her chest, she fought to hold in a scream. A chill worse than the wind necessitated coursed through her.

What was that look?

For a moment he had looked like someone she didn't know.

A heartbeat later she was diving towards the side and throwing up what felt like everything she'd ever eaten, to the sound of gulls cawing overhead.

When the hull scraped on sand, Helga thought she would cry with joy. Nobody had made jokes at her expense or pointed out that she looked a little green, and no one had mocked her for the birdshit. When she'd finished puking her guts up, Freysteinn had handed her a waterskin and told her to drink gently.

All the while, she'd held on to one thought and one thought only: *I am never getting on another boat in my life*. She considered carving the words into her skin.

She watched, still half-dazed, as Haki leaped overboard, one hand on the side, like he'd done it a hundred times before. *He probably has, too*. The land was a little different from their starting beach, with no rocks in sight, only soft white sand topped with tufts of green.

'Come on,' Freysteinn said gently, offering his hand, once again the man she knew and loved.

She took it and allowed him to help her down, but she couldn't get that strange look of his out of her head. She could almost taste the fear on her tongue, the sickness from the up-and-down of the ferryboat, the smell of the horses – and then . . .

Smug.

He looked smug. Smug, and happy that there was birdshit on my face.

'What's the matter? Are you still feeling sick?'

Dragging her mind back to the present, she realised that

Freysteinn was staring at her. Belatedly, she also realised that her face was scrunched up in a grimace, as if to push away the idea that had, just like them, arrived where it wasn't supposed to be.

'No . . . no, I'm fine,' she lied. 'I was just wondering about, uh, how flat it was.'

The smile that always set her heart beating faster was still there. 'They have little in the way of hills, the Danes.'

'Have you been here before?'

There was a moment of hesitation – *Why?* – then, 'Once. A couple of years ago. I had just left home and I jumped on a boat with some traders.'

'Mm,' Helga said, trying to ignore her aching leg muscles, not used to dealing with sandy dunes, particularly after being stuck on the ferryboat for so long. She looked round and saw the others were already lugging the carts off the boat and re-assembling them. Freysteinn saw her looking, leaned in to kiss her forehead and moved off to do his part.

She looked back over the sea to King Eirik's domain. If she squinted her eyes, she was almost certain that she could make out a slightly darker line on the horizon, but the glare of the sun on white sand was making her eyes water. Suddenly, she felt alone – alone, and small, and helpless, and afraid. Looking up, she imagined the traced line of a raven in the sky, but there were none to be seen.

'No wonder the Danes are always so angry,' Big Rolf muttered. 'If I had to live like this I'd be off to raid in a shot.'

'What?' Helga had to shout to make herself heard over the howl of the wind.

'I SAID—' The old man stopped and waved the question away.

Helga looked around. No one else was talking either. Haki was riding off to the side, as usual. Freysteinn, on the driver's plank of his cart, was hunched over looking uncomfortable. Breki was keeping his horse next to Big Rolf's cart, his head turned away from the wind as much as possible. The only people who looked like they weren't suffering were Jorunn and Nazreen, who were riding up front and carrying themselves like locals. Ever since they'd remounted the wheels on their carts and made the long trudge up onto the plains, this had been their lot, riding against a wind that was determined to get in their faces and under their skin. For the first while it had carried a fine grain of sand from the beaches; after that it flung the dust and grit of rarely travelled roads in their faces. From time to time the discomfort was enhanced by more earthy farm smells.

A yearning for the tall, thick trees of Uppsala filled Helga then and leaning over Grundle's flank, she murmured, 'When we get out of this, girl, I'll get you the best feed and add in a little extra. Hazelnuts, maybe, or an apple. A nice, juicy apple.'

A twitch of the ear and a quick, snorted reply was all she got. *Mind you, best conversation all day*, she thought.

Up ahead, Nazreen raised his fist, then pointed. In the distance they could just about make out a deeper shade of green.

'Finally,' Big Rolf muttered.

With the wind still battering them, the caravan continued its lurching journey to the south.

*

As the ground slowly sloped downwards, a forest of sorts spread out before them – if you could call this collection of bent and twisted trees leaning this way and that a forest. The little-used path snaking between the trees was only just broad enough for the carts. As they got deeper in, the trees grew smaller and denser and Helga found her eye focusing on the slightest movement of leaves. *We'd not see anyone until they were upon us.* In the land of King Harald, this was not a comfortable thought. She could see she wasn't the only one feeling nervous; all of the riders sat warily now as the unease spread.

Up ahead, Nazreen swivelled in the saddle and gestured to his eyes, then looked around.

'Of course we'll be keeping our eyes open,' Freysteinn muttered angrily. The rest of his words disappeared down into his chest.

The narrow path had forced them into a long line. Nazreen and Jorunn up front, were followed by Big Rolf in his cart, then Freysteinn in his. Helga had slotted in behind the carts, with Breki and Haki behind her, bringing up the rear. *This is probably the safest place to be.* Then she looked over her shoulder and her stomach told her otherwise.

Haki was no longer riding with his usual practised ease and grace but instead, held himself stiffly. His eyes were darting in all directions.

Helga exchanged glances with Breki and when she gestured, *Is he all right?* the big lad looked back at her, his own eyes wide, slowly shook his head and lifted his shoulders in a shrug. He hadn't the faintest idea.

I do, though and he is definitely not all right. She could see the warrior's nostrils flaring, his chest rising and falling too rapidly. *Herbs?* She thought about that for an eye-blink, then discarded the notion. *There's only one thing to do.* She touched Dagaz, the rune for hope, around her neck, and dropped back until she was riding next to Haki.

'Hey,' she murmured, 'hey. Goat boy.' He looked up at her, and this close, she could see his eyes were wild. 'You know what they call Ludin in Uppsala?' The mention of his chieftain's name reached him. He blinked and furrowed his brow, as if trying to get rid of a headache, but still he didn't respond.

Helga's ribs ached where her mother's bony fingers would have poked her. *Again.* More slowly, she repeated, 'Do you know what they call Ludin of Skane?'

Haki looked like he was biting through something sour '. . . no.'

'They call him the Pine Cone. Do you know why?'

The gaunt warrior's eyes squeezed shut and his features grew pinched in his face. 'No,' he managed.

'Because if he gets in, he's not coming out nicely.'

Breki's indrawn breath was followed by a big, barked laugh as the images caught up to the words in his head.

Haki didn't react at all at first, but after a moment, his eyes twinkled and his lips lifted in a half-smile. For a second, he looked very much related to the fearsome warlord. 'They're not wrong,' he said. 'He's done for a lot of people, has my uncle.'

'So I gather,' Helga said, adopting the same conspiratorial tone.

An angry hush travelled towards them from the head of the column like wind in the reeds and Helga held up her hand as if to acknowledge her mistake, thinking angrily, *You should be thanking me. You'd have liked it worse if the bug-eyed freak had lost his mind and cut his way through the column from the back.*

Up ahead, Nazreen's hand rose again, then he led them off to the right, into the trees and away from the path.

The clearing, if it could be called that, was barely wide enough for the two carts. Breki and Freysteinn had taken the horses and gone in search of better grazing, disappearing behind a stand of gnarled alders. Jorunn was conferring with Big Rolf about the state of the wheels and the path ahead, while Nazreen walked around the camp looking intently at the ground. Helga observed his lithe form and the way he moved over the tufted grass and gnarled roots as if he were traversing a flat boardwalk. *I'd love to see with your eyes.*

She smiled at herself. Her mother had taught her that everyone had something they were better at than other things and the more you could learn from them about whatever their natural skill was, the better. What was it Nazreen looking for? Escape routes, possibly? Traps? Footprints?

Paths between sleeping bodies in the dark?

Her mind raced forward to the night to come. She imagined his strong hand clamped down on someone's mouth – hers? Breki's? She felt the push of cold steel on her throat, the stretched muscles as her head got twisted to the side, the warm gush of blood as the life of her leaked into the ground.

Even though it was warm here, out of the wind, she shuddered.

But was Nazreen the killer?

As there was nothing she should be doing, she returned to

her mental storeroom to organise her thoughts. Nazreen's shelf was empty now – she looked at where she'd left his boots, under Jorunn's shelf, but there was nothing there. Why was that? She could smell the danger on him, and the way the warriors gave him a wide berth told its own tale. But was he a coward? A killer in the night? She reached for something of his to put on the suspects' shelf, but couldn't find anything. First of all, why would he do it, unless commanded to by Jorunn . . . ? No – it wasn't him. And she was less and less sure Jorunn had anything to do with it, either.

On the shelf next to Jorunn's was a bearskin, cut for a small man, but it was almost falling off. She just couldn't see Big Rolf as a murderer: he had guile a-plenty and she wouldn't ever play him at a game that could be cheated, but she had yet to see malice in him.

There was something else bothering her about the idea of Big Rolf being behind the attacks – something simple and annoying, a raven's talons on the roof – but she couldn't quite get her fingers on it.

And then the fog lifted and she remembered her thoughts before that awful sea journey. Of course it couldn't have been Rolf. Drifa was too tall. He would have had to have wrestled her to the ground first, and there had been no signs of struggle. So definitely no. The attacker had to be taller.

She turned to the last shelf, on which sat a well-used, notched axe, and immediately her brain started tingling. *There's an important reason to leave the shed. Now. Now, now, now—*

Squeezing her eyes shut and then opening them slowly, she

breathed deeply, in and out. The smells of an unfamiliar forest tickled her and she felt a tingling sense of discomfort, of being where she didn't belong.

There – Haki—

Whatever she was feeling, though, Haki appeared to be going through quite a lot worse. The warrior looked like a cornered rat, ready to strike at anything and anyone. His hand was hovering too close to his axe. The slightest sound from the woods set his head whipping around to find its source.

Quick, now—

'Hey,' she murmured, and when he snapped round to look at her, Helga caught his eye, pursed her lips, stuck out her tongue and blew at him.

Haki blinked suddenly, repeatedly, and shook his head from side of side, as if to throw off a shroud. Slowly his jaw unclenched and he shook his head again – then almost as if catching himself, his gaze dropped and the colour rose in his cheeks. For a moment he was much less the fearsome fighter and more an awkward half-man, half-boy, and a piece of Helga's heart broke off and drifted away into the woods.

'It's a shitty excuse for a forest,' she said, but the connection, fleeting as it was, had broken.

Haki muttered something incomprehensible, turned and moved off between the trees. Just before he vanished, Helga noticed his bow and arrow had somehow materialised in his hands.

Was he sent to help us, she asked herself, *or to save Ludin the trouble of dealing with him?*

The thought brought a cold smile to her lips. She imagined the old warlord, happily dropping the deranged fox in the henhouse and watching the feathers fly.

She looked around at her fellow travellers and wondered to herself, *How did I end up in this mess?*

When the horses had been seen to and enough wildlife slaughtered to calm Haki down again, they gathered around a small, carefully constructed fire. Breki fetched the water for Big Rolf, who set to creating a stew from the three hares Haki had quickly skinned and quartered, a small bag of turnips Jorunn conjured up from somewhere and a handful of Helga's herbs. The clearing was small and the crowding trees and surrounding carts forced them to sit quite close together. For a moment it felt more like a hut than the wide outdoors – a family home, even.

Helga felt her lips quirk. If this were my family I'd be off like an arrow.

Jorunn finished her bowl, put it to the side and announced, 'Hedeby is less than half a day away. We could have reached it by now if we'd pushed it – but I'd rather not arrive in the evening.'

Big Rolf nodded, but Breki looked confused. 'Why?'

'Because you want people to be working when you first arrive,' Big Rolf said, and it was Jorunn's turn to nod in approval.

'Hedeby is different from Uppsala. It's bigger, but feels smaller.' When Breki looked surprised at this, she explained, 'The town consists of several big longhouses – although King Harald's is obviously the biggest – but there are also huts and dug-down pit houses, and there is a huge vegetable field, the like of which I have never before seen, and it is all enclosed within a wall easily three times the height of a man which is open only on the sea-facing side. Oh, and the smell of fish is *everywhere* – and it never lets up.'

'And the people,' Nazreen chimed in, looking disgusted, which appeared to thoroughly amuse Jorunn.

This is a practised act – they've done this before. The thought popped up, did enough to bother Helga and then disappeared again.

'Their singing – it comes from their throats and sounds like a dog. But worse.' He gave a brief demonstration, which did indeed sound awful.

Big Rolf hummed along, even more out of tune. 'One of my favourites, that.'

'But you're stuck between four walls,' Nazreen said, getting more animated, 'and you cannot escape. And there are loud noises everywhere.' He unleashed a harsh, discordant half-cry, half-belch.

'Hedeby does get tight,' Jorunn said. 'There are people everywhere, and they all want something.'

'And they *smell*,' Nazreen said, scrunching up his nose in distaste.

'They do, a bit,' Jorunn admitted. 'The thralls in the pen and the fishwives, at any rate.'

'Then why are we going?' The words shot out of Haki's mouth like spit.

Jorunn frowned and glared at him. 'We are going to trade what we have – and to find out what Bluetooth is up to, for the king.'

Helga saw it happen, but Haki was too far away and she was feeling like she was swimming in ice-water. She knew there would be no stopping him this time.

'No. No, no, no, no, no.' He stood up, his hand resting on the head of his axe. 'Bad. Bad bad bad. NO!'

Stay away, boy! Helga thought as Breki reached up to steady the man and got a hard blow to his sprained arm for his trouble.

'NO!' Looking truly nightmarish in the flickering firelight, Haki started spewing guttural words in the Southern dialect. Helga was struggling to keep up, but there was no mistaking his stance: he was ready to fight *everybody*.

Breki and Freysteinn, sitting either side of him, inched away as best they could, trying to give him room, but there was nowhere to go.

Slowly, ever so slowly, already anticipating the damage, Helga started to calculate. *There will be broken bones – and screaming – and axe-wounds to treat. If I'm alive to treat them, that is.*

She only noticed Nazreen had already got to his feet when he spoke. 'Friend,' he said softly.

Haki, holding his axe tightly as if ready to split skulls, looked like anything but a friend. His hand flailed, almost a spasm, warding off Nazreen and he started looking feverishly around for a way out. A steady stream of words was pouring from him, but none of them made any sense at all.

'Friend,' repeated Nazreen, very slowly, very quietly moving forward, towards the fire, all the time observing Haki, until he was standing just a hand's-breadth from the flames. His shins must have been burning, but he didn't show any emotion.

'NO,' Haki shouted, 'NOT GOING.' Tears were flowing down the man's face now, and he looked far younger than usual. He appeared to be completely unaware of his fellow travellers.

'Friend . . .' The moment the last syllable landed, he was leaping across the small fire. Haki swung at him, but somehow, lightning-quick, Nazreen contorted himself in mid-air so he was within the arc of the blade. He took the impact of fist and handle on his shoulder as he landed and almost before anyone could blink, he had seized Haki's axe-hand and in one smooth, impossible movement, pivoted and heaved the warrior over his back.

For a frozen moment, Haki's feet were a good deal higher up than his head – then he landed. The air was knocked out of him with a thump as he hit a massive protruding root; a wheezing gasp for air turned into a sore, rasping cough.

Nazreen dropped to one knee next to the fallen man, still firmly holding Haki's wrist, and put a knee gently but firmly on the other arm. '. . . you need to rest now, friend.'

Haki thrashed around violently, and even though Nazreen was holding him firmly, he still had to fight to remain on top.

'I know what you need to do.' Helga's voice sounded strange in her own ears.

Nazreen looked across at her with eyes that briefly said, *Do you, girl?* Then he smiled. 'What would you advise?'

Helga caught Breki's eye. Even with a clipped wing, the young wrestler still looked strong enough to pin down an ox. 'Disarm him, then follow me – Breki, you'll need to help us too.' As she'd expected, she saw Nazreen glance quickly at Jorunn, who nodded: *Permission given.*

The still thrashing Haki was swiftly stripped of all his blades, then Breki wrapped one arm around him, catching him in a firm hold and, carefully keeping his broken hand out of the way, lugged the smaller man off his feet. The fading light was just enough to see the path. Helga led them back the way they came, moving as quickly as possible. Judging by Breki's laboured breathing behind her, keeping Haki under control wasn't an easy job, but when she checked, she could see the scrawny warrior was almost on his tiptoes, being half-dragged, half-pushed along.

She could feel the incline under her feet and soon enough the trees started thinning out. This time when she looked back, she felt the weight lifting off her chest, not to mention the nice, warm feeling of being right. She felt like she was being rewarded when she turned and saw the pure puzzlement in Breki's face.

'He's . . . calming down.'

And you're looking at me as if I am a witch. 'I thought he would be.'

'. . . how? Why?' There was a brief flash of panic in the boy's eyes. 'What's in those woods?'

'Too many trees. Our man here' – she pointed at Haki, who was now hanging listlessly in Breki's arms; noticing his state, the big wrestler laid him gently on the ground – 'needs to see the sky. I saw how calm he was in *our* forests, where you can always see a fair bit of the horizon, and he was the happiest I've seen him when he was looking out to sea. I reckon he's not good with walls.'

Breki stared at the shivering warrior, clearly struggling to see the cold-blooded killer who had been travelling with them. 'You see a lot,' he muttered.

She was surprised to feel herself smiling. 'I think we all need to see better.'

Breki shifted his weight, looking a little nervous, then he gestured for Helga to step away a little bit. When she did, he bent down to her height and muttered, 'Can I tell you something?'

'Yes,' she said. He was close enough that she could feel the warmth of him in the cooling air.

'I think I was sent here to warn Rolf – I suspect our Finn-witch saw something in the bones. I think she thinks the killer is with this group.'

Keep calm. 'Are they, now?'

'I think so. And I thought it was him, definitely.' Breki glanced towards Haki's prone form, who looked like anything but a stone-cold murderer. 'Now, though . . . ?' His voice trailed off.

'Mm,' Helga said, telling herself, *Keep him talking; what else do you know?*

'What do you think?'

'I have to say I thought Styrbjorn's men were behind it,' she lied smoothly, and felt immediately guilty for it. *But I don't know you, boy. Not really.*

'I don't know what to do.'

The silence of the evening enveloped them, broken occasionally by Haki's wheezing breaths.

When she eventually spoke, the truth tasted bad in her mouth. 'Neither do I, friend. Neither do I.'

Going back, Helga kept checking over her shoulder to make sure the boys were all right. Haki no longer needed Breki's support, but he was still a little unsteady on his feet. Helga, noting the worry in Breki's steps, wondered, *When did I become the goose-mother?* Still, one way to stay safe from the murderer was to be in everybody's good graces. Once he'd recovered some, Haki had shamefacedly confirmed her suspicions. He always needed a clear view of the horizon, so on raids he stayed away from houses and tunnels; as long as he did that, he could do his job. He promised he'd be fine with some rest.

Helga politely suggested that he might need to tell Jorunn this, and find a way to be useful when they got to Hedeby.

Making their way down the path to the camp, she couldn't help but admire Nazreen's skill. The wagons blended into the darkness and the fire was only just visible through the trees because she knew what she was looking for. It was almost impossible to see her own feet, but she was pretty sure the number of roots and potholes she was stumbling over had tripled with the sunset.

If anyone does manage to sneak up on us in the night, they're probably worth whatever they've been paid.

The rest of them were talking in low voices when Helga came back into the ring of flickering light. The first person to catch her eye was Jorunn. Her face had a golden glow in the warmth of the flames, reminding Helga more than a little of their shared mother. She didn't say anything, but the look she gave spoke volumes: *Well done*, it said. Helga nodded in response and quickly took her seat as, without breaking stride, Haki stepped straight over the fire and stood in front of the seated Nazreen, who was watching him with sparkling eyes. The gaunt warrior swiftly extended his arm and Nazreen rose fluidly and grasped it in a warrior's handshake.

Helga caught Jorunn gently rolling her eyes. *Men.*

Haki sat down, and there was a moment of silence, then Jorunn coughed, as if to make sure everyone was looking at her before she spoke. 'I think we could do with a story.' Helga marvelled at the effect of her words. *It's like a cool drink of water.* Even Haki visibly calmed down. 'Legend has it that one time, long ago, King Harald wanted to go hunting.'

'Oho!' Big Rolf smiled from ear to ear. 'Sounds like a good one. Do you want me to cover the ears of the youth, in case he gets scared?'

'Would you like me to kneel so you can reach?' Breki replied, making the men snicker, but none of them lost focus on the storyteller, who was waiting patiently for her audience to settle.

'He was young then, maybe twelve summers,' Jorunn started, 'and a long way from his first raid, but he was stubborn.

'Someone said they'd spotted a particularly impressive stag – eighteen points or even more – in a nearby forest, so when young Harald was told that he couldn't go on the hunt because there was rumoured to be a vicious band of wolves roaming that area, he said . . . nothing.'

She had the listeners in the palm of her hand. 'In fact,' she said at last, 'he went to sleep.

'And then, in the middle of the night, he got up, stole his father's best mare and his brother's biggest bow and rode out by himself.

'The next morning, his furious mother sent two search parties out for him, but despite combing the forest, there was no sign of Harald, not that day, nor the next.

'After three days, even old King Gorm was ready to accept that his son was dead and gone.' Jorunn stopped and looked round the fire at each of her fellow travellers.

Then she continued, 'And five days after that, Harald came back: skinny and weak with hunger, and oozing pus and blood from where something large had taken a chunk out of his shoulder.

'But he also had the head of the biggest wolf anyone in Hedeby had ever seen on his back. When his father asked him what had happened, all Harald said was, "I went out. I came back."

'He never told anyone what had happened in the forest – but those wolves? They were not seen again. It is said that anyone standing in Harald's way has a habit of going missing in the forests around Hedeby . . .'

'A good story, well told,' Freysteinn said after everyone had spent a few moments contemplating Jorunn's words.

'Who knows.' Big Rolf glanced towards Jorunn. 'That one might be worth knowing as well. Shows you what kind of man King Harald is.'

Jorunn had clearly been waiting for the moment. 'Those who see truth for truth and tale for tale have misunderstood both. But we will need to hunt in a pack of our own. This is how we will do it.' She paused, as if arranging the commands in her head. 'We will go in at midday and set up ready for trade. 'Rolf, you know where to go, right? You and Breki, you will be on the fur cart.'

'And me,' Haki interrupted.

Jorunn gave him a searching look, but when he did not back down, continued, 'And Haki. Helga and Freysteinn, you come with Nazreen and me to deal in amber, gems and herbs.' When she was satisfied that she had everyone's full attention, she went on,

'We all know what we are searching for: information. We want to know who conducted the negotiations with Styrbjorn and what he was promised – and we need to know what King Harald has learned of his attack dogs since.'

Nazreen smiled, but there was nothing of good humour in his expression.

'We also want to find out whether the King of the Danes is planning to go east. Remember: we should sell our goods for reasonable prices, but do not bargain yourselves too far down in search of knowledge: you never know what's worth the bother and expense – and after all, we must give King Eirik a reasonable return on his investment, must we not?'

She paused, then repeated, 'A reasonable return.' There was the artful suggestion of a wink, the hint of a smile and a lot of weight on the word 'reasonable'.

And just like that, we are Jorunn's crew – on her boat for the raid, for better or for worse. Helga felt a little proud of the woman she was slowly coming to think of as her sister; she certainly admired the sheer skill she exhibited.

The fast-falling dark, the occasional spark of flame as a gust caught the embers and the journey was making her feel sleepy, but Jorunn was still speaking.

'If you want to snake your way into the enemy's graces, here's what you have to do. Compliment them. Be strong, but show a little weakness too – not too much; it goes a long way.' Looking at Breki, she smiled. 'A big lad like you is already interesting: if you ask for directions, maybe, or look a little helpless, any woman worth her salt will be silk in your hands.'

Helga thought she could see Breki's blush even through the darkness.

'Make sure you are good for your word – do not try any cheap tricks. Listen carefully, be agreeable and ask questions carefully.' She smirked. 'And if they think that with some luck and charm they might get a ride? Well, that's no bad thing either.'

Feeling suddenly chilled by the night air, Helga glanced at Freysteinn.

He was watching Jorunn, rapt with attention.

She looked at the beautiful man who had come to Uppsala out of nowhere and won her heart and a place by her side with a combination of strength and weakness, patience and flattery. The man who had asked all the right questions at the right time – except for anything to do with the murders. The man who had tried to convince her that the first death was an accident, who had delayed her going to King Eirik about it. Who had sown seeds of doubt about the dead cook. Who had not been by her side when any of the murders happened.

The idea unfolded slowly, like a green leaf in spring. She rolled her eyes and smiled indulgently at herself. *Ridiculous.* She had to be tired, or losing her mind, or both.

Nonsense.

Of course not.

But there was an ache in her bones and suddenly it was hard to sit still. She rose and walked purposefully out of the circle, just smiling when Freysteinn caught her eye. They'd agreed a rule of walking for fifteen heartbeats to relieve themselves – not too far, but not too close either. Feeling her mind starting to race along to catch the beat of her heart, she pushed against it. *Don't think. Just do.* As soon as she was out of sight, she changed direction and moved as quietly as possible to where Freysteinn had left his travel-sack. Her fingers were trembling and she fumbled the knot, but at last the leather thong was loose enough for her to reach in. Here was his spare tunic, his money pouch, a rag wrapped around a chunk of dried meat – and—

It was so small she might almost have missed it, but as if drawn to it, her questing fingertips found the tightly-knotted little bag no bigger than her thumb.

She eased it out and held it in her hand. She didn't need to untie it to know what the little hemp bag held, for the scent was unmistakeable.

Wolfsbane.

Her wolfsbane, in fact, that she'd so carefully harvested, chopped and dried.

Hot tears streaking down her cheeks, she shoved the poison back into the bag and as she did so, her thumb brushed against metal. She pulled it out and examined it, but with its short, thick blade and fiercely sharp edge there was no doubt about its function. This was a killer's weapon.

Words were stubbornly absent; all she could do was let the fury flow through her like a river in tumult winter.

He was a liar.

He'd made her believe in him, made her trust him – and all the while he'd been creeping around the town, murdering innocent people while she slept. He'd urged her to start thinking out loud and had distracted her with the idea of Big Rolf.

She'd needed him. *Need*. Orifa had even sent her a message – scratched it in her hand when she thought she was dying – and she'd missed it. A fresh wave of anger washed over her and she bared her teeth, standing there alone in the darkness, her mind running to the assassin's knife hidden in his bag and the idea of punching it right in between his ribs while he slept.

Then the part of her who wanted to live hissed at her to *damn well wake up!* Murdering Freysteinn in his sleep would only get her into more trouble – and what if he woke up at the wrong time? He was far stronger than she was, and more importantly, he was used to killing. What if she missed? Would he hesitate to do to her what he'd done to the others? Just because they'd shared a blanket all this season?

No, she'd have to go back to the others and figure out what to do. She forced herself to put the knife back and as she retied the knot, she noticed fury had calmed her down; she was no longer shaking. She replaced the travel-sack where they'd laid out their bedding for the night before tiptoeing back to the camp, her heart thumping.

She was sure everyone would know immediately what she'd discovered when they saw her face, but luckily, Jorunn was in the middle of yet another tale and the men were once again all caught in her snare. Helga eased herself back onto her log, the calm smile on her face belying the storm raging inside her, as much at her own stupidity as anything. It had all become clear now: Freysteinn had been spying on the council, trying to unsettle them. The boy must have been his accomplice; the father would have been asking questions.

But what of the others?

You do what has to be done.

She looked at him again, but now she could not see past his deeds. Underneath that beautiful face was a cruel killer and he was driving their carts straight into the heart of King Harald's lands. And what was she going to do? What *could* she do?

As the stars came out in the black sky above them, she found her answer.

Freysteinn had accepted her wincing explanation that she was still feeling weak from the sailing and after kissing her forehead gently, he had quickly fallen asleep, while Helga had lain awake wondering whether it was safe to close her eyes, whether he'd somehow smell the knowledge on her. Once she'd decided on her only possible course of action she managed to sleep, but it was fitful and she found herself starting awake at every small noise. When morning finally broke, she was the first to get up and get ready. While the men around her set about their tasks, seeing to the horses, reloading the carts and preparing to head off, Helga found Jorunn, as usual standing to one side, watching the others work.

With a light touch on the arm, she leaned in. 'I need to speak to you.'

Chapter 11

ANSWERS

Jorunn signalled for a halt. 'There – that's it,' she said, pointing to the west. Once they had cleared the Troll-forest, they'd found themselves back on heathland. They'd been mostly silent, each wrapped in their own thoughts, as they started making their way southeast, coming down into the land of the Jutes. There had been no other travellers to speak of; they'd seen a couple of riders in the distance once, but no one had crossed their path. The seagulls had been visible for a while, a sign that Hedeby was getting closer, but there'd been no other indications until now.

The lines of white cookfire smoke on the horizon looked like finger-bones, except there were too many of them. *Far too many. A forest of death.* Helga's stomach had been in knots all day as she thought about her choice. *But what could I do – or have done – differently?* The rage still burned in her, but now was not the time. Not yet.

'Freysteinn, you and Helga wait here. Rolf—'

The old man was prepared to go, and did not look like he needed any instructions..

All the same, she said authoritatively, as if they hadn't already discussed this, 'You'll take your boys in first.' Haki, standing beside the Northmen, looked grimly prepared. 'We will wait here until you are out of sight – we don't want them to see us together – but we'll be behind you.'

There were nods all around, but Helga's ears pricked up. *She sounds . . . nervous.*

For what felt like an age, Rolf's cart lumbered forward until at last it had passed Freysteinn's. Once they had an open road they trundled away, looking for all the world like an old man travelling to market with his two sons.

'It's all going to go well.' Freysteinn's voice was soothing.

Helga had to force her shoulders to relax, but she managed to tease a smile from somewhere. 'I hope you're right.'

'With them?' He glanced towards Jorunn and Nazreen, who were deep in conversation. 'I don't think anything could go wrong.'

I'm not so sure. Their body language was distracting; their discussion was animated and Nazreen was scowling.

Doubt crept into Helga's mind and she asked herself, *What's going on?* She focused on remembering to breathe, fighting the urge to slam her heels into Grundle's sides and gallop away. *No*, she told herself sternly, *he is going to pay for all these deaths – for everything he has done.*

Rolf's cart was moving so slowly it looked like it was standing still. *How far had they gone? Was it time?* It was hard to tell. The Northmen and Haki were about the size of a fingernail now.

'Freysteinn,' Helga didn't need to see Jorunn to tell that she was smiling. Her voice was practically dripping with honeyed invitation. 'Could you come here? I need your help.'

It had felt like it would never happen, but now it was, it happened so slowly. He swung off the cart, past Nazreen, who was reaching for something at the back, and moved towards Jorunn – and then there was a flurry of motion as the brown-skinned man turned instantly and leaped onto Freysteinn's back, forcing him down to the ground. He was no longer in Helga's sightline from where she sat safely on Grundle's back, but she could hear a muffled shout and a grunt – then Jorunn was there as well, also diving down out of sight.

There was a thump, an exhaled breath and a hissed command – and then silence. For a moment it was only her, sitting astride her horse in a foreign land, the sound of blood rushing like the sea in her ears and her heart thumping fit to burst – and the thought struck her again. *I could just leave. I could turn the horse around and ride.*

But she knew she couldn't. She had to know, and this was the best way.

The sounds of struggle started up again. Freysteinn gave a hissed curse and she turned around to see Nazreen dragging the younger man to his feet. Jorunn clambered up soon after, grinning fiercely and wiping blood from her mouth with her sleeve. She eyed up Freysteinn, pinned fast by Nazreen's arms, and delivered a vicious punch to his stomach. She glared at him as he doubled over and Helga thought she could see a Viking warlord's face in her features.

'Stand,' she snapped, and when Nazreen yanked him upright he gave a pained indrawn breath.

'What . . . is this?' Freysteinn croaked. Then his eyes flashed to Helga and he gasped, 'They've gone mad – run!' When the moment passed without her obeying him, a vague look of confusion passed over his face and he stared up at her, sitting there. 'Helga . . . ?'

I have no words. The thought was simple and pure in her head and it was accompanied by tears.

She looked at him and remembered and felt her heart shattering.

And then there was a moment: a flash of understanding in his eyes – so quick and cruel and then gone again so fast that she couldn't be sure that it had been real – then his head turned. A bitter cold coursed through her veins, squeezing her heart and filling her mouth. She bit down on the words, but somehow she couldn't stop the tears from falling. Luckily, the other three weren't looking at her.

'Did you kill them?' Jorunn's hand was on Freysteinn's jaw, forcing him to look her in the eye.

'What?'

'Uppsala. Did you kill them?'

Freysteinn stared at her until his face contorted with pain. Helga couldn't see what Nazreen was doing behind him, but it was clearly hurting a lot. 'Yes! Yes, I did.' His face went grey and he was breathing though pursed lips. 'Tell him to stop.'

Jorunn kept her eyes fixed on Freysteinn until he yelped, then she signalled to Nazreen and Freysteinn went limp in his arms.

'Next time, he wrenches your thumbs off. Understand? Why did you do it?'

From where she sat, Helga could see beads of cold sweat form on Freysteinn's forehead. 'I'm not telling you.' His chin jutted out, his nose turned up and for a moment he looked like a spoiled brat princeling. An image flashed through Helga's head involving her kneecap and his nose.

'Try again.' This time it was Jorunn who brought the pain, with a precise knuckle jab to the lower ribs. Freysteinn was trying his best to squirm away, but Nazreen had him in a vice-like grip.

'Please don't hurt me!' Freysteinn squealed, catching his breath. 'Please – I have silver in Hedeby – you can have it all! I just want to see the king – please!'

'Oh, you'll see the king, and we'll happily take everything you own, you snivelling little shit,' Jorunn growled. 'Now listen up: you'll be bound and put in the cart. If you say so much as a word, Nazreen here will eat your liver.'

The dark-skinned man was remaining studiously impassive, Helga noted.

Moving quickly, Jorunn rummaged in the cart and brought out ropes to tie up Freysteinn. Once she'd cleared space for her prisoner, Nazreen hoisted him up and booted him roughly into the corner.

At last Jorunn looked at Helga. 'What do you think we should do with him?'

Helga was quite unprepared for the question. *Think, girl*, she ordered herself, for Jorunn was watching her calmly. She glanced back at Nazreen, who was looking concerned, for some reason, but she brushed that from her mind; she could deal with that later. What made sense?

Go slow: nice and slow.

'What he says suggests he's one of Harald's men,' she started, testing out the logic as she spoke her thoughts aloud. 'So we could turn around, go back to Uppsala and hand him over to King Eirik.'

Jorunn thought for a moment. 'Yes, that would make sense. It's a long trip, though – and we've just sent our hunter ahead to the town.'

'On the other hand . . .' A plan was slowly forming in her head, although she couldn't yet tell if it was any good. 'On the other hand, we could continue on to Hedeby.' She paused to allow Jorunn to ask questions, but none were forthcoming, which made her happy. 'First, we now know something that King Harald doesn't know we know, which means we are in a strong position to get something out of him.' She dared a glance at Jorunn, who was looking delighted. Helga felt a sudden, unexpected surge of pride. 'And,' she continued, picking up speed, 'if we stash him safely outside the city walls, he could be of value in a trade.'

'What kind of trade?'

'I don't know yet.' Somehow, this admission made Helga feel both proud and strong: she was thinking on her feet, moving with the situation and working with what she had. 'But I'm sure we'll think of something.'

'That works,' Jorunn said. After a pause, she added, 'The old witch would have been proud of you.' With that, she moved back to the cart and sat gracefully on the driver's plank. As she started the cart rolling, Nazreen followed like a shadow.

She would have been proud of me. Helga felt warm inside. Everything had turned out far better than she'd hoped. She felt in control, like she'd finally earned Jorunn's respect.

Then she caught sight of Freysteinn and her happiness vanished. He had recovered far too quickly and now he just sat in the cart, staring at her, those bright blue eyes glinting.

With what? Mischief?

'You need to pick your friends better, girl.'

She bit down hard, pursed her lips and exhaled. 'Maybe,' she said, coldly, 'but at least I am not a coward and a liar.'

All she got in return was a wry smile. 'At least I am alive.'

The words came out before she could stop them. 'Did you ever love me?'

He looked at her as if he was seeing her for the first time. With a sneer playing across his lips, he said, 'No.' There was a brief pause, then, 'You were useful.'

'Quiet.' Nazreen's order was barked in the manner of someone who expects to be obeyed.

Closing her eyes slowly, biting her lower lip until it hurt, she turned her head away in order to stifle the first five things she wanted to say. She distracted herself by wondering if maybe Freysteinn's hatred of Nazreen was mutual. There was an edge to Jorunn's man now, like something had greatly displeased him. Whatever it was, he had certainly made Freysteinn shut up.

As the cart rattled on, Helga watched his head bobbing and enjoyed thinking of a number of things she could do to him with a knife, or a piece of string, or a rock, or a variety of other . . . useful things.

The words died in Breki's mouth, but this time Rolf did not chide him.

Haki shook himself. 'This place,' he muttered. 'This fucking place. I have never been here for longer than it took to unload and then set out again.'

'We'll be as quick as we can,' Big Rolf rumbled in a soothing voice. 'Get in, set up, drink with the locals, sell our wares, get out. And don't forget to keep your ears open.'

Breki looked at the massive wall facing them. It had to be the weight of a mountain, and high enough so that the bodies on it were no bigger than the size of his hand. Nothing felt possible here. This beast would swallow them whole.

When they moved slowly forward into the open maw of the wall, Big Rolf glanced back at him. 'If you're going to gawp, boy, look up as you go through.'

So Breki did. The ceiling had rows upon rows of holes. The tips of nasty-looking spears could just be seen in the darkness. They passed through the wall quickly, but all the while his imagination was racing: what would it be like, being caught in that tunnel, hemmed in by strong, crushing bodies? When they reached daylight, Big Rolf looked back at him. 'You saw the murder holes, so now you know that's who we're dealing with. The men, the women, the children – even the chickens are vicious here.'

This drew a chuckle from Haki. 'I've never seen the like,' he agreed. 'Those damn things could take a grown man's eye out.'

To their right, a confusion of huts sprang out of the ground like a mushroom field on a shadowy forest floor. Hordes of children flowed between them in an endless game of catch, dodging around – and occasionally colliding with – corners, people and horses. To the left they could see a field with rows upon rows of various leaves stretching to the curve of the wall. Far away they could see a huge field full of carts and traders' tents.

Breki tried to take it all in – for all Rolf had warned him, the sheer size of the place was hard to comprehend, and the shouts, bleats, cries and screams were already making his head ache. It stretched all the way down to the sea, which was a good long sprint away. He could see a clear, straight line running parallel with the coastline, cutting the town in half. Beyond it rose wooden halls, much grander than the huts and twice, even three times the size of his father's house. The most magnificent of all was the King's Hall, which was bigger than King Eirik's longhouse, if still dwarfed by the Godhouse of Uppsala. It towered over the other buildings, positively radiating menace.

'Old Harald really wants you to know you are in his town, doesn't he?' Big Rolf spat over the side. 'Not much time for big displays like that, myself.'

'That's pretty clear,' Haki said.

The laughter burst out of Breki like a fish caught on a line long before he realised it was coming.

'Hah! It's not just his blade, is it? He's as sharp as they come, and no lie,' Big Rolf exclaimed. 'That's a good one, my half-dead friend, and as such should be celebrated.' An artful pause, then, 'As was your mother.'

Haki grinned from ear to ear, resembling nothing so much as a hungry pike. And so they made their way towards the market-field, talking and joking and trying their best to convince each other that everything was fine.

Every leisurely step led them closer to Hedeby. A cold knot of worry growing in Helga's stomach was made worse by a sharp, barked command from Jorunn to Nazreen when, without any explanation he leaped onto the back of the cart and gestured for Freysteinn to rise. As the cart stopped, Nazreen whistled softly and his horse trotted up alongside.

'Get on.'

'With my hands tied behind my back? I'll fall,' Freysteinn said, sounding half cocky and half offended.

'Do it.' There was a hard edge to his voice.

Freysteinn moved to the side of the cart, but the gap between him and the horse was too wide.

'I can't do it – look, it's too far. I—'

The rest of the words disappeared in a great huff of expelled air as he doubled over from the hard punch to his gut.

Grabbing a handful of Freysteinn's tunic, Nazreen yanked the young man unceremoniously onto the back of the horse where he lay like a slain deer, still panting and grunting.

'I told you.'

Having apparently finished his conversation with Freysteinn, Nazreen looked up at Jorunn and snapped a short sentence in his language.

Helga wondered what they were keeping from Freysteinn – or her. *Are they . . . arguing?*

Jorunn looked serious at Nazreen's words, but when she turned back to Helga, the smile was back. 'He'll take our prisoner to a clearing in the forest we know; it's just outside the town, but safe enough. He'll guard Freysteinn there and await my orders.' While she was speaking, Nazreen had already clapped his heels to the horse's side and started off down the path.

Helga watched the man she had loved being hauled away, feeling an odd mixture of relief and sadness. The ride had taken most of the fury out of her, but there was still a lingering taste of bitterness in her mouth. She had been so determined . . .

She thought back on the sweet times, the closeness she'd never felt with anyone else, and for a moment she hated that she'd *had* to know; that she'd been so determined to search for answers, to find and make sense of things.

Why did I have to care about a stupid boy I didn't even know? She felt her jaw clench.

'He got to you, didn't he?' Jorunn's voice was full of knowledge and sympathy.

'He did.' Helga swallowed the bitterness. 'I believed him.'

'No reason not to. And he's not half bad to look at.'

She scanned her sister's face for any hint that she was being mocked, but there was none; instead, she had the strangest feeling that she had reclaimed her mother, but a softer, kinder version. 'I just . . . I feel like I should have known.'

Jorunn's smile broke her heart. It was wistful, bitter and sad at the same time. 'Oh, but you couldn't have. The only way to learn is to make mistakes.' She paused for a moment, then, 'When I was younger than you were, I ran away from Riverside because a boy asked me to. He was beautiful . . . on the outside. Once he had me to himself he became cruel and hard.'

'What happened?'

'Aslak tracked us down and slit his throat in his sleep.' Helga thought back on the youngest of the family, Aslak with the eyes of the fox, and shuddered. He might have been the runt of the litter but there had been an edge to him that his bear- and wolf-like brothers could not match. 'I cried for him, even when his beautiful face was ruined. Just like I suspect your decisions will make you cry.'

A warmth snuck into Helga from somewhere. After so many years on her own it felt good to have someone worried for her.

And then the path took them around a hillock and the sea opened up in front of them and at the edge where sea and land met, Hedeby sat like an ugly crab.

Jorunn must have seen her staring. 'It's unbelievable, isn't it?'

'It is,' Helga managed.

'I'm sure you're up to any challenge it throws at you.'

'I hope so,' Helga muttered.

Beside her, Jorunn gave a smile that looked reassuring.

They rode along in silence until they were close enough that the enormous wall curving away into the distance was blocking out almost everything in front of them. The guardsmen cast a bored glance their way and directed them through a gate into a corridor that smelled of packed dirt, bones and blood. The eerie silence inside was odd when compared to the constant sounds of wind and weather outside, but the moment they emerged into Hedeby itself, the noise of the town rushed towards them: market sounds in the distance, shouting from the docks, screaming children running after each other. They had gone about fifty paces when Jorunn stopped the cart and jumped off.

'Wait here.' The command was gently given and followed by a twinkling smile, and Helga watched her walk back towards the gate and summon a guard. They exchanged words, and at one point, looking towards her, Jorunn waved. Helga waved back, wondering what they were discussing.

When Jorunn returned she leaped effortlessly up onto the driver's plank.

'Everything going according to plan?'

'Yes,' Jorunn said, smiling. 'Everything is going exactly according to plan.'

The cries of the market traders hit Breki from all sides, but Big Rolf was clearly in his element, yapping questions and barking insults in a mixture of languages and accents as he guided the cart into a narrow space between a leather goods salesman and an old woman with a handcart of caged hens who were all squawking indignantly at their arrival. Before long Rolf had introduced himself and his two sons to the leather man, a Norse traveller named Sigvald, and the woman, Mette, whose meaningless guttural sounds Breki struggled to understand, but the prideful gesture towards the hovels must have meant that she considered Hedeby her home.

'Look busy,' Rolf snapped at him suddenly.

'Doing what?' Breki mumbled.

'Tend to the horse. Listen, watch and learn.'

Almost the moment he'd closed his mouth, a rangy, dark-haired man had approached and was pointing at the topmost furs, glorious black-and-white skunk pelts from the north. Breki watched with admiration as Big Rolf launched into a complicated mix of gesturing and arm-waving, interspersed with nods and shakes, pointing and frowning. It was clear, looking at Haki, that he had no idea what was going on either, but Big Rolf turned out to be very good at the game. The man left muttering, but he was carrying three lush pelts and Big Rolf had already made the plump purse he'd exchanged for them vanish somewhere about his person.

Rolf chuckled. 'I'd forgotten how fun it is to fleece someone.' Practically humming to himself, he went about rearranging the furs so that they showed to best advantage to attract the next buyers.

After a while, Breki began to tune in to the rhythms of the place. There was a certain way of moving, a certain noise to make, a certain sound to the haggling voice. 'It's like the sea,' he muttered.

Big Rolf, still grinning after selling the heavy pelt of a big elk, looked at him appraisingly. 'That is not a bad way to put it, stripling. There's a rise and a fall for sure. Found anything out?'

'I can't understand half of it.'

'No – if you've never met Danes before you really need to be at least half drunk to understand them.' He looked over at Haki, who was deep in conversation with someone selling axe-hafts. 'Bonehead over there looks to be doing a bit better.'

'He has travelled and seen things. I haven't.'

The grey-haired man looked kindly at him. 'You'll find your own wisdom, troll-child. You think, and that's more than can be said for a good half the men I ever sailed with.'

'Should we be worried that Jorunn hasn't showed up?'

Big Rolf's face clouded over, but after a while he said, 'No, they'll have been taking it slow, I reckon. They'll be here soon enough.' With that, he went back to rearranging the furs.

Breki looked around. There was only one way to wisdom, and that was to go and get it. The horses were long since groomed and fed and there was nothing else for him to do right now. He flexed his wounded hands; the sprained one was almost better now, but the left one was still hurting, making him wince. He edged away from the cart, thinking he'd just have a quick look around, maybe try to make himself useful.

He got some inquisitive glances from other traders, which he answered with a smile and a nod, which appeared to work as well as conversation, for the moment at least – but he was supposed to be a trader, so he guessed he should probably be paying some attention to the goods. But what a huge selection there was! He thought Jorunn's cart had been exciting, but this was ten times more. There were whole tents devoted just to amber jewellery! The woman next to them with the hens wasn't the only one selling livestock; a stocky farmer had put down five stakes and tied three healthy-looking sheep to each of them. He was already busy haggling with a shifty-eyed stork of a man, although Breki didn't know how he could negotiate with someone who appeared to be looking everywhere at once. Of course the animals were no match for the noble beasts of the North, but for weak Southern sheep, they didn't look too bad at all.

A little way further he came upon a carver – no, he was surely a master woodcarver, looking at the quality of his wares. He'd set up his cart to display a number of beautifully fashioned figures of the gods.

Breki couldn't help himself. He reached for an exquisitely carved Sleipnir, captured in full flight. When his fingertips touched the back of the figure, he thought he could almost smell the horse.

'Are these to your liking, Northman?' The carver was old, but he looked strong.

'It's . . .' Breki's voice trailed off as his fingers traced the musculature of the horse. 'It's . . . like the real thing.'

'I had a good model.' The old man chuckled at this as if he'd just told a joke. 'Now, what is a Karl of the North Wind's court doing this far south? A bit far away from home, aren't you?'

Breki blinked. Something in his head felt like he was watching a fire break out at night, somewhere far away, but he could neither hear nor smell it, so it couldn't be real. 'I am,' he said. 'But that's where you find the wisdom. Far from home.'

'Oho!' The old man sounded amused by this. 'You are word-wise, young Breki: a skald in the making. Odin's Spear rather than Thor's Hammer for you, I reckon.' Before he had had time to make sense of this, the old man was reaching down into his cart. He rattled around a bit, then pulled out a small sliver of wood, about the length of his thumb, tied up with a leather strip into a necklace.

'Here. Wear this and you will have the luck you deserve.'

In a daze, Breki put out his hand – it seemed to be the right thing to do. The necklace felt oddly heavy, but when he looked closer, he found his head beginning to swim. What had looked like just a piece of wood a moment ago suddenly seemed to be an intricately carved spear. One moment it was there . . . then it swam out of vision . . . then there were two. It was big, then small, then both at once. The leather felt a little warm to the touch as he grabbed it and slipped the loop over his head.

No sooner had he settled it under his tunic than there was a rough hand yanking his elbow and Big Rolf hissing, 'Move!'

'Where?' Idly, he wondered why he sounded sleepy.

'We're going. *Now*.'

Over Rolf's head, Breki could see their cart – and the daze instantly fell away from him. Haki was in front of it, facing off against five barrel-chested men. The way they stood together, the way they were holding themselves, clearly told of fights . . . a lot of fights.

'What's—?'

'It's a trap. Haki saw it and sprung it for us, the crazy bastard. He nearly booted me out of the way. Move now, or we all die.' With that Rolf pulled him to one side with surprising strength, then dragged him behind the leatherworker's tent, out of sight of the five fighters. 'Breki, you'll have to—'

Three men stepped into their path and Breki noticed there was an air of calm command about them, backed by the weight of their leather armour. The foremost one held out his hand, palm up, as if to say *Stop there!* and grinned, showing a missing front tooth.

Two quick steps and a hard right punch and the man went down, screaming silently, clutching his balls.

Breki stared for a moment at Big Rolf, but the old man's foot was already up and aimed at the second man's knee. Sounds of a fight rose up above the market hubbub and swallowed the crunch of cartilage and the scream of pain – and at last his own reflexes kicked in and Breki was bearing down on the third man, leading with his broken hand, but turning it just at the last moment into a sweeping elbow-blow that met the man's nose with a wet crunch. As the fighter sank to his knees, blood flowing from his face, he made a feeble attempt at grabbing for Breki, which was easily slapped away—

—and they were clear.

'What about the cart?' Breki whispered.

'The cart stays,' Big Rolf said, but a moment later he patted his hip, producing a heavy jangle of coin. He gave Breki a smug smile. 'Take only what you can carry. Wisdom, little bear.'

'I'd rather have two horses,' Breki said.

Big Rolf grinned at that too. 'You are not wrong at all, there. Do you think the king will sell us some? Slow down, will you?'

As they cleared the market-field, the main road beckoned. Two large men holding wrist-thick clubs came running towards them—

—and went straight past them.

'Our boy is going to need a lot of care after this,' Rolf mused, 'and if we don't use our brains to get out of here, we will too,' he added. 'Walk as if you've been here five times over and you're bored of the place.'

Breki did as he was told, all the while waiting for the thud of running feet behind him – but nothing happened and soon enough, the wall looming in front of them was stretching out to fill their horizon.

Far behind them, a shout went out from the market square.

'I reckon they'll have found our friend,' Big Rolf said.

'We will get caught.' A cold, bitter feeling was spreading in Breki's stomach – fear, but it wasn't like any he'd ever known.

'Unless . . .' Big Rolf's voice trailed off. He started fiddling with his belt. 'They're looking for two people, not one, so we need to split up. Take this. In a couple of days you'll be a lot wiser.' The purse was airborne. Breki caught it reflexively – and saw the back of Big Rolf, ducking into the warren of huts and almost immediately disappearing. His mouth opened to speak, but it had all happened too fast: Rolf was gone and Breki was on his own: a great flapping fish on foreign shores.

The slow *clip-clop* of horses coming from the tunnel through the wall dragged him to his senses again. Should he flee? Hide? At the last moment he turned and started walking back towards the market – they surely wouldn't expect him to be coming back into the city, he told himself, really hoping he was right. Rolf's advice rang in his ears – *act as if you belong* – so he didn't look back at the riders coming up behind him. He also tried to avoid looking at the riders on some very familiar horses thundering down the road from the market at speed. Five of them, there were, and all fired up for a scrap.

'Where are you headed?' The voice was gruff, coming from behind and above.

Breki turned. 'Me?'

'Don't see anyone else here,' the rider said. He was somewhere north of twenty winters, but already looked hardened enough for thirty. A shock of black hair gave him a furious appearance, not helped by a rough black beard and piercing blue eyes. Another horse trailed placidly after him.

'Towards the boats.' Sound bored and they'll believe you.

'Looking for work?'

'Possibly.'

'I need hands on oars. One of my oarsmen had a . . . listening accident.'

Breki looked at the riderless horse and the absolute lack of remorse in the young man's eyes. 'Unfortunate,' he replied.

The rider grinned. 'Indeed. He wasn't listening when we talked about the shares and how you shouldn't take other people's. Are you good at listening, boy?'

'One of my strengths. However, I am one-handed at the moment.' He raised his left hand. 'Should heal soon enough.'

'You look like you'd equal most men with one hand. What happened?'

'Snapped it while wrestling.'

The rider looked him up and down, critically. 'Who?'

'Ludin of Skane.'

'Hah! And you're alive? You're either a liar, a bastard or a beast. Either way, you're on my boat. Get on the horse.'

Breki did as he was told, soothing the animal as it protested under his weight. The wooden pendant weighed heavy on his chest.

Moments later, riders pulled up in front of them. 'Well met, Ormar,' the first one said, a mixture of deference and dislike in his voice.

'Well met, Thrainn. Why are you stopping me?'

'We're looking for two men – the king wants 'em. Breki and Rolf, they're called. Northerners.'

The guards stared intently at him, but Breki set his face to stone and held on to the reins with both hands.

'And?' Ormar looked utterly unconcerned by the threatening glares as beside him, Breki fought to continue looking bored. 'This is my crewmate, Bjorn.' Looking away from the guards, the black-beard winked at him.

For a moment the man in front of the five looked like he might be thinking about challenging the man called Ormar, then he clearly thought better of it. 'They must have got out. Go!' He put his heels to his horse and charged on, the other four following him out of the gate.

Once they were out of sight, Ormar looked Breki up and down again, apparently mulling something over. 'I think it's time to see what the whale-road offers today,' he said at last. 'I've had as much of this place as I can be bothered with. I think maybe we'll sail off while the king is distracted.'

Breki swallowed. 'Not going to disagree there.'

Ormar studied him again, then at last he smiled. 'And wise, too. You'll do, Bjorn.' Then he turned his horse towards the sea and urged the beast into a fast walk. A moment later, Breki's horse followed.

As Helga's eyes adjusted to the dark of the longhouse, she thought back on what she'd seen since they came into town and found she couldn't remember much of it. The cart had rattled on through the gates and into Hedeby and there had simply been too much to look at and listen to. *Too much to smell, too; Nazreen hadn't been wrong about that*. So many people huddled together stank far worse than anything she'd come across at the farm, or even in Uppsala.

Now she was standing on her own, waiting in the middle of the floor, uncomfortably aware of the men who had come to stand by the door when they'd entered. They looked very much like they would fit right in with Ludin's raiding party. About twenty paces away was a grand dais with an elaborately carved high seat. Jorunn was talking to someone off to their left, a tall man who reminded Helga of a miserable stork. Jorunn looked furious – just a moment earlier she had been berating the man, whom she'd called Frode, for losing something or someone and now she was demanding to see someone else.

She and Jorunn hadn't discussed their plan much further. It had felt so natural, so fluid, as if Hildigunnur had been with them. Last night's discovery had been almost too big to comprehend, but in the swirl of violent emotions it had still taken all her courage to tell Jorunn of her suspicion. She had been impressed by how calm Jorunn had been and how she had made her mind up about what to do in an instant.

And you took that to mean that the two of you could therefore walk into the hall of the most feared king in all the Viking lands and simply – what? She wanted to argue with the voice in her head, to shout at it, but the truth of the matter was that she hadn't thought through the options and now she felt foolish for that. Jorunn had motioned for her to stay and be patient and of course that was the right thing, but Helga was aching to *do* something. She was about to stride over and invent some reason for both of them to make their excuses, leave and regroup when a wave of deference swept the hall and simultaneously, a booming voice announced the arrival of King Harald. All around her, burly warriors and serving thralls alike averted their gaze. *Do it,* her mother's voice whispered in her ear and Helga instantly obeyed. The hard-packed floor looked like it had seen its share of spilled mead. *And here I am, doing what I'm told.* Anger flared and when she heard footsteps, Helga glanced up at the dais.

It took her a moment to add up everything she was seeing. She searched for the right word to describe the man on the throne. *Disappointing.* She had expected a younger version of her father, or someone like Alfgeir Bjorne: a giant leader to strike fear into anyone who looked upon him. But the King of the Danes looked a little . . . well, soft. The kind of man who turned old before his time.

Then Helga noticed Jorunn was striding across the floor to stand next to her and the tall man she had been arguing with had gone straight to the king's side and was whispering in his ear, although whatever it was he had to say didn't seem to be interesting the king.

Then Harald Bluetooth caught her looking at him and Helga felt like she had been nailed to the spot.

This must be what the mouse feels when it meets the cat.

Almost lazily, the king raised his hand and silenced the man, Frode. He took another long look at Helga and smiled. She lowered her gaze immediately, cheeks burning and heart thumping.

'Jorunn,' the king said. His voice was warm and inviting, but Helga didn't dare look up to see what was happening.

'My Lord.' Jorunn, on the other hand, was meek and apologetic.

'You have returned.'

'I have.' There was a brief hint of hesitation in her voice, then, 'Is Sigmar not here?'

For an eye-blink all Helga could hear was the rush of blood in her ears. *You have returned.* She tried desperately to catch hold of her own thoughts and make sense of those words.

'You are late,' the king said. 'Your husband has been sent to attend to . . . other matters.'

If the silence was an invitation to ask questions, Jorunn was wise enough not to take it. Her voice rang out, breaking Helga's heart. 'I can tell you everything about King Eirik's defences, his strength in men and how the town will fare against attacks from the west and south.'

A dull ache started throbbing in Helga's teeth and she realised her jaws had slammed shut.

I can tell you everything.

She started arguing with herself, feverishly. *This is a ploy. Jorunn is stringing him along, like you do with a big fish.*

'Mm.' The king sounded less than impressed. 'And?'

'And I found this rat here, who nearly ruined everything we had prepared for.' Jorunn looked over her shoulder and to her horror Helga became aware of Nazreen, standing by the door, with Freysteinn, still bound.

No – that is not the plan. Nazreen should be outside. We should be negotiating. This is not—

But as her senses returned, so did the realisation that she had lost.

She was overflowing with shame and fury: she had been fooled.

Jorunn is one of them.

She felt like a fox in a den of hounds, condemned to stand still and make no sound, draw no attention.

'Everything *you* had prepared for.'

'Yes, my Lord – of course. I grabbed him and brought him back to you for you to do with as you wish. He says he wants to see you. His name is Freysteinn.'

There was a brief silence as Nazreen pushed Freysteinn forward. Out of the corner of her eye Helga saw him kneel with annoying grace despite having his hands tied behind his back.

There was a touch of amusement in the king's voice. 'I know who he is. Second son of a farmer two days' ride to the north. No one of note.' There was a pause. No one rushed to fill it. 'Tell me what he did.'

Helga could sense the shift in Jorunn's voice, the edge and the accusation. 'He had already been there for a few months when we got there. He killed three people and wounded another.'

'Hm.' There was a brief pause and a scuffing of feet as Harald Bluetooth rose. 'Is this true, Freysteinn?'

'My king.' Freysteinn sounded both deferential and defiant. 'I wished to earn my name by unsettling the council in your favour and breaking the alliance. I was heading towards the market-field when I happened to hear Frode say that King Eirik was a nuisance, and after the Jomsvikings came to stay I figured you might use them to get at the Svear. I went there to do what I could.'

The silence that followed was uncomfortable. Helga wished that she could look up, read the people, but from the feel of tension in the room she guessed that the king was looking at Freysteinn, waiting for him to say more. She didn't need her mother to whisper, *People will fill a silence.*

'He killed a boy in the forest,' Jorunn put in. 'That's what started it.'

'He followed me from here,' Freysteinn added hastily. 'He wanted to steal my glory. I told him to stay out of sight, but then he started going to the farms around Uppsala, asking questions – and I thought he would be of more use dead.'

'Then he crushed the throat of a man named Alvar Dal – just outside King Eirik's house, after a feast. He was my cook.'

And you sound angrier about the loss of a meal than a life, Helga thought savagely.

'He was asking questions,' Freysteinn put in. 'And if I'd known Jorunn had been sent by you, I would still have done it.'

'Why?' The king sounded interested, dangerously so, and despite everything Freysteinn had done, to her and to others – and with no idea why – Helga found herself fearing for him.

The young man clearly did not share her concerns. 'Because she was being too slow to act,' he replied, and just at the edge of hearing, Helga heard Jorunn hiss with contempt. 'Then I wounded Ludin's advisor because I knew that would drive the old dog furious – which it did – and then I mixed a whole heap of wolfsbane in a thick-skulled brawler's drink on the eve of Styrbjorn's attack.'

'You've braved danger to seek your name and acted to bring honour to Jutland, and to me.' The king's voice was studiously neutral, but Helga could hear him moving.

'All I had to do was to lie well enough to get these two to bring me here to you, so I could tell you of my deeds and get what I deserve. I wanted to get the Svear to fear their own shadows, to ready them for the planned invasion.'

'Get what you deserve.' The king sounded calm, and closer.

If she shifted her head a tiny bit, *just* so, Helga could see his feet.

'And what made you think you knew my plans?'

'I – uh—' And for the first time, Freysteinn faltered. Helga wondered if he knew that a note of fear had crept into his voice. 'Defeating the Svear – taking their lands . . . I—'

'You thought you were allowed to make your own decision.' The king's voice was cold.

There was a thud, a wet cough, a sucking *pull*. Something thumped to the ground.

Then there was silence.

'And so you get what you deserve. It is important to follow orders,' King Harald said shortly. 'And I have no time for self-made shadow-walkers. Throw the body to the pigs.' As an afterthought, he added, 'And Frode? A handful of silver to his father. I'm sure he'll understand.'

Unseen feet moved swiftly and the sound of heels being dragged on the ground followed shortly. Unable to stop herself, Helga twisted her head slightly to the side and saw Freysteinn's body hanging slack. A rose of blood was blooming on his chest. She had a moment to register that seeing his eyes wide open and lifeless was hurting her like nothing had before – just a moment – and then the king, sheathing a cleaned and well-used knife, asked, 'Now tell me, who is the girl?'

Pushing all feelings away and keeping her stare to the ground, Helga tried to draw herself into her own body, become invisible – but it was no good. Every eye in the hall was trained on her.

'The girl,' Jorunn said, purring, 'is from my past. She lived with my parents, but she was a cuckoo in the nest. Then she *lied*' – the sudden burst of fury in her voice was subdued just as swiftly – 'she lied to my father and cast my name in the mud. With your permission, my lord, I wish to add her to the pen.'

Helga felt numb. She was going to follow in Freysteinn's footsteps after all. She'd heard tales of fat pigs eating anything thrown in with them. *They are going to slit my throat and throw me to the swine.*

Her mind replayed the conversations with Jorunn: the smiles; her words, the sideways looks. *Compliment them. Show strength, but not too much. A little weakness goes a long way.*

Helga had been too blinded by love in the beginning, but she had at last realised what Freysteinn had been doing to her – but she had never even noticed Jorunn doing exactly the same thing. The daughter of Hildigunnur had baited her and hooked her and reeled her in like a fish.

'Hm.' King Harald looked her over once again. 'She looks

familiar. I reckon I may have met her father once.' He smiled to himself. 'If that is your wish, I will not deny you.' He gestured to two of the hard men. 'Put her in the pen.'

Rough hands seized her by the arms and before she could think of a word to say, she was being half-pushed, half-dragged out of the King's Hall. The last thing she saw was Jorunn, leaning in conspiratorially towards the king, no doubt starting on an exquisitely crafted joke.

The journey was weird, like a bad dream, but one that was oddly calm. She felt nothing, understood nothing and wanted nothing. She was barely conscious of the rough wood of the door hitting her heels, despite the dull pain. She thought the guardsman who was cursing at her in the language of the Danes should probably chew some burdock if he wanted to keep the rest of his teeth. The smell of Hedeby – rotting fish, people stench and offal – slapped her in the face but she didn't recoil because it didn't matter. Nothing mattered. She was about to die.

And then here they were: the pen.

It wasn't so much a pen as a small barn, some thirty paces long by twenty wide, with a door at one end. She could neither see nor smell pigs, and even in her dazed state that came as something of a relief. When the guard opened the door and pushed her in she found the floor had been dug down by an arm's-length and stones that looked like they'd be heavier than three grown men, each with a number of iron loops driven into them, had been placed at intervals on the ground. The loops were clearly for tethering people; Helga didn't need to look at the handful of beaten-down, miserable creatures tied up there to know that. None of them gave her more than a cursory look when she was dragged in.

'What is this?' she muttered, despite herself, not expecting anyone to answer.

The guardsman surprised her. 'It's the thrall pen,' he told her, licking his lips. 'You're to be sold tomorrow.' He looked her up and down. 'You'll make them a bloody fortune, too, lucky buggers. Oh, and you can rid your pretty little head of any thoughts of rescue. No one escapes King Harald's pen. You'll be bound for Rus, lovey, where you'll be chained under some filthy bear's furs for the rest of your life. And if you think to run away, well, you'll die in the woods – cold, starvation, or et by savage beasts. Have fun!' He twisted her arm roughly, pinning it in the nook of his elbow, and she felt the rope biting into her wrist.

Moments later she was just another thrall, roped to a rock.

As she watched the door close behind the departing guard, a growl started somewhere deep in her throat and built up into an ear-splitting shriek, shocking her as much as anyone else in the barn.

'Now, now, let's have none of that,' came a creaky voice from the shadows. 'Be a nice little lamb.' A bent old man shuffled out of the darkness. He spoke softly, but the long cudgel in his hand was sturdy and clearly well-used.

Helga rounded on him and almost without her volition, words burst from her mouth. 'Don't you tell me what to do, you crusty old f—'

The speed with which the others recoiled startled her and she took her eyes off the old man, just for a moment. The gaoler, much lighter on his feet than his looks and age would have suggested, took two steps towards her and hit her hard on the thigh. Helga turned to spring at him, but her leg buckled just as the rope snapped taut.

'Good little lamb,' he crooned. 'You be quiet-like, yes? Or next time you do that, I hit you twice – and I hit someone else as well. And they don't like that, they don't. And you have to sleep somewhere. You want the other lambs to be your friends, don't you? If you make me hit them they might not like you. They might strangle you in your sleep. Wouldn't that be bad? Yes, yes, it would.'

Helga looked up at the old man, silent tears flooding down her face. She dropped her head in mute acquiescence.

The old man smiled. He was missing half his lower teeth and his lips were an uncomfortable purple colour. 'Good little lamb.'

And with that, he shuffled back to a three-legged stool set in the far corner, leaned against the wall and slumped into a position that looked half like sleep and half like death.

Time slowed to a halt in the pen. She hadn't tested her leg after the attack; she didn't think it was broken, but it was throbbing viciously and she could imagine the bruise blossoming there. What she desperately needed was some rest, and time to gather her senses, marshal her thoughts. Helga sank further into herself. Even though she had plenty, this was not the time for questions. Instead, she needed to heal. Heal – and rest. The last thing she remembered was a throwaway line from the king.

I think I met her father once.

*

When the door swung open there was no mistaking the night sky.

Escape.

The idea burst into her head – and was just as quickly quashed as she felt the heavy plaited rope around her wrist. She'd already tested the iron loop hammered into the rock, but as she'd feared, it was as solid as the stone itself, which wasn't budging. She was truly imprisoned.

And now Jorunn stood in the doorway, looking down at her. 'How does it feel?' She didn't wait for an answer as she made her way down to where Helga was lying. 'How does it feel to be' – Jorunn knelt and stroked her cheek – 'helpless?' There was a definite smell of mead on her breath.

Helga searched for words, but there were none; all she had was a cold, crushing feeling in her chest.

'I swung by the pigs before I got here,' Jorunn said. 'They've been well fed.' She looked almost disappointed when Helga didn't react. 'He got what he deserved,' she snarled. 'Harald told me – in confidence, of course – that he never wanted the council to break. He just wanted me to watch them to see how they would react to an invasion – and he wanted them to get Styrbjorn out of his way. The rest was just fun – making the men sit, bark and bite on my command. They were easy to manipulate. Freysteinn was young, greedy and stupid – just like you,' she added viciously.

She stood up and looked down at Helga. Her lip twisted in a sneer. 'I saw you coming a thousand paces away, with your pathetic need to be accepted and recognised . . . *sister*.' The hate in her voice burned hot. 'I thought about keeping my promise from that time, slicing you up, seeing if you've truly got water in your veins.' She leaned in again. 'But in truth, it is more fun to imagine you ripped open by a village full of Rus brutes, again – and again – and again. Maybe they'll not even wait but start on the boat – that'll get you to the place you deserve in the world, you yappy little bitch.' Jorunn stared at her, her beautiful face ugly with rage and hatred.

Is she waiting for me to speak up or lash out? But the words were still hiding from Helga. *I have nothing. I can't . . . Just . . . go away.* She felt herself withering under Jorunn's harsh glare – and then the glob of spit hit her right across the eyes. It was warm and wet and slimy to the touch.

Whatever had been holding Helga up left her then and she sank to the floor.

'You were *never* worthy of Riverside,' Jorunn snapped. 'There's no fight in you. Go and *rot*, Helga of no name.'

From where she lay, Jorunn looked impossibly tall. Helga could see the scorn in her face matching her words. Then she turned around and stalked out.

Helga blinked. Tears were still filling her eyes, everything was swimming and her breath would only come in gasps. She wished the world away, but nothing was changing. At last, mustering all the strength she had left, she wiped the spittle off her face, then, closing her eyes—

—she was interrupted by muttered voices outside.

The door creaked open again and the old guard huffed, 'Now what? My little lambs need their sleep if they're to be their best on the block, you know . . .'

The smell of the outside drifted in behind two forms. In the half-light Helga could just make out their faces: young men, toughened, but not yet set. The other thralls had either edged away towards the walls or were lying completely still, pretending to be asleep.

One of the men spoke. 'Go and take a break, Halvar.' There was kindness in his voice. 'There is mead in the hall – I am sure no one would begrudge you a moment's warmth and a comforting sup against the chill night air.'

'Hmph,' the old man snorted. 'And who told you to come for me, then, Athelstan? Have you been set to watch the lambs?'

'Frode told us to fetch you,' the other blurted out.

Helga's heart started racing and she shivered. *No. Please—* She could feel dread rushing through the pen; she could see it in the eyes of the other thralls. *They know what's coming. They've seen it before.*

Huffing and puffing, the old warden shuffled up, but stopping in the doorway, he looked fiercely at the two young men. 'You look after them proper, mind,' he said. 'Don't let them . . . hurt themselves.'

'We won't,' said the first, Athelstan, smiling as the door closed. Then he turned to the second one and his voice was suddenly cold as he repeated, 'Frode?'

'I didn't know what to say . . .'

In the dim light, Helga could just about make out the difference between them. The first one, Athelstan, the one in charge, was slimmer and had long blond hair. The second one, currently standing with his back to her, had an ornate ring around his muscular upper arm. He had broad shoulders and one thick braid hanging down his back.

Brains and brawn. She filed the information slowly, feeling like high winter inside. *Think!* But her mind wouldn't comply. The inevitability of her fate was almost suffocating her.

'Maybe just keep your mouth shut in the future, Egon,' Athelstan said, 'and let me do the talking? In any case, Frode is busy running the king's errands. We'll break her in and blame it on the old man. After all, Jorunn will want to see the pain on her when she staggers to the boat.'

'And she'll reward us too,' the big man said, licking his lips.

'Yeah,' said Athelstan, turning towards Helga. 'And remember what she said in the hall: the bitch lied about her.' He looked down at Helga. 'So now she will suffer.'

The light from the torch behind them had turned their faces into shadows, but there was no mistaking the set of their shoulders. As they took their first step towards her, Helga pulled on the heavy cord tying her to the stone, but of course it didn't budge. As wordless terror overtook her, she suddenly remembered finding a bloodied leg in a trap back on the farm, and what her father had said to her: *A cornered animal is a dangerous thing.*

The young men were moving towards her, slowly, savouring her fear, as if they had all the time in the world. Her hands balled into fists and she got ready to strike—

—when the blond man's fist smashed into her jaw and sent her spinning to the ground. She was nauseous and dizzied by the impact, but she could still feel his hand on her head – followed by the burning sensation of being dragged to her feet by her hair.

FIGHT! she screamed at herself, fury welling up again, and she flailed at him, but blinded by rage and tears, she missed completely, and before she could gather herself, the wind was knocked out of her with a blow that felt wider than she was.

Bile rose in her throat but all her muscles fought to keep it down. Gasping dryly, she felt the panic rising—

—and a sharp pain lanced across her face and her knees gave way and somewhere, in the back of her head, Hildigunnur winked at her and mouthed something and Helga . . .

. . . laughed.

'Why is she laughing? Make her stop,' the big man growled.

'Good, Athelstan,' Helga hissed. 'That's just what we agreed.'

'What are you talking about?' the blond man snarled, levelling a hard kick at her.

A dull ache blossomed in her hip, but she gritted her teeth together and pushing away pain, thought and hesitation, said firmly, 'I think that's convincing enough.' She twisted her head so she was looking up at the big man and snapped, 'You're Egon.'

'Yes . . .'

'Shut up, Egon,' Athelstan hissed, but he hadn't moved; he'd clearly been thrown by her words.

'That makes sense,' Helga said, salting her voice with disdain and authority, even though that was a million paces from how she was feeling.

What would Jorunn do? The thought running through her head was so bitterly funny that she found herself chuckling.

'Why are you *laughing*?' Egon sounded furious. He grabbed a handful of her tunic in his meaty fingers and lifted her up.

'Slow down, Egon . . .' Athelstan suddenly sounded a lot less confident. 'That's too much—'

Helga fixed her eyes on the blond man and ordered, 'Now! It's time, lover! Kill him!'

As Egon's eyes flashed with fury and realisation, he threw Helga to the ground and whipped around on Athelstan, screaming, 'I *knew* it.'

'You said you'd never forgive him,' Helga rasped. She had to bite down hard to keep herself from sobbing. Every single bit of her was hurting.

'You should have done it properly,' Egon growled. 'You should have declared your intent rather than just sneaking off into the woods for a quick tumble with her.'

'I – what? Sigrun? No! No – I don't care about that—'

'Oh, so my cousin is nothing to you, is she?' Egon took a swipe at Athelstan, who only just managed to dodge out of his way in time. 'You were mad enough about it when I told my father, as I recall . . .'

'That's because you were a shitty little coward about it,' Athelstan snapped, all the while backing towards the door. 'You should have come to me and settled it then and there. Now calm down—'

'I'll fucking calm down when I'm sitting on your broken legs,' the big man growled, lunging for Athelstan, who jumped aside, then turned and ran, with Egon hot on his heels, roaring like a bear.

Moments later, all that remained of the pair of them was a wooden door creaking on rusted hinges. Helga raised herself up on her elbows, winced at the burning feeling in her wrist where the cords had rubbed her raw and stared at the doorway.

Freedom. It was there—

And then she heard the huff and puff of the old guard, muttering to himself as he shuffled back to his post. '. . . not fit for work . . . Idiot cubs . . . chasing and hollering like that . . .' She could only catch snatches of his words, and by then he was back in his corner and sitting on his stool. A faint smell of mead wafted from him.

Helga could feel his eyes on her as he scanned his domain. Satisfied that no one was dead, he settled back and closed his eyes.

Helga sobbed and hugged herself with one arm. Everything hurt, badly.

The throbbing in her abdomen contrasted with the sharp pain in her scalp and she fully expected her fingers to come away sticky as she searched for any open wounds, but she couldn't find anything except a hotness in her skin and the tenderness of blooming bruises. Her cheeks and forehead were warm to the touch as well, and her jaw was swelling where Athelstan had punched her.

She suddenly realised people were watching her. Some of the thralls looked hard and resentful, although she had no idea what she'd done to earn that sort of reaction. Others were clearly terrified. *Well, I can't blame them for that – so am I.* All of the thralls were keeping silent, from years of habit, no doubt, but for some reason it was obvious they were very much against her. She tried to imagine what they were thinking.

You're a trouble-maker . . .

You've drawn attention to us . . .

They'll be back, and this time they might not stop with you . . .

They'll be back.

They'll be back.

It was a whisper at the back of her head, an insistent whistle where the wind got in through the cracks. One or both of them would be back and her ploy would not hold a second time. She might indeed just have made things even worse for herself . . .

She looked at the rope around her wrist. The emptiness in her chest threatened to grow bigger and bigger, opening up until she'd caved in on herself and broken completely. And if that happened, that would be it and she would be lost forever.

But Helga remembered standing up straight and looking the world in the eye, moving under her own strength, going where she wanted, and she muttered hoarsely, 'No.'

No. I will not give up.

'No,' Helga croaked.

Don't let her win.

Don't let her break you.

'No,' Helga whispered.

She pushed herself up to a sitting position – and at that moment there was a loud snore from the corner.

Something ignited in Helga's chest and she stared in wonder at her fingers. Then she knelt and scratched in the packed earth, muttering as she went.

Hagalaz for force.

Thurisaz for conflict.

Laguz for dreams.

Nauth for need.

She blinked at the runes by her feet and felt like she could see them glowing in the darkness. Glaring at the lumpen shape in the corner, she hissed, 'Take what you have so freely given, *shepherd*.' The heat of her rage burned through the pain and made her jaw clench so hard she thought she could feel her teeth break.

The old man guard coughed in his sleep, almost as if he'd heard her. The silence that followed was far deeper than usual.

Uncomfortably aware of the pounding of her own pulse, Helga looked around. The other thralls were nothing but dark blotches, all lying motionless, but she could still feel their eyes on her.

'What?' Helga whispered. 'I didn't – I didn't kill him!' But the old man was neither moving nor making any sounds. *I don't think I did . . . ?* She felt panic rising – and then she remembered the floor of the King's Hall in Uppsala, and saving a dying man.

Why bother saving men? her mother's voice whispered in the back of her head. *They'll only find other ways to get themselves killed.*

She couldn't help but smile at that – and suddenly the rope and the ring were an insult and a challenge and the rock was an opportunity. Kneeling, she let her fingertips search along the base of the stone for anything she could use – and there it was: the hint of a shape in the rock. She followed it down, felt her heart thumping as the shape grew under her hand. Scrabbling in the dirt, she found what she was looking for: an edge, no more than a thumb's worth and buried three fingers deep, but it would be enough. Soon enough, ignoring sore, bruised fingers and nails torn off to the quick, she had shifted enough of the hard-packed dirt to push her arm down and run the rope along the edge. *Don't rush, but don't stop . . . keep it nice and steady, now . . .* Time stretched,

Surely the scuffling sounds of rope rasping against rock must be the noisiest thing in the world – then she felt one strand of the rope give way, not enough to loosen the hold on her wrist, not yet, but soon . . .

Hope swelled in her and she rubbed harder. Another strand went, and another. Her skin was red-raw, but she made it fuel her anger. She lifted her wrist to her lips and tried the rope with her teeth, but it was still too strong for her to tear apart.

Not quite.

She steeled herself and started rubbing again, her shoulders and elbows aching from the odd motion, her wrist feeling like it was being held to the fire – but another thread gave, and another – and suddenly the noose was shifting around her wrist, and she *pulled*. Her thumb joint burned as the rope squeezed the bones in her hand, but she laved her wrist and hand with her tongue before clamping her teeth together against the agony and going back to *pulling* and this time, the rope shifted, a hair's-breadth at a time – until suddenly her hand popped free and she almost fell over.

She stifled her shout of triumph; she might be free of the stone, but she was not yet free of Hedeby and King Harald and Jorunn . . .

And then the old man in the corner gave a gasping breath that became a snore and a cough and she shifted back to her stone, her heart thundering in her chest. He muttered something that she couldn't make out, then, with a decisive '*Hrrmph*' dropped his chin to his chest and went back to sleep.

She could hear loud singing drifting in the night from somewhere: they were already drunk, then. Looked like the Dane men weren't much different from the Svear when it came to holding their mead. And it was dark now.

Don't think. Just run.

But she couldn't run. Terror had all but paralysed her. Now, talking softly to herself as if she were a spooked horse, she forced herself to stand up, to move, until, step by stealthy step, she was making her way towards the door.

No one was saying a word; the only sound now was the soft snoring of the old guard on his stool.

She leaned against the door until it started shifting, flinching as it creaked open, but still nothing else in the pen moved. At last the gap was just wide enough for her to slip through.

The door closed silently behind her and heart pounding, body, throbbing, Helga stood with her back to the pen and fought the almost overwhelming instinct to *run run right now run—!*

The dark blue sky above still held the memory of sunlight, but night had overwhelmed the buildings and everywhere she looked was ominous with the promise of men lurking in shadows. The loudest noises were coming from the King's Hall, but she could hear arguments and shouted conversations from all sides. For a moment she considered diving back in and taking her chances. The old guard might wake at any moment. Maybe she could negotiate?

Move. Move! Now she forced herself to stand up straight, to carry herself like she had a right to be here and she knew where she was going. After a moment more to let her eyes and ears adjust to the darkness, she set off, stopping just a few paces further on and sidestepping to avoid a huge staggering shape – who proceeded to vomit loudly, just on the very place where she'd been standing.

He'll suffer in the morning, she thought, and to her surprise, found herself laughing at herself for even caring. But her mind was clearing despite the pain and fear and now she knew what she had to do.

I have to find her.

She still had to order herself to get moving again, but fighting off tears, she started walking more purposefully, trying to ignore her surroundings, even as the stench of Hedeby, the loud noises, the fear and the memory of Jorunn's hate-filled breath on her face, all threatened to overwhelm her.

And suddenly she heard a horse whinnying in the distance and her heart beat faster. *Grundle!* Just in time, she stopped herself from breaking into a lopsided run, desperate to put the raucous singing of King Harald's hall behind her, but it would not do to draw attention to herself, not now, when escape was so nearly in sight.

The journey through the town had her heart thumping as she jumped at every shadow, but at last she reached the corral, which was set close to an open space housing more carts than she'd ever seen at one time. *This must be the market-field.* She scanned the area for movement, but the place was still. A familiar smell met her nose. *I'd happily stick my face in horseshit to get away from the stench of this hateful place.* She dismissed the thought and her worries fell away as she edged into the corral.

'Grundle?' she whispered. 'I'm here, girl!'

At the far end of the field there was movement and one of the shapes shifted and changed, and as it started to move, Helga's heart moved with it. It felt like moments and a lifetime later that Grundle was standing next to her, nudging her side with her big head and snorting, asking where she'd been.

'Best you don't,' she whispered, and then the words caught in her throat and hot tears streaked down her cheeks. 'But we have to go.'

Grundle nuzzled her for a moment – then she stopped and her ears pricked up.

Behind Helga, a soft voice said, 'She is wise, the horse.'

She turned around slowly. Even in the dark, there was no mistaking his silhouette. Looking at Nazreen, standing by the open gate, desperate pleas and brazen challenges alike died unspoken on her lips.

That's it, then.

'Wh— What do you mean?'

'She knows what you have to do.'

'And what might that be?' She hated how thin and childish her voice sounded.

Come on, then, get on with it. Don't drag it out just for fun.

'She is wise. She knows that the gates are closed at night and so you cannot ride away. And she is sad.'

Nazreen's words caught up with her and Helga blinked.

'She understands goodbye,' Nazreen said softly.

Grundle snorted and nuzzled Helga's hand.

'You must come with me now.' Nazreen turned and walked off.

There is nowhere to run. 'I'll be back, girl,' Helga whispered to Grundle, not believing a word she said, but she had to say something.

Then she followed Nazreen's shadowy form as he left the corral. 'Nazreen!' she hissed, 'please – wait—' She had no idea what she could ask him that he could give her.

Sixty paces more and he stopped and turned to face her.

She cursed the darkness, unable to make out much except the bright flash of his eyes. *What is he thinking? Is he pleased that he has rounded me up, like a stray?* Approaching, she tried to remember how to be attractive, but her mind gave her nothing. Preparing to ask him where they were going she tried to make her voice drip with honey, but it only made her cough.

Nazreen's voice dropped to a whisper. 'Ssh. You must not make noise.'

Hold steady, girl. The memory of Hildigunnur helped her slow down and instead of pleading with him, as she'd intended, she said nothing and just listened to what he had to say.

'Do you trust your horse?'

What? She had expected questions, but not that one. *I do. And she trusts you.* 'Uh – yes.'

'You must take a small boat and sail into the night and hope the djinns in your cold, cold seas will take pity on you.'

The moon chose that moment to peer out from the clouds and Helga saw the carved outlines of Nazreen's unmoving face. There was a glint in the depths of his eyes and a hint of something more . . . a smile? The question came before she could stop it, but she needed to know. 'Why . . . ?'

Why are you not dragging me back to your mistress?

But he only raised his hand and placed a finger on his lips, then beckoned for her to follow. Now she took care to trace his steps carefully, ducking into shadow when he did, traversing open spaces swiftly, and the path down to the shoreline felt quicker by far than her walk to the corral.

Nazreen led her unerringly past the big piers jutting into the bay to a small sandy beach, where he stopped beside a small fishing boat.

'Here,' Nazreen said, motioning for her to climb aboard. Helga looked at the boat and her stomach turned in on itself. *Oh, no. Oh no no no.* She could feel Nazreen's eyes on her and was thankful that the night did not show the colour on her face. Biting down hard on her fear, she grabbed the side of the boat and tried her best to climb over and not fall in. Once she'd planted herself at the back end, following his instructions, he took her right hand and planted it on the rudder. 'Hold this. Steer.'

'How?' she murmured.

He glanced at her. 'You'll learn.' He pointed at the oars and raised his eyebrows, which she took to mean a query that she knew what they were and how to use them.

'Yes,' she said, adding to herself, *Well, I'll learn that too*, which was nearer the truth, but for some reason, she didn't want him to think her a complete incompetent.

He reached over her, picked up something which turned out to be a rope and handed it to her. 'Pull here' – she tugged it, and watched a small sail rising – 'but down in big wind. Understand?'

She released the cord and the sail sank back to the pole it was attached to. 'Yes.'

Apparently satisfied, he reached for something attached to his belt: a bag, tied up. He looked at her solemnly. 'Food and herbs.'

She seized his hand. 'Why are you doing this?'

This time he did not pull away but instead, offered her his other hand. 'Jorunn told me what you do, with herbs and runes. She told me to watch out for your magic – but in my country, we respect people like you. We do not lie to them, and we do not sell them as slaves.'

When he opened his hand, the moonlight caught on the blade of her rune-knife. He placed it, along with her necklace, on the wooden plank next to her. 'Go. Be wise.' He looked in her eyes. 'I will watch the wise horse for you and who knows? Maybe we meet again.' Once again there was a hint of a smile about him. 'I would like that.'

'I—' She was still searching for the words when he slipped from her grasp.

'Pull up the sail,' he whispered, then there was a jolt as he gave the little boat a hard shove and it slid easily over the sand and into the welcoming embrace of the water. She clenched her lips together, determined she would not cry out, and focused on finding her balance for a moment. The pull of the waves felt strange and unfamiliar, but the silvery sheen of moonlight on the deep black of the sea was both unsettling and beautiful.

The wind caught the sail and the boat suddenly shot forward. When she turned to look over her shoulder, Nazreen was gone.

No matter how she tried, the horizon was too much for her. It was too big. The darkness of the skies and even the gentle lapping of the calm waves all spoke of nightmarish horrors like sea-wolf jaws, just waiting to close on her and her little wooden bucket.

But still the wind pushed her along gently until Hedeby was only the tiniest yellow dot on the nearly invisible coastline.

'Now what?' she muttered. 'And where to? And in any case, how do I get there, wherever "there" is?'

She had no idea.

Above her the moon broke from the clouds once again, casting a strange greyish light on this new world, a world devoid of trees and hills and animals but full of gentle, constant movement. She found a carved bit of wood on the side and experimented until she'd managed to make fast the sail-rope so she didn't have to hold it herself all the time, then she sat back and watched with some satisfaction as the cloth swelled and the little boat shifted into a canter.

And soon enough, while the sea sang to her, the waves lulled her to sleep.

Had she stayed awake a little longer, she would have seen a large sail on the horizon, closing in fast.

Acknowledgements

2017 became 2018, and 2018 became 2019. This one took a while – and involved some excellent people.

Thanks for this book – and everything – go first and foremost to legendary agent Geraldine Cooke, who has been an instigator in my life and my writing for about a decade.

Furthermore, for showing kindness, generosity of spirit, abundant stores of patience and an admirable restraint in not going after me with a halberd, publisher Jo Fletcher deserves thanks, delivered while bowing deeply and reversing very carefully out of the throne room.

Thanks go also to Suzie and Eileen for giving me a job, and to Greg, Sharleen and especially Tracy for helping me keep it. Many thanks to Work-Morag, Susan, Becky and Nicole for being endless fountains of joy, banter and occasionally cheese. Furthermore, I wish to thank the students at Inveralmond Community High School for being a constant source of charm, confusion and entertainment. You make an old man feel very happy, and occasionally make a happy man feel very old.

Family and friends have been an unending source of support, as always. Allan, Helen and my dear Mum and Dad have been wonderful, supportive and particularly good at very gently not asking how it was going when it really wasn't. Ailsa and Chris (and Anna and Flora), Andrew, Sarah and Steven, Emily and Khaled, Helen and Gordon (and Euan and Ross), The Extended Armitage Clan and Peter and Simonetta have supplied everything from country walks to cake, barbecue assistance to cinema trips, banter to boardgames and all manner of lovely play time. You feed me more than you'll ever know.

Literary sensei/cattle prod and challenger of ideas Nick Bain gets a nod, as always. You can thank/blame him for most of my writing. The eldritch rituals of gratitude are also performed for the Extraordinary Fellows of Arcane Sorcery.

And finally – my wife, Morag, who has lived with me and this book for way longer than anyone should have to. She has been its champion since day one and has held my hand, endured my fainting spells and gently encouraged me through various slumps with methods that included tea, biscuits and making me a life-sized Editing Helmet, complete with horns, out of tin foil.

Thank you, thank you, thank you.

Snorri